INVASION OF DARKNESS

THE APOCALYPSE : EPISODE TWO

DAVID O. BULLOCK

Black Rose Writing | Texas

ISBN: 978-1-68433-555-8
PUBLISHED BY BLACK ROSE WRITING
www.blackrosewriting.com

Printed in the United States of America
Suggested Retail Price (SRP) $19.95

Invasion of Darkness is printed in Calluna

*As a planet-friendly publisher, Black Rose Writing does its best to eliminate unnecessary waste to reduce paper usage and energy costs, while never compromising the reading experience. As a result, the final word count vs. page count may not meet common expectations.

To Glenda, my beautiful wife and the love of my life
You inspire me, challenge me and love me for who I am
We have survived the darkness and are enjoying the light
I am yours forever

SPECIAL THANKS

To my family and friends who stand with me and believe, not only in me but also in the potential of my books to change lives. Your support means the world to me.

To the businesses of Somerset and Pulaski County, Kentucky who have so graciously supported David O. Bullock Writing. You have been a huge blessing to me.

To all the people who have purchased and read Episode One and are anxiously awaiting Episode Two. Here it is! I know you will love it just as much and be equally excited for Episode Three.

To all the writers of fiction whose books I have enjoyed through the years. You drew me into your stories and made me a part of the action. You taught me as I read, and I am grateful.

Darkness: absence or deficiency of light; wickedness or evil.

Invasion: an act or instance of entering as an enemy; the entrance or advent of anything troublesome or harmful; entrance as if to take possession of or overrun.

December 20, 2029.
It is a normal day. Winter is preparing to make its official arrival at midnight. Christmas is only five days away. But this day also brings a normal event which promises to be not so normal this time around. The event has been hyped more than any event since the *Invasion*, as the world still knows it. It stands the chance of being a historic occurrence, because it follows on the heels of the disappearance of what officials from every country have now confirmed as more than a billion people worldwide. Some see it as so significant they have described it as *apocalyptic*. Such a word is not to be taken lightly, although many do not grasp the extremity of its significance. *Predicting imminent disaster and total or universal destruction.* The approaching date has dominated news, weather and talk shows and been the topic of conversation from water coolers to dining room tables. *Apocalyptic?* That possibility is more like probability in many people's minds.

People would not typically take lunar eclipses so seriously, but this one feels different. No other eclipse has ever held such implications for a planet already reeling from loss and devastation. A total lunar eclipse is rare enough. It can only occur when the sun, earth and moon are all perfectly aligned. At totality, the earth's full shadow falls over the moon, casting it into an eerie darkness. The moon turns red and appears to look like blood. At maximum eclipse, the darkness is at its deepest. The opinions of people vary. Many believe the world will end this evening. Most fear the aliens may return for another *invasion* during totality. But regardless of the extremity of their views, nearly all agree on one thing: somehow the world will never be the same after December 20, 2029. Little do they know how accurate those feelings are.

INVASION OF DARKNESS

INTRODUCTION

It is a beautiful sunny day in New York. It fits perfectly with the condition of the world. Prosperous times have come quickly. The Invasion is all but forgotten, even though it has only been 100 days since it happened. The world has grieved and moved on. There are even those who suggest that such significant lessening of the population has made the world a better place. Most disagree, but if they agree are unwilling to say so. However, one thing everyone admits is, things are good. They are very good, everywhere. Economies are thriving. Resources are plentiful. In America, the stock market has soared to daily record highs. Around the world, currencies are stronger than they have ever been. Joblessness, homelessness, hunger and poverty are almost things of the past. There is hardly such a thing as lower class. The sun has dawned on a new day and ushered in a golden age the likes of which the world has never seen. The last thing people need is anything which will interfere with that.

Another thing most people admit is this: it is all because of one man, Aissa Messai. He has arisen on the scene as the savior of humanity. Savior? People around the world regularly use that word to describe him. It is not a title that should be taken lightly, but in this case it seems appropriate. No one could have accomplished what he has achieved in so little time and not be deserving of such a praiseworthy epithet. It has been nothing short of ingenious and miraculous. Miraculous? That word fits him too. The man can work miracles. Dare they say it? Like God? The God they have heard about but never believed existed may have revealed himself now in the person of Aissa Messai. And now the world is beginning to believe... in him.

CHAPTER 1

Weather reports around the world predicted a cloudless sky on December 20. There was no chance of rain or snow anywhere on the globe. That is not only unusual; it is downright impossible. By the very nature of the universe, some kind of precipitation must fall somewhere on the earth on any given day. But not on this day. Even in places where the eclipse would not occur, there would be nothing but clear skies. Strange. Weird. No, more than that. Eerie. Yes, that is the word... eerie.

4:41:54 p.m.: Chicago.
Evan Ryles, Ally Fromm and John Baldwin sat in the commons area on campus, along with dozens of other students and faculty members who wanted to observe this natural phenomenon. The moon would be difficult to see due to it being below the horizon for most of the eclipse. But the feeling that this event held such significance for the planet caused them to be present, waiting and watching to see what would happen. Every face revealed genuine concern.

5:41:54 p.m.: New York City.
Blake and Beth Jennings Thompson reported for their separate networks from the One World Observatory atop the tallest building in the Western Hemisphere, the Freedom Center in Manhattan. Would be astronomers and a few curious onlookers who were lucky enough to get tickets packed the place. The view was spectacular and unobscured, the mood in the room a mixture of excitement and anxiety. No one could predict what the evening would bring. Blake and Beth knew it would be the beginning of something bad.

11:41:54 p.m.: Germany.

Bruno and Mila Fromm and their two sons watched the eclipse from the countryside near their home in their favorite quiet place, away from city lights. They chose it so they could be alone on this night, which would impact the world in more ways than anyone could understand at this point. It was a cloudless night, providing a perfect view of the moon. They huddled together, close enough to reach out and touch one another. What would happen, they did not know, but they were certain it would change the world... again.

12:41:54 a.m.: Israel.

Ben Abramson and Oliver Barton sat atop the Mount of Olives overlooking the Old City of Jerusalem. The location produced some stunning views of the moon during total eclipses in the past. Photographers crowded the mountain, standing shoulder to shoulder, hoping to get that one award-winning photo which would define their careers. Ben and Ollie were working, reporting live as the event unfolded, so they could not be together. But they had committed to find each other promptly should trouble arise.

Most people thought the world would change tonight, but no one expected it to change in a single second. When clocks around the world hit 41 minutes and 54 seconds of the hour, the earth's full shadow covered the moon. Maximum. The so-called Blood Moon turned red, but a deeper shade of red than anyone had ever seen in an eclipse. In that second, darkness covered the planet, but it was no normal darkness. It was total darkness, an *invasion of darkness*, that entered the world in a single second, just as people had disappeared from the earth within seconds one hundred days earlier.

The entire planet went dark, a worldwide blackout that extinguished every source of light. Darkness covered the globe. Automobile lights, flashlights, every light failed. True totality for the next 26 minutes and 51 seconds until the full eclipse ended and partial began. 26 minutes and 51 seconds that felt like an eternity. The depth of the darkness was like nothing anyone on earth had experienced before. Everyone felt it deep in their souls; intense and suffocating. There were no sounds, only darkness; the entire world silent and dark for 26 minutes and 51 seconds.

Yet something far worse came during that time. Heat. Not heat that increases air temperature, but searing heat, like a laser beam burning into the brains of every person on earth. It was pure evil seeking to claim their minds and force their allegiance. Its origin was none other than the pit of hell. Blake and Beth could hear groans and occasional muffled screams from people in the Observatory as the heat penetrated their minds like a blazing inferno. Evan, Ally and John heard them on the commons, escaping from the lips of students and professors. Ben and Ollie heard them coming from every part of the Mount of Olives. Even from their quiet place in Germany, the Fromms heard them faintly in the distance. Something sinister was taking place. The people of the world were oblivious to it. Blake and Beth were thinking the same thing: much like the day Aissa Messai was first introduced to the delegates of the United Nations...

At last, the earth's shadow moved ever so slowly. A tiny sliver of the moon appeared, signaling the end of the full eclipse. No one understood what had happened or what it meant. If only they were aware, it was an omen of what was coming soon. It was inconceivable that it could come to a world so at peace following such turbulent times, but it would. If people only knew the truth, they would do whatever they must do to avoid it. But they did not understand. How could they? The satanic heat had seared their minds. The Smyrnians knew. And they would do everything possible to save as many from it as they could.

•　　•　　•　　•　　•

As morning dawned on December 21, strangely, people had forgotten the events of the previous night. It was as if they never happened. The world returned to the way things were prior to the eclipse. To the Smyrnians, the way things were made no sense. It seemed impossible to reconcile the prosperity of the world with what they had seen and felt after Aissa Messai's election as Secretary-General of the United Nations. How could this be, considering the two murders and evil spell that accompanied his election? How did it match with the eerie fog they saw spreading in all directions to cover the earth? And most recently, how did it jibe with the darkness and searing heat of the preceding night? The feeling and chill had all but disappeared. Neither had been present in weeks. It was natural for them to feel what the rest of the world enjoyed: peace. Something changed during the night. But this morning it appeared nothing had changed.

To top it all off, the big announcement that just came out of Israel created a worldwide buzz. While many had spoken of it, no one expected to see it happen: peace in the Middle East. But this went beyond the realm of possibility in anyone's mind. Aissa Messai had negotiated a peace treaty between Israel and her Arab neighbors that also tore down the greatest wall which divides them: their religious beliefs. "We are family," he proclaimed. "We come from the same spiritual root, our Father Abraham." Seemingly out of nowhere, Judaism and Islam now accepted and understood each other. Rabbis and Imams sat at the same table and reached an astonishing agreement. It involved one of the most sacred places for both.

The Temple Mount in Jerusalem is Judaism's holiest site. As its name suggests, it was the place where the Jewish Temple had once proudly stood. Built first by King Solomon in the 10th Century B.C., many proclaimed it to be the most magnificent structure in the known world. It symbolized the place where God's presence dwelt on earth, where the Jews housed the holy chest, the Ark of the Covenant. The Babylonian army destroyed it in 586 B.C. The Jews rebuilt and rededicated it in 515 B.C. after the people of Judah returned from Babylonian captivity. That structure paled in comparison to Solomon's Temple, but Herod the Great expanded it, beginning in 20/19 B.C. He restored the extravagance and grandeur of the original temple. It served as the center of Jewish worship until the Roman General Titus destroyed it in 70 A.D. The Jews continue to mourn that destruction to the present day. Some Jewish traditions also taught that creation began on that site. They believed the stone over which Solomon built the temple was the place where God created the world and the first man, Adam. And they thought it to be the place where Abraham offered to sacrifice his son, Isaac.

But the Mount, the most important place on earth to the Jews, was now under Muslim control. Yet, religious Jews believed they would rebuild the temple during the Messianic age, fulfilling Old Testament prophecies. The Messiah would then sit on his throne in Jerusalem. None of that could be possible without the temple standing again where it had once stood. They had prayed for years for those two prophetic events to occur. And they believed both may happen any time.

For Muslims, the Temple Mount is their third holiest site, the first two being Mecca and Medina. They believed it to be the place from which Muhammad ascended to heaven on a white horse. Atop the Mount, where the Jewish Temple had once proudly stood, sat the Dome of the Rock Mosque. They built it to ensure it would stand on the exact site of the original temple, thus replacing it. As had been true with the temple, the sight of the gleaming golden dome greeted people when they arrived at the summit of the Mount of Olives. Sitting to its right at the southern entrance of the Temple Mount stood the Al-Aqsa Mosque. Together they made a powerful statement about the Islamic dominance of the Mount.

Though under Israeli sovereignty, the Muslim Waqf controlled the Mount. They took advantage of every opportunity to showcase their authority over that special and unique place. When you walked on the Mount, you saw groups of Muslim men, women and children. It was a place for Islamic education and prayer and served that purpose well. They allowed Jews little to no presence anywhere on the Mount, with Jewish prayers specifically prohibited. Sharing the Temple Mount would never be possible. Or would it?

Ben and Ollie remained in Jerusalem for the special announcement. Aissa Messai had set December 25 as the day to share his big news. It was his way of including people who were neither Jewish nor Muslim, or even religious, in this important event. Many of them still celebrated Christmas with gusto, even though they gave no thought to what the day was about. Messai had also reached out to other groups, telling them this was the time for all religions and all people to come together and unite for the good of the world, a plan that was clearly working.

December 25 came with Ollie reporting for BBC and Ben also putting his reporter skills to work again. The press conference began at noon on the Temple Mount. Messai stood at the top of the steps leading up to the Dome of the Rock. A delegation of reporters joined select Rabbis and Imams standing at the bottom of the steps. He began with a surprising announcement.

"Before I get to the real reason we are here today, you may already know there are multiple reasons I chose this day to reveal news that will change the world, beginning at this very spot. But the reason of which you may not be aware is this: today is my birthday! On this day when many people once celebrated the birth of one who claimed to be the Messiah, I want to say thank you for your trust in me and willingness to follow me into the New World Order. Today, we are being liberated from past beliefs which kept us divided and limited in what we can achieve as human beings. On this day, formerly called Christmas, we begin a new day, a day when all people of the world come together in a one world religion. We will do away with the archaic ideas of the past and come together to worship as one. 'As one what?' you may ask. As one people who share a common belief in the ability of humanity to achieve anything we can conceive as we work together. I ask you to follow me into a glorious future and a more prosperous world than any of us has ever known!" His voice rose in a loud crescendo, followed by thunderous applause.

"Instead of receiving gifts from you today on my birthday, I come to offer this as my gift to you. It is my joy to announce that on this day, the two major religions of the world, Judaism and Islam, are uniting to lead the way into a beautiful new world. They will show their solidarity by sharing this sacred piece of land on which we stand, known as the Temple Mount. Jews have long dreamed of rebuilding their temple on this site where it once stood. Today, the Muslims of the world are extending a hand of peace to the Jews, allowing them to construct their temple here on this sacred site. They have agreed to build it directly behind me on the large open area sitting beside the Dome of the Rock!" His voice rose again, followed by more thunderous applause.

"Construction on the temple will begin immediately. The building will conform to the exact specifications of their former place of worship. We will commit every available resource to ensure the completion of this project as expeditiously as possible. Nations around the world will contribute to the cause, as they will all benefit from this decision. As preparations to build are being made, both sides have agreed that the Jews will erect a tent, or tabernacle as they called it in times past. It will stand near the construction site so they can begin worshiping there prior to the completion of the temple. This will also be a replica of the structure they used in antiquity prior to the temple being built. My hope is, they can complete the Jewish temple within 3 months. Let us all get behind this effort and walk into the future together!" Another round of thunderous applause. "Now I will allow a few leaders from each group to speak."

As Rabbis and Imams spoke, few listened to what they had to say. Most eyes focused on the man of the hour as he shook hands, smiled and posed for pictures and interviews. One of the first to get to him was Ben Abramson.

"Mr. Messai..."

"Please, I want to be on a first name basis with everyone. Call me Aissa, or in writing, you may use the abbreviated form, Isa. Now, please be quick. I have others with whom I need to speak."

"Okay, but I will at least stick to the given spelling, Aissa." Messai smiled. "As a Jewish American with roots in Israel, I only have one question. Why do you see the rebuilding of the Jewish Temple holding such significance? It seems to me there are other ways you might bring our two groups together, without appeasing one's desire to the neglect of the other receiving anything in return."

"Well, Mr., I am sorry. I did not catch your name."

"Benjamin Abramson."

"Well, Mr. Benjamin Abramson. Based on your name, I would assume you are an Orthodox Jew whose life has been steeped in the Jewish teachings. Is that correct?"

"Yes, that is correct. My parents taught me the Mosaic Law from childhood, and I have lived by its precepts my entire life."

"Then you surely know the teaching of your scriptures that the Jews will rebuild the temple during the Messianic Age. And the Messiah will come to his temple and rule on his throne in Jerusalem."

"I am well aware of that teaching."

"Then, Mr. Benjamin Abramson, maybe it is time for the fulfilling of that promise. Following the construction of this temple, the Messiah may indeed come and rule. Do you believe that is possible?"

"Yes, I do," Ben answered confidently. "But I wonder if he will be the Messiah we have expected?" He stared Messai directly in the eye as he asked that final question.

With a wry smile, Messai returned his stare with a look that said, "You know who I am. And I know who you are."

Ben felt the chill crawl up his spine, but one thought consumed his mind and overcame it: "And I am determined to tell my people who you really are."

Ollie got in the briefest of interviews with Messai. He had never been one to be at a loss for words, but his conversation with the world leader ended with Messai's answer to his first question.

"Mr. Messai, my name is Oliver Barton. 1 am with BBC. How do you think people around the world received your announcement today?"

"Well, Mr. Ollie Barton." Messai used his nickname. How did he know that? Then, as Messai continued, Ollie recalled with complete clarity his previous encounter with the man.

"On my flight over, 1 was reading a newspaper. You have read a newspaper on a plane before, haven't you Ollie?"

The moment came racing back to Ollie's mind, as fresh as if it had just happened. The chill was so strong it left him speechless, almost as if he was suddenly rendered mute.

Messai abruptly ended the conversation with these words: "Thank you, Mr. Barton. 1 am sure we will see each other again soon."

As he walked away, Ollie stumbled toward Ben, shaking all over as he walked. Ben saw things were not well with his new partner.

"Are you okay, my friend?"

"I thought 1 was ready for this Ben. But 1 suppose 1 wasn't." He recounted his plane encounter with Messai again, followed by the man's response to his interview question.

"We both know what we signed up for, Ollie. We have put it all on the line. There is no turning back, regardless of what happens. Now, let's go. We need to get back to New York. We have work to do."

"Right you are, Ben. Thanks for the reminder. Let's do this thing. 1 am ready!"

CHAPTER 2

With the holiday break in full swing, the entire group of Smyrnians gathered in New York City. In less than 3 months since the invasion, they had become followers of Jesus. They now understood the disappearances were not the result of an invasion of aliens. September 11 had brought the Rapture of the church, the day Jesus took his people home to be with him, as he had said he would. They had also learned that event started a 7-year period known as the Tribulation. At the end of the seven years, Jesus would come, defeat evil, and set up his earthly kingdom. But it was the events of those years that gave them their name and their purpose. They were the Smyrnians, a name taken from Jesus' message to the church in Smyrna in the Book of Revelation, Chapter 2. Verse 10 foretold how they would suffer, many of them imprisoned or even killed, because of their faith in Jesus.

An evil world leader would arise to power and proclaim himself to be the Messiah, demanding that people worship him. He would persecute and slaughter those who refused to do so. They now knew Aissa Messai was that man. He would be their enemy for the next seven years. Their determination was to fight him, even if it meant dying for Jesus. And they committed their lives to telling everyone about Jesus and helping them turn to faith in him instead of the Antichrist, Aissa Messai.

Blake and Beth were taking some time to celebrate their honeymoon. They were unable to do that after their wedding because things broke so fast following the election of Messai as the Secretary-General of the United Nations. And now their celebration would include eighteen other people, as the Smyrnians got serious about their plans for the next seven years. Anders had taken the time off. Blake did not need a cameraman during his break. Evan, Ally and John were on winter break from college, and Ollie had taken time off to ring in the New Year in New York City, something he had always wanted to do. Ben could take off anytime he wanted as the producer of the network. He, Miriam, and their seven children lived in New York and could meet with the team whenever necessary. He and Ollie had flown back from Israel and gotten a night's sleep under their belts. Bruno and Mila Fromm and their sons flew in from Germany to be with their daughter, Ally. Bruno was especially ready to make plans to fight the enemy.

On Thursday, December 27, they gathered in Blake and Beth's spacious high-rise luxury apartment in Manhattan to begin their meeting. Despite the peace and prosperity in the world, they knew perilous times were coming soon. They reaffirmed their belief of that truth, regardless of how things looked at the present time. The darkness of the eclipse and searing heat that attacked people's minds signaled the nearing onset of dark days and a total disregard for human life. The world would soon go crazy and they would need to combat the craziness with the truth about the real Messiah and King. Those titles belong only to Jesus, the Son of God and Savior of the world. Each of them began reaching out to their list of contacts in hopes they would turn to faith in Him. Most were on the list because of what they would bring to the team, although helping them come to faith in Jesus was paramount in their minds. But they were also cognizant that doing so had the potential to blow their cover and put their lives in danger. And it may drive them underground much sooner than they had planned. But then, they were already planning for that too.

Doc Sanderson was the owner of Protection Services Inc. in Wichita, Kansas. His parents gave him the nickname "Doc" because as a child, he always said he wanted to be a doctor when he grew up. He reasoned he still met people's protective needs through the products of PSI. They built and installed storm shelters for the people of Tornado Alley, and business was booming. Their services had saved countless lives through the years. But while tornado shelters were their primary products, they were not the only ones. They also built and sold massive steel bunkers used for everything from storage to protective shelters. There were smaller ones which provided short-term protection and larger ones that made it possible for groups to survive as long as necessary underground.

His childhood friend, Professor John Baldwin, who taught at a university in Chicago, had contacted Doc. He expressed an interest in purchasing the largest underground bunker they made at PSI. Why would John need a 3,000-square foot steel bunker in Chicago? Beyond that, how could a college professor afford to shell out a million dollars to buy one? Those were not questions he needed to be asking. If he made a sale like that, who cared how John used it? Those deals were rare and helped to fund Doc's extravagant lifestyle. But John said he needed to meet with him and talk about it before he made the purchase. Something about a discovery he had made that gave him insight into things that would soon come upon the world. He told him he not only wanted to buy a bunker, he also wanted to share those things with his childhood friend. And he said a well-known personality was coming with him. He told Doc he would recognize him when he saw him.

They would fly in on Saturday, December 29, and leave the following day. Doc was off this week, but stayed in town instead of taking his usual out of the country trip with his family. Since he was in town, why not meet with them? A sale this big would be worth the time, for sure. But who could this famous personality be that John was bringing? His old friend had long been a conspiracy theorist. What celebrity had he convinced to buy into one of his theories? To be honest, he did not want to take the time to listen to any of John's foolishness. He needed to make the sale, then get back to his break between Christmas and New Year's Day. There were things he wanted to do, including spending time with his family, even though they stayed in town this year instead of traveling abroad. He loved having some time with his children and grandchildren.

John opened the Smyrnians meeting by sharing what he, Blake and Anders were getting ready to do. They were flying to Kansas tomorrow evening for a Saturday morning meeting with a childhood friend of John's who owned a company that built and installed underground shelters.

Beth rolled her eyes, shook her head and said, "There goes my honeymoon."

"Face it, Beth," John said. "It will be hard to have a honeymoon with all of us around. I promise to bring him back so the two of you can ring in the new year together and celebrate however you want. Then we will all leave you alone for a few days. Will that work?"

"You know it will. We have to do whatever we need to right now. But I am warning you, you had better have him back here the next day!"

"Here's the deal." John got back to business. "We plan to talk to him about Jesus after we talk about shelters and bunkers. But man, that is dangerous. Doc has always been a tough guy to convince about anything. We have to feel him out and be careful. He's a high roller, well established in the political arena. He has been a financial contributor to a lot of big time election campaigns. He may blow our cover and turn us in, just like that. Or he could believe us and put his faith in Jesus. The results of that would be much more far-reaching than him providing us with a bunker. Although, if he gave us one, that would be nice too."

They all agreed with that and continued the meeting. They would pray hard for Blake, John and Anders, and for Doc Sanderson. The man would be a huge answer to their prayers. Bruno reported that he had researched and also found a few businesses in Germany that built and installed underground bunkers, one of them located less than 100 miles from his home. He would get in touch with them after they returned home the second week of January. He needed prayer for that, too.

Evan was working on a system that would allow them to communicate with one another anytime, from anywhere in the world. He could also track their every move and be aware of their locations at all times.

Ben was planning to create an underground network from which he could speak to Jews all over the world. He would talk to them about Jesus and warn them about the dangers of following Aissa Messai. Being a genius at things like that, he would make it virtually impossible to track down.

Blake and Beth would continue reporting for their networks until Messai discovered them. And they planned to enjoy marriage as much as these turbulent years would allow. Despite everything they were doing, they would make that a priority!

Anders would keep doing his thing as Blake's cameraman. He often saw things Blake had overlooked. It would begin with a trip to Kansas.

Reporting would continue to be Ollie's gig too. His role was essential because of his trips to Israel to provide coverage. Those trips would be many during the construction of the Jewish temple. He would be on the inside in a way that was not possible for the others. For the time being, Ben would make several of those trips with him. He could fly under the radar because Jews traveling back and forth to their home country led to no suspicion from authorities.

Ally was making plans to infiltrate Messai's camp and bring information back to the team. Her activity would put her in constant danger, but she decided she was up to the challenge, even though she still battled fear. Her plans caused her parents to cringe, but they understood why. Being a spy was what she had been born to do. Her role on the team was vital. They just had to pray she did not get caught.

Mila and Miriam were talking about how they could be mother hens for the group and try to take care of their every need; Miriam for the American group and Mila for the German contingent, at least until their number grew too large. Miriam would also help with research. But both of them wanted to be out in the field too. Miriam hoped to take the youngest Abramson kids with her and allow them to gather information. They were very cute, which gave them the ability to get close to people and situations where others could not. The older two could work with Ally. Ally's brothers would try to build a youth movement in Germany, beginning at school and reaching out to their friends.

The team was forming, roles were being determined, and they were ready to get started. Darkness had invaded the earth. Now they would invade the darkness and shine the light of Jesus to show people the way to safety, if only they would heed their warnings and follow the light. Having encountered the darkness in such an intense way, surely they would do that.

As the meeting neared an end, Beth had been waiting for an opportunity. She wanted to save the best for last. "Hey everybody," she called out. "I have one more thing to tell you. Some of you remember my pilot friend, Trey, who flew Blake, Anders and me back to New York to cover the UN story. We sure could use him and his plane. Well, he flew a charter flight in here a few days after the eclipse and called me. He had a lot of questions about Messai and the things that happened during his election, and a lot of concern about the peace treaty between Israel and the Arab nations. He wanted to know the truth. When I told him, he believed it immediately! He is now a follower of Jesus and a member of the Smyrnians! He is ready to do whatever he can to help. He will still have to work his charter business, but he will also fly us anywhere in the states we need to go. He couldn't be here today. But you will meet him soon." That was an exciting way to end a meeting! They were all fired up! Trey would be a huge addition to the team.

Friday evening came, and John, Blake and Anders landed at Dwight D. Eisenhower National Airport in Wichita, Kansas. After grabbing a bite to eat, they headed to their hotel to discuss how they would approach Doc Sanderson about their need for an underground bunker. They had questions, and there were things they must decide before they arrived at PSI.

"What if he asks me what I plan to do with a 3,000-square foot bunker, Blake? What do I tell him? Do I try to talk to him about Jesus? I brought a flash drive with the pastor's message."

"You had better feel him out as you go. We don't have a lot of time, but you still need to take it slow. And remember, Anders and I are only here to film this story as you try to prepare for a worldwide emergency. We need to be impartial and stay undercover as much as we can."

"Okay, man. Let's go to bed and try to get a good night's sleep so we'll be ready in the morning."

They were up at daybreak, and after eating a hearty breakfast that came with their room, they were off to meet Doc Sanderson at 8:00 a.m. Their GPS led them straight to PSI, and as promised, Doc met them there.

"Doc! I hardly recognize you. You have changed a bit since we were kids." John smiled.

"The same would be true here if I hadn't seen you on the news once or twice talking about earthquakes and such. It seems you have made quite a name for yourself."

"Do you recognize this guy?" John asked as Blake and Anders stepped around the corner.

"Blake Thompson! You are my favorite newscaster. I watch you just about every night."

"It is good to meet you, Doc. John has told me a lot about you. It seems the two of you got into a fair amount of trouble when you were kids growing up around here."

"Don't believe everything he tells you about me. I'm not such a bad guy. I have grown out of some of that stuff, but not all of it, I must confess." His smile displayed a mischievous streak.

"Blake is following me around on a few of my stops. This is his cameraman, Anders Norstrom."

"Pleased to meet you, Anders. I suppose if you guys put me and PSI on television, it has to be good for business." But his actions revealed that Doc was apprehensive about the whole thing.

"Doc, you don't have to worry," Blake threw in. "We are focusing on John and the theory he is espousing. He is an expert in the field, so he bears listening to. Besides, it is an appealing story, don't you think? You understand I am about reporting news that people want to hear."

"I do. And you do an outstanding job! You can film and report as much as you like. It's about time I got on television." Doc had warmed up to the idea and lost some of his concern about the project.

"Is it okay if I get set up to film?" Anders asked. "I just want to be ready to shoot some footage when the time comes." Doc agreed, and Anders left to get his camera and tripod.

"John, you said you wanted to talk to me about this theory you have before we discuss bunkers. I would like to hear it, but I don't have all day. Get on with it, while there is time."

"Okay, here goes. I have done a lot of research into the disappearances, especially the worldwide tremor that followed them. How is such a thing possible without it having some significance, right? But as rough as this one was, it may have been minor to what is coming."

"I have done a lot of thinking about that myself. They're saying it may be a sign that another quake is coming soon. So, are you saying what you have discovered in your research is part of why you want to buy a bunker?" Doc tried to shift the conversation from research to discussing bunkers. He wanted to make this sale.

"I think so, Doc. I have concluded that the trauma caused by the disappearances led to the quake which portends another quake stronger than the world has ever seen. I believe it will approach 10.0 on the Richter Scale. I'm not sure the earth can take much more. The end of the world may be close. But if not, I still believe the planet is about to go crazy, so we need to prepare for that."

"John, you always were a conspiracy theorist. Even when we were kids, you were constantly coming up with hair-brained ideas about things that would happen. It seemed like you came up with one of those after everything you saw on the news. Mr. Thompson, you may need to know that about my old friend here. If I remember correctly John, you were into the

Y2K thing too, were you not?" There was little doubt that Doc would be a hard sell.

"True, Doc. I have always been a conspiracy theorist. But the Y2K thing? Yes, I thought about buying a bunker then and hunkering down for a worldwide disaster. But when my research ultimately showed it would not happen, I didn't pursue that any further. I am convinced enough about this to purchase one. That's why I am here."

Anders had gotten set up. Blake asked, "Mr. Sanderson, is it okay if I ask you a few questions?"

"First off, you can call me Doc. Now go ahead. Just remember, I have a limited amount of time."

"Okay Doc, I will be prompt. My time is valuable too. I have to be back in New York this evening. So, let me cut right to the chase. Anders, are you ready?"

Anders nodded and counted down: "3, 2, 1, and go." He pointed at Blake.

"This is Blake Thompson reporting from Wichita, Kansas. Here with me is Doc Sanderson, the owner of Protection Services Incorporated, a thriving business that sells storm shelters to help protect residents during the large number of storms here in Tornado Alley. They also sell larger shelters, such as underground bunkers up to 3,000 square feet in size. Also, with me today is Professor John Baldwin, a renowned expert on earthquakes and other natural disasters. He has been researching the recent tremor that rocked the entire world and looking into the idea that it is a portent of a worldwide quake which will be the strongest to strike the planet. Doc, I will start with you. John believes that worldwide quake is coming soon and we may be near the end of the world. As an expert, his opinion would seem to be more credible than others. Would you agree with that? Can you see a possibility of those things happening?"

"May I be transparent with you, Mr. Thompson? John... uh, Professor Baldwin, and I grew up together. He has always been a conspiracy theorist. But I am a realist. People have been talking about the end of the world longer than you or I can remember. It has not happened. However, I understand when he talks about the trauma caused to the earth by the Invasion. I have to admit, that makes sense."

Blake wanted to jump in and say, "It was not an invasion!" But he had to keep quiet, for now. The time for that would come soon enough.

Doc continued. "I have no problem believing something might affect the planet like that. But the earth has withstood a lot of traumas before, and it is still here. As for the worldwide quake, it may happen. I'm not an expert like Professor Baldwin is. But even if it does, I don't presume that means the end of the word is near, if that is what you are asking."

"As we were talking before we came on the air, you told me the professor also became convinced about the Y2K scare at the end of the millennium. He even researched purchasing a bunker back then and storing up items that would help him survive the collapse of everything controlled by computers and cause the end of life as we know it."

"Exactly," Doc interrupted him. "That didn't happen either, just as no other conspiracy theory has panned out. What about all the groups that have moved away from society and lived in communes because they thought the world would end on a certain date? Many of them believed 'Jesus would return' when that date arrived." He feigned quotation marks with his hands. "People have said that for 2,000 years, and it has never happened either. I just don't get into that stuff."

The time came for Blake to involve John in the conversation. "Professor Baldwin, what do you have to say about all of that?"

John was more than ready to interject his thoughts.

"Well, Blake, as for the Y2K thing, we are talking about manmade disasters. With what is happening today, we are talking about natural disasters, or dare I say supernatural disasters, over which we as human beings have no control. There is an enormous difference between the two. This earthquake is a natural disaster we cannot control."

"People have also believed in life on other planets and that aliens would invade the earth someday. We did not see them either, but people seem certain that happened."

"We have scientific proof that happened, John. That makes it easy for me to believe." Doc had gotten combative.

John was not backing down either. "I am a scientist, Doc. But I have found no proof that happened. All the world is doing is taking other people's word for it because they deem them to be experts. Why is it difficult to believe one thing you can't see, but not another?" John had to be careful. He was treading on dangerous ground and needed to be sure he did not give away his belief about what happened and what was coming, though he desperately wanted to.

Then Doc turned the conversation in another direction Blake had hoped to avoid. Thankfully, this was not live, so he could edit out anything he wanted to. But this also gave him a look into the thinking of most people in the world.

"This is my belief," said Doc. "As I mentioned, I am a realist. I believe what I can see. And what I see is, the world is better off than it has ever been. Things have improved more than ever in history after the Invasion. Please understand that I am not saying the Invasion made that possible. Because I didn't lose anyone in my family doesn't mean I have not grieved with those who did. The world is better because of the efforts of one man: Aissa Messai. I believe in him. What he has done in such a short time since being elected as the Secretary-General of the UN is nothing short of miraculous. He is what the world needed after enduring such a tragedy. He has restored hope and brought peace and prosperity. That is something I can see and something I am living. I think we can all say we are better off now than we were before he came on the scene."

That made the skin crawl on the other three men. They knew it was a lie, but they were not free to say so on the air just yet. Blake had to end the interview so they could get on with their purchase of the biggest underground bunker Doc had to sell. Thankfully, Ben had made it clear that money was no object. They would purchase a bunker before they left Kansas, although Doc was not aware of that yet. The only question was whether he would join them in the cause or reject it.

"Okay Anders, turn the camera off. I think I have what we need. We had better let John and Doc get down to the reason we are here."

"I am more than ready to do that, Blake," said John. "Doc, I want to get down to business, but I would like for you to hear my reasoning for this whole thing before we do. I even brought a video on a flash drive that will help you understand. Then you won't just be selling me a bunker. You will be part of a cause, if you will, understanding that you are living up to your company's name in an even bigger way. You will be protecting people from utter destruction."

"I told you John, I am not interested in any of that. My realism and your conspiracy theories just don't mesh. Do you want to see the bunkers I have in stock, or not?"

"Yes, but please give me a minute to explain. This is something you desperately need to hear."

"I told you John, I am not interested. If you want to buy a bunker, I want to sell you one. But if I have to listen to your theory about the end of the world, we'll forget about it. What will it be?"

"Okay, Doc. You have always been stubborn. You call it realism. I call it a closed mind. Hopefully, you will listen to me later. But for now, let's look at bunkers."

"Okay, now you're talking. I have a 3,000 square footer on hand. I always keep one around in case someone finally wants to buy it. I have sold some big ones, but if you take this one, it will be my biggest sale ever. It is 30 feet by 100 feet, if that works for you. Come back here with me to the last building. It takes a good-sized warehouse to hold this baby."

The four of them walked to the building together. When they entered, what Anders, Blake and John saw amazed them.

"Doc!" said John. "This is amazing! Lots of people could live in this thing for a long time." He chastised himself for saying that. Even the tiniest slip of the tongue could give them away.

"The 30 by 100 is a great setup: living quarters, kitchens, bathrooms and most everything else you need. It is a house underground."

"What if I told you I may be interested in more than one?"

"It would take me a little while to build another one, but the more you take, the better deal I can give you. I don't know what your budget is, but here is what I can do. As I told you, the price for one is a million bucks. If you take two, I can let you have them for $850,000 apiece, and if you take three, the price goes down to $750,000. That is a lot of money, but it is a great deal."

"I need to check with the others first to see if we have space and funding for three. It would be hard to pass up that kind of savings if we do."

"And if you take three, I will even throw in delivery and installation."

"Depending on the situation, I think we will do that ourselves."

"I don't know how far you plan to haul it, but if it is all the way to Chicago, that is no easy task. Not to mention installation. You need a trained crew for that. But if you think you can handle it, it will save me money. It won't change the price of the bunkers."

"I understand. We will definitely take one. I will get back to you on the others. For now, we need to get out of here. Blake and Anders have to get back to New York. I'll call you after the first of the year, if that is okay."

"Sure. I'll wait to hear from you. In the meantime, we'll get this one ready to move."

The three Smyrnians left for the airport, hoping nothing they had said would cause Doc Sanderson to be suspicious about their intentions. Doc walked out of the warehouse feeling even better about Aissa Messai's New World Order.

CHAPTER 3

New Year's Day had come and gone. Blake and Beth were thankful for some time alone. Albeit brief, they had now had a honeymoon. They had made it a point to not see any of the others. And the others had made it a point to leave them alone. There were no two happier people on the planet than Blake and Beth Jennings Thompson. But their happiness would soon face tests even the strongest of relationships would struggle to endure. The Smyrnians and other followers of Jesus in the world, if there were any, would face them too.

Now that 2030 had begun, the news immediately shifted back to Jerusalem, Israel. Aissa Messai was back in town overseeing his favorite project, the building of the Jewish Temple on the Temple Mount next door to the Dome of the Rock Mosque. For many years, the Jews had been collecting the items necessary for temple worship as commanded in their Bible. That would make the project move far more quickly. Everything was ready now. They had just finished setting up a tent of meeting, patterned precisely after the Tabernacle described in the Torah, the five books of Moses. It sat to the left of the spot where the temple would soon stand and would serve as their place of worship until the completion of the temple, as the first Tabernacle did following their exodus from Egypt.

Today was a big day, thus calling for Aissa Messai's presence from a purely publicity standpoint. The cleansing of the people of Israel, and of the tent itself, required the sacrifice of a red heifer with no defect or blemish, as commanded in Numbers, Chapter 19. The search for such a heifer had been ongoing for years. One had finally been identified a few months earlier, interestingly, just in time for this moment. Messai watched, along with the world, as they carried out the entire ritual. They led the heifer to the priest in charge, who they chose after identifying him as being from the tribe of Levi, the priestly tribe of Israel. They then ceremoniously took it outside the city and slaughtered it there in the priest's presence. He brought some blood from the heifer and sprinkled it seven times toward the front of the tent. They burned the animal and gathered up its ashes to save for ongoing ceremonial use. It was a bloody, but elaborate ceremony.

Aissa Messai despised these Jewish rituals. They were silly, petty things designed to appease the adherents to their outdated religion. In fact, he liked nothing about the Jews. They were living in the land Allah gave to his own people and claiming it belonged to them. From his perspective, they rubbed that in the faces of the descendants of Ishmael every day. His people knew the inheritance of the father belonged to the oldest son and his descendants. Ishmael was their forefather, the oldest son of Abraham. The land of Israel, which God promised to Abraham's descendants, naturally belonged to them. He was one of them.

The Jews sprang from Abraham's youngest son Isaac, who they believed received the inheritance as the promised son, the one through whom they believed the promise would come to pass. They believed the land belonged to them. "They are wrong," Messai growled to himself as he watched the ceremony mercifully end. He smiled and waved at the cameras, concealing his thoughts, as he granted interviews to those who wanted to hear from the newly crowned leader of the world. He had to play the part to his loyal fans and win the admiration and adoration of humanity.

Ben and Ollie were there again, too. Ben could not make every trip to Israel, as his work of broadcasting to the Jews would require him to be in the bunker in Missouri. But he would be there every time he could. Ollie would spend a lot of time in Israel and occasionally be able to bring some of them with him. When things went down in Jerusalem, he would almost have to live there. His life would be in constant danger then. But today, both of them focused on the imposing man who dominated the day.

Jews worldwide were in awe of the ceremony and the fact that they would once again have a presence on the Temple Mount. It excited them that the temple would soon stand proudly there again. Even if they had to share it with the Muslims for a while, their Messiah would soon come and give them ultimate victory. The rebuilding of the temple was a sure sign of that prophecy being fulfilled.

Ben was among those who had waited and prayed for this day all of his life. But he now knew the Messiah who would come and bring true and eternal victory was Jesus. As he watched the ceremony, he longed for his people to recognize that truth. But for now, Jewish worship had begun again on the Temple Mount, and construction of the temple would begin soon.

Ben had spent some time with Jewish leaders during the previous day. There was a little-known fact that they knew. The location where they were being allowed to build the temple was the right spot. Those who had erected the Dome of the Rock thought they were building it exactly where the temple previously stood. But they were wrong. If they had done their research, they would have known. They did not.

A fact from the Mishnah they overlooked stated that the Holy of Holies in the Temple, the Holy Place into which only the High Priest could enter once per year on Yom Kippur, must align perfectly with the Golden Gate. It is also called the Eastern Gate because it faces east toward the Mount of Olives. It was obvious when one stood on that mountain that the Golden Gate did not line up with the Dome of the Rock. It stood to the left of the gate. What aligned with that Gate was a little covered portico known as the Dome of the Tablets. Many understood, including Ben, that this dome sat on the exact site of the Holy of Holies. They named it the Dome of the Tablets, referring to Moses' two stone tablets housed in the Ark of the Covenant. The Ark was the most important element of the Holy of Holies.

Without realizing it, Messai had negotiated an agreement allowing the Jews to rebuild the temple on the exact spot where it had originally stood! Ben could not help but smile as he thought about that. He already envisioned the magnificent structure proudly standing on that site facing eastward toward the Mount of Olives. Standing atop that Mount provided a view directly into the front entrance of the temple, looking through the Golden Gate. The Jewish Rabbis had smiled along with him as they discussed that fact.

Ollie was oblivious to all of that, but he also took pleasure in hearing that Messai was wrong about something. The man had many things wrong, but he would eventually answer to the one had everything right. Ollie would be on the side of the right. He was thankful for that.

Back in New York, Blake and John were trying to plan for the purchase of steel bunkers which would serve as the secret hideaway and command central for the Smyrnians during the remainder of these seven years. Ben had okayed the purchase of three bunkers, but only if they confirmed there was space for that many on the property in Missouri which had belonged to Beth's parents. The clearing was more than an acre in size, but they had to be certain three 3,000 square feet bunkers would fit on that acre and function as they needed them to.

That meant a flight to Missouri and the first time Trey would get to do his job as a Smyrnian. He could hardly wait to pick up Blake, Beth, Anders, John, Evan and Ally in New York and fly them to Missouri the next morning. The latter three were ecstatic about finally getting to see the property for themselves. They would take as long as they needed to inspect the property, determine whether three bunkers would fit and decide what layout would work best to fit their purpose. They would also check the ground to ensure that digging would not be too difficult. Because of the absence of precipitation for months, it was dry and hard. They would give specific attention to how they could best move in and out without being seen and to the overall security of the site. Then there were the other questions. How were they going to get the bunkers into the clearing, and who would install them? None of them had any experience with that. They would have to figure it out.

The next morning they boarded Trey's charter jet and took a few minutes for introductions and welcoming him to the team. But with no time to waste, the plane climbed into the air bound for Missouri. The flight was smooth and seemed to last only a few minutes as they talked and planned the entire time.

Once on the ground, Trey had a Suburban waiting. It would hold all seven comfortably for the drive to the farm, with him being the seventh. He wanted to check out any potential sites to create a landing strip for a plane, or at least set down a chopper in the clearing. Beth drove and soon made the turn into what appeared to be a grove of trees, but was actually the lane leading back to the clearing. Everyone except Blake and Anders jumped and braced for impact until they realized they were on a lane entirely covered by limbs hanging from each side and overlapping in the middle, concealing the drive.

"This is like driving through a long tunnel," said Evan.

"Wait till you see the clearing," said Anders. "We could probably build houses in there and no one would ever see them. You'll wonder why we even need underground bunkers."

When they reached the clearing, Ally whispered, "What do you mean build houses? This is a house. There is a roof overhead and walls on each side. Nobody is getting in here. And that grass looks like the softest carpet I have ever walked on, even though it is dry."

"Remarkable, isn't it," asked Beth. "As soon as we started talking about a location for our safe place, I knew this was it. I am certain God already had that planned when he gave this farm to my parents and that he prepared it all in advance."

"Let's get out and start taking measurements." John was eager to get down to business. He had a visual picture of the bunker in his mind and knew three of them would easily fit in this space. As he looked around, he spread his arms and said enthusiastically, "Home sweet home!"

He then continued, "Beth, did you say there is more than an acre in here?" She nodded. "There are 43,560 square feet in an acre, 208 feet square. You don't have to be a math whiz to know we can easily put three 3,000 square foot bunkers in this area. But spacing them is key. I'd like to ask Doc if there is a way to connect them, creating a 9,000 square foot building underground that will allow all of us to be together instead of staying and working in separate bunkers. I'm not sure if that's possible, but if it is, it will make a major difference in how we work together as a team. If we can't do that, maybe we can dig tunnels to connect all three. We will have to wait and see once we get them in here. If we put them side by side, they will be 90 by 100, plenty of room in this field."

"That would be perfect, if it can happen, John." Evan was seeing John's vision for the bunkers.

Anders filmed the property, allowing them to have a visual aid when they planned off site. Beth had a plat of the property which would serve that purpose on paper, or online if they preferred.

John kept saying, "This is unbelievable. I can't believe a place like this even exists. We have to seal this deal on those bunkers and figure out how to get them here, then install them."

"I think I have a solution to your first dilemma," said Trey. "I have a pilot friend who has a large cargo plane. I'm sure I can convince him to let me use it for a few days. If weight is not a problem, I can fly them in one at a time, or more if his specs will allow."

"Now we are making progress," John said with a big smile. "I'm seeing them buried in this area, probably next to each other. We can use the remaining square footage for lots of things. We will need parking, but we need to keep vehicles to a minimum. We can figure all of that out later."

"One thing I can see," said Trey, "is there is no place for a landing strip or helipad in here. I will scope out the surrounding acreage for a spot to land."

"I have this feeling, call it women's intuition or something else, that we will need this place ready to go soon," said Beth. "John, you need to get on with purchasing those bunkers."

"I sense that too, Beth," said Ally. "Maybe it's because I am the only other woman here."

"I agree with both of you." Blake had kept quiet until now, allowing the rest to check out the site for themselves. "I can feel it in my spirit. The invasion of darkness is about to get real. I say we get the most specific measurements of this place we can and get on our way back to New York. I honestly don't believe we have a minute to wait." They were all thinking the same thing, so they did what they came to do and were on their way to Trey's plane. Then it was back to Blake and Beth's high rise, which would serve as command central and their safe place until they got this place ready to go. As they boarded the plane, Blake called Ben's phone and got a quick answer.

"Blake, how are things going there. Have you been to the property?"

"We were just there and are getting on the plane now to head back to New York. We all agree on two things. One, the site is perfect, and three bunkers will fit easily, more if needed. Two, there is no time to wait. We know things will break any minute."

"Ollie and I can sense that strongly here in Jerusalem. As people were celebrating on the Temple Mount, we could sense the storm coming. It is here, Blake, days at most. Something is getting ready to happen. I can't be certain what it is, but I know it is coming. We have to get ready."

"That is the plan. John will call Doc while we are in flight. He worries me. I'm not sure why, but there is something about him that makes me not trust him. However, we need his bunkers, so we will have to work with him the best way we can."

When they were in the air and leveled out, John punched in Doc's number. He answered.

"John, how are you? What did you decide about the bunkers? One, two or three?"

"We need three, Doc. How fast can you get them ready?"

"If we put every available man on them, we can get them ready for you in less than a week. I was pretty sure you would take them, so we got a head start on building them."

"That's perfect. I will make plans to transport the one you already have."

"Are you sure you don't want me to bring them to you and put them in? No extra charge for delivery and installation."

"No, we'll get them. We have people who want to do that. You just concentrate on getting them ready. I'll bring your money when we come." Doc wanted to know where the bunkers were going and what his childhood friend was up to, but John refused to yield that information.

Blake and Beth sat talking on the return flight about something they had been discussing, and they knew in their hearts the time had come. It would change everything for them, the Smyrnians and the people of the world. If it was not on, it would be after this.

•　　　•　　　•　　　•　　　•

Ben and Ollie were waiting in Ben Gurion Airport to board their flight back to New York. Ollie would only be there two days before he had to go back to London. All of them had to get back to work, but how long would they be able to do that without being identified as followers of Jesus? He knew it would not be long. They were heading straight into utter darkness.

"Blake and Beth, what were the two of you talking about on the plane? I can tell it is something important. Are you going to let us in on it, or not?" John's patience was wearing thin. That was not at all surprising with all the things he had on his mind.

"We will tell you, but not today. We want to wait for Ben and Ollie to get back. Then we can let everybody in on it at the same time. We need to do it while Bruno, Mila and the boys are here too. They only have a little time before they need to head back to Germany."

"Okay, but I'll go crazy until you tell us. I can tell it is big."

"It is big, John. If the war hasn't already started, this will kick it into high gear."

* * * * *

Two days later they were all gathered to see the video of the property, get a report from Ben and Ollie, and finally hear about Blake and Beth's plans. Things seemed to move at warp speed now. Beth's property. The bunkers. Doc Sanderson. The temple. And whatever Blake and Beth had up their sleeves. It was a somber time. Yet anxiety filled them, as they also tingled with excitement, the way a soldier feels as he is preparing to go into battle.

As the video played, Ben and Miriam, Ollie and the Fromms sat in amazement at what they were seeing. "Barmy!" exclaimed Ollie. They looked at him with a look that said, "What in the world does that mean?" Beth explained.

"Barmy means crazy! What he means is 'Wow!' See Ollie, my time in England came in handy."

"Well, I meant what I said. That place is barmy, crazy if you prefer. I've never seen anything like it anywhere. It's completely hidden."

Ben said, "I agree. I can't imagine us ever being discovered in there, especially underground. But we will still have to be careful of our every move so we don't give away our location."

"I can't think of any place like that in Germany," said Bruno. "Even if we can buy a bunker, I don't know where we will put it."

"Now, my friend..." The team expected words like these from Anders. The man's faith often seemed stronger than any of theirs. "God will provide the bunker and show you where to put it. He hasn't let any of us down yet, and I don't expect him to start now."

Bruno seemed humbled. "I'm sorry. I believe that. And I can't wait to see it happen!"

Mila reached over and placed her hand on his arm. "You're right, dear. I would love for it to be just like Beth's farm, but it will be perfect, wherever it is." Her smile melted his heart even more now since he put his faith in Jesus than it ever had before. All of them recognized it.

"So, Ben and Ollie, can you get on with what you saw in Israel? I want to hear from Blake and Beth, and they won't talk until you do." John's patience was really being tested now.

"I can tell you," said Ben. "Messai is not who he claims to be."

"What do you mean by that?" asked Ally. "We already know he's the Antichrist."

"That he is," Ben explained. "But he has my people, and the world fooled. He hates the Jews. I am not sure anyone else realizes that, but I do. I saw the disdain for them in his eyes. And I was standing close enough to hear a growl escape from his throat. I didn't catch what he said, but he unquestionably uttered it from his hatred for my people. I fear the world will see that soon."

"I agree with Ben," said Ollie. "The man is so fake I can see right through him. His actions and words are all one big show. His intentions are evil, and his motives are impure. But none of the Jews realize that. They think he cares about them. The world believes he wants peace. Both are wrong. Israel and the Jews are falling right into his trap, along with everyone else in the world."

"There is one bit of humor in all of this, though," Ben chuckled.

"How can you find humor in any of that, dear?" whispered Miriam. "He is the enemy of our people and seeks our destruction. That is not funny to me." She spoke softly, but there was no questioning her serious tone.

"Not humorous in that way, Miriam." Ben wanted to reassure her. "Maybe I should have said ironic. You have read what the Mishnah tells us about the location of the temple."

"He is allowing us to build it on the right spot!" Ben did not have to explain further. She got it.

"That's right. The Dome of the Tablets. The front of the temple facing the Mount of Olives, lining up with the Eastern Gate. Let him think he is right. We know he is wrong!"

"What are you two talking about?" asked John. "Let the rest of us in on it, please."

"Messai thinks they built the Dome of the Rock on the exact site of the Jewish Temple. But they missed it by that much." Ben held up his thumb and forefinger, barely apart. "The Mishnah says when you stand atop the Mount of Olives and look through the Golden Gate, or the Eastern Gate as we often say, it aligns perfectly with the temple entrance and straight into the Holy of Holies. We built the Dome of the Tablets on the exact site where the Holy of Holies stood at the rear of the temple. If you stand on the Mount and look through that gate, you are looking right into that little dome."

"So, Messai is allowing the Jews to build the temple right where it stood. That has to be another God-thing." Blake could not help but smile at that too.

"We have always taught that Yahweh is a serious God and there is no place for fun. Now that I have accepted Jesus as the Messiah, I see that God has a sense of humor!"

"I know," chimed in Evan. "Just look at John! I'd say he is funny looking, wouldn't you guys?"

"Ha, ha," said John. "That is enough of this. Ben and Ollie, if you have nothing else to add, it's Blake and Beth's turn. I can't wait any longer to hear what they have on their minds!"

"Anything else, Ollie?" asked Ben.

"Nothing at all. Blake and Beth, the floor is yours. We are all ears."

The newlyweds sat side by side. Blake took her hand in his as he prepared to speak. The group saw the seriousness of the moment. The mood turned from light to heavy in a matter of seconds.

Blake went first. "There is no doubt the time is short. Things will start happening any day. But the time is also growing shorter for us to tell people about Jesus. We don't have any time to waste. Neither Beth nor I have any doubt that the time is here. It is time to act. Beth?"

"Blake is right. People must hear the truth. Each of us will get permission from our networks to host simultaneous 90-minute special programs. That should be easy for Blake." She glanced at Ben, who smiled and nodded. "In the first twenty minutes, we will talk about September 11, then move to things that have happened since. Before a commercial break we will promise viewers that when we come back, they will see something that will explain it all. After the break, we will show the pastor's video and finish without commercial interruption. We will promote the specials heavily in advance, so the ratings should be high. We can tell millions of people about Jesus in an hour and a half!"

"But..." Blake took his turn again. "We must have the bunkers installed and ready to move in before we do this. Doc said he can have them ready in a week. Okay Trey, it is time we hear from you. Tell us about your friend's cargo plane."

"His name is Rickie, short for Enrique. We were in the military together. I flew fighter jets, and he flew cargo planes. When we got home, we stayed close and have borrowed each other's planes several times. He will have no problem with me using it, if we can arrange our schedules. I will call him when we finish here. Can one of you give me a copy of the pastor's message? We are so close I think he will hear me out. I will tell him I discovered something that changed my life, then show him the video. I believe I can win him over. He will be a big plus for our team. It may take three separate flights, depending on the size and weight of the bunkers. I will need John to get that info for me. But I will do whatever it takes to get them there. Don't worry about that."

"Thanks, Trey. It sure is good to have you on board, no pun intended." Blake grinned, though it was half-hearted. "Now let me tell you more about our plans. There's a man who has been trying to buy my place for a few years. I will sell it to him and try to close on the loan as soon as possible. After we do, we will have 30 days to move out. Hopefully, all of that will give us time to get the bunkers installed and finished enough to live in. We will air the specials after we move out, which means we will have to move into the bunkers immediately. The two of us will be public enemy number one after that night. The rest of you may fly under the radar for a while, but not likely for long. Beth and I are ready to roll with this, so we need to plan accordingly."

The room fell silent for what felt like an eternity. Ben eventually ended the silence.

"I will create my studio in one bunker, just as Blake and Beth will. The three of us will broadcast securely so they can't find us. I will speak specifically to the Jews. Blake and Beth will speak to the rest of the world. Miriam and I are selling our house too. And Beth failed to say so, but she already has a buyer for hers. Between the sale of our houses, our bank accounts and cashing in our retirement funds, we will have enough to purchase the bunkers, set them all up and provide our needs for much of the next seven years. Are the rest of you in?"

"I'm all in," said Anders. "This guy is ready. I'm fighting this war for my Angie and our three kids."

Everyone was in and ready to go on the offensive. No defensive mindset here. Trey would call Rickie and set up the use of his plane. Beth shared about a barn in a wooded area on the farm that housed a bulldozer and backhoe, along with a tractor and some other equipment. They came with the property when her parents received it. Her dad enjoyed playing around on them, though he never accomplished much. But he kept them in good working condition. She would teach some of them how to operate both. Her dad had allowed her to do that a few times. Blake was becoming more amazed by his wife every day. She was skilled at more things than he had even imagined.

So they set the plan in motion. They would work to prepare the property. Trey would fly in the bunkers, but only after he had found a place to land the big cargo plane. Then they would install them, and everyone who needed to would move in. They would have to work hard to make it all happen, but they could do it. Then Blake and Beth would air their specials in prime time, and things would go crazy. Hopefully, there would be many new believers in Jesus after that night. Go time was getting near, and one thing was sure. The Smyrnians were ready.

CHAPTER 4

In Kansas, Doc Sanderson stood inspecting the work on the bunkers. Everything was going according to plan. His employees were happy because they would receive a nice bonus for working hard to get them ready in time for John to pick up. Doc would receive his biggest payday in a long time. He smiled at the thought of how he would use the money. He had already promised Kathie the new car she wanted. She was a supportive and helpful wife, and it would not be possible to run the business without her. She deserved the car and much more. They already lived in their dream home and had houses in Florida and the Rocky Mountains.

But Doc lived with an insatiable desire for more. No amount of money or things was ever enough. He had delved into an illegal venture here and there, but what people did not know would not hurt them, right? And it sure helped him! His wealth had not all come from his highly successful business. Some of it had come through unscrupulous means. Doc would do just about anything to make more money. Yes, he would sell his soul to the devil, if that is what it took.

The bunkers were almost ready to go, but they needed a few more days. Doc waited for a call from his old friend, John Baldwin. His phone rang. "John! How's it going? Bunker number one is sitting here waiting for you to come and pick it up. You haven't changed your mind on your old pal now, have you?"

"No way. I'll have a truck there day after tomorrow to get that one, if that is okay. Then if they are ready, we will get the others the next two days."

"That works on our end. Don't forget to bring the money with you. It will take an enormous suitcase to carry that much cash."

"You said you take credit cards, didn't you, Doc? Oh, stop worrying. I will have your money."

"Sure wish you would tell me what you are doing with those bunkers and where they are going."

"I tried to tell you why I am doing this, remember? You wouldn't listen to me."

"And I'm still not interested in your conspiracy theory. Just come and get your bunkers."

"That is exactly what I plan to do. I will see you day after tomorrow."

"I will watch for you. It is a pleasure doing business with you, John."

"The pleasure is all mine, Doc. But I wish you would take a few minutes to hear me out. This truly is important, earth-shattering stuff."

"That is not happening, John. But it has been good to see my old childhood buddy again."

"Same here. I wish you well. But I fear for you at the same time. Talk to you later, Doc."

The call ended. What did John mean by that last comment? He feared for him? John did not need to fear for the man who had it all. It sounded to Doc like John was the one who was afraid. Bunkers? Hiding away? A conspiracy theory? John was the one who had surely lost his mind.

In Jerusalem, work on the Jewish Temple progressed at a rapid pace. They were well ahead of schedule. There was potential for an earlier completion date. Aissa Messai had thrown all of his resources behind the project. The man would stop at nothing to bring peace to the world. But something had not been right since the night of the eclipse. It brought reminders of the Invasion to people's minds. They felt something was wrong that night after the deafening sound and blinding flash of light. But they would not understand it until they got word that billions of people had disappeared, taken away in a flash. Now people were going about their lives, and those lives were prosperous and good. But something was still not right. The inhabitants of the world did not know what it was. But the Smyrnians knew and were prepared to face it head on.

Blake and Beth were sleeping soundly, enjoying the comfort of their posh high-rise apartment for a few more days. The others had returned home, and now they had the place to themselves again. They had a couple more days off before returning to work. At least, that is what they thought.

Almost simultaneously, their phones jarred them awake. The contrasting sounds of their opposite but loud ringtones almost caused them to jump out of bed and land on the floor. Each grabbed their phone and answered in sleepy voices.

"Blake, this is Ben." The call brought vivid memories of September 11 racing back to his mind.

"What's going on, Ben? I still have two more days off, remember?"

"Listen to me, Blake. Your time off is over. In fact, after last night, I feel sure all of our time off is permanently over. I need you up and out there covering the news again."

"Wh... What..." Blake knew he was stammering again. "I'm sorry, Ben. Tell me what is up."

"Gang war. Hundreds dead. Cars and houses burned. New York is on fire! And the same thing is happening all over the world. Sound familiar?"

"Yes, it does. September 11... worldwide. The tremor, the eclipse... worldwide. I will get out there. And I will report the news. But honestly, I can't wait for the day when Beth and I share Jesus on the air. People are dying without him. And every day that goes by, many more will die."

"You're right, Blake. It is imperative that we reach the point of being able to spread the word without worrying about whether we are giving ourselves away. We need to get our faith and opposition to Messai out in the open so that can happen. But none of us can do it until we get those bunkers installed. Number one should arrive tomorrow night. I would love to be there to see it come in."

"Me too, Ben. I want to go so badly. Trey said he could fly us anytime. After we report today, maybe we can hop on his plane to Missouri this evening, if he can come and get us. I'm sure Beth will want to do that, too. But her job is more in jeopardy than mine. Her producer is not a believer, and he has already been lenient with her. But I'm not sure she cares about that either. Okay, I am off here and out there. Talk to you after I am on the scene, Ben."

"You got it. But we're not talking about a scene. We're talking about scenes. You can't cover them all. We have other reporters out there too. Do what you can and don't worry about the rest. I will call Trey and see what he says."

"Blake," Beth said. "I can tell we both got the same news. The peace brought by the man of peace sure was short-lived, wasn't it? Let's get dressed, get out of here and get to work. But it is hard to act like my heart is in it, when you and I both know it isn't."

"I'm with you on that. But we have a few more weeks before we can be free to speak as much as we want. Ben told me he wants to check with Trey and ask if he can fly us to the farm tonight. He would love to be there when the first bunker arrives. What do you think?"

"I'm not sure about that, Blake. I can't afford to lose my job. I have to keep it and maintain my standing with the network until we air the specials."

"Maybe neither of us should go then. I don't want to go without you."

"I think we need to wait until all three bunkers are there. If we can get away then, we can help get the digging started. Anyway, Trey will be there with Evan, Ally and John. I have also thought about something else. We need an entrance into the bunkers. John hopes to find a way we can connect them so we have one huge house underground big enough to hold all of us and our equipment, with plenty of room to spare. What if we build a cabin over the site that has a hidden door leading to a secret stairway that goes down into the bunkers?"

"That is a great idea! I have wondered how we plan to get in, unless we leave a walk-in entrance above ground, and that would be too visible. It blows my mind that we haven't talked about that. It just never came up. Okay, we have to get out of here. I'm heading to the shower."

Within 30 minutes, both had showered, dressed, eaten a bagel and were out the door. Back at work. Neither wanted to be, but as soon as they hit the streets their adrenaline kicked in and they were once again the two top reporters in America. The world waited to hear from them.

Trey had done his homework. He could land the big cargo plane on the small road that went past the tree-covered lane leading back to the safe place that would be home for the Smyrnians. They would use the lowboy trailer, that had transported the dozer, to haul the bunkers down the lane. The backhoe would lift it from the cargo hold to the trailer, while pulling it with a Chevy Silverado 3500 and a Grade 120 chain. Trey planned to bring both. That should get the job done.

The tricky part was how to do all of that without being seen or heard. Almost no one traveled the road, so hopefully no one would drive on it either of those nights. The darkness would conceal the big plane flying over, although if someone caught the sound of it descending, they may run outside to check it out. But very few people would get out for that at midnight. The isolation of the farm made that even more unlikely. Yet even with careful planning and extreme caution, it was still a risky effort. However, the team looked back on all that God had done for them already, and they believed he would do it again. So they prayed...

Blake could hardly wrap his mind around the scene that greeted him as he walked the streets of Manhattan. The streets and sidewalks were strewn with dead bodies, most of them teenagers or young adults. Sadly, others had gotten caught in the crossfire. Blood literally ran in the streets. As he looked into the faces of the dead, he knew they were not ready to die because they had not believed in Jesus. His heart broke for them. All the more reason to get on with the program. He and Beth could not afford to wait much longer.

First responders flooded the area, trying to find and care for anyone who may still be alive. Curious onlookers stared at the carnage. Family members mourned loudly over the lifeless bodies of sons and daughters. Anders pointed the camera at him and said, "3, 2, 1 and go." Blake was not ready, but he had to report. It was his job.

"Good morning, everyone. However, this is anything but a good morning. It is not a great way for me to get back on the job either. I have never seen anything like the carnage that lies in the streets of Manhattan, and all of New York City this morning. These images are far too graphic to show on television. I cannot even describe them to you. You can likely hear sirens, but I can only hope they are loud enough to drown out the screams of those who are grieving. This is tragic. It is just like September 11, and the tremor that stuck later. Scenes like this one have greeted people all over the world today. Violence is rampant. Young people are dying needlessly. Others have gotten caught in the crosshairs of this senseless bloodshed and perished. I am appalled at what is happening. Where is the peace Aissa Messai promised? Did he not tell us that is what he came to bring? But where is that peace now? From what this reporter sees, this has nothing to do with peace; not here in New York City or in any other part of the world."

Blake was treading on dangerous ground by calling out Messai like that, but he did not care. He'd had enough of the man and his arrogance. The Smyrnians knew who he truly was, and they had to tell the world. Their personal war with him and his forces was weeks away at most. Why not tell them now? Then realizing how close he may be to opening up the entire team to danger, he caught himself and spoke to the panel in the studio.

"I am sorry. This has just sickened me to such a degree that I am struggling to control my anger. I suppose I am looking for someone to blame. And I am calling on Aissa Messai to step into his role as leader of the world and bring the peace he claims is already here. Because this morning I don't see it. The world desperately needs his leadership right now."

He had said enough. "I am sending it back to you in the studio. I will be eager to get your thoughts on all of this."

Beth. He looked for her and saw her reporting too. He could tell she was struggling as much as he was. It was time to promote their prime time specials. They needed to move up the date, but there was still much work to do in Missouri before that happened. How many would die before then? What would Messai say considering last night's tragedies? The world was waiting to hear.

Evan was doing his job as the organizer for the Smyrnians. With the opening day of the Spring semester three weeks away, he was organizing efforts to get the bunkers installed before classes started. He had seen Blake's report and knew he would not wait much longer. He had heard it in his voice. The reporter had turned rebel overnight. He was ready to unveil the real Aissa Messai to the world, revealing his true identity, and telling the truth about what happened on September 11. When both he and Beth did that, many more people would turn to faith in Jesus. But Aissa Messai would declare war on Christians the minute their specials ended. And it would not be long until he declared war on the Jews too. That would make Ben's role vital.

So much on a young man's mind. It was more than a college student should have to deal with. He should be able to focus on his classes and have a good time enjoying college life. But all of it made his role essential. And time was of the essence. They had a small window of opportunity to get the bunkers installed and ready for the team to take up residence in them. To do that in such a brief time seemed impossible, but Evan intended to make it happen. Besides, he knew who was on their side. And the Bible said all things are possible through Jesus. Once they were in, they planned to get set up and operational. The first would arrive tomorrow. And he and Ally would be there to greet it.

Trey was there already, looking things over one last time before bringing in the bunker the next day. He had told Ben his busy schedule would not allow him the time to bring the news crew in from New York and also be ready for everything that needed to happen. Ben agreed, saying they needed to stay put and not leave town until after all the bunkers had arrived.

John would fly with him. It was a covert operation, so they decided doing it at night, under the cover of darkness, offered the best opportunity for a clandestine mission. He had arranged for the transporting of the bunker from PSI to a private airstrip where they would load it onto the cargo plane. He could not help but be a little nervous, because each bunker put the plane at or slightly above its maximum weight capability. But he would take the chance.

He and John would drive from Springfield to Jefferson City Memorial Airport, where Rickie kept his plane. They did not have commercial flights, so it provided the perfect location for them to depart. They would land at the airstrip in Wichita at 5:00 p.m. John would make the drive to PSI and complete the transaction. He had told Doc he would be there shortly before 6:00. It would be dark by then. The driver of the transport would leave immediately after John inspected the bunker. He would get to the plane and be ready to load by the time John returned. The moment they finished loading it, they would be in the air headed back to Missouri.

They hoped things would go well, and they would arrive at the farm by midnight. Evan and Ally would be there waiting and on the lookout for any activity in the area. Evan would have the lowboy trailer at the end of the lane. Both he and Ally would use flashlights to guide the big plane to the roadway. They had confirmed there was sufficient width and length to make the landing. But testing had not taken place, so they would not be sure until the plane was safely on the ground. If all went as planned, they would deliver one of three bunkers before dawn. They would then have to repeat the process each of the next two days.

Meanwhile, in Belgium, Aissa Messai fielded questions about the violence that had broken out in places all over the earth. Regardless of the pressure, he never seemed to become frustrated.

"Friends, there is no need for concern. Achieving peace cannot happen overnight. I remind you we have been seeing progress around the world. These things are nothing more than isolated incidents and minor setbacks. I would like to point out the one place where there is complete peace right now: the Middle East. Israel and her Arab neighbors have come to the table and arrived at a peace settlement which has led to a time of unprecedented tranquility in that part of the world. That has not happened in recorded history. Our focus has been for peace to begin there, then spread to all parts of the earth. If it can happen there, it can happen everywhere. As the Secretary-General of the United Nations, I commit to you that we will continue to seek peace on earth, all the earth, as we are seeing in Israel at this moment. Let us stay the course together."

"Blake Thompson, the leading reporter in America, called you out today. Have you seen that? And if so, how would you respond to his criticism of your leadership?"

"I know well who Mr. Thompson is, although I have not had the privilege of meeting him personally. We shared a few seconds when the UN Security Council presented me for nomination to this position, but it was not a verbal encounter. I am sure Mr. Thompson remembers it well. We will have future personal encounters where I will get to express myself more clearly to him. For now, I am not concerned about his statements. I understand them considering what he witnessed today. I hope he will see the truth of what is, rather than what appears to be. Now, I must be going. To Mr. Thompson, I offer this opportunity. Meet with me face-to-face and let's discuss your concerns man-to-man. That will give you a chance to see what kind of man I really am."

As their day of reporting came to a close, Beth and Blake were back together. She came to him and wrapped her arms around him in a tight embrace. "Blake, please be careful. I can't believe you called Messai out like that. I don't want to lose something I have waited my whole life for. I need you, Blake. This world needs you. We have to air the special programs and play the video for everyone to see. People will put their faith in Jesus when we do. Please Blake, for me, and for people who need Jesus, don't get yourself killed."

"I know, Beth. I love you so much. And I want to share the good news about Jesus with the millions of viewers who will watch us that night. I just got so angry as I looked at all those young people who died without believing in him. I know who is the ultimate cause of it all. But I also know nothing I, you or anyone else does can change what he will do and what the next seven years will bring. If I can hang in there for a few more weeks, we will be out in the open in the public eye, and with Messai. But we will have the bunkers as a haven when we need to hide for a while, or just get away from the action and refresh. Help me keep my anger under control until then. We both need to survive for seven years, if we can." His phone rang.

"Hello, Ben. Before you say anything..."

"Blake, what were you thinking? Don't start this war before it is time. I now think we need to get out of here. Can Beth convince her boss to give her a few days off? She can tell them she is doing research. Isn't that what you told me all those times you were in Chicago and Missouri?"

"Are you thinking what I'm thinking?"

"Without a doubt. We need to go to Missouri and get away from New York for a few days. Every one of us wants to be there when the bunkers come in. Ask Beth to check with her boss. Your boss is giving you three days off right now!"

"I will have her do that and let you know as soon as I can. Then we need to schedule a flight."

"No, not a flight. Records would show where we flew. We can't take any chances on giving away the safe place. Are you up for a 20-hour drive? We will drive through the night until tomorrow afternoon. We can each take turns driving while the others sleep. I say others, assuming Beth can get away."

"I am definitely up for it! I will talk to Beth right now."

Beth waved her hands around and shook her head up and down, trying to get his attention. She had been on the phone with her boss too, unbeknownst to Blake.

"Can you call and ask if they will give you few days to leave New York and go out of town to do some research? Ben thinks we need to go to the farm and be there when the bunkers make it in."

"I heard you talking to Ben, and I have already called. I didn't ask; I just told them I need to be somewhere doing research for a few days. They didn't question it. They said go."

"Ben says we need to drive so we don't take a chance of leaving flight records behind that can trace us to Ozark. We can leave in an hour or two. Do you think you can take a turn driving so we can go straight through?"

"Sure! Let's call and tell the others we are heading their way."

"Ben, we are in! What time can we leave? Is Miriam coming and bringing the kids?"

"The kids have started back to school. They can't go. Miriam will stay here and take care of them. Besides, we would need a bus to have room for eleven of us."

"Make that twelve. Anders is in too. So there will be eight of us there to help. That will make a huge difference. Too bad Bruno can't be there. We could use the big man's help. Another thing: if you don't mind, can we take your car? You are far more under the radar than Beth and me. Can you pick us up at our place in an hour?"

"I will get there as soon as I can. Just be ready."

Blake, Beth and Anders headed back in to pack. Anders said, "Missouri, here we come!"

CHAPTER 5

In Germany, Bruno Fromm was ecstatic. He saw his first two people put their faith in Jesus! Hans and Heidi Meier were a young couple who lived down the road. God had given him their names that morning while he listed people he wanted to speak with or show them the pastor's video that had helped him and all the others believe. Evan put the translation at the bottom of the screen so people who spoke other languages could read the pastor's words as he spoke. That boy was sharp! He could handle just about anything involving technology. He would without a doubt be one of the key cogs in the Smyrnians wheel. And why not? He was the first to believe in Jesus, so God had undoubtedly prepared him for his lead role on the team.

Hans and Heidi took very little convincing. The invasion, which they now knew to be the Rapture of Jesus' church, took their grandparents. They married only one year before and had no children. They were excited and wondered how soon they could get started. They were ready to join Bruno and Mila in the search for a safe place where they could install bunkers when they could purchase them. They believed that would happen! Their families were wealthy, so if they brought them to faith in Jesus, it may bode well for those being funded.

The German unit was growing. Bruno had reminded them their group was closer to the action because of the proximity of their countries. Germany and Belgium bordered each other, and Aissa Messai now called Belgium home. Five to six hours separated them from him. Bruno had to share the news with the group in Missouri. They were ecstatic! They looked forward to the day Hans and Heidi would meet the rest of the Smyrnians.

Go time had arrived in Missouri, and Trey and John were on their way to Jefferson City to board Rickie's plane and make the relatively short flight to Wichita. The four New Yorkers were only a few hours away. Evan and Ally awaited their arrival, and the six of them would get started right away preparing for the installation of the bunkers. Back in New York, Miriam worried about her husband. He had reassured her, "Don't worry. Jesus didn't visit me personally and call me to go tell our people to let me die before I get to do that." She knew he was right, but she could not help being anxious.

Blake, Beth, Ben and Anders arrived at the farm around the same time Trey and John flew out of Jefferson City bound for Wichita. A much-needed surprise awaited them: thermal carafes with Blake's favorite Red Eye coffee. The carafes would keep it hot all night. Beth and Anders had learned to like the strong stuff, too. For Ben, there were two carafes of the sweet tea he loved so much. The caffeine would keep them awake all night if need be. And by nature of all they had to do, they would likely need that for each of the next three nights. They may find some time for a little sleep, but most of the time, they would have to work.

Shortly after 5:00 p.m. Trey landed at the private airstrip in Wichita. He arranged in advance for a car to be there, which John would drive, and for a tractor and trailer driven by another of his military buddies to haul the bunker. He and Trey were close and the man was 100% confidential. No one else was around, just a vacant airstrip and one lone car. John climbed in and sped off for PSI while Trey readied the plane for its precious cargo.

John pulled in at 5:30 and saw the tractor and trailer sitting there with the large, impressive bunker already loaded on it. It looked even more impressive than it had sitting in Doc's building. Per their discussions, as he walked inside carrying his flashlight, he found rooms divided off which could serve as living quarters, TV studios or other things. A kitchen and multiple bathrooms were a welcome sight. Doc had told the truth. This baby was amazing! It was unquestionably worth a million dollars. John now saw that they were getting a bargain at the reduced price for purchasing three. The others would be identical, with each having separate entrances.

Beth had shared her idea about the cabin above ground with a hidden door and a secret stairway leading down. With the bunkers buried in the middle of the clearing, the stairs would end in a hallway from which they could access all three doors. It would be the safe place to top all safe places when they finished it.

Doc approached him from the office. "I'm glad to see you made it. I wasn't counting on that until you showed up and I had your money in my hands."

"Here is your money, cash just like you wanted. $750,000. Count it to make sure it's all there. Is it okay for the truck driver to head on with it while we wrap things up here?"

"Sure. Let him go on."

"Doc, I still wish you would let me talk to you about why I need these things."

"As I told you, John, that is not happening. I am not the least bit interested in your conspiracy theories. But I am happy to take your money." He grinned.

John thought his grin almost looked evil. Doc was a secularist to the core. He believed only in himself and what he could accomplish. "Not all that much unlike me before I put my faith in Jesus," John thought.

"Although," Doc continued, "I would still like to know where you are taking them and what you are using them for."

"That is not happening either, Doc, unless you let me tell you about *why* I need them."

"Then I guess we're at an impasse. We'll have to let it go without either of us being satisfied."

"I suppose we will. Okay, let's get this deal completed so I can get out of here too."

As the truck pulled away, John and Doc walked into the office where Doc counted the money then said with a grin, "It sure is a pleasure doing business with you, John." He held a stack of bills up to his nose and breathed in the smell of new money. "Same time tomorrow?"

"Same time. Everything will be just as it is today. The truck will be here and have the bunker loaded, and I will arrive at the same time. Now, I need to be going. Thank you, Doc."

"Again, my pleasure. I will see you tomorrow, buddy."

John drove away, checking behind him to ensure he was not being followed. They could take no chances of giving away their location. When he got back to the airstrip, he found the bunker ready to load. That required special equipment, which they had rented and would leave at the airstrip for the remaining two trips. That and securing it took well over two hours.

Ready to fly at last, they sped down the runway and lifted off, bound for the farm. It was 10:00 p.m. Just right for their planned midnight arrival time. Both had a sense of relief as the plane climbed into the sky. Each knew they exceeded the weight limit, but they trusted God to get them there safely.

•　　•　　•　　•　　•

At the farm, the rest of the crew anxiously awaited their arrival. They had everything in place and were ready. A call from Trey informed them they were fifteen minutes away. Evan and Ally stood on both sides of the road with flashlights in hand. Blake and Beth hid in the trees near the turn off the main road, ready to signal the others should someone turn onto the side road, which would serve as the runway. Anders positioned himself two miles down the main road to keep an eye out for any approaching vehicles. Ben stationed himself two miles down the other way. A few trucks passed by, but there was almost never any traffic on this road, especially at this time of night. Trey was now approaching, having begun his descent. The plane headed down, and he clearly saw the flashlights being waved up and down by Evan and Ally. Blake's phone vibrated with a text from Anders.

"An old pickup truck just came flying by us. It didn't show any signs of slowing down, so I would guess we are okay. But I wanted to tell you, in case they come your way."

Blake and Beth saw the lights of the pickup coming in the distance. It came toward them like a bat out of Hades. Then suddenly, as it neared the side road, the driver slammed on the brakes and made a sharp turn onto it. It sped toward Evan and Ally and left Blake and Beth scrambling. She called them while he called John and Trey.

"Evan, you and Ally have to turn off your flashlights and hide, now! There is an old pickup truck coming right at you. Hurry!" They knew Beth was serious, so they turned off their lights and ran.

"John, Trey, ABORT! ABORT! Intruders! ABORT NOW!" Blake screamed.

Trey pulled up hard. He had performed *go arounds* in the past on aborted landings, but not in a big cargo plane carrying a heavy load. As he throttled up, the engine roared loudly, and the cargo shifted in the rear. Both thought they had secured it well! As that happened, the big plane lurched to the right, leaving John staring helplessly out his window at the ground below. He saw the lights of the pickup truck in the distance. The ground appeared to be getting close. He held on for dear life and prayed. Trey was fighting hard to level out the plane and get it headed back up. Trees were right beneath them. And there was a $750,000 bunker in the back.

Below, the others watched in horror. The truck seemed oblivious to the plight of the plane, and even to the plane itself. It appeared to be two good old boys out for a drive after having too much to drink. With windows down, they were whooping it up, yelling and waving their arms out the windows. The driver slammed on the brakes again and spun around, headed back toward the main road. Going through the ditch on the side, he bounced and scraped a tree before speeding off again, leaving the scene behind. They had gone right past the lane to the farm without even realizing it.

Beth said no one else was ever back there, and almost no one ever drove down the lane. It was the land time forgot, even though Ozark and Springfield now abutted it on each side. It never came up in discussions about property for sale or development, another God-thing. It did not take long for the truck to be on the main road and out of sight. But that did not help the men in the plane fighting for their lives. Looking up from the ground, the group could only stand and watch the frantic scene that had the potential to end badly. Blake yelled into the phone again.

"Trey, they're gone. You are clear to land. I repeat, you are clear to land!" But there was no response.

The plane started leveling out slowly, but as it did, the bunker shifted again and slid to the other side, sending the aircraft into another roll, this time to the left. Trey fought it with everything he had. Below, the flashlights were in plain view and being waved vigorously by Evan and Ally in the roadway. He yelled at John, "If I can get this thing close to level, I will try to take it down. We can't keep this up, or we will never make it. Just hang on."

They started down with the plane leaning to one side. Blake and Beth had sped back down the side road to reach Evan and Ally and be there to help if needed. Anders and Ben were hurrying to get back, too. Trey yelled at John again, "We're going down! There is no turning back now. Prepare for a rough landing!" John took him at his word. The others had gotten there just in time and had headlights from every vehicle shining on the roadway.

They just cleared the trees, and the tires touched the road. Coming in at an angle, the left wing clipped the road, and sparks flew. The load in the back shifted again, sending the plane to the other side where the right wing scraped the road, causing sparks to fly again. The aircraft bounced and swayed from side to side. Trey throttled back hard. The engines roared, and the plane shook violently. But it continued to slow, eventually coming to a stop. Trey jumped out as John rolled out, looking green.

"That was smooth," Trey said with a big grin. "One down; two to go!"

John crawled to the bushes on the roadside and lost his dinner. In a few minutes, he half staggered back and said, "If that was smooth, I'm not sure I want to be with you tomorrow night if we have a rough landing."

"Oh, I have had a lot worse than that. We're standing here on solid ground, aren't we?"

"As hard as it is to believe, yes we are. I suppose I should say 'thank you' for that. I have no idea how you did it, but I am thankful you did. I thought for sure our time had come."

"You're welcome. You had better be ready because you and I get to do this two more times!"

"Don't remind me. Somebody may have to tie me in my seat tomorrow. But one thing I can tell you is this. Securing that bunker will be a big priority before we leave Wichita this time."

"With that, I agree. That is on me. I haven't hauled a lot of heavy cargo before, but I should have known better. We will get that right tomorrow night."

"Are you two going to stand here and talk all night?" asked Evan. "We have a bunker to unload and haul back to the farm. There is a lot of work to do and not a lot of time to do it."

All of them needed that reminder. It took all hands on deck to get the bunker from the plane to the trailer. They backed the lowboy up against the cargo hold of the plane. Then they wrapped the chain around the bucket of the backhoe and attached it to the front of the bunker, lifting it up. They placed two heavy-duty cargo dollies as far underneath as they could get them after raising it up. The backhoe then lowered the front end slightly to allow the dollies to support the weight. Then another chain connected the truck and bunker and eased it from the plane to the lowboy. Good planning plus the right equipment equaled success!

Beth, being the expert, drove gently back the lane to the open area, being sure not to harm the tree canopy which framed and covered it. It was almost a perfect fit, barely scraping the trees on each side. Thankfully, the lane was not narrow. When the bunker was off the trailer and on the ground near where they would bury it, there were embraces and tears of joy all around. They celebrated the accomplishment of step one. Now it was time for the real work to begin. There was no time for sleep.

Beth had the dozer out, ready to go, and was operating it, with vehicles again providing light so she could see. She wore the hard hat her dad always insisted she wear. The others stood watching and learning. She had dug around on the farm with her dad and even cleared a little brush. She would teach Evan and Blake, too, if he would try it. He may be more difficult to convince. Then they would take turns until they got it done.

The job required a space 110 feet wide, 130 feet long and 10 feet deep. That would allow for all three bunkers to fit side-by-side with a 10-foot walkway around the sides and back for access to the exterior, should they need it. A 20-foot entryway across the front would lead to all three doors. That would allow ample space for moving things in. Fortunately, the dirt on the farm was soft and not frozen, with the warm, almost hot, temperatures. Neither was it rocky, a key component to their success because it made for easy digging.

Beth moved a lot of dirt in the next hour. Evan finally climbed on the backhoe, pulling out dirt and piling it to the side, acting like a kid with a new toy. A large hole in the ground took shape. They pushed the topsoil to one side, with the subsoil piled by itself to use as fill dirt to cover the bunkers. The rest would be hauled and dumped in the edge of the woods so no one would see it. The topsoil would then cover the fill dirt above the bunkers, and they would sow grass around the outside of the cabin. They had one goal in mind: Should someone find their way back there, they would only see a nice little cabin with landscaping around it.

By the time bunker number two arrived tomorrow at midnight, they hoped to have the hole completed. If not, they were sure it would happen by the following night. Once all three bunkers were in, they would construct a framework around the perimeter which would allow dirt to cover the top. And since none of them wanted to be walking on or smelling dirt, they would enclose it with walls and have gravel for the walkway. If they were to be here a lot, they wanted it to be nice.

They decided building a cabin would take far too long, so Ben purchased a tiny house that was a mansion in size compared to most tiny houses. It would cover a good portion of the area above the bunkers. They hauled the cabin on 24x8 utility trailer they also found in the barn, pulling it with Trey's truck. The cabin was wider than the trailer, making it necessary for Evan and Ben to drive in front and back, signaling a wide load. Nothing would be suspicious about a wide load being pulled on the main road. They waited until evening, just after dark, to bring it in, allowing for a time when the coast was clear before pulling onto the side road that led to the farm. They were learning survival skills which would benefit them well for these years of Tribulation.

The next two days were perfect. It seemed clear to them that God was directing this show, and they thanked him for that. It was good to have Jesus in charge of the project. Trey and John made their trips with no trouble. There were no intruders or landing problems. They took precautions to ensure they had the bunkers tightly secured in the cargo hold so there would be no shifting this time. They had mastered the art of unloading them and moving them to the open area.

Things were going better than they could have hoped. And they had a brilliant mind in charge of the intricate details. John was diagramming, and they were doing the work. Each was doing things they had never done before. But they were getting it done, and John was inspecting every aspect to make sure it would function as it should and last seven years.

He mapped out the ventilation, heating and cooling. It amazed them, watching it all take shape as they worked together. Who needed Doc Sanderson's help, anyway? The Smyrnians were a resourceful group, not professional by any stretch of the imagination, but able to do the job, and do it well. Leaving the bunkers unconnected, but side-by-side, abutted tightly against each other would give them three different locations from which to work and broadcast. Yet it only took walking out one door and into another to be together.

There were other necessary elements they must take care of. A deeper hole five feet wide, eight feet long and seven feet deep was dug behind the bunkers. At the bottom of a slight downhill grade, it held a septic tank that should easily last seven years. Electricity came from the barn in the underground conduit, which allowed it to remain hidden from sight. A generator would serve as a standby in case of an electrical outage. Water would come from a spring in the woods that surrounded the area, using a pump and piping to bring it into the bunkers. They also needed to store up water in case of an emergency. But the spring had slowed because of the dry weather. Water collection would have to begin soon. A hidden ventilation system and heat and air would take more time, but they would get it done. They could not take a chance on bringing anyone in to do it for them.

This was their safe place. No one could know about it but them. It would have all the comforts of home and be fully functional with everything they needed. They were doing it all themselves in just a few weeks. But they were fully aware it would never have happened without God's help. Blake, Beth and Anders had to tear themselves away and drive back to New York after taking two additional days off. Ben, Evan, Ally, John and Trey stayed to continue working on the project. It would take a few weeks to complete it, but they would have it ready to move in, if that became necessary. After Blake and Beth did their thing, it would definitely be a necessity.

Back home, the two reporters started planning the date they would air their specials. Three weeks gave them ample time to promote and prepare. So they announced to their colleagues they would host individual presentations on February 2. Somehow, Groundhog Day in America seemed like the right day since their home would soon be an underground shelter. In fact, they had decided that would be the name they would use for the bunkers: the *shelter*.

Regular announcements on both networks set the tone for millions of people to tune in on that day to watch the pastor's message, although they did not know what they would be watching. Some would turn off their TVs when they saw the word church, or a pastor beginning his sermon. But many would watch and listen because they had been told this would answer their questions about September 11, 2029 and the events that had happened since, including the lunar eclipse of December 20 and the deep darkness. They would be told to email and let Blake and Beth know if they put their faith in Jesus. Unknown even to their networks, the address was private and secure. The emails would come only to the Smyrnians.

Blake contacted the would-be buyer of his luxury apartment and informed him he was ready to sell. They signed the contract, and the Thompsons agreed to vacate the premises within thirty days, or less. There was no turning back now. As violence continued escalating in more places, they all eagerly awaited February 2. It would be a life-changing day for many people in the world. And it would be a life-changing day for all the Smyrnians.

One such life change happened in advance. Trey had shared the video with Rickie after returning his plane. It did not take long for him to see the truth and place his faith in Jesus. He and Trey would form an invaluable duo for the team. They could get them anywhere they needed to be in the U.S. and transport anything they needed to haul.

The pieces of the puzzle continued to fall perfectly into place. Ollie also had his first convert in London. This was a big one: a member of Parliament named Amelia Clarke. His standing as the most well-known reporter in England gave him access to those in government and national leadership. Talk about a win! Amelia was a leader in her party and well respected by her peers. She would have an open door to talk to them about Jesus, although she would also have to walk a thin line. She could not take a chance on giving the Smyrnians away. However, being bold in politics would translate well into her new role as a follower of Jesus Christ. What an incredible blessing it was to have her on board! It almost guaranteed the British group would explode with members. Ollie's voice overflowed with joy and pride when he called Beth and asked her to inform the others about Amelia.

Back in Missouri, the project was coming together. They now had Rickie helping. He and Trey had gained valuable education and experience in the military. They were excited to use those skills for Jesus and the benefit of their fellow Smyrnians. Their biggest priorities centered on electricity, heat, water and functional bathrooms. Oh, and the kitchens were vital. They were sure Evan would want to eat... a lot.

Ben, Blake and Beth were purchasing all the things they needed for their studios, from which they would broadcast to the world. All of them, except possibly Evan, would be out in the field much more than they would be underground. His primary role would be traffic controller from command central, AKA the shelter, keeping track of everyone and making sure they were all aware of each other's locations and activities at all times. Home base would be vital to their success.

Every day they worked from early morning until midnight, taking brief breaks for food and rest. It was definitely taking shape. They were sending the New York, German and British groups pictures daily of the progress they had made. The final thing was setting the cabin over the bunkers and creating the hidden door and secret stairway that led down to them. They needed to move everything in before that could happen. As they worked, they lived in anticipation of the evening of February 2, Groundhog Day, when two identical prime time specials would air simultaneously on the two most popular networks by the two most well-known and respected reporters in America. The day was getting closer.

In New York, Blake and Beth were carefully planning for that time. Both wanted to not just be on the same page, but say the same things at the same times. Because they were on different networks, precision was key. They created similar scripts which would keep them on the same track. Commercials would air simultaneously if their breaks coincided as planned, and the pastor's video would play after they ended. There was no guarantee it would perfectly sync, but it would be close. When the programs ended, they and Anders would be out the doors and in an automobile bound for Ozark, Missouri.

They sold their cars and purchased a normal car that no one would suspect them of driving. Beth struggled with letting go of her Bimmer. It was part of her. Any true BMW owner will tell you to never call it a Beamer! "It is a Bimmer!" they will say. A Beamer refers to a BMW motorcycle. And Beth had totally been a Bimmer girl. But this was a new day that called for all things new, or used, as in the car's case. They had purchased it from an individual using assumed names Evan created for them.

They each had a new look on their fake driver's licenses. Evan had digitally altered their photos, so they looked enough like them in case they needed to show their IDs, but also different enough that it would be difficult for anyone to recognize them. As for Anders, no one would recognize him, anyway.

After getting to the shelter and settling in, Ally would help give Blake and Beth a new look. But for that night, they would have to look like themselves for their specials, and for the 23-hour drive to Ozark. Hopefully, they would arrive without being spotted on the way. That would mean no speeding, not an easy task for either of them. They would need to be as inconspicuous as possible.

They had enough snacks in the car to keep from stopping to eat. They would have to stop for gas four times, but would try to fuel up at little out of the way places so no one would see them anywhere near Missouri. To further avoid traceability, they would take an unusual route, planning it carefully so their final stop for gas would appear they were heading somewhere other than the Show Me State. The different route would cause the additional 2-3 hours of driving time. They had everything from clothes to personal items to electronics packed into the trunk of the car and ready to roll.

Anders brought a minimal amount of stuff. The most important things were his camera and other equipment. He had it stored in the back seat where he would be sitting. Sure, it belonged to the network, but it would be their donation to the cause. They packed the car, with no room for anything else. Blake and Beth left nothing behind, except the furniture. They left the apartment fully furnished for the new owner. That had been an excellent selling point, although he would have taken it empty. He had finally convinced Blake Thompson to sell him one of the most sought after high-rise apartments with one of the best views in New York City.

The group at the farm furnished the bunkers and cabin. The cabin furniture was merely for show since all of them would live underground. They had assured Blake, Beth, Anders, Ben and Miriam the place would be ready to live in when they arrived. Not 100% finished, but suitable for habitation.

Ben would stay in New York, feigning anger and disappointment at his top reporter. He and Miriam planned to leave a few days later, unless he came under suspicion before then. If that happened, they would flee without a moment's hesitation. The world would figure it out when the producer of the most viewed network in America and his family disappeared. People would initially presume they were missing until Ben showed up on computers and TV screens worldwide speaking to Jews about Jesus.

His goal was to create his own network, aimed specifically at reaching his people, God's chosen people dating back to the days of Abraham. He had always prided himself that his family name came from the name of the Patriarch of Israel. The Abramsons were ready to get started telling the Jews about the real Messiah, Jesus, whom they had rejected for 2,000 years. But he loved them enough to give them a second chance during this seven years known as the Tribulation, just before Jesus returned to bring all things to an end. Bring it on...

CHAPTER 6

The day had arrived: February 2, Groundhog Day. The day that would change everything. Blake and Beth were ready. The world waited in eager anticipation of their prime time specials. They would air at 8:00 p.m. on their separate networks, shown worldwide. Subtitles would translate their words and the pastor's video for viewers in other countries. The number of viewers should be huge. People wanted to hear what the two top reporters in America would say during identical programs airing at the same time. There had to be something unique about them. No reporters had done anything like this before.

Blake and Beth had spent the day preparing. They had also prayed often that God would prevent anything from happening that may interfere. The day was sad for them in some ways. They had just spent the last night in their posh apartment in the Theater District in Manhattan. Tomorrow night, they would sleep in an underground bunker, which would be their home for the next seven years, or less, depending on whether they survived that long. They would trade a life of luxury for a life of simplicity. They would trade an incredible view of Downtown Manhattan for a view of steel walls. And they would trade the life of celebrities for a life on the run.

But neither of them would have it any other way. Jesus had radically transformed their lives. He had changed their futures and their eternal destinies. They wanted everyone to have what they had. They would spend the rest of their lives, even give their lives if they had to, so they could tell everyone the good news and warn them about Aissa Messai, the Antichrist, the epitome of evil, Satan's man. They were ready to declare war, and they would fire the opening shots tonight.

Anders packed their things into the car for them. He knew they needed to prepare. And he wanted them to have time alone one last day in their home. It was difficult for him to part with his house, too. The memories of life there with Angie and the kids flooded his mind. Even though he was more than ready to get on with the battle against the forces of evil, it still overwhelmed him. The tears came naturally. One last time he slept in the bed he and Angie had shared. One last time he spent precious moments in the kids' rooms. One last time, he prayed and read the Bible in his living room chair. As he did, he prayed the new owners would sense Jesus in the house and believe in him as their Savior.

After packing his stuff, he walked out for the last time and drove to Blake and Beth's apartment. Having moved his things into the car with theirs, he delivered his vehicle to its new owner at the office complex where the man worked. Then he made the short walk back to Blake and Beth's place. Now, he was eager to get to Missouri. There was nothing left for him in New York City.

In Germany, Bruno and Mila Fromm, their sons, and Hans and Heidi Meier were spending the day praying for everything that would happen tonight. In London, Oliver Barton and Amelia Clarke were praying. In Ozark, Missouri, Evan Ryles, Ally Fromm, John Baldwin, Trey Butler and Rickie Cruz were praying. In New York City, Ben and Miriam Abramson and their seven children were praying. And Blake and Beth Jennings Thompson and Anders Norstrom were praying.

They prayed this would be a miraculous night. They prayed for the 90 minutes of the special programs which would air that night to be problem free. They prayed for the people who would see the pastor's message to trust in Jesus as they had. They prayed for Blake, Beth and Anders as they traveled to the farm. They prayed, then prayed again and again. Neither Messai nor the world knew what was about to hit them. God had answered the prayers of the Smyrnians many times in some amazing ways. They believed without a doubt he would do it again tonight and tomorrow. The next 24 hours would prove whether they were right.

Evan had the email addresses set up and ready to receive mail. They would ask people who prayed and invited Jesus to be their Savior to send emails informing Blake and Beth of their decision. The emails would notify all the Smyrnians, as well. They would then receive an automated response, giving them instructions for next steps, and a website where they could find answers. They included what the team considered FAQs, or frequently asked questions. The website also gave them an opportunity to register as new followers of Jesus. Encouraging emails and teachings from the Bible would also be sent to them each week.

The team would do everything possible to prepare them for what they were about to face and the potential ramifications of being believers in Jesus. And they would inform them about Aissa Messai and things to watch for from him, beginning soon. They may consider it dangerous to do so, but they would provide lists of new believers in specific areas, allowing them to connect with each other. They would encourage them to gather some others and start house churches for worship, prayer, and Bible study. It would be paramount for them to share Jesus with their families and friends.

A copy of the pastor's message would be available for download. They had tried to think of everything, but then, they were still learning themselves. The name of the website? *Smyrnians.com*. It was time to come out of the closet, so to speak. Closet Christians would have no place in the Tribulation. Hiding away was not the Jesus way. Smyrnians. The entire world would be familiar with that name by the time this night ended.

7:00 p.m.
It was almost go time. Blake and Beth sat in their studios making last-minute preparations. Every member of both crews understood they were not to stop the programs, regardless of what happened. Blake and Beth knew their colleagues would hear about Jesus, too.

7:30 p.m.
Everything was in place. Both reporters received final touches in makeup. Anders sat in the studio but planned to leave 15 minutes before the program ended to have the car parked nearby and ready for them to hop in and go. He would drive the first leg, because he was less recognizable than the other two. It would also allow Blake and Beth to get changed, then be online checking email and watching the website for people who had put their faith in Jesus.

7:55 p.m.

Both reporters stood in front of the cameras at their networks, awaiting the signal to begin. They had prepared, prayed and done anything else they could think of to be ready for this moment. The rest was up to God. Jesus would be with them as he had been so many times before tonight. "Take this, Aissa Messai," Blake thought to himself. "We are declaring war!"

8:00 p.m. Lights, Camera, Action!

"Good evening, folks. I am Blake Thompson, and this is the most important night of your life. The things you are about to see and hear during this 90-minute program are the most life-changing truths you have ever been told. Our world has been through a lot in the last 144 days. First, we endured September 11 together and shared each other's pain as over one billion people disappeared in an instant. Then, as we struggled to cope with that trauma, an earthquake rocked the planet. Scientists called it a tremor but also told us it was a portent of a major worldwide quake to come. We then watched together as the news came of the assassination of the Secretary-General of the United Nations. The death of another delegate followed that before a new Secretary-General could be elected."

"Then came the lunar eclipse of December 20. The world was already anxious before that night arrived. But nothing could have prepared us for what came. Darkness. Darkness deeper than any of us had ever seen. Darkness that covered the entire planet, even in places where the eclipse was not visible, and rendered all of us blind. Darkness in places where the eclipse occurred in broad daylight. If you were outside on that night, you not only saw the darkness, you also felt the darkness; an *invasion of darkness*. Further, you may have had a sense that something happened during the darkness. What I am about to show you tonight is, something did happen; something sinister; something evil. And I will show you how all the events I just mentioned are connected, interwoven into a plan that existed from the beginning of the universe."

"When I finish, you will understand why some people disappeared on September 11, while you and I remained here, left behind. You will learn how men wrote about each of those events thousands of years ago and hear from a man who explains what they mean for you and me. Tonight it will all make sense to you, if you will listen to what he has to say. You will connect the dots and realize that while these events were devastating for many of us, they brought deliverance for others. Some of you lost family members and friends on September 11. Tonight you will discover who took them and where they are now. How is that possible, you ask? You are getting ready to find out."

"I can tell you there are people for whom this realization has already revolutionized their thinking. It has replaced their pain with peace, their sorrow with a smile, their hopelessness with hope. The best terminology I can use for the truths you are about to hear is life-changing. When you believe them and act on them, they will change your life. How do I know? They changed my life. In an instant on one day, I made a decision based on this man's words that changed everything for me. It literally changed my past, present and future. It gave my life purpose and meaning. I hope that you will receive it as I did and let it change your life as it has mine."

"We will take a commercial break now. I encourage you to make preparations to spend the next hour watching a video that will explain everything I just said. Visit the bathroom. Get something to drink, and some snacks, because you cannot afford to take a break until the video has ended. When we come back, I will give you instructions for watching. It is vital that you pay close attention and do exactly as I say. You have trusted me as a reporter, bringing you the news. I ask you to trust me again tonight."

With the camera off and the network gone to commercial, Blake felt good about what he had said. Even if he had gone off script, it came from his heart. Most of all, he knew it came from Jesus speaking through him. Next door, Beth had the same sense of satisfaction. The big moment was about to happen. It would be a declaration of war and call to action. After this, the number of Smyrnians would increase exponentially. There may be hundreds of thousands, or hopefully millions. A formidable army, for sure. They were excited about new troops, but more excited about new followers of Jesus. Messai had his work cut out for him! But sadly, many of them would also die at his hands. However, when that happened, they would go immediately to be with Jesus! The thought brought a momentary tear to each of their eyes and a smile to their faces.

Blake was so deep in thought he barely heard the commercials end and saw it had come back to him. He caught himself just in time.

"Okay folks, it is now time to unveil the news for which you have been waiting. It is why you tuned in tonight. My colleague on the network next door, Beth Jennings, is airing the same video. We are giving you one minute to call someone and invite them to watch too. Then I will give you instructions for watching. They are important, so you will need to listen closely."

He paused for 60 seconds as soft music played. When the minute ended, he was back on the air.

"Now, here are your all-important instructions. We will also show them on the screen. To get the most out of the video you are about to see and experience genuine life change by doing what it says, you must follow them carefully."

1. Watch the entire video without stopping or leaving your seat for any reason.

2. You may hear things with which you disagree or dislike. Keep watching anyway.

3. Pay close attention to details. They will fall into place like pieces of a beautiful puzzle.

4. Watch with an open mind. If you will, you cannot miss the truth. And I believe you will receive that truth.

"It is time to start the video. I will not be back with you until it ends. I am not there with you in person. But as you have done for many years, by tuning in, you have invited me into your home once again tonight. As if I am sitting there with you, I ask you to promise me you will watch to the end. At that point, I will give you an opportunity to make the most important decision of your life. I hope you make that decision when the time comes. The video will start now."

The pastor started talking at almost precisely the same time on both networks. Blake and his wife had nailed it. Both sat and watched again as the pastor delivered his powerful and accurate explanation of the events that had happened in the last 144 days. They saw their own colleagues battle their personal beliefs as they watched. They had no choice. They were at work and had to watch the monitors to ensure that everything ran smoothly. They observed them as their emotions ranged from shock to anger to intrigue.

They saw the amazement on their faces when the pastor gave the date of the Feast of Trumpets for 2029. That date was September 11, the same day of the event they had spent the last 144 days believing was an alien invasion of Planet Earth.

Now the pastor confronted them with the truth of Jesus' words. Jesus said the day he took his people home to be with him would be the Feast of Trumpets in the year 2,000 years after his death and resurrection. God raised him from the grave in A.D. 29, not A.D. 33 as many people assume. That meant the year he would take his people home would be 2029, and the day, September 11.

The pastor explained that world leaders may say it was an invasion of aliens, when it was in reality the Rapture, when Jesus sent his angels into all the world to gather his people and take them home. No one could deny the facts. They may reject them, but they could deny nothing the pastor said. Understanding he had spoken these things over four years ago and they had happened exactly when and how he said they would, tied it all together.

The moment of truth arrived. The pastor asked everyone who believed the things they had just heard to stop right then, tell Jesus they believed, then open the door of their lives and invite him to come in. Both Blake and Beth felt the magnitude of the moment. The other Smyrnians felt it too as they watched from their locations. All of them prayed for every person who had tuned in and watched to the end. Blake allowed the video to play until the pastor had explained the seven years that would occur after the Rapture and the man of evil who would rise to power.

No one who heard it could deny who that man was: Aissa Messai. And those who understood the terms recognized what they meant: Jesus Messiah. The name Isa, an Arabic translation of the name Jesus, in its longer form, Aissa. Messai, an alternate spelling of the word Messiah, meaning Christ. It left no doubt that the man who had risen to power through the United Nations was the Antichrist. That is anti-Christ, anti or opposed to Jesus and his followers. Anti can also mean *instead of.* He would furthermore set himself up to be the Messiah instead of Jesus.

He would eventually call on people to worship him. That call would then become a demand. He would persecute and kill those who failed to obey it, as the verse from which the Smyrnians took their name revealed. Revelation 2:10 came from Jesus' words to the first century church in Smyrna. They understood it also foretold what followers of Jesus would face at the hands of the Antichrist during the final seven years of the earth before Jesus comes again and wins the ultimate victory over him.

"Do not be afraid of what you are about to suffer. I tell you, the devil will put some of you in prison to test you, and you will suffer persecution for ten days. Be faithful, even to the point of death, and I will give you the crown of life."

The video ended, and the screen went blank. Blake and Beth spoke immediately to make sure no one missed the opportunity to do this last thing that would solidify their decision and give them their purpose and mission.

"If you believed what the pastor said is true and prayed to receive Jesus as your Savior as he instructed you to do, and as I did, 'Welcome to the family of God!' I understand exactly how you feel. As you know by now, there is no better feeling in the world! You will now live with Jesus forever when your life is over, guaranteed to be seven years or fewer."

"Now, please listen closely and do these next two things. They will be vital for you going forward. Email *blake@smyrnians.com* or *beth@smyrnians.com* and tell us about your decision. Then go to our website, *smyrnians.com*, and you will learn all about your new life and receive instructions for your next steps. We are getting ready to experience an invasion of darkness like the world has never seen. It began on December 20. Be prepared. And for now, welcome to Team Smyrnians."

"Beth and I, and others, will be in touch with all of you who email us and/or reach out to us on the website soon. We invite you to join us as we serve Jesus and fight for him on behalf of everyone else in the world. The war is on! And we are ready to fight! I look forward to communicating with you soon. God bless you. This is Blake Thompson signing off for tonight."

With that, Blake and Beth exited the studios at a brisk pace. They had no time to stick around and talk to any of their coworkers who may have put their faith in Jesus. They would have ample opportunity to speak with them digitally via email and the website. Anders was parked outside where he promised to be. They got into the car hastily, and he drove away. Their destination was a remote and well-disguised farm outside of Ozark, Missouri. There they would join their friends and fellow followers of Jesus before tomorrow ended.

Blake donned a ball cap, something he had not done in years. Before tonight, he could not afford to mess up his perfect hair. Now that no longer mattered. He wore dark glasses, even in the darkness of night. He changed clothes as they drove, not an easy thing to do in the front seat of a car driving down the road. An old pair of jeans and faded t-shirt made him look like anybody but the reporter in the sharp suit who had been on TV a short while ago.

Beth changed too, telling Anders to keep his eyes on the road and away from the rear-view mirror. She chuckled at that. Faded jeans and an old, worn New York Yankees jersey replaced the fancy dress she had worn as millions of people watched her earlier. A ragged cap covered her head with her long blonde hair hanging below it. They were no longer socialites. They were Smyrnians. Their mission had changed, and they were excited about it.

Their anticipation rose as New York City disappeared behind them. They did not know if they would ever return. But if they did, their lives would be far different from what they had been in the past. Thoughts were no longer on former houses, automobiles, or the finer things of life they had once enjoyed. They were ready to begin a new life, fighting for their lives, possibly even giving their lives for the cause of Christ. Survive or not, they knew the crown of life would be theirs. They tingled with excitement at the thoughts of what lay ahead. And it began right now.

"Missouri, here we come," said Anders.

The smiles on the faces of the couple riding with him said it all. They were madly in love and loving life together, and come what may, nothing would change that.

"To Missouri and beyond!" exclaimed Blake, raising his hand and pointing forward.

Beth leaned forward and gave him a kiss which lasted longer than either had intended. Anders had to interrupt. "Do I have to put up with this twitterpation again?" he asked jokingly.

"You just may," said Blake. "Remember, you were the one who coined that phrase and were so eager for us to get together. So, you are part of this, buddy."

"I am and proudly so, partner," beamed Anders. "Now, let's get this party started. Where are those snacks, Beth? This guy is starving!" She handed out the goodies, and they ate well. It had been a busy day and an intense evening.

They had eaten very little, so they were making up for it now. On they rolled with a tank full of gas and food to spare. Yes, this trip would be fun.

Aissa Messai was on the air within minutes to make an announcement of his own. The world watched to see what their leader had to say following what they had just seen. Millions of them had already decided on his true identity and chosen to follow Jesus. Nothing he said would deter them from their faith in Jesus Christ, the true Messiah. Yet many others remained in his camp.

Messai appeared on the screen: "Ladies and gentlemen of the world. After what we just saw and heard, the peace which now defines our world is under attack. There is a group of people who are seeking to overthrow the things we have accomplished. The things you heard from Blake Thompson and Beth Jennings tonight are lies, blatant lies. The Smyrnians have arisen out of nowhere and are enemies of the cause."

"I can endure their personal attacks and slander of my name. But I cannot abide their efforts to rob you, the citizens of the world, of the peace and prosperity you deserve, the peace and prosperity I am determined to give you. We must stop them! And we must begin now. Every day we wait only gives them more motivation and belief in their divisive cause. They were likely few in number prior to tonight, but their numbers may have multiplied now. And they will continue to increase if we do not stop them."

"Many gullible people easily fall for hoaxes like this. Here is what I am asking from you. Be on the lookout for anyone who acts suspiciously or does things that appear to be irrational. I suspect these rebels may search for ways and places to hide. If you are aware of anyone who has been seeking a place of asylum, please turn their names over to us. If you encounter anyone who exhibits the behavior or espouses the things we heard about tonight, please let us know. If you have any suspicion at all that someone may belong to the cult known as the Smyrnians, we have set up a tip hotline which will come directly to my office. For any tip that leads to the discovery and arrest of such persons, there will be a significant reward."

"We cannot allow anyone to interfere with the progress we have made. In the interest of worldwide peace and prosperity, I ask for your help. Thank you for being good citizens and helping to make our world a better place."

The Smyrnians were watching Messai's announcement. They wasted no time connecting on a conference call with each other, using secure phones.

Their lives were in imminent danger and would remain in danger for the next seven years. But their mood was not somber; it was joyful. As a Bible verse they had read stated, they counted it all joy to suffer for their Lord, Jesus Christ.

The group in Missouri gave an update on the progress made at the shelter. Yes, they called it a house underground, for that is what it was. They assured Blake, Beth and Anders they would love it when they saw it. The German and British groups got fired up after watching Messai's speech. But the most important thing had to be the vast amount of emails that kept pouring in from all over the world. The number of visits to smyrnians.com astounded them. Their number had exploded in one night. Now to mobilize these new believers and turn this massive group into an army to battle the forces of evil and be victorious.

But they would achieve victory differently. They had laid claim to another verse: Revelation 12:11. It reminded them of their theme verse. It gave three keys to defeating the enemy. "They have defeated him by the blood of the Lamb and by their testimony. And they did not love their lives so much that they were afraid to die." They knew the blood of Jesus, who died and rose again, made that victory possible. They must spread the news about him to all the world. They were not afraid of death, because it led to real life. Yet they would fight to stay alive for all seven of these years. They were God's army, his warriors of the Tribulation. They were the Smyrnians.

CHAPTER 7

Doc Sanderson sat alone in his den after watching Messai's speech. He had one man on his mind: his childhood friend and conspiracy theorist, Professor John Baldwin. John had to be one of them. He would never have imagined that his old friend would get caught up in something this serious. Sure, John had always been one to fall for every doomsday prophecy that came along. But this was too far across the line for even him to step. As hard as Doc had been on him, he still did not want to accept what he feared might be true. But there could be no other answer.

First, John came to buy an underground bunker. Messai had said these people may seek for places and ways to hide. Why else would someone need an underground bunker? Second, he had bought not just one bunker, but three, at a cost of $2,225,000. Where would John get that kind of money? The professor surely did not make enough money to afford that. He must be part of a group of people who were wealthy enough to fund such an expensive project. Third, John had refused to allow PSI to haul them or send a crew to install them. He did not want Doc to be aware of where they were going. He wished he had put a tail on him so he would have that information. Fourth, John had wanted to talk to him about something he deemed urgent. He suspected it must surely be the same thing Blake Thompson and Beth Jennings talked about tonight. Last but not least, who had been with John when he came to check out the bunkers? Blake Thompson. Even if the other evidence against John was not so overwhelming, that unquestionably meant guilt by association.

Doc had to admit, it made sense. It was impossible to deny, but that did not mean he had to accept it. It appeared he had a choice: accept what the pastor said and Blake Thompson so strongly espoused or accept the prosperity Aissa Messai had brought to the world. Maybe what the reporter had said was true. And yes, Doc had trusted him with the news for a lot of years.

But even if it was true, did that have to mean Aissa Messai would not be the one left standing at the end of it all? The man had it all together. In a few months, he had helped the world move on from the Invasion and brought peace and prosperity far greater than any previous generation had known. Doc had been the beneficiary of that himself. Sure, the huge bunker sale to John was a big part of it, but even that came through the New World Order Messai had brought into being.

Doc was better off than he had ever been. But regardless of how much he had, he always wanted more. Messai had said there would be a significant reward for any tip that led to the discovery and arrest of people like John Baldwin and Blake Thompson. He cared about his childhood friend, even if he thought he was insane for believing in all the conspiracy theories. But he cared more about himself. He had a call to make to a tip line.

Anders, Blake, and Beth were methodically making their way toward Missouri. Anders had given way to Blake on the driving. Midnight had come and gone now, and the journey was going well. Blake had the cruise set to make sure he did not break the speed limit. Traffic was light on the Interstate because of the late hour. He longed to step on it and go. Driving the speed limit tested his patience and drove him crazy. But tonight, he could take no chances.

As they crawled on through the night, if you can call driving 70 miles per hour crawling, Beth slept soundly in the back seat. He would rather have her sitting in the front with him, but he would not wake her. He had glanced around a few times at her lying peacefully with her head toward the passenger side door. He saw her from that position when he turned his head to get a brief glance. She was no less beautiful in her ragged cap, faded jeans and Yankees jersey than she was in a nice dress with her long, blonde hair falling on her shoulders. He loved that woman. And while they fought side-by-side during the Tribulation, he would do everything he could to protect her, even if it meant laying down his life for her.

Anders had nodded off too in the front seat. Blake drove on in silence, thinking about all that had changed in his life in less than five months. But he also contemplated what life would be like during these seven years. With those thoughts filling his mind, he barely noticed a patrol car's lights flashing behind him. He was not speeding! He glanced at the speedometer and found it to be right on the limit.

Thoughts raced through his mind. Should he try to outrun the trooper? No, that would be crazy. Would his fake ID be enough to fool the man? He hoped so. He drove on for a mile, hoping either the trooper would pass him and pull someone else over, or if he stopped him, let him go, possibly with only a warning. But he eventually had no choice but to pull to the side of the road.

Anders roused up and asked, "What are you doing, Blake? We don't have time to be pulling over. Besides, it is dangerous!"

Blake pointed behind them. Anders turned and saw the flashing lights. "Should we try to outrun him? Maybe you should take off as he walks toward the car. If he recognizes us, we're goners."

By now, Beth was awake too. "Blake, what are we going to do? Were you speeding? No, you weren't speeding. You had the cruise control set, didn't you?"

"I did, even though it was driving me crazy to creep along like that. I don't understand why he would pull us over unless he somehow got a tip or someone turned in our license plate number. We just need to play it cool. Remember your aliases!"

The trooper walked cautiously to the driver's window. "Excuse me, sir. May I see your license and registration, please?"

As Blake honored the request, he asked, "I'm sorry. Can you tell me why you stopped me?"

"Your third brake light is out. People usually forget about those, but they are an important safety feature. That is one of the things we are focusing on right now."

"I am so sorry. I hadn't noticed that. We just got this car. I will replace the bulb tomorrow."

"Wait right here, and I will be back in just a moment." He took Blake's license and registration back to the patrol car with him.

Beth said, "I don't think he recognized you. And he did not even mention Anders and me."

"We need to stay calm and take the ticket, if he writes me one, then thank him and drive away. We don't want to cause any trouble. We can't *afford* to cause any trouble."

The trooper was returning. When he walked up to the car, he looked closely at Blake. He said, "Here are your license and registration. I won't write you a ticket this time. I'll take your word that you'll get that light taken care of tomorrow."

"I promise you I will. Thank you, officer. I appreciate you doing that for me."

The man looked more intently at Blake and glanced in the back seat at Beth. Blake thanked him again and pulled the car into Drive, preparing to pull back onto the Interstate.

"Wait, a minute. I think I know who you are. Yes, I recognize you. How lucky could I get? You are Blake Thompson. And that is Beth Jennings in the back seat. I have been fans of both of you for a long time. In fact, I saw your special programs tonight."

Now Blake was sweating. "I'm sorry, but my name is Ryan Davis, like it says on my license. And that is my beautiful wife, Kelly, in the back seat."

"Look, I saw what Aissa Messai said tonight after your programs. You must have created fake IDs to cover up who you are. But I recognize you, even with the disguises. You can't fool me."

"I truly am sorry, but you have us confused with someone else."

"I need all three of you to step out of the car, please."

Blake noticed the man did not draw his gun. That was unusual. He saw that Anders noticed it too. Looking at Beth, he saw a look of fear on her face he had not seen before. He wanted to grab her and hold her close, but that would not be wise at this point.

They stepped from the car and walked to the side of the road. Blake assumed backup was already on the way. He watched for the flashing lights he was sure would come any second and listened for the sirens they would hear. Could this be it? Why would Jesus allow their capture before they even got started as his warriors? That did not seem right. But they had fired the opening shots tonight that started the war and understood the danger they had put themselves in.

He needed to think about what to do now that they already faced their first dangerous situation. Should they fight to protect themselves, or remain calm and wait on Jesus? He needed to make a split-second decision. There was not much time, if backup was on the way. He tried to get Anders' attention so he would watch him and jump in to help when he made his move. The man had not drawn his weapon, but he was a large man. They would have a fight on their hands.

They reached the shoulder of the Interstate, a dangerous enough place in its own right. The trooper asked them to step further off the road and into the ditch, out of sight of oncoming traffic. He may shoot all three of them right there on the spot. Messai had probably already put a bounty on their heads. Blake's pulse quickened, and his heart was racing. Just as he was deciding whether to rush him, the man spoke.

"Mr. Thompson and Miss Jennings, I am positive it is you. I would recognize you anywhere. Thank you. I want to say thank you for being so bold tonight and showing us the truth. My wife and I prayed when the pastor invited us to and asked Jesus to come into our lives and be our Savior. As you promised, what we felt at that moment was indescribable. We emailed you and have been on the website. We now know where our baby and 2-year-old are. Aliens did not abduct them. They are with Jesus. And we will see them again! Thank you!"

Blake, Beth and Anders broke down, and tears poured from their eyes. They were not sure whether it came more from relief or the happiness they felt inside. This couple were now followers of Jesus because of what they had shared with the world tonight! And Jesus had brought him straight to them. It was another miracle, so much like the ones they had already seen. The trooper grabbed Blake in an embrace only true believers in Jesus can understand. They had gone through the same experience with others. They would never grow tired of it. But this one had caused them a fair amount of consternation before the man got around to telling them who he was and what had happened.

"My name is Malik Williams. My shift started at 11:00. I wanted to stay home with my wife, but I had to come out on patrol. Jesus is already showing me he is with me. He led me right to you!"

"I believe you are right, Malik. We have seen him do things like that again and again since we put our faith in him. Welcome to the Smyrnians. And welcome to the family of God!"

They took a few minutes to celebrate, then Anders said, "We need to get on the road. But Malik, won't your superiors get a little suspicious when your dashboard cam shows you walking us out of view, staying this long then bringing us back to the car?"

"I'm not worried. I have ways to handle that. I've been doing this for a while. I am just so thankful I found you tonight. Tell me what to do next. I am ready to follow Jesus, no matter the cost. He is my Lord now! I will fight Aissa Messai as long as I live. And I will tell others what Jesus has done for me. Did you say we can download the pastor's video on your website?"

"Yes, you can. And you can get answers to all of your other questions, too. Study it carefully. Do everything it tells you to do. And in a few days, you can tune in and hear Beth and me on our private channel where we will give regular updates and share insights from the Bible. We will be out fighting the enemy a lot, but we will make sure to take time for that."

"Thank you so much. My wife and I will get started with that as soon as I get home in the morning. We know where our babies are now. And knowing we will see them again has changed everything for us! Let's get you back to the car. I don't know where you are going, and I will not ask. But I feel sure you need to get on your way."

"It was a pleasure meeting you Malik. We love meeting people who have turned to faith in Jesus! I don't know if we will see each other again on this earth. But if we don't, we will see you in seven years, or less, in the presence of Jesus!"

One more hug and they were back on the road praising Jesus for what had just happened. He was a miracle-working Savior. But they also knew a change in their appearance had to happen soon after they arrived at the shelter. If Malik Williams had recognized them for who they were now, it meant other people would too.

Members of the media had already contacted Ben Abramson multiple times about his top reporter, but he was not taking questions. That would allow him to lie low for a while. He decided it was better to not make any statements and let the chips fall where they may. Then he would disappear, and everyone would figure it out for themselves.

Evan would have his studio ready to set up when he arrived at the shelter. Once he got the equipment in and confirmed it was secure and not traceable, he would begin broadcasting to the Jews. He expected a great movement among his people, with many of them turning to Jesus. The world, including Aissa Messai, would take notice of that! But in taking notice, he would pursue the Jews with a vengeance, and peace in the Middle East would be a thing of the past.

What would happen then, Ben did not know. He would deal with that when the time came and trust God to give him the answers he needed. For now, he was ready to get to Missouri, and get started with his work. Nothing else mattered to him at this point.

In Missouri, the group moved the cabin into place, with the back half sitting over the top of the bunkers and the front half extending out in front of them. They made the foundation from rocks they had brought from around the spring. The rocks were flat enough to work with. They mixed cement and sealed the gaps. The foundation was solid and the cabin steady.

In a small walk-in closet in the bedroom, the back wall became a secret door which led to a hidden stairway going down to the bunkers. The door spun around when pushed, allowing them to walk through, but no one could tell it was not the back wall of the closet and nothing more. Hunting clothes hung inside, further concealing the wall at the back. It was an ingenious idea.

Thus, the location of the safe place was on a hidden farm that was only accessible via a camouflaged lane that led to a covered clearing which housed a cabin built over three steel bunkers completely entombed underground. It was perfect.

Rickie's family operated a lawn care company where he had learned the ins and outs of growing grass. Most people would not sow grass seed in February. But he knew dormant seeding done in February grows better and covers more quickly than seeding in other winter months. It typically has good coverage in April and full coverage by May.

They covered the bunkers with the subsoil, then worked the topsoil over the top of it until it was smooth. It left no evidence of bunkers underneath. They sowed the seed and covered it with straw. Within two months, a mixture of ryegrass and weeds should cover the area, making it look like they had never touched it. They would let it grow high and not cut it above the shelter so it would conceal the vent pipes that were sticking up out of the ground, providing ventilation for the bunkers and their inhabitants below.

They did everything they could to make it appear that there was nothing on the lot but a cabin in the middle of a beautiful and spacious field.

The shelter and the Smyrnians inside would be completely out of sight and non-existent to anyone who may somehow accidentally wander onto that hidden acre of ground. As unlikely as that was, they still needed to take every precaution to ensure they never compromised their safe place. It was not just a place they had discovered, but a place God had provided to serve them as a place of respite whenever they needed a break from their war with Aissa Messai and the forces of evil. From it, they would also report the good news about Jesus to the world.

Doc picked up his phone and dialed the number that Messai gave and showed on the screen. Realizing the possibility that had hit him about John Baldwin, he had grabbed a pen and written the number down. It surprised him when someone answered his call, but it was not Aissa Messai.

"Thank you for calling Aissa Messai's Tip Line. How may I help you?"

The call did not go directly to Messai's office, as he had said it would. Momentarily stunned when someone else answered, he stammered, "Uh, I would like to speak with Mr. Messai, please. I need to report someone who I know is a member of the Smyrnians."

"Okay, sir. I can take that information and pass it on to our security forces."

"This one is important. I would rather talk to him personally. I guess I could tell one of them."

"Sir, all of our people in that department are out or busy with other calls, as is Mr. Messai. As you might imagine, many people are calling with tips. I will make sure they receive yours."

"I think I would rather leave a message. The information I have needs to get directly to someone in charge. This is no normal tip. This is a sure thing. I'm nervous about turning this person in because he is a childhood friend. But I'm a huge supporter of Mr. Messai and want to do my duty as a civilian and make sure he gets this. Can you have someone call me back?"

"Sir, I can take your information. If you will please just..." He interrupted her in mid-sentence.

"No, if I can't give it to someone in charge, I will just keep it to myself." He ended the call.

Anders, Blake and Beth were making good time. Beth was driving now after getting a little sleep following their encounter with the trooper. She kept saying under her breath, "Hi. My name is Kelly. Kelly Davis. This is my husband, Ryan." She said it again and again. "I am Kelly Davis. Pleased to meet you." She had to get used to it. That is who she would be from now on, Kelly Davis, Humanitarian Aid Worker, helping those in need. She had insisted on that title when Evan suggested things like Medical Researcher, the official title being Physician-Scientist, or possibly Freelance Writer, allowing her to get the inside scoop on things happening in the world.

But Beth, no, Kelly, wanted to make a difference in people's lives. The need for that would be huge with war on humanity getting ready to break loose in the world. When human beings are in desperate need, they are much more open to ideas about things that can help them. She would go where the needs were greatest and assist those who were suffering. And she would tell them about Jesus, the one who could provide the help they needed most. She was up to the challenge, knowing the role would also get her into some places the others could not infiltrate. "Hi, I am Kelly Davis. Pleased to meet you." She would have to adapt to that. It would be her persona for the next seven years.

A ding from the message center on the car interrupted, alerting her it was time to stop for gas. The road sign beside the Interstate showed one place that would be open where they could purchase gas. She woke up the guys to tell them she would get off the next exit to find the place. It was the ideal location because it seemed to be in the middle of nowhere. She exited and turned left, heading in the direction the sign pointed. She drove over two miles on a deserted road before seeing a food mart in the distance. It sat on the outskirts of a small town and thankfully was open all night. She turned in and pulled up to the pumps.

Blake went inside to prepay with cash, not wanting to use a card with their names on it. They would not complete that detail until they reached the shelter. When they got there, Evan would have new credit cards waiting for them with their new identities. But for this trip, it was cash only. The man behind the counter appeared to be the only one working tonight. He took Blake's money, and Blake motioned through the window for Beth to pump gas. Blake asked for a pack of cigarettes and a lottery ticket. He wanted to look like a normal customer.

When the man turned to get them from the display behind him, Anders slipped in and went to the bathroom down a short hallway. Beth finished pumping gas and came in to grab a coke, keeping things as routine as possible. The man rang up their tab, took the money and placed it in the drawer. Then, as quick as a flash, he pulled a handgun from under the counter and pointed it at them. Coming around the counter, he ordered them to face the counter and place their hands on it. This guy was not like Malik. He meant business.

"Okay, now turn around slowly and face me." They complied. "Take off those caps. And you take off those glasses. Did you think you could walk in here and me not recognize who you are?"

"I am not sure what you are talking about," said Blake. "My name is Ryan Davis, and this is my wife, Kelly. We are on a trip and almost ran out of gas, so we got off and found this place."

"Blake Thompson and Beth Jennings. I know exactly who you are. I was looking forward to your programs tonight until you started the video of that preacher. I watched as long as I could and turned the thing off. You are not making me believe that stuff. I never have and never will. I saw you talk about the violence that is going on in the world, and you even tried to blame it on Messai. Religion has caused a lot of the wars the world has faced throughout history. And it looks to me like you two are trying to start another one. Then I saw the replay of Messai's message. There is a big reward for anyone who turns you in. So, I will do that right now. It is my duty to this country and the world. We need to stop this thing before it starts."

"Once again sir, I don't have a clue what you're talking about. I am well aware who Blake Thompson and Beth Jennings are. I have watched them many times myself. I have been told by people I look like him, but..."

"Shut up! I know who you are. Now don't move while I call 911. I need that reward money. It will be another way Messai has put more cash in my pocket."

They both saw Anders come out of the bathroom and notice what was happening. Fortunately, the man was unaware that there were three of them. They tried to remain calm and not show any sign that they saw him. Anders quietly slid a glass beer bottle out of a 6-pack and approached the man from behind. Just as he opened his cell phone and prepared to tap 911,

Anders raised the bottle and brought it down hard on his head. The man collapsed to the floor in a heap.

"I didn't want to do that, but I had no choice."

"You had to do it. Grab his gun and let's get out of here."

"What do you mean, grab his gun?" asked Beth, sounding both angry and frightened.

"We have to have some protection. I don't want to kill people any more than Anders wanted to knock that guy out cold. But I think I could do it if that's what it took to keep us from getting killed. This has already happened twice tonight. These disguises aren't working. Everyone recognizes us. We have to get to Missouri and start changing the way we look." Then trying to alleviate her fears and calm her down, he said, "And Babe, I promise you will love the new me!"

His attempt at helping her seemed to work. She half smiled and said, "But I already love the way you look. That's the Blake Thompson I fell in love with." Then she winked and added, "But I will love the new you too!"

"Look," said Anders. "You can continue this twitterpation in the car. We need to get out of here before someone comes in!" He rolled his eyes.

They ran to the car. Anders said, "I'm driving this time. You guys try to stay down and out of sight. If you don't, you may get us killed."

He peeled out and headed back toward the Interstate so fast it threw both of them back against their seats. They would have to stop for gas two more times. Next time it would be Anders going in. Blake and Beth would stay in the car, hunkered down in their seats. It might be their only chance to stay alive until they reached their destination.

Doc Sanderson had fallen asleep wondering how he should handle the information about John Baldwin. He was not about to give it to someone low on the totem pole in Aissa Messai's chain of command. That was a sure way to get left out and miss that reward money. Doc would do whatever he had to do to get it. Money was far more important to him than his childhood friend.

John had always been crazy and fell for every hoax that came along. But he could not believe even he would get caught up in this Jesus stuff. He was a scientist and biology professor. He had to know better. And yet Doc was sure it had happened. Now he had no choice but to turn his friend in. That crazy group of people who called themselves Smyrnians would mess up everything Messai had accomplished if someone did not stop them. He hated to turn his old pal in, but too much hung in the balance if he did not. His phone rang, waking him out of a dead sleep. He had been dreaming about John Baldwin as he slept.

"Hello," he mumbled, answering on the fourth ring, barely catching it before it went to voicemail. Who in the world would call him at this hour of the night? Did they not realize he would be asleep?

"Is this Doc Sanderson?"

"Yes, it is. Who is this?"

"This is Aissa Messai."

Doc sat up in bed, trying to determine if someone was playing a prank on him. But he recognized the voice. It was the same voice he had heard on TV many times. The voice of the man who spoke after his election as Secretary-General of the United Nations. The voice that had celebrated the decision to build the Jewish Temple in Jerusalem beside the Muslim Mosque. The same voice he had heard on TV last night promising a handsome reward for turning in any rebels who were trying to destroy the peace and prosperity that had come to the world. Violence and killing may be on the increase, but things were good for Doc. And he wanted to keep it that way.

"Mr. Sanderson, are you still there? I am an impatient man and have a lot to do."

"Yes, Mr. Messai, I am here. I just can't believe you are calling me."

"Well, I *am* calling you Doc. I understand you have some information for me pertinent to the threat of the group of rebels who are part of this Smyrnians cult."

"I do, but how did you know I called. I didn't give them my name or any other info."

"Doc, Doc, Doc. I know everything about you. You cannot keep anything from me. Now, give me the name of the person or persons you suspect may be a part of the Smyrnians."

"I am sorry, Mr. Messai. Forgive me. His name is John Baldwin. He is a professor at a university in Chicago. We were childhood friends but had not seen each other in years. He approached me about buying an underground bunker a few weeks ago. I own Protection Services Inc. here in Wichita, Kansas. We sell underground shelters to people who live in Tornado Alley."

"I did not ask for your life story. Just give me the info!" roared Messai.

"I... I am sorry, sir. John ended up purchasing three 3,000 square foot steel bunkers from me. He paid $2,225,000 for them. I'm certain he doesn't have that kind of money..."

"Where did he take them?" asked Messai, growing more impatient.

"Well, I don't know. He insisted that we not deliver or install them. He said they would do that themselves. All I know is, some guy drove them out of here on a tractor trailer."

"What do you mean, you don't know where he took them? You didn't get that information?" Messai was yelling now and growing more impatient and angry by the minute. "What kind of businessman are you? They are planning on hiding out underground. Did you say he lives in Chicago?" Doc felt severely chastised. He was certain Messai cared nothing about him.

"Yes, sir. That's correct. I would have to assume he is using them somewhere in that vicinity. You said there would be a handsome reward for any person who gave information."

"I thank you for the information, Mr. Sanderson. I will reward you well for calling us with this tip. Tell me where I can send your money."

Doc gave him the address, and just like that, the call ended. He was in a state of shock that Aissa Messai had called him. The reward money would come because Messai was a man of his word. But he struggled with what he had just done. He knew it would be bad if Messai found John and his group. He may have just cost his friend his life. But could he really call John his friend? He had been, but that was years ago when they were kids growing up in Kansas. Yet he knew what he had done, and it was eating him up on the inside. Was money worth a man's life?

Doc finally slept again, but his sleep was restless. He dreamed over and over about John Baldwin. There was John, then Aissa Messai, then Blake Thompson and Beth Jennings. He saw John with his hands bound behind him, kneeling at a guillotine. The blade came down and John's severed head fell into a waiting tub covered in blood. John's lifeless body fell sideways to the ground. Blake and Beth were next. Same thing. He woke up in a sweat, shaking all over. He fell asleep again. The same dream. He eventually got up, went to his man cave and walked the floor.

What had he done? How could he do such a thing? In that moment, he hated himself. But Aissa Messai was the savior of the world. He had done more for the planet than anyone before him. But tonight, on the phone, Doc had sensed something else in the man's voice. Evil. Darkness. Something sinister. A chill ran down his spine. Fear seized him. He wished he had a way to warn John, but he did not. It was too late anyway. Messai was onto him. He hoped John could survive AMPP hunting him down. For the first time, he now understood what they were about. Doc collapsed into his chair, as hopeless as he had ever been in his life.

CHAPTER 8

Aissa Messai yelled as he met with his staff. "Underground! They are going underground! And we must find them and exterminate them! Chicago. I want every available man we have in Chicago. Find out anything you can about Professor John Baldwin. Search everywhere there till you find where he and the others are hiding away like moles. When you find them, bring them to me immediately! Do not kill them. I want them taken alive. People need to see an example made of them so they will understand how important it is not to interfere with my plans for the world!"

Daylight had arrived as the three Smyrnians continued making their way to Missouri. Anders fought drowsiness but kept going. There was no time to stop. Blake and Beth talked to him nonstop to keep him from falling asleep. Trying to stay awake, he put his window down to let cool air hit his face. It was a struggle. Beth pulled up her tablet as she lay in the back seat. The first headline she saw said, "Wanted: this man." There was a picture of John Baldwin. "Blake!" she said louder than she intended. "Look at this!" She practically threw the tablet at her husband.

"Doc Sanderson," said Blake.

"Doc Sanderson? What does he have to do with this? There is a bounty on John's head!"

"I guarantee you Doc turned him in. He is a money grubber. He wanted that reward."

"Do you honestly think so?"

"In my heart, I *know* so. Am I right, Anders?"

That snapped Anders out of his slumber. "Without a doubt. I wonder if John knows about this?"

"I think I will call and make sure he does. Are we sure these phones are secure?"

"They are 100% secure. Call him."

Blake dialed the number, and John answered.

"Blake, how are you guys coming along. Is everything going well?"

"I guess that depends on your definition of well. Let's see, a trooper stopped us and recognized us. He made us get out of the car and took us down over an embankment out of sight. Then, as I was trying to decide whether to rush him, he told us he and his wife had seen our specials and prayed to receive Jesus. He wanted to thank us. The Rapture took their baby and 2-year-old, and now they know where they are and that they will see them again. That was an awesome experience!"

"I am sure it was! I wouldn't really call that smooth, but I am thankful you are in the clear now."

"Oh no, that is only part of the story. We had to stop for gas and found this little Food Mart on the outskirts of a small town. Thankfully, they were open all night. I went inside to pay for the gas while Beth pumped it. As the owner had his back turned, Anders slipped in and went to the bathroom. That guy recognized us, too. He held a gun on Beth and me and was ready to call 911 and turn us in. But Anders came out of the bathroom, and the guy did not see him. He grabbed a beer bottle out of a 6-pack on the shelf, came up behind him and smashed it over his head, knocking him out cold. I am hoping he didn't kill him. We took the man's gun and ran!"

"You took his gun?!"

"Absolutely! We have to protect ourselves. I do not want to kill anyone, but if it is kill or get killed, I will do what I have to do. We have been on the road about an hour since then. But that is not why I called. Have you seen your picture on the news?"

"*My* picture? We have been too busy here to watch the news. Why am *I* on the news?"

"You are a wanted man. I assume there is a bounty on your head too now. I think your old buddy Doc Sanderson called Messai's Tip Line and turned you in. There is a big reward for anyone who gives a credible tip. Had you heard about that?"

"Yep, I saw that. But I never thought one of those tips would be about *me*!"

"Well, you are a wanted man now. We thought we should let you in on that little tidbit, in case you had not seen the news. Trust me, everybody else has seen it."

"I am honored to join you and Beth on that list. I thought I would have a little time to be out and about unrecognized and able to use my work as a seismologist on the earthquake stuff to get on the inside. I guess that idea is out of the question now. Sounds like it is time for me to get my new face on too. I am going for the sexy look, wavy hair with a goatee and mustache."

"That would be a big change," Blake laughed.

"Hey, I know very well how I look. You don't have to point it out." John laughed too.

"Well, I am going for the gruff look, long hair and full beard. Beth assured me she will still love me, no matter how I look. Okay, I need to get off here. Just stay in for now and don't show your face outside the shelter."

"You don't have to worry about that. I am not leaving this place. I can't afford to get myself killed this early in the Tribulation. But I am worried about Doc. By calling Messai, I am afraid he is now in league with the devil. I wish I had a way to speak with him."

"Is your phone secure? If it is, call him."

"Get him on the website to watch the video. I would also guess he didn't watch it all last night."

"That is a good idea, Blake, I may do that. It is worth a try."

"Do it! I have to get off the phone. Anders is driving, and Beth and I are trying to stay out of sight. Pray that we do not run into any more trouble."

"Done deal. You can count on it. We will see you guys later today. Be safe."

Doc's wife worried about her husband. He had always been the upbeat, happy-go-lucky one. But this morning he was not his normal self. He was quiet and reserved, and she knew something was bothering him. However, he would not talk to her about it. In fact, he would not talk to anyone; employees, customers, no one. He had not eaten breakfast, his favorite meal of the day. Every morning, he wanted gravy and biscuits, eggs, two or three meats, and pancakes or waffles. He had never been much of a lunch guy. He ate well enough at breakfast that it lasted him all day until dinner. He did not seem physically ill this morning. No, something else was bothering him.

She heard him on the phone when she was in the kitchen getting something to drink in the middle of the night. She often got thirsty after eating certain foods and could not sleep without getting a drink. That normally involved several minutes of being up. By the time she got back into bed, he was sound asleep again. She assumed it must have been a customer on the west coast. That happened occasionally too, and he never wanted to miss a customer's call, even though it always made him angry that they called and woke him.

He had a nightmare an hour or so after that and murmured in his sleep. One time he uttered John Baldwin's name and screamed just before he woke up. He was sweating when he sat straight up in the bed. She had held him when he laid back down and told him she loved him and things would be okay. But this morning, they were not okay. He seemed to be a shell of the man who had been her husband for 35 years.

She wanted to help him, but did not know how. Then she had an idea. She walked into Doc's office and rummaged through the paperwork for the huge bunker sale he had made to John. She wrote John's phone number down and placed the call. The number was no longer in service. What was going on with Doc and John? She needed to know. She walked back in the house and searched for Doc until she found him sitting alone in his man cave without the TV on. He sat, staring at the wall. His phone was vibrating, but he did not even look at it. The sound did not faze him. She walked over and picked it up. Too late. She missed the call. She checked the number. Unknown caller. Who was it? Was Doc in trouble? Or was it just one of *those* calls? Neither of them answered *those* calls. She and Doc only called back if the caller left a message. The phone dinged. She looked at it. New voicemail. This caller had left a message. They never do that. She walked out of the room and listened to the message.

"Doc, this is John Baldwin. Look, man, I need to talk to you. I just found out I am a wanted man. Aissa Messai has put a bounty on my head. I saw that he set up a tip line and asked people to call if they had information about anyone who may have been acting suspiciously and could be a part of the Smyrnians that Blake Thompson and Beth Jennings talked about on their special broadcasts yesterday evening. And he suggested this group may seek ways or places to hide out."

"l recall how suspicious and inquisitive you were about the bunkers, where l would put them and what l would use them for. So you are the only one l can think of who may have turned me in. Look, Doc, l am not blaming you. l *am* a member of the Smyrnians. l gave my life to Jesus Christ and am now a Christian. l wanted to tell you, but you would not let me. l can't give you my number, but if you will have your phone available, l will call you again in a few minutes. If you don't answer, l will continue trying every thirty minutes throughout the day. Please, Doc, take my call. l care about you and desperately need to talk to you."

That explained it! She looked at her husband and wondered how it had been possible for him to turn his childhood friend in to Messai. Now it was killing him on the inside that he had done it. She lay the phone back down on the arm of his big recliner he loved so much. She stepped back and waited. Doc did not act as if he even heard her come into the room. Five minutes went by, then ten. Doc had not moved. He still sat, staring straight ahead. Fifteen minutes. Still no call back from John.

She had never met John, but Doc had told her stories from their childhood and teenage years. No matter what Doc said, she knew they had been close. She could tell that he still had an affinity for the man, even though they had not been close for many years. She had seen it in his face after John came that first time to talk about the bunkers. She could tell it did Doc good to see his old friend. That evening at dinner he had shared stories with her from their childhood and guffawed at some of them. He talked about John's conspiracy theories and found humor in most of them. He laughed about how John had fallen for the Y2K scare until he realized at the last minute it would not happen. He said these bunkers were part of another of John's crazy ideas.

She did not want to believe Doc would turn his friend in, but she knew in her heart he had. The phone vibrated again. Doc remained motionless, as if he was still unaware that someone was trying to call him. She walked over, picked it up, and answered as she moved out of the room.

"This is Kathie Sanderson. May l help you?"

"Kathie, this is John Baldwin. We haven't met, but l am sure Doc has talked to you about me, especially these last couple of weeks."

"Hello, John. Oh yes, Doc has talked to me about you and him growing up together many times. And after you were here, he told me stories of when you guys were kids and teenagers and laughed all the way through them. John, I know Doc has been elusive with you, but he cares about you and misses your friendship."

"It is vital that I speak with him. There is something I desperately need to talk to him about."

"I know that. I listened to your voicemail. I was not trying to snoop. But I knew Doc needed help. He is sitting in his man cave staring straight ahead, with the TV off and talking to no one. He has not eaten. I am very concerned about him. I know he turned you in, John. He has not told me that, but I know you are right. He woke up sweating heavily last night, calling your name. It took a long time for him to go back to sleep, but when he did, it happened again. I can't snap him out of his trance. Something happened to him yesterday evening. I just don't know what it was. It is like he is under a spell, or something."

"If I tell you something, Kathie, will you hear me out? It is very important."

"Yes, I will. If you can tell me what is happening to Doc, I need to know."

"I can't get into all of it over the phone. But I can give you a website where you can watch it for yourself. Just let me say this. Aissa Messai is an evil man. In fact, he is the epitome of evil. He is from Satan. I don't know what you believe about God and Jesus. I know Doc has never been a believer. Neither was I, trust me. I was a biology professor and self-proclaimed atheist."

"But when I heard truths about everything that has happened, which were impossible to deny, I became a follower of Jesus Christ. He has changed my life, Kathie. If Messai claims Doc's mind first, he will destroy his life now and forever. Messai wants his mind and soul, and Doc has opened the door to that by contacting him. Please help me tell him the truth. And please go to our website and watch the video on there for yourself. It is *smyrnians.com*. Will you do that?"

"I will do it right now! I don't believe Doc can watch it with me. What can I do? I believe you are right. Messai has cast some kind of evil spell on him. Doc is under his control right now. I can feel it and see it. Please help me, John."

"I would love to come and talk to him myself, but I'm not sure it is safe. There is a price on my head now. Messai will have his forces on the lookout for me."

"I am so sorry about this, John. I can't believe Doc did this to you. I need to go and check on him again. Then I will go to your website and watch the video. Can you call me back in an hour or two so I can give you my thoughts? Here is my phone number. You can call me directly. I just hope we can help Doc, John. My heart is breaking for my husband."

"I will do everything I can, Kathie. And we will all start praying for him right now."

"I don't even know if I believe in praying. But you do whatever you need to do. If it helps Doc, it is what I want. I hope to talk to you later today."

John wrote the number down and shared the news with the others at the shelter. They immediately started praying for Doc Sanderson and his wife.

Morning had barely dawned over Kentucky as Anders crossed the state line. They had taken what some may consider an unconventional route for a trip from New York City to Ozark, Missouri. Neither of them had ever been to the Bluegrass State, and this route would take them through the heart of horse country. The unfortunate thing was, they did not have time to stop. If they had the Kentucky Horse Park and some larger horse farms that raised thoroughbreds, including Kentucky Derby winners, would have been on the agenda. They would make no stops in Lexington or any of the other larger cities. Once again, when they stopped for gas, it would be in an outlying location with few people around. That would happen farther to the west and should be their last fill-up before they reached the farm.

Their conversation centered on the beauty of the landscape, from the mountains of West Virginia and Eastern Kentucky to the rolling hills of central Kentucky to the lowlands in the western part of the state. The differences were striking, but not all that much unlike the state of New York; they reasoned. They would enter Missouri in the south and work their way north to Ozark. That included a drive through a portion of the Ozark Mountains with their beautiful scenery, even in winter, and a better option for driving unnoticed.

They would make their final gas stop between towns in far Western Kentucky. With Anders being the only one getting out of the car, filling the tank with gas and going inside to pay, the third stop had gone off without a hitch. They could not believe they had not thought about that before. They should have realized Blake and Beth would still be identifiable, even with disguises. But no one would recognize Anders because he was never on camera.

After that final gas stop, they would be just over 300 miles away from their destination with a full tank of gas and a car that got 30 miles to the gallon. It should be smooth sailing from there. Until then, they were driving and talking about the future and what it held for them when Blake's phone sounded the old car horn that had become his go-to ringtone. John was calling to tell them about Doc Sanderson's situation and asking them to pray for him. But not just for him, for his wife Kathie also as she watched the pastor's message alone.

They needed Doc, his business and his connections on the team. But even more, they wanted Doc and Kathie to put their faith in Jesus. Messai had his hooks in Doc, and Jesus was the only one who could set him free from his spell. Blake and Beth had seen a room full of United Nations delegates under that spell, and they were well aware of how intense and mesmerizing it could be. So they would pray hard for both of them. Then John threw a bombshell into the equation.

"I think Trey will fly me to Wichita later today so I can see Doc for myself. I need to prepare him for the video and sit with him as he watches it. Then I can be there for him and hopefully help him give his life to Jesus."

"John, you can't take that chance. Messai has people out looking for you. It is too risky."

"I don't think I have a choice. Jesus is telling me to go. It feels urgent, more urgent than anything I have ever felt before. And it is my place to do it. I don't believe anyone else can do it for me."

"I wish you would reconsider," Beth said from the backseat. Blake had his phone on speaker. "We need you on the team. You may jeopardize that by going. You may jeopardize your *life* by going. We all know how careful we have to be. Please think about that."

"I have already decided, Beth. I am going, and Trey is flying me. We would love to wait for you guys to get here before we leave, but we need to be there before dark and in time for me to watch the video with Doc before bedtime. So, as it stands now, we plan to leave in the middle of the afternoon. I also want to call Kathie again before we go. She is probably on the website watching the video right now. She asked me to give her time to watch it, then call."

"I know we can't talk you out of it, John," said Blake. "Please be careful. If you get caught, my guess is, we won't see you again on this earth. As Beth said, we need you. And as she told me after I called Messai out that morning when I saw the carnage of gang war on the streets of New York, don't get yourself killed! Do you have an exit strategy if things go south?"

"Well, not a complete one. Trey will fly me into the private airstrip we used before when we went to get the bunkers. He has arranged for a truck to be there for me this time, instead of a car. I will drive to Doc's place, trying to be careful and lie low. If anything bad happens, I will get out of there and back to the airstrip so we can get in the air immediately. That is about the best I can do."

"I don't like it any more than Blake and Beth," said Anders. "I don't have a good feeling about this, and my intuition is on the money most of the time."

"I hear you, Anders. And I understand everybody's concern. But this is something I have to do. I will trust you guys to pray for me. That is the best coverage I have in case of an ambush. I just know Doc is worth it."

They called Ben, who called John and also tried to talk him out of going, but to no avail. "He has the video," Ben said. "Some people have put their faith in Jesus after watching it, me being one of them. Give that a chance. If he still doesn't believe, then you can go."

"I wish it was that easy, Ben. But I have to go. Doc is under Messai's spell. Kathie says he is sitting and staring at the wall in his man cave. He didn't eat breakfast, which is his favorite meal. I hope you understand that."

Ben surrendered as well and promised him the Abramson clan would cover him in prayer too. All of them believed John may get himself killed.

The time came to call Kathie Sanderson. John moved to a private area of the bunker where he now lived and tapped her number. He had saved both it and Doc's number in his contacts. She answered on the first ring.

"John, I am so glad you called. I am shaking all over right now. How did I miss the truth all of those years? How did Doc miss it? How did anyone miss it? When I watched the pastor's video, it became clear. I believe it with all my heart. I believe Jesus is the Son of God and he died on the cross for me and rose from the grave. I know what happened on September 11 was not an alien invasion. Jesus took his people home to be with him."

"I am suddenly so happy for those people! I wish I had been ready then, but I am ready now! John, I put my faith in Jesus like the pastor said and asked Jesus to come into my life and be my Savior. And he did, John! I can feel him. It is like nothing I have ever felt before. I am not proud of this, but I did drugs for a little while in college. But I never experienced a high like this. You can't believe how good I feel!"

"Oh trust me, Kathie, I can. I have been there, done that. It took a lot to get this atheistic college professor to believe, but when I did and accepted Jesus as my Savior, it was the most awesome feeling I have ever had! Welcome to the family of God! Welcome to the Smyrnians!"

"I want to hear more about the Smyrnians. I can't wait to hear it! I watched the last part of the video too. I know about these seven years. I know who Aissa Messai is. I haven't gotten to watch the other things yet, but I will. I want to know more. I am hungry for more. I want all of Jesus I can get! But John, please help Doc. I tried to get his attention, but he still hasn't moved. There has to be a way to break the hold Messai has on him. Please, John, tell me how to help him. He has to hear the truth about Jesus!"

"I will do more than that, Kathie. A friend and fellow Smyrnian is flying me there. We are leaving soon. I should be there by late afternoon."

"Oh John, how can I ever thank you? After all Doc has said and done to you, especially ratting you out to Messai, I can't understand why you still want to help him. He really cares about you. That is why he is so broken now. But wait. There is a bounty on your head. It will be dangerous for you to come. They will kill you if they catch you! But I want you to come. Doc needs you."

"I know how dangerous it is, but I am coming. Doc is worth it to me. I will be in a black truck. My friend will wait for me where we land. If you don't mind, keep an eye out for anything out of the ordinary, any movement or people, any noises. I don't want to frighten you, but Messai is dangerous. He has what he calls his *Peace Patrol* out looking for me. While it makes little sense to me, he may think I will return to the scene of the crime, so to speak. Who knows? Doc may be on his hit list too. Whatever happens, he will explain it in a way that the world sees it as good and something he had to do to protect the peace and prosperity of the world."

"I will keep a close watch and all the doors locked. And I will keep trying to get through to Doc. It is almost as if he is not even here. His body is, but it's like his mind and spirit aren't. I don't want to put you in danger, John, but I am glad you are coming."

"Watch for my arrival. Is there a way I can come in unnoticed and a place I can park that will be out of sight and easy access to the truck if I need to leave in a hurry?"

"There is. Doc often used it when he didn't want people to see him coming in. He is a salesman and people person at heart, but sometimes he has to back away for a bit. That is why he built his man cave, to watch sports, yes, but also to escape the rat race for a few hours. I usually leave him alone when he is down there. A few hundred feet past the entrance to the PSI parking lot and our drive, there is a little lane that turns into the woods. It is also a trail Doc rides his bike on occasionally. Unfortunately, not as often as he used to. He has gotten too busy for recreation. That lane circles around a grove of trees and into our back lawn. It's surrounded by trees too that shelter it. If you take that route, no one should see you, unless they are watching every square inch of this place. Let's hope they aren't and the coast will be clear for you to come and take all the time you need to help my husband. Thank you again, John."

"You're welcome, Kathie. I look forward to meeting you. Doc and I never talked about you much, but I know he is crazy about you. And I know you are crazy about him, too. I am sure you haven't done a lot praying, because neither had I. But do your best to pray for my pilot friend and me as we fly, and for Doc to believe in Jesus. And throw in a prayer for protection while I am there. I will see you in a few hours."

"I will try. I'm just going to talk to Jesus like I'm talking to you. I suppose that is praying. I will wait and watch for you. Please be careful."

"We will."

After ending the call, John started making preparations to leave. But there was no escaping the nagging thought in his mind that all was not well. He knew he had to go, but something was not right about the whole thing. Anders had said he did not feel good about it either. And he insisted that his intuition is nearly always right. It was a trip he now dreaded, but he had to go.

Aissa Messai was on a rampage in his private, soundproof office, and was the only one present for this one. He was loud, boisterous and out of control. If anyone else had been in the room, they would have seen the jagged streaks of lightning darting about and heard the screeches of the demonic creatures flying in and out of them. They would have witnessed him transformed into something inhuman. But outside his office, no one was aware of what was going on inside.

"They think they can fool me. They think they can hide from me and run from me. But they cannot! I will hunt them down. Let them crawl into their holes. I will find them. *Professor* John Baldwin, you should not have fallen for their lies. But you fell for them. For that, you will pay!"

"Doc Sanderson, you are a weak, spineless, selfish creature for betraying your friend. You will not collect your reward money. You will get your reward, but it will not be the reward you are expecting. It will be the reward for a man who attempted to take advantage of me. No one can take advantage of me. I am all-powerful! War has been declared, and its first casualties are about to be claimed!"

He called his secretary. "Get me the captain of the Peace Patrol." She did and transferred the call into Messai's office. "Send units in the U.S. to Doc Sanderson's house in Wichita, Kansas. Watch for the rebel, John Baldwin. Tell them if they do their jobs well, they will receive generous rewards for their service. And do not allow Sanderson to escape."

CHAPTER 9

2:00 p.m.

John boarded Trey's plane at another private airstrip Trey used outside of Springfield, Missouri. On this day, no one needed to know they were flying. The mission was as secret as their location. Covertness must be essential at this point. Soon they were in the air, bound for Wichita. John tried to get his plans together as they flew. He was nervous, very nervous.

Anders' words kept coming to his mind: "I don't have a good feeling about this." He shook them for a minute or two, then they came again: "I don't have a good feeling about this, and my intuition is on the money most of the time." *He* did not have a good feeling about it either, but he felt compelled to do it. Still, the closer they got to Wichita, the more nervous he became.

Anders, Beth and Blake had made their final gas stop in Kentucky and were on the last leg of their journey. Before long, they would be at the shelter. Exhaustion had set in, but their minds were on John. He was not only putting himself at risk; he may put the entire team in danger. He cared about Doc, but they believed this was a bad decision and perilous venture. He might walk into a trap. Who knew if Doc was on the up and up? None of them trusted him. But maybe John was right. Doc's wife may be serious about what was going on. Perhaps Doc would turn to faith in Jesus. Their minds struggled with those conflicting thoughts. Once again, they did the only thing they knew to do. They prayed.

• • • • •

Trey and John landed at 4:00 p.m. The old abandoned airstrip was perfect for an undercover mission. Trey called it private, and that it was. No one had used it in years, but it was still safe for landing and taking off. Trey had contacts, plenty of them. Most were old military buddies who would do anything for him, asking no questions. The truck he had arranged for John to drive sat to the side of the runway.

Trey's friend had said, "It's not much. I don't care what happens to it. I plan to junk it, anyway. But it runs good enough to get you where you need to go." When John saw it, he understood what the guy meant. He had told Kathie he would drive a black truck. It was a black truck, with lots of rust. But it was all he needed.

Trey prayed with him and sent him on his way. As he neared PSI, he saw Doc and Kathie's house sitting a few hundred feet away. He followed her directions and drove on past the house. The narrow dirt lane was so small, he would have driven right past it had he not been looking closely for it. He turned into it and circled through the grove of trees.

He understood why Doc liked to ride in here. It was quiet and peaceful. As he circled farther around, traffic noise disappeared. He noticed the lane continued on past where it circled left into Doc and Kathie's backyard. It was beautiful and as secluded as Kathie had said. He circled the yard and parked with the truck headed back toward the lane. It was a basic precaution in case he needed to get away quickly. Before he even got out of the truck, he saw Kathie hurriedly walking toward him. She grabbed him and hugged him.

"John, please come in. Doc still has not moved. Oh, I'm sorry. I should have welcomed you to our home. This means the world to me."

"Let's get to him. Has there been a hint of anything suspicious? Has anyone you haven't seen before been hanging around? Have there been any strange noises? I'm sorry. Again, I don't want to scare you. But then, I don't want to put you or Doc in danger either."

"Everything is fine, John. Nothing out of the ordinary has happened. Thank you so much for sharing the video and helping me give my life to Jesus. I am happier than I have ever been!"

"I can see that all over your face. Now let's see if we can help Doc experience the same thing."

They walked into the house, and she led him down the stairs to Doc's basement man cave. It was awe-inspiring. The man was an expert at living the life of luxury. The room was large enough to be multiple rooms. One end contained plush side-by-side theater seats, which he presumed were for Doc and Kathie. Both reclined and had cup holders and places for setting snacks.

The wall prominently displayed an enormous movie screen. Perfect for a man's hideaway or a place to watch movies with your wife. The opposite wall held a 75-inch TV. In front of it sat living room furniture where he watched sports with his pals. "They had plenty of parties down here," Kathie told him. It contained a full bar and kitchen.

In his recliner several feet away from the big screen TV sat Doc. He stared straight ahead and did not move. John waved his hand in front of his face, but Doc did not budge. Then he felt it. The chill. He shuddered. It was strange. He had not experienced it for a while, but he understood what it meant: Messai. He had taken control of Doc's mind following one phone conversation, and the man did not even realize it had happened.

Now, Messai was in the room with them, even if they could not see him. He could feel his icy glare and his eyes burning a hole right through him. Fear. He should not be afraid, but he was. Kathie felt it, too. He saw it on her face and in her eyes. She was shaking, her hands trembling. There were goosebumps on her arms. It was not cold in here; it was evil. Darkness. Kathie had turned the lights on, trying to bring Doc out of his trance, but it did not work. Despite the light, the room was dark and cold. John had to combat the darkness, but how was he going to do that?

He recalled his first glimpse of Messai, knowing he was a man he could not outwit. He prayed silently and asked Jesus for answers. He prayed for a plan of action. His friend's life and eternity hung in the balance. He felt the magnitude of the moment. The presence of evil fought against his mind as he tried to think. Messai's face loomed before his eyes, and a demonic voice exploded in his brain. He closed his eyes and shook his head to clear it. Fear clawed at him. Faith struggled against it. A thought. An answer, maybe? Where did it come from? He touched Kathie's arm, and she jumped.

Quietly he said, "Turn on the TV and put in this flash drive. It is the pastor's message. We have to bring light into the darkness of this room. Let's see what happens when it plays." She complied. The opening words showed, then the pastor appeared on the screen.

Trey had some time to kill until John returned, so he walked through the wooded area by the airstrip until the highway came into view. Traffic was busy as rush hour had started in Wichita. He stood on the outskirts of town and watched as thousands of people headed home from work. He considered how his life had changed in the last few weeks. He loved using what he had to serve Jesus. He knew life would not be easy or safe during the next seven years, but he also knew he was ready.

Suddenly he noticed something that caught his eye and brought him back to the moment: black SUVs that looked like official government vehicles of some sort. There were four of them. They were obviously in a hurry, weaving in and out of traffic. They were on a mission to somewhere. Then he saw the circular logo with the emblem of a dove and the bold letters **AMPP**: *Aissa Messai's Peace Patrol*!

The Smyrnians knew Messai had not founded the patrol to keep world peace, but to enforce his will. The people of the world did not realize that because they did not know who Messai was. They celebrated the founding of the Patrol. They believed the man was truly about peace. Nothing could be further from the truth. Anyone who opposed him would face the wrath of AAMP, although the world would be told he had aimed it at those who stood in the way of world peace. By nature of who they were, that put the Smyrnians and other followers of Jesus square in their sights.

Then it hit Trey. Is it possible they were here because of John Baldwin? He was now an enemy of the state. But how could they know John was here? Did they know, or were they just keeping surveillance on Doc Sanderson's house? Trey knew in his heart that was where they were going, and they were going because John was there. How they knew, he had no idea. He grabbed his phone and called John. No answer. He called again. Still no answer. He sent a text. No reply. "John, what are you doing? Answer me! You are in trouble!" he said aloud.

As the pastor spoke, Doc remained in the same position. No movement. John and Kathie did not even see him breathing. Had Messai stolen his soul right out of his body? Were they too late? Then came the pastor's first mention of Jesus. Movement, albeit slight. Another mention. More movement. As the pastor continued, Doc sat up and listened. As he explained about the 6,000 year mark, the Feasts of Israel, and Jesus saying he would return to take his people home on a Feast of Trumpets, Doc's eyes filled with tears. When the pastor gave the date of September 11, 2029 as the likely day that would happen, he wept. John allowed the video to play to the end, then went to Doc and knelt beside him.

"Doc?"

He turned his head and looked at him, his face streaked with tears. "I am so sorry, John. I turned you in. Can you forgive me? Can Jesus forgive me?"

"None of that matters now, Doc. Do you believe in Jesus?"

"I do, John. I never have, but I do now. I have been so foolish. I have wasted my life. Why didn't I see the truth?"

"I didn't see it either, Doc, until I watched the same video you just saw. That is when I put my faith in Jesus and asked him to be my Savior. That was the best day of my life, Doc. The best day ever. Kathie watched the video and did that today too. I tried to call you and left a message. When I called back, she answered. She is a follower of Jesus now. You want to follow him too, don't you, Doc? I know you do. I can see it all over your face."

"Yes, John. Please help me. I want to do what the pastor said. Can you help me?"

"Just do what he said, Doc. Tell Jesus you believe in him and ask him to come into your life and be your Savior. You believe Jesus died on the cross for you and rose from the grave, don't you?"

Doc did not answer. He had a faraway look in his eyes, as if he was looking straight into heaven and seeing Jesus. He prayed the most humble, poignant prayer John had heard. He thought Doc may go home to be with Jesus right then. He had gone from being under Messai's control to falling in love with Jesus. His look was one of longing, a longing for home. Not this home with all of his *stuff*. His home with Jesus. John motioned to Kathie, and she came to him, sat down beside him and took his hand in hers. She looked into his eyes.

"I love you, Doc."

"I love you too, Kathie. With all my heart, I love you. And I love Jesus. I feel his love for me. It is amazing. I want to be with him, baby. This world isn't home. This stuff doesn't compare to what Jesus has prepared for us. I don't want this stuff anymore. I just want Jesus."

They wrapped their arms around each other and kissed. They had always loved each other, but never like this. Jesus had changed everything for them. But there was something more powerful, more intense. It was not just his newfound faith in Christ. As she had sensed the pull of Messai on his life before, drawing him into his web, she felt the pull of Jesus on him now, drawing him into his presence. She did not understand what that meant. She just sat and held him close.

John glanced at his phone only to see that time had gotten away from him. It had to be dark outside. There were texts and missed calls from Trey. He read a text. "AMPP just rolled by here with four black SUVs. They were in a hurry. Just wanted to give you a head's up. You never know..." John looked at the time of the texts. 5:15 p.m. It was 7:00 p.m. now, almost two hours since Trey had sent them.

"Doc and Kathie, I don't want to leave you here by yourself. We have a place where you'll be safe. You can fly back there with my friend and me. I fear for you if you stay here. Messai will know Doc followed Jesus. And he is already looking for me. Why not grab a few things and go with me right now? There is a group of Jesus' followers who will be excited to see you!"

"Let's go, Doc," she whispered. "I want us to be safe."

He still had that faraway look in his eyes. John was certain he was looking into heaven at the face of Jesus. He had seen nothing like it before. It amazed him. What did it mean? Kathie packed a few clothes in two duffel bags. As they were getting ready to lead Doc to the door, there were voices outside. Bright lights suddenly shone through the windows.

"This is AMPP. You in the house, come out with your hands up. Doc and Kathie Sanderson, John Baldwin, we know you are in there. Surrender now, or we are coming in to get you."

"John, what do we do? We can't surrender to them. They will kill us!"

"You're right, Kathie. We have to get out of here. I parked the truck in the back where you told me to. If we can get out the back door and reach it, I already have it facing the lane. We can take off, try to get to the main road and lose them. I need to call Trey before we make a break for it."

Trey answered his phone. "John, are you all right? Man, it has worried me sick since I saw those AMPP vehicles."

"You were right, Trey. They were coming here. The good news is, Doc gave his heart to Jesus. The bad news is, they are outside with lights shining through the windows demanding that we come out and saying they are coming in to get us if we don't. We are making a break for the truck in the backyard and will try to outrun them. I don't see how we can get to you, though. I can't give you away. Besides, if they are in hot pursuit of us, we would never have time to get out of the truck, then get into the plane and take off."

"I don't know what to do. I don't have a vehicle to come and help you."

"Just have the plane ready. If we're not there or you haven't gotten a call from me within an hour, get out of there and head back. If I don't make it, tell the others about Doc and Kathie. And Trey, tell them I said it was worth it."

"John! John, wait. I am not leaving you! I will help you! I don't know how, but I will!"

"No, Trey. Don't even think about it. Just stay there and pray. And call the others."

Trey did that immediately. Smyrnians were praying from Missouri to England to Germany to New York City to a car getting closer and closer to the shelter at the farm.

John and Kathie were trying to get Doc to the back door. He was limp and kept saying, "Jesus." There was something different about how he said it, something unique, something special.

Doc's legs were steady now. There were sounds at the front door. A voice said, "You have 10 seconds, or we are breaking down the door." He started counting down, "10-9-8-7-6-5-4-3-2-1." The front door burst open, with the sounds of glass shattering and footsteps running in.

John yelled, "Go!" He grabbed their bags, and Kathie pulled Doc out the back door. They dashed for the truck. As they neared it, the sound of voices reached their ears. They were getting close.

"They are out the back door and making a run for it. They're headed for a black truck. Hurry!"

John reached the truck and threw the bags in the back. "Get in!" he screamed at the two struggling to make it. He started the truck and reached over to grab Kathie's hand and pull her in. Doc stepped in beside her. Then came the loud cracks of gunfire. Doc slumped over the dash, a gaping hole in his shirt and blood soaking through it.

"Doc!" screamed Kathie, tears rolling down her face. She kept screaming his name. Doc spoke, his voice weak. "Baby, give everything I have to John and the people who are following Jesus. I want them to use it for him. And John, please take care of Kathie for me. Will you do that?"

"You know I will, Doc. But hang on until we can get out of here and get you help." But he knew it was too late.

Doc spoke again, his voice growing weaker. "Look! I see the heavens opened and the Son of Man standing at the right hand of God! Lord Jesus, receive my spirit." The smile on his face looked rapturous. He gleamed with the glory of God. Then these words, "Lord, please do not hold this against them. Let them find you like I did." With those words, he was gone, not just gone, but gone home to be with the Jesus he just met. Kathie held him and wept. As John stomped the accelerator to the floor and spun toward the lane, Doc fell into her lap. She knew he was gone. But there was no questioning where he had gone. That made it hard to grieve. She said, "Enjoy Jesus, Doc. I will see you in seven years, or less."

When John reached the lane and prepared to turn right toward the highway, she said, "Turn left."

"Left?" he asked. "I can't go that way. There is nothing but woods!"

She said calmly, "Turn left."

Not knowing what else to do, he turned left. In the dark, he could barely make out the dirt road winding through the trees. In the distance behind him, he saw the lights of the SUVs turning down the lane to follow them. He still had the accelerator to the floor, even though he had no way to know where he was going. First, straight ahead, then a sharp curve, then straight again. As he was sliding around a sharp curve on two wheels, she said, "Turn right."

"There is nowhere to turn right! There is nothing but trees!"

She said, "When I tell you to, turn right hard."

"Now!"

He jerked the steering wheel to the right, toward the woods. Bracing for impact, he had both arms extended and pushed hard on the floor with his left foot. Then he noticed he was on another dirt road. It had frozen just enough that they were not creating any dust, but it was rough. He thought the truck may bounce off the road and into the trees any minute.

"Turn off the lights."

What were his options? She had been right every time. He slowed and shut off the lights. The SUVs went flying by without turning.

"Let's get out for a minute."

John complied again. His life was in her hands.

"Help me drag this pile of brush over the road. There is a fallen tree right over there that is small enough to drag too. If they come back, it will look as if no one came down this way. It is an old logging road Doc used."

They covered the road with the brush and tree.

"Now, let's go. There is another logging road down here to the left. That is where we are going."

She confused him, but he followed her directions. The truck bounced along. He made the turn.

"Just ahead about 400 yards and turn right."

In the dark, he was driving blind as they bumped along on the logging road, but she seemed to know where they were going. So, he crept along until he turned right, this time before she even told him. A short distance farther and she said, "Okay, we are here."

On the left sat a small, but beautiful log cabin. It amazed him. "How in the world did this get back here? This is gorgeous. I'll bet it is even prettier in the daylight."

"Doc built it for us to get away and hide from everybody. He had his man cave at home, but that was for him and his friends. He built this place for *us*. We would come out here, sit on the porch, listen to the birds and watch the deer and squirrels play. He said it was better than the beach. Believe it or not, there is great cell service out here. You should probably call your friend, Trey."

Trey! John hoped he had not left! Had it been an hour? He called, and Trey answered. John could hear the roaring of the plane's engines. No! He had already left! Now, what?

"John! What has been happening? I was just about to take off. Talk to me, man!"

"So, you have not left? Man, I am glad to hear that."

"Is everything okay? How about Doc and Kathie?"

"Doc didn't make it, Trey. They shot him. He made it to the truck, but he was the last one in. He took a bullet right through the back. But you will love hearing what that was like. Kathie is with me. She is okay; shaken up, but at peace with everything. The way Doc died changed everything for her. Can you get something to drive? I don't think I can explain how to get to where we are, but Kathie can. We are in a cabin deep in the woods. We made a turn onto an old logging road and lost them."

"Let me talk to him." The calmness in Kathie's voice amazed him. He knew it came from Jesus. John handed her the phone. "Trey, this is Kathie Sanderson. How long will it take you to get here? I have an idea. I haven't even told John yet. But just so you know, Doc always said I was the idea person behind the success of PSI. This thought just came to me."

"Tell me your thought. It will have to be good to throw Messai's troops off course."

"Okay, here you go. It seems to me this old truck John is driving has just about had it, although it was the perfect truck for our joyride tonight. There is a hill on down the lane from where we turned off. From the top of that cliff, it is a long drop onto a bunch of big rocks below. When you come and get us, I say we take the truck to that hill, set it on fire and push it over. Then get out of here as fast as we can!"

"You want to burn the truck?"

"Yes. They will eventually find it. If it burns up, they will think we died in the fire. If it burns hot enough, hopefully they will think there was nothing left of us. There are gas cans here. We will fill it with gas, pour gas all over the engine and inside the cab, then set in on fire and push it over. It will be a good thing if they believe John is dead, don't you think?" She looked at John.

He had to admit; it was a brilliant idea. If they honestly believed he was dead, it would free him up to get out in the world, disguised by his new look. No one would be on the lookout for him.

"I love the idea. If you two can get everything ready and you can tell me how to get there, I will find a vehicle. I have enough friends around here. I will just tell them I flew in and have to stay overnight. I can leave their vehicle at the airstrip when I leave."

Kathie gave him the directions. Trey had been in a few combat missions on the ground in the Middle East. He could find almost any place. And with good directions, he would find this one.

Doc still lay in the truck in a pool of blood. "Let's bury him here," Kathie suggested. "He loved this place. This is not the real Doc. We know where he is. He is with Jesus. He would want his body to be here." They found shovels Doc kept in the cabin and dug a grave behind it. They gathered brush and laid it in the bottom, then put more brush on top to cover his body. It was a makeshift grave, but Doc would have been good with it.

When they finished, Kathie took a few more minutes to grieve alone. Then they filled the truck with gas and placed the other cans in the back. They drove back out and parked behind the pile of brush they had used to block the first logging road. They sat and waited for Trey to arrive, all the while keeping watch and listening to make sure the men from AMPP did not return. They did not. The lane ended back at the main road. John and Kathie were sure they convinced the men they had escaped on that road.

It took nearly two-and-a-half hours for Trey to arrive, but he finally made it. He called as he drove down the lane, and Kathie guided him on in. Soon he parked at the end of the lane where they sat. He helped remove the brush and tree that covered the logging road, then replace them.

They got in the truck, sped to the edge of the cliff and slammed on the brakes, skidding to a stop and leaving deep grooves in the dirt. They followed Kathie's plan, poured gas inside the truck and on the engine, started it, put it in gear, threw in a box of lit matches and saw the flames leap as the truck rolled over the edge.

They watched as it tumbled end over end until it crashed on the rocks below and exploded in an enormous ball of fire. Then as fast as possible, they jumped in Trey's truck and headed out the lane back toward the main highway.

As they drove, John called Blake and filled him in. He could hear the celebration over the phone, then it quieted when he told them about Doc. Getting to the shelter was their only goal now. They knew the group was waiting for them and anticipating their arrival. They would be there to welcome them home. The three of them could not wait to get there and feel safe and loved again.

Kathie took one last look at her home as they drove by. AMPP would likely tear it apart looking for evidence and confiscate whatever they could find. Despite everything that happened to her in one day and night, her face showed the peace that only comes from Jesus. "I assume we have work to do," she said. The other two nodded, "yes."

"Trey, this is a nice truck. But I am guessing it looked better than this when you borrowed it. Shouldn't you wash it before we take it back? We don't want to make your pal suspicious."

They stopped in a self-service car wash outside of town, gave it a good washing and vacuumed the inside. It looked as good as new. Then it was on to the airstrip to climb on board and get away from Wichita as fast as the plane would fly. They would be more than ready to watch the lights of the city disappear behind them as they flew.

In Belgium, Aissa Messai was on another rant as he talked on the phone with the director of AMPP. "How did you lose them?" he yelled. "What kind of incompetent fools allow three people in an old truck to escape driving through the woods? I will fire somebody for this. In fact, heads may roll, literally."

"I want every man we have back out there tomorrow searching those woods. Do not leave any stone unturned. Cover every nook and cranny. Turn Wichita upside down. If they are there, find them. If you cannot find them, get back to Chicago and find John Baldwin. I want him! Wherever he and Blake Thompson and Beth Jennings are hiding, flush them out!"

"Sir, we hit one of them. I am sure it was Doc Sanderson. And I am certain he is dead."

"At least you bunch of losers did one thing right. Make sure we have not sent him a check. He was a weasel. That is one down, but there are many more to go. And who knows how many after those crazy reporters aired that story last night. We cannot allow them to stop our progress. They will if we let them. Keep me informed on the search tomorrow. And please get it right this time!"

"Don't worry, sir. We will make sure we do. You can count on your men from AMPP."

CHAPTER 10

Anders, Beth and Blake arrived at the shelter a few hours earlier. The progress the others had made blew them away. The outside looked amazing. The vent pipes were visible as they stuck up out of the ground for now. But once the ryegrass came up, it would hide them. They would never cut it, so it would easily keep them obscured for seven years. It should cover the area well by April and fully by May.

"Impressive!" Anders exclaimed.

"If you think that is impressive, come and see the inside," Ally said.

The cabin was impressive in its own right. But the closet with the secret wall leading to the hidden steps was ingenious. As they descended the spiral staircase to the bottom, they walked all the way around the exterior before entering. Then they entered each bunker and took the grand tours. All three were identical and fully furnished, having all the comforts of home.

"Do we get to pick which one we live and work in, or is that already decided?" Blake asked.

"Neither is up to the standards of your previous abode," Evan grinned. "But I think you will find them to have everything you need and more. You still have the option to choose which one you think works best for you."

"I am ready to move in!" There was no doubt about Beth's excitement. "We need to set up our studio and start broadcasting ASAP. People will expect to hear from us, and we can't let them think we are not doing what we promised."

"I tried to determine the best places for everything to go. Hopefully, you will agree. If not, we can always make adjustments. Let me show you what I mean."

It was then that they received the call from Trey, and a crisis drove them to their knees in prayer. Then all they could do was await further word and pray for the safe arrival of their colleagues. That word had come giving them cause for celebration, followed by grief because of Doc's passing. When their teammates and Kathie Sanderson arrived, they would be there for them. In the midst of the craziness of this time, they always made sure they were there for each other.

Trey landed in Springfield at 4:00 a.m. After getting the plane settled inside the hangar, John and Kathie ran to his truck and jumped in. He hunched down in the front seat, and she lay in the back seat. Fortunately, no one was anywhere near the hangar at this time of the morning. But then, they could not take any chances either, not even on possibly being spotted during the short drive to the farm. That would surely not happen with it still being dark. But they had to take every precaution and leave nothing to chance.

If Messai's AMPP men could convince him that John had died in the fiery crash, it would change things big time. Maybe in the long run, Doc had done him a favor. Had he not turned him in to Messai, Doc would have never watched the video and put his faith in Jesus. Neither would Kathie. And if they had not run from AMPP, she would not have come up with the idea to burn the truck allowing him to disappear, being presumed dead. It was sad in one way that it cost Doc his life, but happy in another way that he wanted to go be with Jesus and got to do exactly that.

John would have to stay in the shelter long enough to change his appearance. Then he would be ready to get out on the front lines and go toe-to-toe with Messai and his henchmen. That would not take long. Trey drove carefully to make sure he stayed under the speed limit on the way to the farm. He did not want to have an encounter with Missouri's finest. When they drove up to the cabin and stopped, Kathie raised her head for the first time.

"Where are we?" she asked.

"The safe house. We call it the shelter."

"The shelter?" she asked, looking around.

"Come on," John said. "Let me show you why we call it that."

They walked into the cabin. "This is not as nice as the one Doc built for you, but it is homey, don't you think?"

"Very homey. I thought you said there were others here. I don't see anyone."

"That is why we call it a safe house. *This* is why we call it the shelter." She followed Trey and him into the bedroom and watched as he opened the small closet door.

"You hide in this little closet? There is only room in here for two or three people, at most."

John pulled the clothes to one side, stepped in and pushed on the back wall. It spun open.

"What in the...?"

"Ladies first. Trey and I will be right behind you."

She stepped in, saw the staircase and started down holding onto the rail to be sure she did not fall. Trey and John followed. When they reached the bottom, they stepped out into the long corridor that extended one hundred feet, passing all three bunkers. The door of the middle one opened, and Evan, Ally, Rickie, Anders, Blake and Beth greeted them. Her face lit up.

"Blake Thompson! Beth Jennings! I have seen both of you on the news many times. I am sorry, I don't know the rest of you, but I look forward to getting to know you!"

"Kathie," said Beth, "we are so sorry to hear about Doc. I am sure you are heartbroken, but we will be here for you. All of us are here for each other. John told us you believed in Jesus and received him as your Savior, so you probably know about the Tribulation. We will need each other during the next seven years as we fight Messai. You need us, and we need you."

"Thank you, Beth. But don't be sorry about what happened to Doc. We just got here, but if you have a few minutes, I would love to tell you the story of how he died."

"Come on in. I can't wait to hear that!"

Anders never grew tired of what he called *Jesus stories.*

"We have coffee ready and some cereal and pastries, if you three are hungry. I promise there will be a bigger breakfast tomorrow once all of us get settled in."

•   •   •   •   •

The sun had risen, and the day began with a sunny sky on a chilly morning. The AMPP guys were back on patrol in the woods, searching for any sign of John Baldwin or Kathie Sanderson. They had already turned everything in the house upside down to make sure they had not returned and were hiding somewhere inside. Then they had gone through the PSI buildings, once again finding no one, except the employees, and they were oblivious to what had happened.

When daylight came, they turned their attention to the perimeter of the property, carefully combing every square inch. They were leaving no stone unturned. No one wants to be on Aissa Messai's bad side. Honestly, most of them hated the man, but they had the best paying job of their lives. So, they kept their mouths shut and did what they were told to do. They knew a far different Messai than other people knew, but none of them would ever divulge that.

Then they were back on the dirt lane that led into the woods on the Sanderson property. Doc owned hundreds of acres, much of it woodland. They drove along the lane with their eyes peeled on both sides for any sign of them. There were several of what appeared to be old logging roads. But they were all blocked with brush and downed trees, so there is no way they escaped down one of them.

Suddenly, one of them in the front SUV threw his hand out the window and motioned for those behind him to stop. He got out and pointed to skid marks leading to the edge of a high cliff. They walked over together, and holding onto small trees so they would not fall to their deaths below, peered over the edge. Barely visible at the bottom in a pile of rocks was something, but it was too far away to tell what it was. Pulling out a pair of binoculars, one of them zoomed in on it.

"It's a wrecked vehicle, but it doesn't look like there is much left."

"Some of us will have to rappel down there and check it out," said another.

They readied the rappelling gear, and three of them made their way down the face of the cliff, doing their best to navigate the jagged ledges and avoid the tree branches stretching out from the sides along the way. They reached the bottom and walked to the charred remains.

"It was a truck, all right," one of them yelled up at the others. "But *was* is the key word. It appears to have exploded when it hit the rocks and burned up. It must have had a full tank of gas, because the frame melted. This was a real inferno."

"Do you see any sign of bodies?" one of them yelled down from the top of the cliff.

"Nothing that we can see, but we will look around. The crash may have thrown them out before hitting the rocks down here. It looks like the truck was rolling and flipping all the way down. Can two of you rappel down and inspect the side of the cliff? It is craggy, but they would surely be down here, in or out of the truck. But we need to be one hundred percent certain."

Two of the others started down, looking for a ledge or tree that may have caught the bodies on the way down. There was nothing. As they neared the bottom, they examined every tree thoroughly to be sure no bodies had lodged in any branches.

"Nothing in the trees or on the ledges. Have you guys checked everything too?"

"We have looked everywhere. Nothing down here either. They must have stayed inside the truck. If they did, incineration is the best word to describe what happened to them. This thing would have been hotter than a crematory. There was nothing but ashes left of anyone inside."

"It was definitely them. You can tell it is the truck they were driving."

"How did we miss seeing it and hearing the explosion? We were not far behind them."

"I would say they went over the edge and we flew by. If you remember, we were flying. It took a bit for the truck to reach the bottom and explode. We were well out of range by then."

"Okay, that settles it. We can tell the boss all three of them are dead. We hit one as he was getting into the truck. I know it was Sanderson. Baldwin was driving, and he had no clue where he was going in these woods. As fast as he was going, not knowing all the curves, it is no wonder he blew right through one of them. And Doc's little woman was probably crying and blubbering over him so much that she was not talking. So, we got all three. The boss ought to be happy."

Aissa Messai was on board his private jet, bound once again for Israel when he got the call.

"Are you sure? All three? Incinerated, huh? Tough way to go," he laughed.

"Yes sir! Like I told you last night, we got one of them with gunfire as he was getting into the truck. So, he was dead before they hit the rocks. Lucky for him, I would say." The AMPP man returned the laughter.

"A job well done. You men have saved your jobs, and possibly your lives. Your reward will be great for this accomplishment."

"Thank you, sir. We do our best. We always try to get our man, or woman."

"Yes, you do, and for that I am grateful. Remember, our work has just begun. There are many more of these rebels that we must stop. But the leaders are Blake Thompson and Beth Jennings, who we now know to be Mrs. Blake Thompson. That adds an interesting little wrinkle to things, doesn't it?"

"I am not sure I follow you, sir."

"A man may do a lot to save his life, but even more to save his wife. She may be the answer to taking down Mr. Thompson. We shall see. If the opportunity arises to take him out, do it. But bring the beautiful Mrs. Thompson to me. I may have plans for her."

"Whatever you say, boss, uh, Mr. Messai."

Trey, John and Kathie had eaten a light breakfast and were sipping coffee as they talked with their fellow Smyrnians. "It was beautiful," Kathie explained. "After Doc talked to Messai on the phone and turned John in..." she paused. "I am sorry for that. Doc was not a bad man, but he loved his money and his stuff. He turned John in for the reward money, but after talking to Messai, he wasn't the same. There was something different about him. He wouldn't eat or drink. It was like he was in a trance. He wouldn't look at me or respond to anything I said or did."

"We know that feeling," Blake interrupted. "The same thing happened to the UN delegates when the Security Council introduced Messai and he walked to the podium. Ben Abramson can tell you a thing or two about that also when he and his family get here. The same thing happened to him. Messai hypnotizes people under his evil spell, and they can't break free on their own."

"I know that now. But it took watching a certain video before I realized what was happening. I am grateful to John for his help. If it hadn't been for him, neither I nor Doc would have believed in Jesus. You're right, Blake. Nothing moved Doc until John came and put the video on the TV directly in front of him so he couldn't miss it. He had to see it and hear it. After he believed in Jesus, John called Trey and learned that AMPP was on their way."

"They broke through our door as we fled the house for the old truck John was driving. John got in and started the truck. Then he grabbed my arm to pull me in the passenger side. Doc was the last to get in. I was trying to help him because he was still weak from the trance he had been in. But as I was pulling him in and John was trying to take off, they started shooting..."

Her voice trailed off for a moment. They sat and gave her time.

"Doc had this faraway look in his eyes from the time he trusted in Jesus. He said he wanted to be with Jesus, that this world and all of his stuff didn't matter anymore. It was as though he was looking straight into heaven and seeing the face of Jesus. I heard the gunshots, then saw Doc slump over the dash of the truck. There was a big hole in his shirt and blood all over it."

The others' eyes were filling with tears now. Kathie had lost her husband just hours ago.

"I started screaming at him, but he was calm. His voice was weak, but he told me to give everything he had to the Smyrnians. He wanted it to help you. And he told John to promise he would take care of me. Then he did something amazing. John said he thinks this is in the Bible. I don't know because I have never read the Bible. And Doc didn't know because he had never read the Bible in his life. His parents raised him in a secular, materialistic home, and he lived his life that same way. He wanted nothing to do with religion. In fact, I would say he hated it."

John quietly said, "I'll bet Anders can tell us where we can find that verse in the Bible, Kathie. He has read it through many times since he put his faith in Jesus. He can tell us where to find just about anything we need to know."

"As soon as I hear the rest of the story, I can tell you if I know," said Anders. "Go on, Kathie."

"Well, as Doc was dying, he was looking toward the sky, and he said, 'Look!' It is like he wanted us to see what he was seeing. We may not have been able to see what he saw, but we could see it written all over his face. It was unreal. He said, 'I see the heavens open and the Son of Man standing at the right hand of God!' John told me the Bible calls Jesus the Son of Man."

"Then, his voice even weaker, he said, 'Lord Jesus, receive my spirit.' You should have seen his smile and the look on his face. We could tell he was seeing Jesus and knew he was on his way to be with him. But it was like he had one more thing he had to say. There is no doubt Jesus had changed him because Doc would never have said something like this. He said, 'Lord, please do not hold this against them.'"

"He finished by praying for them. 'Let them find you like I did.' He prayed for Messai's men who shot him to put their faith in Jesus too! How can I grieve for Doc when I saw him go home to be with Jesus like that?"

The others sat in silence, their eyes filled with tears. But there were more tears of joy than tears of sorrow. Doc's story could easily be their story before the seven years were over. That thought was both somber and celebratory at the same time. They only hoped if they died for their faith, they would have an experience like his and be able to pray for their killers.

"Acts Chapter 7!" Anders broke the silence. "Stephen was one of Jesus' first followers. He was a mighty man who did signs and wonders and preached to people about Jesus. His boldness caused the Jewish leaders to kill him. He was the first martyr, the first one to give his life because of his faith in Jesus. Doc was saying the same thing Stephen said in Acts Chapter 7. Kathie, you need to read that as soon as you can. Do all of you realize what that means? Doc was the first martyr of the Tribulation."

Wow. The first martyr of the Tribulation. The first of many, perhaps even some of them. It was a sobering thought. They returned to silence, but Kathie Sanderson soon broke it.

"Why are we sitting around here looking so sad? From what I understand, we have a war to fight. And I have a real reason to fight now. I am fighting for Doc! He is with Jesus, so I'm not sad. But I know he would want me to fight and help other people turn to Jesus like he did. I'm ready if you are. You have been at this longer than I have. But I say we get on with it!"

"I assume all of you have roles on this team. Make me your idea person. That is who Doc said I was. When you get stumped, let me come up with solutions. When we are brainstorming plans, I can help with those. So, what do you say? Let's get this party started!"

Her enthusiasm revived them all. The bunker was abuzz again with conversation. Messai had fired a shot he may regret in the weeks and months to come.

In New York City, Ben Abramson was completing a laundry list of plans and tying up every loose end he could think of. Having sold their house, he and Miriam only had a few more days to vacate the premises. When they moved out, they were moving into the shelter with the rest of the team. Being the one out of the action drove him crazy. He hated leaving the network in a pinch after all his years with them. But he had no choice. There were some great younger people coming up the ranks who had the ability to fill his shoes well. Maybe even better than him, he thought.

He had spent very little time watching the news since Blake and Beth's specials ended. In fact, he had not even turned on the TV. He had more important things to do. But perhaps he should take one quick look at his network to check for anything newsworthy which may have broken that would affect the Smyrnians.

He had not gotten word from any of the others after the call to pray for John, and Doc and Kathie Sanderson. Surely they would have called him if something had gone wrong. Since they had not called him, he assumed everything was okay. However, it still gave him cause for concern. He needed to call, to be sure. He froze as the TV came on and the panel in the studio reported on a breaking story.

"This is just in. Sources say Professor John Baldwin, who taught at a university in Chicago, has perished in a fiery crash when the truck he was driving plummeted off a high cliff outside Wichita, Kansas. A recent call to Aissa Messai's tip line identified him as a member of the rebel Smyrnian group."

"Riding with him in the truck were Doc and Kathie Sanderson, owners of Protection Services Incorporated in Wichita. Preliminary reports say they also perished in the crash. We have no further information about this developing story. We will update you as more details become available. Now, back to our regularly scheduled programming."

"No!" Ben's voice was louder than normal. He jumped to his feet and grabbed his phone. Miriam came running into the den.

"Ben, what is wrong? I heard you yell."

He hit rewind on the remote control and let it go back to where he had first turned on the TV. He pointed at it as he left the room to make his call. He heard Miriam say it too. "No!" He dialed Blake's number as he walked to the next room. Blake answered immediately, as he always did.

"Hello, Ben. How are things in New York this morning?"

"Blake, have you seen the news about John? They are saying he died in a truck crash last night. I can't believe it. If you knew about that, why didn't you call me?"

"Oh Ben, I am so sorry for not calling. We got caught up in conversation around here this morning. But I am glad to let you know you are right. You *can't* believe it. At least, you don't *have* to believe it because it is not true. John and Kathie Sanderson are here with us. They barely escaped with their lives, but they are alive and well."

"I am so relieved to hear that! Wait," Ben said as it hit him. "You said John and Kathie. We were praying for them *and* Doc last night. What about him?"

"Doc didn't make it, Ben. They shot him, and he died in the truck. But Trey, John and Kathie made it back here safely after a harrowing night."

"I am so sorry about Doc. Did he... I mean, did he trust in Jesus before he died?"

"Yes, he did. And you will love hearing that story when you come. Who knows? Maybe we will even tell you before then. It is an awesome story! Where did you see the news about the crash?"

"On our network, Blake. Our network is reporting breaking news that all three died in a fiery truck crash last night. Man, I am glad that's not true!"

Blake turned and yelled, "John, did you know you are dead?"

"I am?" asked John. "I sure don't feel like it. Who says?"

"Ben saw breaking news saying you, Doc and Kathie all died in a fiery crash last night."

"Man, Messai sure gets the word out fast, doesn't he? I am thrilled to know that because it means he honestly believes I am dead. That means he will leave me alone and stop chasing me. I can change the way I look and get back out there! Woo-hoo!"

"Kathie is doing well, Ben. Her new faith in Jesus is strong. Once you hear her story about how Doc died, and what he said, you'll understand that. There is something else we realized. Doc was the first martyr of the

Tribulation. Read the story of Stephen being stoned to death in Acts Chapter 7 in the New Testament. He was the first martyr for Jesus after the resurrection and ascension. I know you never read that part of the Bible before, but you love it now! Read that and you will be ready for Kathie's story when you get here. When are you coming?"

"I am tying up loose ends. It is almost time for us to be out of our house. It won't be long!"

"Great! I can't wait for you to get here. Again, I am sorry for not calling you with an update on John and the Sandersons. I will try to not make that mistake again."

The call ended, leaving Ben with his thoughts. He hated to hear about Doc Sanderson. It struck him that he was the first martyr among Tribulation believers. It was only the beginning. Many Jews would meet the same fate after turning to faith in Jesus. Maybe he, Miriam, or one of their children would be among them. He forced himself to stop thinking those thoughts. It was time to focus on the task at hand. In a few days they would be in Missouri with the others. He was ready.

The group knew they had to call the others, in case they had seen the breaking news in Germany and England. Ally called her mom and dad, and Beth called Ollie. He had just gotten the word and was dialing her when her call came in. Fortunately, Bruno and Mila had not heard yet. Everyone was sad and celebrating at the same time.

Who knew how many of these times they would go through during the next seven years? There may be many, although they hoped there would be none. But that hope had little chance of becoming a reality. They knew in their hearts those times would come, and when they came, those remaining would get through them together.

Aissa Messai stepped off the plane at Ben Gurion Airport in Tel Aviv, Israel. He was his usual charming self as reporters surrounded him. But he was even more gleeful than normal after the news he had received this morning. He would squash those who stood in his way. His plans were right on track, and nothing would stand in the way of them. He would make sure of that.

He smiled and waved to his adoring fans as he stepped into the stretch limo and rode away toward Jerusalem. The limo struggled to make it through the thronging crowds when it neared the Old City. It stopped to allow Messai to step out. He made his way up the side of the street and entered through the Dung Gate, the entrance that leads directly to the Mount.

"An appropriate name for a gate leading first to the Western Wall, the famed place where Jews pray for their Messiah to come," he thought. Surrounded by large crowds and heavily guarded by security, he walked through the gate by the Wall and across the wooden bridge to the Mount. He ascended the steps up to the Dome of the Rock, then walked around behind it to observe the work on the Jewish Temple. It was nearing completion.

This would be the jewel in his crown, the one thing that would lead to his acceptance as the leader of the world. He had brokered peace in the Middle East and brought Jews and Muslims together. No one had ever done that before. And now, he had done it. *He* had done it. The Jews, who Jesus referred to as his own people, had rejected him as their Messiah when he walked there 2,000 years earlier. But they had received and welcomed *him*, Aissa Messai. They would now believe their Messiah had arrived.

He walked into the beautiful structure. It was ornate on the outside, and even more so on the inside. He prided himself on rebuilding it in all of its original glory. Cameras were forbidden inside while he was there. He came out and addressed the crowd.

"Ladies and Gentlemen, it is a pleasure to see this dream of the Jews so close to becoming a reality. But it gives me even more pleasure to see the world's dream of peace in Jerusalem and the Middle East becoming a reality. This place will serve as the example to the rest of the world of what can happen when people and nations come together. I call on all of you regardless of race, background or religion to be at peace with one another."

"Let us put war and strife away and dwell together in a world united by common goals and purposes. Lay down your weapons. Lift your hands to help your neighbor. Love one another as I have loved you. As I leave this place today, peace I leave with you. My peace I give to you. Let us continue to seek peace with one another. I will return here upon the completion of the temple. On that day, we will celebrate its dedication. I look forward to that time. It is coming soon. Peace be with you. Peace be with all of you."

With that, his entourage swept him away, and he left as rapidly as he had come.

In the shelter, the Smyrnians watched the press conference. Anders had become their resident theologian and scholar, though Evan was close behind. He shared his view of Messai's remarks.

"The words of Jesus. Messai was quoting Jesus in John Chapters 13 and 14. And 'peace be with you' were the words Jesus spoke to his followers after he rose from the grave as recorded in John Chapter 20. Messai is claiming to be the Messiah, but people don't understand that. Only those of us who believe in Jesus get it. Now the question is, what are we going to do about it?"

Evan rallied the troops in his typical fashion. "I'll tell you what we will do about it. We will fight him tooth and nail and spread the good news about Jesus to everyone we can. We will be his band of warriors for the next seven years. We are ready! And we are all up to the task!"

CHAPTER 11

It was moving day for the Abramsons. They had decided it was safe to fly with Trey. There would be no tickets to trace or flight schedule with their names on it. They would also avoid the major airports and fly out of Teterboro in New Jersey. They would take the train to its stop nearest the airport. It was a mile away. They would walk from there. Not the easiest thing to do, but a one-mile walk for their family was no problem.

They had donated most of their clothes to a help center in the city, so they packed lightly. Since turning to faith in Jesus, Ben and Miriam seldom dressed in Orthodox Jewish attire. But both kept enough to help them identify as Jews. Ben especially needed to wear Orthodox attire in his videos. That would make him acceptable to them. He and Miriam were still Jewish but were now Messianic Jews, proudly claiming the title of Jews who accepted Jesus as the Messiah.

Trey would be at the airport waiting for them. They were quite the sight as nine of them trudged along. Ben led the way, and Miriam brought up the rear, with their kids from youngest to oldest in the middle. The walk took twenty minutes and felt good with the temperature in the mid-50s. Their excitement about joining the group in the shelter made it feel like a mere five-minute stroll.

Trey had the plane ready. He met them and led them to it, then loaded their stuff and helped them get on board. He looked around at them and asked, "Are you ready for this?"

"More than you know," Ben replied.

"Then let's get this thing in the air."

At the shelter, the team was busy. They had all chosen to make it their home, except for Trey and Rickie, who lived close enough to stay in their own homes and come and go as needed. They would do that until Messai discovered that they were members of the Smyrnians. And they knew that day would come.

John was no longer a professor, especially since he was dead, as he liked to say. Even if they did not believe he had died in the crash, being identified as a follower of Jesus had done him in. Evan and Ally had also opted to drop out of school and be full-time Smyrnians. In life, getting an education was important. But with only seven years remaining for the earth, doing the work of Jesus was far more urgent.

Today, Evan, Blake and Beth were poring over emails received on and since February 2. It was an impossible task, but they were reading each one they could find the time to read. The emails totaled well over a million; it appeared up to as many as a quarter-billion. There was no way to reply to all of them or build an email list that extensive. But they had instructed converts to visit the website for further instructions, and the number of hits there seemed as large as the number of emails.

Their focus would now be on teaching via the site and building networks of churches everywhere. They double-checked the instructions for new believers and made a few minor changes and additions, but mostly everything was there. They hoped all of those who said yes to Jesus would follow them.

One addition was more instructions for anyone who wanted to host a church in their home. Those leaders would be vital to the spread of Christianity during the Tribulation. They would visit some of those house churches in different parts of the world as they traveled, fighting the battle with evil and spreading the truths of Jesus.

Taking a break from that, they began planning how to best change their looks to most conceal their identities. For now, that would only apply to Blake, Beth and John. They knew what they would do. John stuck to his previous assertion that he was going with the sexy look; wavy hair with a goatee and mustache. But he would dye those gray and make himself look much older.

"You can laugh all you want," he said, "but we all need to go with the opposite of what we looked like before. And I didn't look like Adonis then. Now I'll look like a sexy senior citizen!"

It would take a while for Blake's transformation. He would allow his hair and beard to grow long. He would have no change in hair color because he planned to travel to the Middle East a few times and wanted to fit in while he was there. His jet black hair fit the bill. However, he would get a good tan. A change in skin tone would make a big difference. With a smile, Beth said she was excited about seeing her *bronzed hunk*.

She would trade her beautiful long blonde hair for a dark color with a much shorter cut. She would add glasses, even though she had perfect vision, and most often wear a scarf when out in public. Blake was not all that excited about the change in the way she looked, but said he would sacrifice for the cause. No one would be able to easily identify either of them. Beth would get her new look tomorrow. Blake would be impatient with his process because he was champing at the bit to get out on the job. But he had plenty to do inside prior to that time. They would start setting up their studio, from which they would broadcast to the world. Obviously, it would be on radio, and not on television. No one must know how they looked after their makeovers.

Ally had a plan, and none of them liked it. They would do whatever they could to keep her from it, but it was doubtful that they could. Her determination was too strong for them to stop her. It would be dangerous, but if she was to be a Smyrnian spy, as she planned to be, it would be top of the line. It may or may not pan out, but she would try it and hope for the best. She had not told her parents yet and was not sure she wanted to. Both would undoubtedly vehemently oppose it.

But Ally was a bright girl who should have lots of appeal to Aissa Messai, especially in the position of personal assistant. She had found multiple positions posted online by his office, with that one at the top. The other jobs would still have her on the inside, if she had to settle for one of them. If one is to be a spy, she may as well go all out. She had applied online earlier that day to ensure she did not change her mind. The application was in, and she could not withdraw it.

The only drawback was her limited number of references. Her best one, Professor John Baldwin, had gone by the wayside. The positive note was,

Aissa Messai liked attractive young women. And Ally was easy on the eyes when she cleaned up and dressed the part. If she got the job, she could no longer get by with being *one of the guys*. She needed no makeover. Her appearance was fine just the way it was and unknown to the world, and to Aissa Messai.

Being so close to Messai would give her access to the most crucial and confidential information. The team would always have a leg up on his next moves. But then, if he discovered she was a mole in his organization... She did not want to think about the consequences of that. One thing she was not aware of was that Messai had his eye on another blonde beauty, one Mrs. Beth Jennings Thompson.

Trey landed at Springfield-Branson Airport and taxied straight to the hangar. His truck awaited him there. Cramming Ben, Miriam and seven kids into it would have been interesting if it were not for his roll up bed cover. He had chosen it because it gave him the freedom of carrying things in the back which needed to stay dry or hauling larger items that needed more space above the bed of the truck. All nine of them crawled in the back, and he rolled the cover over them. They would be uncomfortable in there, but would be okay for the 20-minute drive to the farm.

Even though Ben was not on the hot seat yet, he would be when word came that the publisher of the largest news network in the country had disappeared with his entire family. A lot of folks, most likely including Aissa Messai, would put two and two together at that point and figure out that he had joined his top reporter as a member of the Smyrnians. If not, they would know once he started broadcasting to the Jews. So, it was vital that no one see them with Trey, or in Missouri. Secrecy was paramount at this point.

Trey left the hangar and pulled onto the highway, headed for the farm. He drove just under the speed limit so as not to draw any attention. As he neared the farm and slowed to turn onto the side road leading to it, the sound of a siren caught his attention. He looked and knew who it was; his buddy Justin, a deputy for the Christian County Sheriff's Department. He drove on a little further until he found a place to pull to the side of the road. He put his window down, and Justin came up and punched him in the arm.

"You are driving slow for you today, aren't you buddy?"

"Just enjoying the scenery on a beautiful, chilly day, my man."

"Why are you heading this way? I saw you leave the airport and figured you'd be going home."

"I have to run into Ozark and pick up something before I head to the house." His mind was scrambling now to figure out how to explain being headed toward Ozark when he lived on the other side of Springfield.

"What do you have to get in Ozark that you can't get in Springfield? Did they close all the stores back there?"

He said the first thing that came to his mind. "I'm going to the Farmer's Supply Store on this end of town. I'm having a big problem with rats in the barn and need to get some rat poison. They have the kind I'm looking for. It will kill any rat that touches it. I have to get rid of those things."

"How about I just escort you on down there? Stick with me and we'll get there in no time. I know how you like to drive. So, here's your chance. Follow me!"

Trey had no way to get word to his passengers in the back. The temperature was hovering right around the freezing mark. And there was no heat back there. That cover provided shelter from the wind, but it did not do much to keep out the cold. He had to think quick. Justin peeled out. Trey waited a few seconds, then pulled onto the road too. It was not far to the road that turned off and led past the lane to the farm. If he could turn there without Justin seeing him, but how?

There was a curve on up ahead of the road. Knowing Justin, he would think he had left him behind and get a kick out of it. He let him get a good head start. He saw his turn coming up and sped up to get to it since Justin was nowhere in sight. He swerved onto the road, trying not to throw his passengers all over the bed of the truck. Just as he turned, he saw Justin's patrol car coming flying back in his direction. Now what? Should he drive on and hope he had not seen him? No, he could not take the chance of leading him to the farm. He got his answer to that question when he saw the lights on Justin's car flash again. He made a U-turn, whipped in behind him, stopped the car and got out.

"What happened, Trey?" He dragged the name out slowly for emphasis. "Did something go wrong, or is old Justin just too fast for you?"

"Nope. I got a call and have to get back to Springfield. I guess the rat poison will have to wait."

"Whatever you say, man. You sure are acting strange today. Is everything all right with you? You're not in any kind of trouble, are you? If you are, all you have to do is ask, and your old buddy Justin will help you out."

"I'm not in any trouble, but I *am* tired. I've been flying all day and need to get some sleep. I don't think I can wait till tonight. I am worn out."

"Whatever you say. I still say you are acting funny. And you don't look all that tired to me. But whatever you say. I guess I'll let you go. Watch out for those rats!" He wiggled his fingers crazily.

"Sure thing, Justin. Hey, before you go, I wanted to ask, can we get together sometime soon? I need to talk to you about something. It is an important deal. I would like to run it by you."

"Sure you can. Let's do it. What are you up to tomorrow night?"

"I don't think I am flying anywhere tomorrow. What time? Can you come over to my house?"

"I will be there at 7:00, if that works for you. You'd better throw me a steak on the grill!"

"You got it! I know, medium rare. I still don't see you how you eat them half raw. They taste a lot better when they're cooked."

"One day you'll grow up and learn how to eat meat like a man. See you tomorrow night at 7:00!"

Justin was out of sight headed back toward Springfield. Trey asked, "Ben, are you guys okay?"

"If by okay, you mean frozen half to death and cramped up from being back here so long, I guess we are. But I would appreciate it if you can get us to where we're going so we can get out."

"I am sorry, Ben. Justin is hard to get rid of. I'll head on back this road. When I get out of sight on the lane to the farm, I'll stop and roll the cover back so Miriam can see it."

"We are all ready for that. So, stop talking and start driving!"

Trey made sure there was no traffic coming or going before he proceeded down the side road. And he kept a close check on his rear-view mirror to make sure no one was coming behind them before turning into the grove of trees that covered the lane. He wanted to be 100% certain that his friend had not come back and followed him to see where he was going.

Justin was a loose cannon at times. But tomorrow night, he would hear about Jesus. That could pull the plug on Trey's anonymity too, if it did not go well. He prayed it would, because crazy or not, Justin would make a great addition to the Smyrnians. He pulled several feet down the lane, stopped and rolled back the cover. "Feast your eyes on this, Miriam. Do you see what we have been talking about?"

"Unbelievable!" she exclaimed. "I can't even see the road. How far have we come?"

"Only about 20 feet. If you look back, where we pulled in looks like a wall of trees, doesn't it?"

"It does for a fact. I'm ready to see the rest of this place. And these kids need some heat."

They drove back the canopy-covered lane to the open area, that, even though it was an acre in size, also looked covered. It blew Miriam away, just like everyone else who had seen this place.

"I have never seen anything like this in my life. It's the perfect place for the Smyrnians to hide and stay safe."

"Yes ma'am, it is. Hop out kids and let's head inside the cabin." When they were inside, he said, "Let's play a little game. The first one to find the entrance to the shelter wins!"

He only gave them a minute, and said, "You all lose! Come with me."

They walked into the bedroom, and he opened the closet door.

"This is a cute little closet," said Miriam, "but can we get to the shelter now? I'm beyond ready."

Trey shoved clothes aside and pushed on the back wall of the closet. It spun around. Miriam's mouth flew open, as did Ben's. He had not seen that part yet either. "This is crazy," he said. "Amazing..."

They climbed down, and everyone was there to meet them at the bottom.

"You guys are a sight for sore eyes!" Blake grabbed Ben's hand, then gave him a hug.

"Well, your pilot friend just about froze us to death, Blake," said Ben, shivering.

"Get in here and warm up," invited Ally. "I have a pot of hot soup on the stove."

The soup was delicious. It warmed them inside and out. Ben wanted to take the grand tour as soon as they finished so he could see where he would set up his broadcast station. But first they needed to get their stuff inside.

Before Ben could say anything, Evan spoke up. "You guys stay put. Ally and I will get your things from the truck and bring them down. You need to stay in where it's warm."

They headed to the steps. When they got outside the cabin and were walking to the truck, Evan suddenly stopped.

"Listen, Ally," he whispered. "Do you hear that?"

She nodded. "It sounds like a vehicle driving past the lane."

"It is going on by, but let's stand here a bit and keep listening. Maybe we have time to walk out the lane and hide in the trees to watch. Are you up for that? We'll have to walk fast."

"Let's go," she whispered.

They half walked and half sprinted out the lane. They got to the end and hid in some dense brush covered with tree limbs. A perfect lookout spot. The vehicle was coming back. When it came into view, they saw that it was a patrol car.

"A cop!" Evan whispered.

Ally nodded. They watched as the car crept along, with its driver peering closely at their side of the road. Their hearts were pounding. Surely no one would discover their safe place so soon. They had just finished it and moved in. They now saw that it was a deputy sheriff. It seemed he would stop right in front of them. It felt like they were inches apart, and he was staring right at them. Could he see them? They were barely breathing, much less daring to move even a finger. The car continued and passed on by. They stayed put and listened until it was out of range. They could make out the distant sound when it screeched onto the main highway and sped away.

Both of them were shaking all over as they ran back to the truck, grabbed some things and ran to the cabin door. It was obvious they could not get everything in one trip. But they needed to tell the others what they had just seen. By the time they reached the bottom of the steps and rushed inside, they were breathless.

"What took you two so long?" asked John. "You look like you saw a ghost. What is wrong?"

Evan explained. "When we got outside, we heard a car driving down the side road past the lane. It had to turn around and come back out, so we hurried to the end of the lane and hid in all that brush covered with limbs, and watched."

"Yeah," said Ally. "It came back driving slow. The driver was looking at our side of the road. He almost stopped right in front of us. It was like we were face-to-face with him. He was that close! But he never stopped. He was creeping, but he kept rolling."

"It was a deputy sheriff." Evan's concern was obvious.

"Justin," said Trey. "I was afraid he would come snooping around. He probably pulled over somewhere and watched to see if I drove back toward Springfield. When I didn't, he came to figure out where I went. I hope he thinks I went on to Ozark."

"Who is Justin?" asked John.

"He is a friend who is a deputy sheriff. He pulled me over out on the main road, just for kicks. He does that a lot to freak me out, or just to chat. I had to lie to him and tell him I was on my way to Ozark to buy rat poison because I had a problem with rats in the barn."

"Boy, that was a whopper!" said Ally.

"He's right. We heard the entire conversation," said Ben. "I sensed the same thing as Trey. I feared that guy would come snooping around too so he could find out where we may have gone. I thought about suggesting we turn around and head back toward your place, Trey. I wish I had. But we were freezing back there, and I wanted to get these kids someplace warm."

"I learned a lesson in that situation. During the next seven years, there will be many times when we have to think of ourselves *last*. Our first inclination will be to put our needs and wants ahead of the mission. We can't do that."

"You're right, Ben." Blake understood what his ex-boss was saying. "I suppose there is a lesson in this for all of us."

"I'm on the hot seat with Justin," Trey interrupted.

"You sure are," Ben agreed.

"What are you two talking about?" asked Beth.

"I told Justin I want to talk to him about something important. He is coming to my house tomorrow night at 7:00. I'm grilling him a steak and plan to show him the video and talk to him about Jesus."

"Wow, that is dangerous after he came looking around today. I mean, Justin would be a good one to have on the team. But if he doesn't believe, he will be on the lookout for sure," said Blake.

"I pray he'll see the truth. Justin can be a wild man sometimes. But Jesus can use wild men too. I need you guys to pray for him tonight. And for *me*!" Trey knew this was a defining moment.

Ally whispered, "I wish my mom and dad were here. I miss them. They need to see what we have done with this place. They will do the same thing in Germany as soon as they can. Besides, I have something I need to tell them about my plans."

"Boy, do you ever," said Evan. "I still don't like it."

"Okay, some of us are behind the times on things," said Ben. "Please enlighten us on what you are talking about, Ally."

She told them about her application for the position with Aissa Messai. Neither Ben nor Miriam liked it either.

"You will put yourself in grave danger, young lady," Ben warned.

"He is right, dear," Miriam said in a motherly tone. "You don't want Messai to find out what you are up to. He is ruthless and heartless. The world doesn't know that yet, but it will. If you go through with this, you could be the first to experience his wrath, at least the first after Doc."

"Remember the dream you had, Ally?" asked Evan. "The one you told John and me about? It just may come true. I don't want to scare you, but a lot of people will face exactly what you saw in that dream. I don't want you to be one of them. I can't bear the thought of that happening."

It was Kathie's turn. "Ally, I saw what Messai is capable of firsthand. He wanted us dead. He got Doc and almost got all three of us. Surely there is another way for you to get on the inside."

"I appreciate all of your concern." Ally was resolute. "But I believe this is what Jesus told me to do. If I am right, he will open the door for me to get one of those positions."

"If you truly believe that is what Jesus is telling you to do," John said, "then I want you to know your old professor believes in you. And I am here for you whenever you need me."

John's sentiment touched Ally. She walked over and hugged him. Then she hugged them all, one at a time. "Thanks, everyone, for caring about me. I will be okay, whatever happens. But now I am more concerned about Trey's meeting with Justin tomorrow night. We have to pray for him. I am going to call mom and dad right now. I wish they would come. I need to see them."

"I hope they will, dear. We would all love to have them here. They are a part of us." Miriam definitely had the potential to be a mother hen for the group.

"Okay, I need to get started checking out my future studio," Ben said. "Evan, why don't you and Ally go back out and get the rest of our stuff. Do you have all my electronics here already?"

"Yes sir," said Ally. "They are already in your studio and ready to hook up." She smiled.

In Germany, Bruno and Mila Fromm and their boys were with Hans and Heidi Meier, studying the Bible and praying together. They were reading Matthew Chapter 9 and the story of the ruler whose daughter had just died. He came to Jesus, told him the news and said, "... but come and put your hand on her, and she will live." As they discussed the passage, Mila spoke up urgently.

"Bruno, I suddenly get the sense Ally needs us, and she needs us now. We have to go to her."

"Now, Mila, are you just saying that because we are reading this story?"

"No, Bruno, I'm not. We have seen many times that Jesus speaks to us when we are reading the Bible. I know he is telling me that!"

"Mr. Fromm," said Heidi, "I mean no disrespect, but that is what you have told us. If Mila senses so strongly that Jesus is speaking to her, you need to listen to what she has to say."

"Now, sweetheart," said Hans gently, "let Bruno and Mila handle this."

"No, she is right. Thank you for reminding me, Heidi. If you feel that strongly about it, Mila, we should go to her. You know how much I love my little girl. I will call about tickets first thing tomorrow."

"Thank you, Bruno. I believe we need to go right away."

"Then we will go, dear. We will go tomorrow, if we can get tickets."

"I have a thought," said Mila excitedly. "Hans and Heidi, why don't you go with us? You need to meet the other Smyrnians. Can you go?"

"Why not?" asked Hans. "Heidi?"

"Sure. Let's go!"

Right then, Mila's phone rang. "It's Ally," she said, and hurriedly answered.

"Mommy, I need you guys. Can you come? How soon?"

They were all listening and looked at each other in amazement.

"Honey, we have already planned to come. We are calling about tickets first thing in the morning. Jesus spoke to me a few minutes ago and told me you need us and we need to come. Hans and Heidi are coming with us. They are eager to meet everyone."

"Thank you so much, Mommy. Tell daddy I love him."

"I heard you, little girl. I love you too. We will see you soon."

Incredibly, in England, Ollie Barton and Amelia Clarke had just had the same experience. She called him to talk about what she was reading in the Bible. Remarkably, both were reading Acts Chapter 16, although neither was aware of that until she called. The Apostle Paul saw a vision of a man of Macedonia standing and begging him, "Come over to Macedonia and help us."

"Ollie, I believe we need to go to America and meet with the other Smyrnians."

"I was sitting here thinking the same thing, Amelia. Sounds like we have a trip to take."

Jesus was working in three different countries, miles apart, bringing his army together. The war was intensifying, and he was calling them to action. And they were heeding his call.

"Mommy and daddy and the boys are coming!" squealed Ally running back to the others. "I called them to tell them I need them, and Jesus had just told them the same thing right before I called. They were reading the Bible with Hans and Heidi, and he spoke to mommy. Isn't Jesus awesome?"

Beth walked in as she was telling them. "Guess who just called me? Ollie Barton. Jesus spoke to him and Amelia at the same time and told them the same thing. They are coming too."

"Something is about to happen," said Blake. "Jesus is bringing us together for a reason. This isn't what *we* did; it is what *he* did. He has everything ready. This place is ready. There are new believers all over the world. They are ready. Jesus is preparing the hearts of the Jews to believe in Jesus, and Ben is ready. But I wonder what else this means?"

"I fear the Tribulation is about to become just that: tribulation. Darkness has invaded the earth, but it is about to become darker than we have ever seen. Not the absence of light, but wickedness and evil like the world has never known. I thought we had seen it. I thought I saw it on the streets of Manhattan that morning. But what we *have* seen is nothing compared to what we *will* see. We must be ready."

The shelter fell silent after Blake spoke. They could remain in here and be oblivious to what was happening in the outside world. But that was not their purpose for existing. If darkness invaded the earth, then they must invade the darkness. Their lives would be in danger daily, but the people of the world were worth it. There were now millions of Jesus' followers around the globe. Yes, they were ready... ready to invade the darkness in the power of Jesus.

In Jerusalem, the finishing touches were being put on the Jewish Temple. It was ready. Messai would be there in a few days for the dedication. That event was significant. They did not know why, but they knew it was. The feeling filled the shelter. But it came not from Aissa Messai. It came from the presence of Jesus in their midst. He was Emmanuel God *with* them and they knew it.

CHAPTER 12

The shelter was alive with excitement this morning. The German and British contingents would arrive in three days. They were eager to meet Amelia, Hans and Heidi. They would fit right in. They looked forward to getting to know them. They were understanding more every day how special the bond is between followers of Jesus. When they meet, it is like they have known each other their entire lives. Tonight would be Trey's big meeting with Justin, and they could tell he was nervous about it and feeling the pressure. So they were praying for him.

But their focus today was on Transformation Tuesday. This was the day they started changing how they looked. Ally and Kathie were the makeover artists. They had formed a fast friendship. Kathie feared for Ally because of her decision to apply for work with Messai. Ally felt for Kathie because she had lost her husband, turning her world upside down. But she also drew strength from this woman who seemed to exude it after turning to Jesus.

Despite everything on their minds, today was a fun day for both. They had hair color products and other items lined up and ready. "Who will be our guinea pig and go first?" they asked. John volunteered, partly because he did not mind and partly because he felt sorry for Beth. She was stunningly beautiful, and that was about to change. It did not mean she would not still be beautiful, but she would look different from the way she had looked for years. He also felt for Blake. He had always seen her as the most gorgeous woman in the world. He loved her long blonde hair. Now it would be short and dark. So, he stepped up and said, "Why don't you start with me? I don't mind being a guinea pig."

While the others worked on important projects, they got started. John's goatee and mustache would take a few weeks to fill out well, but his hair would get its makeover today. Everyone in Bunker A heard them working and laughing. They assumed the laughter was at John's expense. They could hear water splashing, a hairdryer blowing and John groaning. When they finished, they were ready to introduce their first victim, or lucky customer, to his waiting fans. John came out strutting and flexing.

"Voila!" he said.

His black hair was now gray. He had not cut it in over two months, so it had grown out plenty long enough to style. They had permed it and styled it so the top lay in waves across his scalp.

"How do you like my new wavy do?" he asked.

Whistles and hoots came in response. John seemed pleased. He liked the new John Baldwin look. He had not shaved for a few days either, so his facial hair was growing. He pointed out that they had a good start on the gray with his hair. His look would be different enough to fool just about anyone. The question was, would it fool Aissa Messai and his men from AMPP?

Beth was next. She bravely entered their makeshift salon and sat down in the chair.

"What would you like us to do for you today, ma'am?" Ally asked.

"Just take a foot or so off the top and give me a color while you are at it."

"We can do that. Will this dark brunette work?" they asked, holding up a box of hair color.

"I think it is perfect. But we had better get it done before my husband gets in here."

With that, they began. The sound of snipping scissors reached her ears as her long blonde locks began falling to the floor. Her hair now hung only to her neck. It still conformed perfectly to her face. Next came the color. Styling was not necessary. The straight look was what they wanted. She donned her glasses, wrapped the scarf around her head and stepped out for the others to see.

"Who are you, and what did you do with my wife?" asked Blake.

"You don't like it," Beth teared up.

"Oh baby, you know I like it. You are beautiful regardless of the color or style of your hair. I love you, Beth Jennings Thompson. Besides, maybe I have secretly always wanted a brunette!"

She smiled and said, "I hope so because you will have one for the next seven years!"

"You never know. You may have to change it several times to stay a step ahead of Messai. If you do, I get to pick the color and style every time after this!"

"Blake, stop it. I think it looks good. Do I look like a Humanitarian Aid Worker?"

"Absolutely. You could be out there right now with no problem."

"Well, I can be. You and John can't. You will both have to wait a little while."

"I won't deal with that very well. How about you, John?"

"No way. I already want to be back in the action. Getting killed once wasn't enough for me!"

"Just do your best not to get killed again. Getting killed once is tough, but getting killed twice is brutal. Besides, we can't afford to lose you. You will probably be out there before me. It will take some time for this hair and beard to grow as long as I need them to be." Blake rolled his eyes.

"Don't worry, honey," Beth said. "You have plenty to do from in here. Between showing the video, teaching the Bible and helping organize the new believers, you will be plenty busy."

"Transformations one and two are complete," said Kathie. "We will perform others as needed."

Beth walked back in and swept up her locks of hair from the floor. "I will keep these in our room so you won't forget what I looked like, Blake."

"I will never forget that," he said. "One suggestion, though. I think you should lose the scarf."

"I agree. I thought it would help disguise me even more. But it doesn't make any difference."

Transformation Tuesday was over. Blake was eager for his own metamorphosis, allowing him to get back in the game. But his would have to happen naturally. He would check the mirror daily to see if his hair and beard were long enough to make him look like a different man.

While the previous day had brought its fair share of excitement, Trey's big moment had now come. It was almost 7:00 p.m., and he was awaiting Justin's arrival. There was never a guarantee that Justin would be on time. He was a happy-go-lucky sort of guy who took life as it came. He was not the most prompt man in the world and was just as apt to be 10 minutes late as 10 minutes early.

At 6:55, it was apparent this would not be one of his 10 minutes early times. Trey had just put the steaks on the grill. He did not want to take a chance on them getting cold if Justin was late. It did not take long to cook his medium rare, half-cooked steak. To Trey, that was like eating raw meat. Then, as he was taking them off the grill, Justin came whipping up the drive in his truck that was loud enough to scare some people half to death. He skidded to a stop.

"Sorry, I am a few minutes late, buddy. Got a little tied up on the way. The steaks smell great!"

"Yes, they smell great, and yours looks raw."

"Ah, you know how I like them. I know you wanted to talk to me about something, but I sure hope we get to eat first."

"You'd better believe we do! Look, man, I am as hungry as you are. And I have had to smell this stuff cooking for the past 45 minutes. I have a salad to start us off, baked sweet potatoes with all the good stuff to go on them, corn on the cob that my mom froze last summer, green beans and yeast rolls. That ought to make your stomach growl and your mouth water!"

"Oh, it does, trust me. You just took the steaks off, and I assume everything else is ready. Are we going to stand here and gab, or are we going to eat?"

"Come on in. It is time to eat!"

After dinner, they stretched out in the living room for a little while, chatting about stuff that did not matter. Trey knew that he was stalling. The magnitude of this moment weighed on him. It was his second time to talk to someone about Jesus. It was the opportunity for Justin to become one of Jesus' followers. But Trey's status as a local Smyrnian might also become known, or it may even blow their cover right after they had gotten moved in. Justin was already suspicious after yesterday. His mind was spinning with all of that when Justin left him no choice but to proceed with his plan.

"So, what is this big thing you wanted to talk to me about? Does it have anything to do with why you were acting so strange yesterday?"

"It is not about yesterday; it is about *you*. I have to tell you what happened to me. Come to think of it, it may cause me to act a little strange, at least as far as other people see it."

"What in the world are you talking about? What happened to you? Is it bad?"

"Oh no, it is not bad. It is very good!"

"All right! You hit the lottery! What are you going to do with all that money? New bass boat? New truck, I assume. Maybe you can take a bunch of us boys on a 'guys only' trip. I am happy for you!"

"Would you stop it? I didn't hit the lottery. It is something much better than that."

"What in the world could be better than winning the lottery?"

"I am glad you asked, because I am about to tell you! Did you see Blake Thompson and Beth Jennings specials the other night?"

"Come on, man. Don't tell me you fell for that stuff."

"Did you watch them?"

"Well, no. I started watching, but the game was on, and I wanted to see it. It makes me mad when they put stuff on that interferes with my games. They were getting ready to play some video about something. They said it would give us answers about what happened on September 11. I don't need answers about that. We already know what happened. Alien invasion, man. Little green men. I guess they were afraid to take guys like you and me, huh? Anyway, I already know everything I need to about all of that. So why would I waste my time watching a video?"

"I thought I knew everything about it too, but something always bothered me about it. Have you ever wondered, if it was aliens, why didn't anyone see them? Space agencies and government leaders said they had confirmed it, but you saw the satellite images. Did you see any spaceships or little green men?"

"No, I guess I didn't. But that doesn't mean it's not true."

"I had never been comfortable with their answers. In my mind, I always believed it was something else. Then someone told me what happened, and I know it is the truth. In fact, when I believed it and accepted it, my life changed! So, I guess that's why I'm acting strange. I should be, because I am a different man! Let me show you the video. That is all I ask. It can explain what happened and everything you need to know about it far better than I can."

"Is that why you asked me over here? To watch a video?"

"Yes, that, and to eat steak. Come on man, you owe me this. Watch the video with me."

"Okay, okay. I will watch the video. But it had better be good. My eyes are getting heavy after all that food."

"Trust me, it is good. It is an hour long, but it is worth every minute."

"An hour?"

"How long was that game you watched instead of the video?"

"You made your point. Put in your video. What is it? A scientist or someone trying to give some scientific explanation for the disappearances?"

"Nope. It is better than that. Here is what I need you to promise me. No matter what you think when you watch, you will watch it all the way to the end. Promise?"

"Do I have to? Okay," he said, throwing his hands up in surrender, "I promise."

"If you need to go to the bathroom, go now. I don't want you to stop once it starts."

"Man, you are serious about this thing, aren't you? I'm good. Let's see it. If it is an hour long, we had better get started. I have to work tomorrow."

"Here we go." Trey popped the flash drive in and hit Play. The church name came up, followed by the pastor.

"Come on, man. You brought me here to show me a sermon? You know that's not my thing."

"I know that. It wasn't my thing either. Just sit back and watch like you promised."

Justin watched as the pastor went through his explanation of the 6,000 years. He told how God created the universe in six literal 24-hour days and the Bible says with the Lord, a day is like a 1,000 years and 1,000 years are like a day. So, he explained, each day of creation represents 1,000 years of the history of the earth. God created for six days, then ended his creation and rested on the seventh day. That, said the pastor, means the earth will last for 6,000 years and we are at the 6,000 year mark right now. Justin stretched and feigned a big yawn. But he settled in and watched as he promised he would.

The pastor told how the seven Feasts of Israel all point to Jesus, and specifically to the events of his first and second comings. They crucified him on Passover as the lamb of God, who takes away the sin of the world. He was the perfect, sinless lamb, as represented by the Feast of Unleavened Bread. He rose from the grave on Firstfruits, being the first of everyone else who would rise later because they believed in him. Pentecost represented the 2,000 years that Jesus' church would be on the earth. Jesus' first coming fulfilled the first three feasts, and the fourth is being fulfilled by his church now.

Justin's intrigue showed, but he was not yet convinced. Then the pastor talked about how the Feast of Trumpets pointed to the Rapture, the day Jesus would send his angels to take all of his people home to be with him. Justin glanced at Trey with a questioning look. Trey told him to keep watching.

Next, the pastor explained how Jesus gave us the day that would happen. He said we should watch and wait for his coming, as the priests watched for the sliver of the new moon before they blew the trumpets, calling God's people to come to the temple to celebrate. And he said he would come with the blast of a trumpet. The pastor said that would likely be the loudest sound anyone had ever heard. And he would come as lightning flashes from the east to the west. That he said would likely be the brightest light anyone had ever seen. Justin glanced at him again.

Trey mouthed, "Sound familiar?"

Then when the pastor said it would likely occur on a Feast of Trumpets in the year 2,000 years after Jesus resurrection, Justin looked at him again.

"Didn't that happen in 33 A.D.?"

"Keep watching."

The pastor told how Jesus was born in 4 B.C. and not 0, as many people say. So, he said, his death and resurrection was in 29 A.D. And if he was right, Jesus would return on the Feast of Trumpets in 2029. Trey hit Pause because he saw Justin's question coming.

"What day was the Feast of Trumpets last year?"

"September 11," Trey said with a big smile.

Justin's face grew pale. "Do you think he was right? If I saw correctly, he preached that sermon over four years ago. Did he really get all of that from the Bible?"

"Yes, he did. Justin, think about something. Did you know any of the people who disappeared on September 11?"

"Yeah, I knew several. I had an aunt and uncle and some cousins and friends taken."

"Can I ask you a question?"

"Sure."

"Were they all Christians? Did they all believe in Jesus and go to church?"

"Every one of them," he mumbled.

"And you and I were not Christians and did not go to church, and we are still here. Okay, watch this part."

The pastor's words rang clear. "If you happen to be watching this after the Rapture has occurred, listen to me. You still have time to put your faith in Jesus and receive him as your Savior. If you are listening, please stop this video and do that right now. Tell Jesus you believe in him and ask him to come into your life. He said, 'I stand at the door and knock.' That door is the door to your heart and life. If *you* open the door, *he* will come in! Decide that you will follow him for the rest of your life, no matter what!"

Justin was quiet for a moment. Trey sat and silently prayed for him. He eventually spoke again.

"Trey, thank you for showing me this. I believe. Can I ask Jesus to come into my life right now?"

"Go for it. I did, and it was the best thing that has ever happened to me. Far better than winning the lottery." He grinned at him.

Then Justin prayed. He told Jesus he was opening the door of his heart and life and asked him to come in. The look on his face was unmistakable. Trey knew it well. He had been there.

"I know exactly how you feel, Justin. I experienced the same thing when I said yes to Jesus. May I show you the last part? It explains what happens now." Justin nodded, and he hit play again.

"Listen closely to me for another two minutes. No more, I promise. If you just said yes to Jesus, this is very important. There are seven years of time remaining before Jesus returns to conquer evil and set up his earthly kingdom. Those years will be the *Tribulation.* That will be the most horrible time the world has ever seen. The entire earth will be shaken. Evil will prevail."

"You will be hunted, chased down and possibly imprisoned for your faith. The Antichrist and his evil forces will murder some of you. Whatever you do, keep the faith! Do not turn back. Do not receive the mark of the beast. You will understand that when the time comes, if you survive that long. Be God's witnesses to the truth during those seven years. Tell everyone you can about Jesus. And to you I say, Welcome to the family of God! I will see you in seven years... or less."

"Wow," said Justin. "Sounds like it will be tough for us."

"Yep, it will. But there is a group of us who are ready to fight. Are you in?"

"Count me in. Tell me what I have to do. I'm ready!" And there was no doubt he was!

"Our army has a name. Do you want to hear it?"

"Sure, why not?"

"We are the Smyrnians."

"The *what*?"

"The Smyrnians." He read Revelation 2:10 and explained it to him. He got it. "I will take you and introduce you to the rest of them tomorrow."

"I am ready to meet them right now! Who cares about work tomorrow?"

"Let's wait until tomorrow. You and I can talk more tonight."

They did that and had a real celebration. Trey felt like he was walking on air. "Meet me here tomorrow at 9:00 a.m. and I will take you. Will that work?"

"Yes sir! I will be here. And I *will* be early this time, so you had better be ready!"

Trey called the team when he left and gave them the good news. They would meet Justin tomorrow. They celebrated his new life in Jesus, unaware that meeting would not happen.

They were all up early the next morning, excited and eager to meet Justin. But the news captured their attention. Shootings, bombings, rioting, home invasions, murder, all over the earth. What Blake and Beth had witnessed on the streets of Manhattan had only been a preview of what was coming. There was no war on earth, but neither was there peace on earth. It was clear on this morning that the absence of war does not equate to peace. Nations were not killing each other; *people* were killing each other.

Overnight, there had been bombings in at least one major metropolitan area in every country in the world, except for the Middle East. That last part was strange. There were drive-by shootings during the night at clubs and restaurants. There were heart wrenching stories of kids killing their parents and parents killing their children. Bruno had called. There was a shooting at the school where the boys attended, and where Ally had gone to school.

Many students and teachers died in the attack, but the boys had miraculously survived. They called Ollie. The same was true in England and all of Europe. Every continent. Networks could not keep up with the stories. Peace seemed to have disappeared in a single night.

"I have to get out there," said Beth.

"No, it is too dangerous," Blake warned.

"I have to go. People need us, and we need to get a glimpse of what is going on. I love you, Blake, but I have to go. Besides, it is a great chance to try out my new look, right?"

He knew that look. It was one of determination. "Go on, but please be safe. I can't bear the thought of losing you. I wish I could go with you, but I know I can't. Perhaps there is someone who can go so you don't have to be alone. Evan, Ally? Are you in?"

Both said at once, "Yes!" They started getting ready to go.

"I will go too!" said Kathie.

"Oh no, you won't," said John. "Remember, you are dead too. No one can see you outside of this shelter until you change the way you look." She knew he was right. She would stay.

"I think the three of you are enough for tonight," said Ben.

"I don't think so!" said Anders. "I will take a smaller camera and do some recording. And if I recall correctly, Ally is an excellent photographer. She may as well put that to good use now!"

"I will!" Ally ran to get her camera.

"Maybe you should just use your phone for today," said Blake. "You don't want to be too conspicuous. Try to get pictures when no one will notice you. You and Anders can bring what is out there back here to us with your pictures and videos. Evan, we will all have our phones on. Call and let us know what is happening. And especially call us if you need us. We will be right there. In that case, nothing else would matter."

"Got it," he said. "Come on, gang. Let's get going."

They were out the door in a flash and climbing the steps to the closet. This would be mission number one. Not nearly as dangerous as those to come, but a good way to start.

Beth wanted to drive into Ozark first. It was her hometown, and she needed to see it for herself. Maybe it had been spared. It was a smaller town, not near any large cities, the most peaceful place she had ever known. It was the perfect place to grow up and a great place to live. She wanted to drive by her mom and dad's place first. It was one of the most safe and quiet neighborhoods in Christian County. That is why she had bought a house for her parents there. It was in the suburbs on the outskirts of town.

As they came down their street, what she saw horrified her. Police cars and ambulances at their neighbor's house. Next to her mom and dad, they were two of her favorite people. She had always found some time to visit them when she was home. She saw them. One was lying on the front porch and the other on the steps, both covered with white sheets. They were dead. Then it hit her. They had died without believing in Jesus. She wept. Evan, Ally and Anders tried to console her, but she was inconsolable at that moment.

As they continued to drive through town, the scenes did not change. How many had died in this one small town in one night? If it was true of Ozark, Missouri, what must that number be in the world?

"Let's get out of here," she said. "Maybe we can drive to Springfield. No, it will be the same. Let's go back to the shelter. Did you two get any pictures or video?"

"I took a few pictures," said Ally.

"And I got a little video, but not much," said Anders.

When they arrived at the shelter, Beth broke down weeping as soon as she saw Blake.

"Beth, what's wrong?" He grabbed her and hugged her. She explained about her parents' neighbors and everything else they had seen. The whole group wept with her. Tribulation was increasing.

"Where is Trey?" wondered Ben. "I thought he was bringing Justin to meet the team at 9:00? It is almost 9:30. It is not like him to be late. He is always early."

Trey was sitting in his truck, ready to leave. Where was Justin? The guy was famous for being late, but he had been so excited about meeting the team, he had promised he would be early this time. He had tried to call him, but gotten no answer. He had better drive over there and wake him up. Justin could be a late sleeper. He had almost gotten fired a few times for being tardy. The sheriff was an early guy and did not like for his deputies to be late. He started the truck and backed out of the driveway. He had not seen the news this morning and had slept till the last minute himself. He pulled into Justin's driveway. Both his truck and patrol car sat in their usual spots. He had not even gotten out of the house yet. Sleepyhead.

He would pound on the door till he woke him up. He walked on the porch and up to the door. As he pulled back his fist to knock as loudly as he could, he saw something that made his skin crawl. The door was ajar, and the latch broken. Home invasion! Trey was shaking as he walked inside. He did not have his gun. He should have brought it. He had not walked far when he saw him. Justin was lying in a pool of blood on the living room floor. Whoever broke into his house had murdered him. His gun lay nearby. He had not gotten the chance to use it. The first blow had been a sneak attack from behind. As he got closer, he saw the brutality of it. Beaten. Stabbed multiple times. Trey turned aside. He nearly threw up.

He stumbled out the door and called 911. The operator said there were so many calls they could not get to all of them, but she would get someone there as soon as possible. Trey told her who it was, one of their own. That seemed to change things. She would send someone immediately. She asked him to wait. He complied. He went to his truck and sat in silence.

It suddenly occurred to him. What if he had not invited Justin over last night and let him hear about Jesus? What if Justin had not said yes to Jesus? He prayed and thanked God for allowing him to do that. He thanked him for giving Justin an opportunity to receive Jesus. Right then, it hit him just how vital the Smyrnians mission was. This would put it in an entirely new perspective.

Then the thought entered his mind: what if he had taken Justin on to the shelter last night as he had asked? He wanted to go right then, but Trey had said no. They would wait until tomorrow morning, he had told him. It was his fault! If he had done as Justin wanted, he would still be alive.

His mind raced back and forth between thoughts of grief, grace and guilt. Justin was his friend. His friend was dead. He could have prevented his death from happening. Justin had watched the video and believed. Justin was with Jesus! Back and forth. Good news, bad news. Blame, thanksgiving. From heartbreak to hallelujah. From celebrating with his friend last night to seeing his bloody body on his living room floor this morning. It was almost more than he could take.

He wished first responders would get there soon. He only wanted to do one thing, get to the shelter and be with his fellow followers of Jesus. This was a reminder of how much they would need each other during the next seven years. And he thought about how dangerous those years would be. How could they survive them? He hoped they would, but if he did not, he would see Justin in less than seven years.

The thought of that reunion brought a slight smile to his face. Last night, his crazy friend had gone to be with the Savior he had just met. That brought a sense of relief and peace to his pain. He needed to call Beth. He picked up his phone. Before he could make the call, his phone rang first. It was Blake.

"Trey? Where are you? We were getting worried. Have you heard about all the stuff that happened last night? Murders, killing, brutality, violence everywhere. It has definitely begun."

"I haven't heard about it, but I just witnessed it."

He told him about Justin, and Blake put the phone on speaker so the team could hear too.

"I will get there as soon as I can. I need you guys." Yes, he needed them, and they needed him. They would need each other for seven years.

CHAPTER 13

The three days for the expected arrival of the overseas contingent had come and gone, and the date of their coming was now uncertain. Airlines canceled flights worldwide as they hustled to place more security personnel on both domestic and international flights because of the intensifying violence that had covered the globe. Angry patrons killed passengers, flight attendants, and even a few pilots. They flew into rages and murdered them with their bare hands. Other passengers had often stopped them, but not until it was too late for the victims. Some crashes had occurred, resulting in many more deaths.

The world had become barbaric, a place of savagery and bloodshed, even as Aissa Messai continued to spread his message of peace and prosperity. The populace continued to buy into his rhetoric and propaganda, except for the ever increasing number of those who were now following Jesus Christ. They were snowballing. Though there was no one who was not a potential target, the attacks continued to focus more and more on them. This occurred as Messai stepped up his pronouncements that those who were a part of the cult known as the Smyrnians threatened peace and prosperity, and people must stop them. That led those who believed him to invade house churches across the globe and murder worshipers in cold blood.

The group in the shelter focused their daily emails on teaching new believers everywhere what the Bible said these seven years would bring for people who missed the Rapture of the church. They strongly encouraged them to find safe places to meet and take every precaution as they followed Jesus. But their warnings went unheeded as people who had discovered Jesus kept spreading the news about him, with no regard for their own lives. They had discovered real peace in Jesus and determined that they would bring as many others to him as they could, regardless of the cost. What had begun in Evan Ryles' dorm room in Chicago was now a worldwide movement that proved to be unstoppable. And yet, Aissa Messai was determined to try.

The battle was raging all over the planet, except in the one place it had raged most throughout history: the Middle East. Peace reigned there as Arabs and Jews had bridged the gap of their differences and come together as one. Ben and Ollie longed to get back there while the possibility of being unrecognized remained. But they would have to wait for air travel to start back up.

That also prevented both the German and British groups from traveling to the states. The team was eager to meet and spend time with each other, but that would not happen for a while. Trey could not fly, as the FAA had also issued a ban against private and charter flights. It seemed the world had come to a standstill, yet people continued with their daily lives despite it.

The team in Missouri decided they would not sit back and fail to be out helping those in need. They could drive to areas that would allow them to return by nightfall. The increasing daylight hours as Spring approached gave them more time for that. But Blake, John, Ben and Kathie must stay in until they were certain no one would recognize them, regardless of how much they wanted to go. However, the others were ready to get to work caring for people, while also trying to tell them about Jesus, even though they had to do so carefully. They continued showing the video of the pastor's message online daily, allowing believers from everywhere on earth to gather others to watch. People were putting their faith in Jesus every day as they watched the message and discovered the truth.

Those Christ followers. Nothing seemed to deter them from what they saw as their God-given task for these seven years. In Germany, the Fromms and Meiers, and in England, Ollie Barton and Amelia Clarke were all still under the radar and able to be out without being detected. They were making the most of that opportunity. Amelia was seeing members of Parliament turn to Jesus. Ollie's job allowed him free rein to get into just about anywhere, giving him access to vast numbers of people and situations.

Bruno and Mila Fromm were methodically building the team in Germany, while Hans and Heidi Meier were also adding new believers, starting with several of their own family members. Those believed for much the same reason they had. The people in their family who had gone missing on September 11, 2029 were Christians who lived for Jesus. As Hans and Heidi told them the truth or showed them the video, they instantly said yes to Jesus. They gave daily reports to the American group but felt it was God's plan for them to stay in Europe for the time being to continue the work.

Beth was going out every day, with Miriam and Ally by her side, using her new identity as a humanitarian aid worker to help families who lost loved ones in the violence. Many times, it softened their hearts when she spoke to them about a way to find real peace. People are often more open to a message of hope during times of heartbreak and difficulty. She had chosen the right occupation to go along with her disguise. And her appearance had everyone fooled. As yet, no one had even suggested that she resembled Beth Jennings. Kudos to Ally and Kathie!

Trey, Rickie and Anders were teammates too, traveling about and also trying to help. Trey and Rickie were locals, so their efforts came as a surprise to no one. And Trey's friend, Steffen, who was visiting and could not leave because of the no fly rule, was helping too. Anders liked his new name.

Ally had received an email which left her tingling with excitement. It stated that they had selected her as a candidate for the position of personal assistant to Aissa Messai, or one of several other roles within his organization. Applicants hailed from several countries, and all had one thing in common. She would not discover what that was until after she had met the others.

That forced her to call her parents and tell them what she had intended to share with them face-to-face when they came. Her call upset them. It broke their hearts because she had not told them before. She assured them it was because she wanted to tell them in person. But since air travel was suspended, she had received confirmation and had no choice but to tell them over the phone. They would probably miss seeing each other, as she would likely fly to Belgium at the same time they were flying to Missouri, or possibly before. She read them the email from Messai's office:

Dear Ally,

Thank you for your application seeking a position in the organization of United Nations Secretary-General Aissa Messai and desiring to help him bring peace and prosperity to our world. He gave careful consideration to which candidates will best work alongside him and assist him in achieving his goal. Congratulations on being selected as one of them. We will schedule interviews the moment flights resume. I am happy to inform you that each applicant chosen is guaranteed a job in one of the available positions. We wish you well as you serve alongside the Secretary-General, assisting him in making the world a better place. When you come to Belgium for your interview, your travel expenses will be paid in full. We will be in touch with you soon. Mr. Messai looks forward to meeting you and getting to know you.

With Regards,

The Office of Aissa Messai

They guaranteed her a position! Ally was about to fulfill her calling to be a Smyrnian spy. The thought sent shivers up her spine, a combination of excitement and fear. Her dream from a few months ago came rushing back into her mind: being captured by Messai, her hands bound and her neck placed in the guillotine, then waking up at the sound of the blade releasing. She recalled waking in a sweat and shaking all over.

She knew that she was preparing to tread upon dangerous ground. She understood the consequences of being found out as a mole who was secretly relaying inside information to the Smyrnians. The punishment would be swift and harsh. Yet she believed this was her role on the team during the Tribulation, and she would fill it, regardless of how it ended.

She would not go back out with Beth because she could not take the chance of being seen by anyone on the outside before she flew to Belgium to meet with Aissa Messai. She had a few days to prepare for that meeting. She would be ready.

Beth and Miriam, now a team of two, had been making the rounds for a few days. They had yet to come under any suspicion, but this morning they encountered an AMPP checkpoint while attempting to enter a community that had experienced a significant loss of life the night before. They heightened security, with citizens on edge and AMPP on hand to protect them and ensure that no further violence would happen today. As Beth and

Miriam drove up to the checkpoint, a member of the patrol questioned her thoroughly.

"What are your names?"

"I am Kelly Davis, and this is my partner, Abigail Isaacs." She knew to only give the requested information and nothing more. "Just answer their questions," Blake had reminded her.

"What is your purpose here?"

"We are here to help the injured and those who have lost family members."

"Are you with an organization? We allow no reporters or curious onlookers; authorized personnel only."

"We are with *People of Peace*, a humanitarian aid organization that works in crisis situations to help people find peace amid their pain. We have been on the field every day since the violence escalated." Both she and Miriam produced badges bearing the emblem P.O.P., an appropriate name chosen to appease Messai's troops. Evan had done well again.

"I have never heard of this organization," the man said gruffly. "How can I know you are on the up and up?"

"Here is one of our cards. Please check out our website, which you can see there on the bottom of the card. Or you may call our 800 number."

"Okay, I will do that," the man said, watching to see if that drew any reaction from them.

It did not, so he proceeded with calling the number. It was one Evan had set up, complete with an answering machine and a recorded message. The man listened to the entire message.

"Hello. You have reached the People of Peace Humanitarian Aid office. No one is available to take your call. Because of the current crisis, all of our people are out helping those in need. Please leave your name, a call-back number, and a brief message after the beep, and we will get back with you as soon as we can. If you would like to report a need, please include the specific location from which you are calling."

"Okay, it seems legit enough." He bent down to look through the window at Miriam sitting in the passenger seat. "Ma'am, you are Jewish, is that correct?"

"Yes, I am," Miriam proudly proclaimed.

"Aissa Messai wishes to thank you and your people for your willingness to work for the cause of peace. I only wish the rest of the world would follow your example."

"Thank you." It shocked Miriam to hear that from him. What more could she say?

As his eyes drifted back across the car, he looked closely at Beth. "You look familiar. Are you local?" She was trying to discern whether he lived in the area himself and may recognize her, or if he was not and was trying to figure out who she was. She did not recognize him.

"No sir. People of Peace sent us here to work with the people in this area and any surrounding areas with serious needs. We have sent our workers all over the United States. We will be here as long as needed, so you may as well get used to seeing us around."

"Okay. I am not local either. You just look like someone I have seen before. Maybe we have passed each other on the street in the last couple of days. If you don't mind me saying so, you are beautiful. I would not forget seeing you. If a night on the town would interest you, I would be happy to oblige. Even you humanitarian aid worker types need to have a little fun now and then."

"I appreciate that, sir, and thank you for the compliment, but I am happily married."

"Well, if you are from out of town, that means your husband is not around. What he doesn't know won't hurt him, right?" He winked. Looking back over at Miriam, he said, "Sorry, ma'am. We just get a little lonely out here on patrol. The company of a beautiful woman is the perfect remedy for that! Okay, get to your work. But I must warn you, it is ugly in there."

Miriam smiled at Beth as they drove on. "Apparently you have not lost your appeal to men after changing your appearance. Blonde or brunette, it seems you have what it takes! Maybe that will come in handy somewhere along the way during these seven years."

"I would not hesitate to play that card if it would help us. But only if Blake was okay with it." She smiled, not knowing just how true those words may be.

Meanwhile, Trey, Rickie and Anders were working in areas around Springfield. The savagery had touched every place. No one had a clue what had happened in such a short time that turned some people into animals, while others became their victims. The Smyrnians knew, and the Bible told them things would only get worse before the Tribulation ended and Jesus returned. In a beautiful and popular suburb of Springfield, the three men helped with cleanup from the looting of the past few days. As they walked out of a ransacked building, the sheriff came by.

"Trey, I sure am sorry about Justin. He worked for me, but I know you guys were close. We will miss him on the force. I understand you were the one who found him."

"I did, and I would just as soon never think about it or talk about it again. We were together the night before and had a great time. He came over, and I grilled steaks, and we sat and talked and laughed and watched TV. Our typical good time. Then the next morning I walked into his house and saw him dead on the floor."

"It tore up the guys on the force pretty badly too. He was the clown of the group. They will miss him a lot. I understand you talked to some of them at the scene."

"Yeah, I know it was hard on them. And it is hard on me too, but honestly, I am happy for him."

"Happy for him? How can you be happy for him? The guy is dead. Someone brutally murdered him."

Trey meant what he said, but should have thought better before he said it. "What I meant was, he is better off not having to deal with all this junk we are going through."

"But he is dead, Trey. There is no way that can be a good thing. You can't be happy for him."

"If you only knew," Trey thought. But he had to drop the subject or risk exposing the team.

"Rickie, it is good to see you too. I don't think I have met your friend."

"Steffen Janssen." Anders stuck out his hand. "Pleased to meet you."

"I can tell by that accent you're not from these parts."

"No, I am not. I am from up on the East Coast. Trey and I were college buddies back in the day."

"Well, you boys continue doing what you have to do. I have other business to attend to."

They had only walked a little farther down the sidewalk when they saw an elderly shop owner and his wife standing in the rubble of what was once their cute little boutique. It was very popular in the community, but now it lay in shambles. The two were holding each other as they surveyed the devastation. Rickie knew the couple and started talking to them.

"John and Mary, I am so sorry about your business. Many people will miss this place. Do you think you can clean it up and reopen?"

"No, Rickie, we are too old for that. But it breaks our hearts. This shop was our lives. Our kids practically grew up in here. We should have retired and sold this place a long time ago. We kept it open for far too long. Now, I don't know what we can do. Everything seems so hopeless."

Hearing that word and seeing the heartbroken couple triggered Anders. He could not hold himself back. He walked over to them and said, "You don't know me. I am Steffen Janssen, a friend of Rickie. I know things look hopeless now, but what if I told you there is someone who can give you more hope than you have ever had?" He was getting much bolder with his faith.

"What do you mean? Is this someone who can rebuild our store for us?" Their heads came up, and he saw a faint glimmer of hope on their faces.

"No, he does not give silver and gold. But what he has, he gives to you. And what he gives is life, real life. I know that because he gave it to me. I can introduce you to him." The couple was interested, so he began telling them about Jesus using the pastor's sermon.

They teared up, and the husband said, "We know what you are talking about. We saw Blake Thompson's special when he talked about the same thing. We didn't do what the pastor said that night because we were afraid. Then when we heard Messai afterwards, it terrified us. But we have talked about it every day since. Can you help us? We believe what the pastor said. We had friends who were Christians taken on September 11. Now we know what happened."

"Do you remember what the pastor told you to do if you believe?"

"He told us to talk to Jesus and tell him we believe in him. Then open the door of our hearts and lives and ask him to come in and be our Savior."

"That is exactly right. I did that, and it changed my life! Why don't you do it now?"

They did, standing right in the middle of the rubble that sought to define their lives. When they had finished, their faces seemed to glow. Trey, Rickie and Anders understood how they felt.

"Welcome to the Family of God," said Anders, his face lighting up too.

"How can we ever thank you?" asked Mary. "We didn't think we would have another opportunity to do this. Jesus sent you to us today."

"John and Mary, how would you like to meet Blake Thompson and Beth Jennings?" asked Trey.

"What do you mean? How can we meet them?"

"We can go where they and some others are. It is a safe place. If you want to go, hop in my truck with us, and we will take you right now."

They knew their day of helping was over as the couple walked with them to Trey's truck. God had led them to the place where they needed to be today. It was a day none of them would ever forget. They helped John and Mary into the truck and drove toward Ozark.

Blake was poring over names on the list of people who had emailed saying they had put their faith in Jesus. There were millions. He thanked God as he scrolled through each page. He did not know them, but he still prayed for them. Continually scrolling and taking no time to stop, he extended his hand toward the screen as he asked God to guide them.

Something caught his eye in the middle of one page. There is no way he could have seen it, but neither could he miss it. It may as well have been in bold print and highlighted in yellow. He stopped scrolling and stared at the screen, hardly believing his eyes. Was this his imagination? No! It was there. One name among millions. His source. The guy who had so often given him the inside scoop that gave him a leg up on other reporters. Blake had forgotten. His number had changed. The man could not contact him. But Blake still had *his* number. He jumped up from his chair and called. Voicemail.

He left a message, ending with, "This number is private and secure. You can't call me on it, but I will call you back in exactly thirty minutes. Please take my call."

This was amazing! Jesus had shown him the man's information on a list that would amount to looking for a needle in a haystack, if he had been searching for it. But he was not looking for it. He was just occupying the hours of the day while Beth was out, since he had nothing else to do. "I may as well pray for new believers," he thought. Now he knew it was Jesus directing him to do that. The thirty minutes were up. He called again. The source answered!

"Blake, is this you?"

"It is me. I saw your name on the list. Is it true that you put your faith in Jesus?"

"It is true! When I watched you that night and saw the pastor's message, it suddenly all made sense to me. I knew what had happened and why it happened. I have been on the website and have read the Bible every day. I can't get enough of it! But I have wanted to talk to you. I am amazed that you called me. It had to be Jesus who showed you my name. Can we get together?"

"I am nowhere near you. As you might assume, it forced us into hiding and doing our work from here. Soon we will broadcast to the world from a secure site where no one can find us. But I have to tell you, I want you on our team. We need you on Team Smyrnians!"

"How do I join? Tell me what to do!"

"You have already joined. You did that the moment you asked Jesus to be your Savior. But I would like to have you here with us and fighting alongside us. If you are ready to give up everything for the last seven years of this planet before we all go home to be with Jesus, come and join us!"

"I don't know where you are. Can you tell me how to get there?"

"No airlines are flying right now. But we have a pilot on the team who can come and get you as soon as they lift the ban and allow flights again. If you are ready to turn your back on everything else and give it all for the cause, I will make that happen."

"You are on, man! I will get everything ready now so when the time comes, I will be free and clear. I am not married and have nothing to hold me back. I cannot wait to see you and get to work helping the Smyrnians fight Messai! I can't thank you enough for calling me."

"Don't thank me. I would never have found your name without Jesus. Thank him! Let's stay in touch through email. We can also talk on the phone every day. The airlines should be open again soon. So you had better have things ready. Our man will come and get you as soon as they are!"

He could not wait to tell Beth the news. But she would have to settle again for not being the first to hear. He ran to tell the others who had to stay in the shelter with him. This was news that had to be told. Good news would come from the others too when they returned. It was a day to remember!

When Blake told Ally, she was packing her things so she would be ready to leave for Belgium at a moment's notice. She also assumed flights would be on again soon. Blake told her the source would be her partner in spying. She would be on the inside in Messai's office, and he would be on the outside gathering information. Together they would make a formidable team. Ally could not wait to get on the plane. She feared it may take that to keep her from backing out. But when Aissa Messai has your application, there is no going back.

In London, Amelia Clarke was leaving the Palace of Westminster after an evening meeting with some fellow members of the House of Commons. As she opened the door of her car, a black SUV pulled up behind her, blocking her exit. She knew what that meant.

"Amelia Clarke?"

"Yes, I am Amelia Clarke. Who wants to know?"

"Aissa Messai's Peace Patrol. You are under arrest for spreading the dangerous propaganda of the rebel Smyrnians and threatening world peace and security. We need you to come with us."

She knew going with them meant not coming back. She looked for a blue sedan that was coming to pick her up. He was seldom late. Sure enough, right on time, it pulled into the parking garage and parked in front of the SUV. Oliver Barton stepped out.

"What do we have here, gentlemen?" he asked. "Why are you harassing Miss Clarke?"

"Oliver Barton, the best reporter in England, and the best Middle Eastern correspondent too, I might add. It is a pleasure to meet you, sir. Do you mind if I get an autograph for my wife?"

"Not at all," said Ollie. He took the paper and signed his name. "We reporters like it when we are in the right place at the right time. This seems to be one of those occasions for me. Do you mind if I gather some facts for a story? You can see yourselves on the news tomorrow."

"Not at all, sir. It will be a privilege to have you interview us."

"It appears Miss Clarke here is being arrested. Can you tell me why? I know her well. She is a highly respected member of the House of Commons."

"Well sir, she is being charged with treason and working to spread the dangerous propaganda of the Smyrnians. They are being sought by the regime so we can put an end to their lies, and their efforts to destroy the peace and security of the world."

"Well said. But it sounds rehearsed to me. Are those your words, or the words of your leader? What you mean is, Messai has put a price on their heads. Am I right?"

"No sir, I would not say that at all. They are being arrested and brought to trial as all criminals are."

"Miss Clarke, what do you have to say to these charges?"

"I suppose I would have to plead guilty. If I am being accused today of speaking to others about Jesus who has changed my life, then I must agree that I have done what they say. I can only say I wish these men were as I am, except for those handcuffs they intend to put on my wrists. I would also say that, as far as being a threat to world peace and security, I believe my many years of service in Parliament speak for themselves. I have worked tirelessly to *bring* peace and security, not *destroy* it!"

"Gentlemen, do you have a reply to that?"

"I have great respect for Miss Clarke," said one. "But we have our orders and must carry them out. So, ma'am, if you would not mind, come with us peacefully. Please face your car and put your hands behind your back."

"This is big news," said Ollie. "If you will give me a minute before you proceed with her arrest, may I get my camera from the car and film this? It will only take a moment."

"I guess we can wait. We have no reason to be in a hurry. What matters is taking the prisoner into custody."

Ollie got into his car, watching the AMPP men from the rear-view mirror. One of them bent down to pick up something he had dropped. The other was lighting a cigarette. He threw the passenger door open and shouted, "Amelia, get in!" Amelia sprinted and dove into his car. He started it as she did, jerked the gearshift into Drive and sped out of the garage, going through the entrance instead of the exit. He crashed through the gate and turned onto the busy highway. Behind him, he saw the AMPP vehicle following the same track he had taken.

"Thank you, Ollie," she said. "But what do we do now? You know you just implicated yourself, right?"

"That I do, but I told you I would pick you up, and I never go back on a promise."

Seeing the SUV gaining ground, he turned left onto a side street, running a red light and clipping another car as he did. Speeding down the street, he saw the SUV making the same turn, with lights flashing.

Amelia was holding on for dear life. She yelled, "You drive, and I'll pray!"

"That is the plan," he said, never slowing down.

As they turned onto another small street, they found it empty. But Ollie also saw that the AMPP guys had circled around another side street and were trying to cut them off. He roared past them just before they pulled out in front of them. But now they looked attached to their rear bumper.

"Didn't anyone teach them you're not supposed to tailgate?" Ollie asked, attempting to smile.

Then something hit the car. They were shooting at them! Bullets pinged off the trunk. They heard a tail light shatter. Ollie was swerving, hoping to elude the gunfire as much as possible.

"Amelia, get down," he yelled. Just as she did, a bullet crashed through the back windshield. He knew more AMPP vehicles had to be on the way to assist this one. He was approaching the end of the side street and the entrance onto a busy avenue. A traffic light stood on the corner. It was red with no other vehicle waiting that would cause it to change. He yelled at Amelia again.

"Hang on. This may be rough!"

"What choice do I have?" she yelled back. "Just keep driving and don't worry about me."

As he approached the light, he noticed the men had stopped firing and assumed it was because they were coming upon the busy thoroughfare. They were expecting him to stop, he thought, so he slowed and noticed them slowing behind him. Then, some 20 meters before he reached the light, he stomped the gas to the floor. Ahead, he saw that the street was busy, but at least with vehicles spread out and traffic not stopped. He saw the SUV also speed up behind him. As he reached the light, he jerked the steering wheel to the right and turned on two wheels onto the avenue, just missing an oncoming garbage truck. The SUV was not so lucky. He saw it crash into the truck at full speed. The impact lifted the truck into the air as the SUV slammed into it and disappeared underneath it. He was certain the two men inside did not survive. Ollie sped away, fleeing the scene like an Indy car driver racing for the checkered flag on the back straightaway.

"I didn't know you could drive like that, Mr. Barton," said Amelia, appearing calm despite the perilous situation through which they had just come.

"There are a lot of things you don't know about me, I am sure," he smiled, without letting up on the gas. "So, where do we go from here? We obviously can't go to either of our houses."

"I have a friend who owns a house about an hour from here. She is almost never there. I know where she hides the key. If we can get there, maybe we can talk about our next move. We're both finished as a reporter and politician. And if AMPP catches up to us, we are dead. They will have our faces splattered all over the news tonight. We will be the two most wanted criminals in Great Britain. I wish we had a way to get to Missouri, but with no airlines operating, I don't see how we can. Even if they were, they would arrest us in the airport if we tried to board a plane."

"All I know is, we must have a plan. Talk me through the drive to your friend's house, and I will call Blake Thompson from there. I am sure they have everyone available out looking for us right now. And the way I have banged up this car, we will be easy to spot. We need to take the most isolated route possible. If they come this time, there will be more than one SUV and two AMPP men. We wouldn't stand a chance. So, lead on fair lady, and I will keep the wheels rolling."

She directed him along back roads to the house in the country. It was more isolated than he would have imagined. From all appearances, it looked like the perfect hideout. He parked the car at the rear of the house behind some fruit trees in the backyard. Once inside, he called Blake and told him about their plight.

"We have to get out of England, Blake, or they will capture us or kill us. We can't fly, so I am clueless about what to do. Do you have any suggestions?" Blake was quiet on the other end. Ollie knew he was thinking. There was no answer, unless it came from Jesus.

CHAPTER 14

The UK was abuzz with the news of Oliver Barton and Amelia Clarke's dramatic escape from AMPP. Their pictures were on every news network. Fellow correspondents and Parliament members expressed their beliefs that neither of the two highly respected citizens were a danger to society. Members of Parliament, both the House of lords and House of Commons, gathered as one at the Palace of Westminster to stand up for their colleague. Some had been her opposition in government matters, but they cared for her.

Fellow journalists rose in unison to support their esteemed comrade, Oliver Barton. This was a defining moment for Aissa Messai's leadership. He would need to convince the world that members of Parliament and the media were wrong. The public waited to hear from him. His press secretary introduced him, as he prepared to make a statement in typical Messai fashion.

"Ladies and Gentlemen of the world, I come before you tonight with utmost respect for the men and women of the Parliament of the UK and the members of the news media. I support their efforts at keeping the peace, just as we do. Tonight, I fear they do not comprehend the gravity of the situation at hand. We have worked very hard together to bring peace and prosperity to our world. Setbacks have occurred in recent days, linked to the group of rebels who call themselves the Smyrnians."

"We have found undeniable evidence that Miss Amelia Clarke became one of them. She has been openly promoting their beliefs and agenda to her colleagues in the House of Commons, and to those in the House of lords, as well. We believe she has also been espousing those false and destructive beliefs in the presence of many others."

"It has become apparent tonight that the journalist Oliver Barton has joined her in this destructive behavior. We have suspected him for some time but have failed to investigate his activity due to the sheer nature of the high regard in which the public holds him. That is true not just of the people in the UK, but also of the people around the world. However, tonight we know he has also joined the rebel cause."

"So, it is with a sad heart that I must tell you we have issued a red alert for the capture of these two people. AMPP is out in force attempting to locate Miss Clarke and Mr. Barton. As always, I ask anyone who has any information about their whereabouts to call our tip line. The number is on the screen."

"Per our normal protocol, any tip which leads to the arrest of these two people will bring a handsome reward. Because this situation is so critical, the reward will be £400,000 for each of the fugitives or £750,000 if one tip leads to the capture of both. As the Secretary-General of your United Nations, I am working hard to maintain the peace, security and prosperity of your world. Thank you for standing with me in this effort."

With that, he was off the air, and the debates were on. Some argued that AMPP had caught both Amelia and Ollie red-handed, and they were undoubtedly guilty. Others argued that Amelia was the guilty party, and Ollie was an innocent reporter in the wrong place at the wrong time. He was only trying to report the news and felt compelled to help the lady, not understanding the gravity of the situation.

The debates continued throughout the night as violence continued to rage around the globe. As that occurred, people remained blinded to the way the violence stood in stark contrast to what Aissa Messai was saying. But regardless of the varying opinions, the amount of the reward offered for their capture had much of England searching for Oliver Barton and Amelia Clarke.

At her friend's house, Amelia and Ollie were desperately seeking answers. They knew the group in America were doing the same thing. And they knew that all of them, including the Fromms and Meiers in Germany, were praying for Jesus to intervene. A potential solution came to Trey. It was risky in every way, but it was worth a try.

He had served for some time at Royal Lakenheath Air Force Base in Suffolk in the UK. It is a military base operated by the United States Air Force and home to only American troops. He had a friend there who was a career military man. They had flown combat missions together, and Trey had once shot down an enemy plane just before it fired the missile that would have sent his buddy's plane to the ground.

Their friendship was unbreakable, and there was nothing they would not do for each other. But this was a huge ask. He needed the man to arrange a flight to the states, for two of his friends who were in grave danger. His comrade-in-arms was not living in a cocoon, so he was well aware of the situation with Amelia Clarke and Oliver Barton. He was not an Aissa Messai fan. Neither was he a believer in Jesus (at least, not yet, Trey thought), but he was a loyal friend. He would find some way to pull this off with a no fly order in place, since the military was exempt from civilian orders. If he could fly them from Suffolk to the nearest military base in Missouri, the Smyrnians would pick them up. He agreed, and Blake was on the phone with Ollie.

"How long will it take you to get to RAF Lakenheath in Suffolk? My calculations say it is about a 2-hour drive. Trey has a buddy there named Bradley Rodgers who will fly you to the states. The military can get by with flying missions, even with passenger flights cancelled. If you can get to a base in Missouri, we will pick you up and get you to the shelter."

"We can leave now! I banged up my old car pretty badly, but hopefully it will get us there."

"From what I saw on the news, I am sure it is! You are a reckless driver, my friend. Remind me not to ride with you while you are here."

"Just ask Amelia about my driving. She was calm and relaxed the entire time."

"Good for her. I assure you I would not have been. Now, get off this phone and get to Lakenheath so we can get you over here where you will be safe. We need you to stay alive. It also sounds like a change of appearance will be in order for both you and Amelia before you can get back out. Don't worry, we have ladies here who will take care of that for you."

"Aye, don't worry about it, Matey. This Bloke could use a makeover, anyway. I can't wait!"

He and Amelia instantly got into his car, back window out and barely holding together, and headed to Lakenheath. Their destination was the bunkers in Ozark, Missouri, where they would receive protection from Aissa Messai. At this moment, their lives depended on the ability of Trey's friend to make it happen.

Taking back roads and driving carefully, it took two-and-a-half hours for them to arrive at Lakenheath. Bradley Rodgers had cleared them at the gate and was waiting just inside. He directed them to a place where they could leave Ollie's car. It was now a clunker which the base would dispose of. Then they got into a jeep, and he drove them to the plane.

"We are taking this monster?" asked Amelia.

"Yep, unless you want to crash somewhere in the middle of the Atlantic," Bradley answered. "It is all we have that will make it across without in-flight refueling."

"What is this one?" asked Ollie. "I have seen a lot of military planes in the Middle East and even flown in a few. Is this a C-130?"

"You got it right." That impressed Bradley. "I guess as a news correspondent you have to know your stuff about everything, don't you?"

"Well, not everything. But I know a lot about a lot of things. That comes with years of research and experience. So, how long will it take us to get to Missouri?"

"It should take around 12 hours, give or take a minute or two. If you two are ready, hop in. You get to ride up front with me. You can be my copilots. We have a long night ahead of us. I am putting my career on the line for you. I hope you understand that. But there is almost nothing I wouldn't do for Trey Butler. I owe him my life. Did he tell you that story?"

"I haven't even met Trey," said Amelia. "But he sounds like a guy who would do that."

"Maybe I can tell you the story on the flight over. We have to get in the air. As far as the military is aware, I am flying a top secret mission. I suppose you could say that is exactly what I am doing. But we are not all alone. I can't make the round trip by myself. I have a real copilot asleep in the back. You won't see him. He will stay back there until after we land. Then after you have securely disembarked and gotten with Trey, he will take over for our return trip while I sleep."

"I appreciate what you are doing for us," said Ollie. Amelia seconded that and Bradley acknowledged his thanks with a nod of his head as he prepared for takeoff.

With no further hesitation, they were in the air. Ollie and Amelia were exhausted, but far too fascinated to sleep. They had never been in a cockpit before, especially that of a military cargo plane. They were in awe. The two of them settled in for a long flight.

Mila Fromm was praying in Germany. She was brokenhearted and frightened for her daughter.

"Jesus, please protect our Ally. I believe the Bible story you gave us about the synagogue ruler's daughter dying shows us she will be in grave danger. You raised his daughter to life. I believe that was your way of telling us Ally will be in danger of losing her life. I beg you like he did, please save Ally's life. When she doesn't know what to do or say, and there is no one there to help her, give her wisdom. Messai is powerful, but you are more powerful. He can't defeat you, and Ally belongs to you. Please Jesus, keep her safe and spare her life."

She would pray that prayer every day and constantly watch for Bible verses or other signs that told her when Ally may be in danger. It frightened her and Bruno for their little girl.

Around the world, the violence continued to rage. The death toll climbed daily. Many people were afraid to even go out, but they were not safe inside their homes either. Businesses suffered from absentee employees. The economy slipped from its near perfect status after Messai's election. Many people felt like they had gone back in time to the Middle Ages. If that is what they thought now, they would feel that even more soon, because what was coming would mimic one of the Middle Ages most horrific periods.

After a long night, Bradley Rodgers landed at a military base some two hours from Ozark. He had special clearance for the top secret emergency mission. Trey and Rickie were there to pick up Ollie and Amelia. Though they were no longer active in the military, they could easily arrange clearance for themselves. They rapidly transferred the passengers from plane to vehicle with faces covered to conceal their identity.

Bradley and Trey took a few moments to hug and talk as the plane was being refueled. Then he boarded, allowing his copilot to take the controls for the 12-hour trip back to England. Trey and Rickie hurried to the truck and jumped inside. They turned to their passengers in the back, and Trey greeted them.

"It is good to see you, Ollie. And this must be the infamous Amelia Clarke. Good day, ma'am. My name is Trey Butler, and this is Rickie Cruz. It is good to meet a new Smyrnian! Now, keep your heads down until we get through the gate and back out on the road." They gladly complied.

Once on the road, Ollie said, "You don't know how good it is to be alive and on American soil."

"Oh yeah, I hear you had a harrowing experience over there last night," smiled Rickie.

"Oh, it was nothing, really." Amelia returned the smile. "We just had a little joyride, and I got to find out what a good driver Mr. Barton here is."

"You two wouldn't think I am a good driver if you saw my car," chuckled Ollie.

"Well," said Trey, "the main thing is you made it, and you are here safe and sound. There are a bunch of people at the shelter who can't wait to see you. They will have hot coffee and breakfast ready when we get there. Then I assume you want to get some sleep."

"I'm not sure we can sleep with all the excitement. It will be good to see everyone and introduce them to Amelia. She proved tonight that she will make a great Smyrnian!" She smiled and flexed her arms, showing she was ready.

Trey drove the speed limit and was very careful so they would have no problems. In just over two hours, they turned onto the deserted side road leading toward the farm.

Amelia said, "I am a city girl, so this should be interesting." A smile formed on her face.

"Oh, I guarantee you it will be... starting NOW!"

Trey made a sharp turn into what appeared to be a grove of trees, causing his new passengers to grab for anything they could get ahold of. Trey and Rickie laughed out loud.

"Don't worry. You aren't the first to have that fun little adventure. Each of us who had never been to this place had the pleasure of experiencing it, too. That includes all of us, except Beth."

"I suppose it is okay for you to have a little fun at our expense." Still visibly shaken from what he thought would be a sure crash, Ollie said, "You had better be glad I didn't have breakfast, or I would have lost it all over your truck."

As they drove through the covered lane that looked for all the world like a tunnel, Amelia was awestruck.

"This is the most amazing thing I have ever seen," she exclaimed. "If this leads to the shelter, I can see why it is a safe place."

"This is just the beginning," said Trey. "Wait till you see the rest!"

They pulled into the clearing in front of the small cabin, parked and got out.

"No one will ever find this place," she exclaimed, looking around in wonder and amazement.

"I suppose they might find it, but the question then would be, can they find *us*?" asked Trey.

"What do you mean by that?" asked Ollie. "Where are these bunkers I have heard so much about?"

"Come with us," Rickie offered. They followed as he and Trey walked inside the cabin.

"This is so quaint and peaceful," said Amelia. "Can I take a tour before we go to the bunkers?"

"Sure," Trey said. "Be our guest."

She walked throughout the cabin, taking it all in. "I wouldn't mind living here," she said.

"You will!" exclaimed Rickie.

"What do you mean? I thought we would be underground."

"Come with us again," said Rickie. Ollie and Amelia followed them into the bedroom.

"Check out this great little closet." Trey pointed it out.

"It is tiny," she said. "But I still don't get what you are saying or where you are taking us."

Rickie shoved aside the clothes hanging in the closet, pushing on the back wall. It swung open.

"No way!" exclaimed Ollie. "Barmy!"

They stepped into the closet for the first time and peered at the steps leading down to the shelter.

"Well, what are you waiting for?" asked Trey. "Welcome home!"

They descended the steps and entered the first bunker. The entire group who had eagerly awaited their arrival greeted them joyfully.

"Ollie!" squealed Beth, reminding him of that morning she met him at JFK Airport when he flew in to cover the UN Session and Aissa Messai's election. It brought back memories of the short time after that when he put his faith in Jesus. A smile came to his face too.

"Beth, and everybody else, it is good to see you! There are a few of you I still need to meet. And speaking of meeting, this is Amelia Clarke. She has already fought battle number one as a Smyrnian and survived! I wish you could have been there to see her in action!"

"Amelia, it is great to meet you. I never tire of meeting new followers of Jesus. Welcome to the team! I just have *one little question.* Is there more going on between the two of you than meets the eye? I think I am seeing something that reminds me of myself a few months ago."

"Blake!" exclaimed Beth. "Why would you ask something like that? Ollie and Amelia just got here. That is no way to greet them. It's not good to speculate that out loud for everyone to hear."

"You are right again, Beth. This is another of those times when I stuck my foot in my mouth. I am sorry, Ollie. My apologies to you too, Amelia."

A twinkle came to her eye as she said, "You have a keen sense of perception, Mr. Thompson. Just why do you think Ollie was there to come to my rescue last night when the AMPP guys showed up? He was not just in the right place at the right time, as he suggested to them. He was picking me up for our date. We have been seeing each other for a few weeks. I would say love is definitely in the air. What do you say, Ollie?"

"It is good to get that out in the open," chuckled Ollie. "The last thing I wanted us to do was to be here trying to hide our relationship. Yes, love is definitely in the air. I can say it here in front of all of you. I am in love with Amelia Clarke!"

"Oh Ollie, I am so happy for you." Beth was tearing up as she hugged both of them.

Anders shook his head and spoke loudly enough for everyone to hear. "Twitterpation. More twitterpation. It seems I can't escape it." He grinned from ear to ear. "And I kind of like it!"

"What are you talking about?" asked Amelia. "And I don't think I caught your name."

"I am Anders Norstrom, alias Steffen Janssen, Blake's cameraman. And not to worry, you will find out what I meant soon enough." He smiled at her again.

"I get it, luv," Ollie told her. "And trust me, he is right! I am twitterpated!" He laughed.

Amelia shook her head and shrugged her shoulders. "I suppose that means so am I." Then she added, "I can already tell I will love being around this group!"

They served breakfast and introduced everyone. Ollie had yet to meet Kathie Sanderson and John and Mary. They all wished the Fromms and Meiers were present so the entire team would be together. Ally prayed they would arrive before she left. She needed to see her mom and dad.

The day finally came for the lifting of the airline travel ban. Passengers packed airports as they were told it was safe to travel again. However, overcrowding and delays created even more havoc. But this time, airport security was being provided by AMPP, and few people wanted to be on their bad side.

Tickets purchased prior to the shutdown would receive top priority. Flights would pick up where they left off, as if no shutdown had occurred. That created some anger among would be travelers who sought to purchase tickets now. But it meant Bruno and Mila Fromm and the boys would fly early the first morning of the reopening. Hans and Heidi had decided it was important for them to stay in Germany and oversee the growing work there.

Ally was still awaiting word about her flight, so if the timing worked out right, she would see her family before she left. The reason for her delay may give her an extra day with them. At least, that is what she hoped. They set the Temple dedication in Jerusalem for the next day. Messai would be present, as he was the central figure in that celebration. Other dignitaries from around the world would be there, too. But two who would not be present were Oliver Barton and Ben Abramson. They had planned to be there and wanted to be there, but this was not the right time. Both sat quarantined in a bunker in Ozark, Missouri. The day would come when they would be out again, but that day was not here yet.

Ally eagerly waited for her family to arrive. They were flying into Atlanta, Georgia, then a quick flight to Springfield-Branson. Trey would pick them up there. Their flight would depart Germany early that morning. They should be in the shelter no later than 6:00 p.m. Ally was planning a big meal for the entire team, but this time she had a secret weapon.

Mary was one of the finer cooks in Greene County. She and John had sold her sweet treats in their boutique in Springfield. For meals, she referred to herself as a country cook. She promised a meal like most of them had never eaten. Along with Ally's specialties, pot roast with potatoes and carrots and her cakes, they would have a feast of massive proportions!

She and Mary got an early start, and the aroma filled bunker number one. The others moved to bunkers two and three to keep their hunger from getting the best of them, except for Evan, who stuck around to sample the dishes one-by-one as they finished them.

The flight was on time, and Trey rolled in with the Fromms fifteen minutes earlier than expected. Ally, Bruno and Mila hugged and hugged. Tears flowed, and expressions of love came again and again. Even her brothers felt the gravity of the moment and did the same, unlike their typically mischievous selves. They all ate, then spent time after dinner getting acquainted with each other and sharing Jesus stories from the time since most of them had last seen each other.

Bruno and Mila showed photos of Hans and Heidi. The day would come when they would get to meet them. Tomorrow they would all tune in and watch the Temple dedication. It would be an important day for these seven years. They did not understand why, but they knew it would somehow define the world in the years to come. After a long and tiring day, they went to bed and slept soundly throughout the night. Even thoughts of things to come did not hinder that. Their sleep was sweet and peaceful.

The ding of her phone awakened Ally, signaling a new email. It was from the office of Aissa Messai and contained her flight schedule. Her flight would leave the next morning. Messai planned to take part in the Temple dedication, spend the night in Jerusalem, then fly back to Belgium the next day and be ready to interview candidates for the position the following day.

Ally shuddered at the thought of sitting down with the man who was the Antichrist, but knew it was her purpose and one she had to fulfill. She made sure the others understood that. She would spend today with her family, and they would make the most of their time together. The possibility that they would not see each other again until they met after Jesus' return hung over them like a cloud, but they refused to allow it to spoil the day.

The Jewish Temple sat proudly atop the Mount, resplendent in all its glory. This time Messai led a procession of Jewish and Muslim leaders from the Mount of Olives, down the steep and narrow road which led to the valley below. They entered the Old City of Jerusalem through the Eastern Gate, beautifully restored and opened for this occasion. This led them straight into the Temple. It was a glorious and defining moment.

To the surprise of many, Messai relinquished the spotlight to the Rabbis and Imams. His moment was walking through that gate, a feat reserved only for the promised Messiah when he arrived. Then Messai defied every law and custom as he entered the Temple, walked to the back, parted the curtain and entered the Holy of Holies. No one could enter that sacred place except the High Priest, and then only one time each year. That stunned the Rabbis, but they dared not say anything to him.

They offered burnt offerings and conducted a ceremony of dedication that reminded the Jews of the same event which took place some 3,000 years earlier when King Solomon dedicated the first Temple. Rabbis and Imams spoke, and Jews and Muslims alike celebrated the day together. Messai stood and watched, knowing he had already fulfilled what he came to do this day. It was not the last time he would do it. He was eager for his day to come.

As the group watched in the shelter, Ben provided commentary throughout the event. "He is doing what only the Messiah can do," he explained. But Messai entering the Holy of Holies shocked even him. "He is saying that he is both the Messiah and High Priest," he said. "Now I understand the significance of this day for him. But does he understand who the real Messiah is?" They knew what he meant. The real Messiah is Jesus. The final battle was taking shape.

Ally did not sleep well that night. She dreamed again and again. The same dream as months before, being caught and eventually placed in the guillotine. But this time dreams of being Messai's personal assistant and sending intel back to the team followed it. By the time she awoke, she was ready.

Her family drove her to the airport and lingered with her until the last second before she walked through the gate, entered the boarding bridge, and after one final wave, disappeared from their sight. Mila wept. Bruno was shaking all over. They and the boys came together in a group embrace that defined the gravity of the day. They watched through the window until the plane was out of sight. Then they turned and departed the terminal, left the airport and walked to the car. There would be more moments like this one, but for now, this was the most difficult day of their lives.

Ally learned her tickets were in first class. She had never flown first class, but she could get used to this! It was the finest flight she had ever taken. When she arrived in Belgium, she found that her hotel was posh. She knew everything with Aissa Messai would be the best she had ever had. She was a common girl from a common family in a small town in Germany. But there would be nothing common about her life from this point on.

She settled in for the night and tried to prepare herself for the next day, although there was no real way to prepare. She would walk in and be herself. That would have to be good enough. All interviewees had received instructions to arrive by 8:00 a.m. and stay until Messai completed all the interviews. She would be there.

• • • • •

At 8:00 a.m. the next morning, Ally sat in a spacious room with 24 other girls. One thing was obvious to all of them. Every girl was blonde. Messai had an affinity for blondes; that was apparent. He had asked them all to include a recent photo of themselves. She had wondered about that, but now she saw why. The form required so much information that she thought surely he needed no more. They called the names in alphabetical order. No interview lasted over 15 minutes. Ally heard her name. She got up and walked into the spacious grand office of the Secretary-General. He sat behind a large, impressive desk.

"Come in and take a seat, Miss Fromm. I see you are from Germany, our neighboring country. You are young, but your answers on the application impressed me. I have only one question. What makes you want to serve as my personal assistant?"

Ally could not tell him the real reason and hoped he did not see through her answer. "Well sir, I believe I have spent my young life preparing for this. It is my reason for being. I too long for the peace and prosperity of the world

(She knew only Jesus would bring that) and will work alongside you to bring it about. *(The real reason was to gather intel and allow the Smyrnians to stay a step ahead of him.)* I will do everything I can to see that dream become a reality. I also believe I can make your life easier. Your role can be a stressful one. You need an assistant who can be serious when necessary, but who can also laugh and have fun. That is who I am. Not to mention, I am also a good cook." She smiled. "So sir, if you will give me this position, I will give it my all. And together, we can succeed." She relaxed and smiled.

"Thank you, Miss Fromm. May I call you Ally?" She nodded, and he smiled. "Well said, Ally; very well said."

Ally left his office, pleased with how she had done. "Lord, please give me this job," she prayed.

It had been six months since the Rapture. Only a half-year of the Tribulation had passed. The man of sin had been revealed. The barbaric nature of human beings had claimed countless lives. How could it possibly get worse? It was a question no one should ask. For what had been would pale compared to what would be. Who could survive? Time would tell.

CHAPTER 15

Mila was out with Beth and Miriam helping as a fellow humanitarian aid worker. She was still in the clear. No one had any idea who she was, or that she was a member of the Smyrnians, so for now, she needed no change in how she looked. Evan had still created fake IDs for her and Bruno. If someone discovered them, their real names would be unknown. However, if that happened, a new look would be necessary for both.

Helping people who were hurting was becoming harder by the day. Desperation was setting in, and desperate people resort to desperate measures when they reach low points in their lives. There were many families traumatized by the deaths of family members and friends at the hands of murderous individuals whose rage had come from somewhere other than inside them. Yes, some of those killings had come from addicts who were frantically searching for the drugs their bodies craved. Others were premeditated and carefully planned attacks against groups by mentally unstable or angry folks. But most came at the hands of normal people who inexplicably turned into raging lunatics in an instant.

On this day, the three of them were driving to a small town a couple hundred miles away where a disastrous school shooting had just taken place. A man had gunned down dozens of children only because of his anger at school leaders for expelling his child from school. With their credentials, Beth, Miriam and Mila could get into just about any crisis area. Their role was to help provide counseling to grief-stricken parents, school employees and fellow students. It was no simple task, but for them, it was an opportunity to meet needs, while simultaneously mentioning Jesus when opportunities arose.

As they neared the school, traffic suddenly came to an abrupt halt. Two police cars with sirens blaring came screaming by them on the other side of the road. From where they sat, they saw the vehicle involved in the incident. They were only a few cars back. They jumped out of their car and sprinted toward the scene. Two policemen stepped out to stop them. They were wearing their credentials around their necks and flashed them at the patrolmen.

"I am sorry, ladies. We allow no one other than first responders near the scene. Please return to your cars now," said one officer.

"We are with *People of Peace*, a humanitarian aid organization that works with people in crisis situations. We are on our way to help those involved in the school shooting that just happened. But this situation takes priority since we are here at the scene. If there are survivors or others who need help, please allow us to go be with them."

"What do you think, Dirk?" he asked his partner, as he looked closely at their badges.

"They seem official to me. I say let them go."

"Evan is good at what he does," Beth thought to herself as they accepted his fake credentials once again.

"Okay, we will let you go, but I must warn you, it is a gruesome scene. A case of road rage. A guy apparently lost his cool because they were going too slow and holding him up. He got out with a shotgun holding five shells. There were five people in the car. Must have been carpooling to work. Five shells were all he needed to do what he did. But we are told there is one survivor. Maybe you can help her somehow before the ambulance gets here."

"Thank you," Beth said as they ran for the car. One policeman radioed another at the scene to inform him they were coming and who they were.

The scene was almost more gruesome than they could bear. But as they opened a rear door and found the surviving woman trying to speak, their helping instincts kicked in.

"Ma'am, we are here to help you," said Beth.

"You may as well forget it," said one cop. "She won't last till the ambulance gets here."

The three paid him no attention. Miriam already had the woman's head in her hands, lifting it up. Mila was attempting to attend to her wound, but knew her help would not make a difference. Beth was down on her knees talking to the woman.

"Honey, can you hear me? We are here to help you. Just hold on; an ambulance is on the way."

The woman looked into her eyes. As she did, her eyes lit up, and she spoke.

"Beth Jennings. It is you!"

"Excuse me, ma'am, but my name is Kelly Davis. I am a humanitarian aid worker with P.O.P."

As a smile crossed the woman's face, she interrupted her in mid-sentence.

"No, it is you, Beth. I would recognize you anywhere. Please let me talk. I don't have long."

Beth motioned for Mila to stand guard so the patrolmen would not hear what was being said.

"You're right. It is me. What do you need to tell me?"

"The five of us... we watched your TV special. Thank you for being brave enough to tell us the truth. That night, each of us put our faith in Jesus. We emailed and registered on your website. Then we followed the instructions and started meeting as a group, studying the Bible together. We have also been reaching others..." She coughed. She was getting weaker.

"This was not a random case of road rage. That guy, he came to our meeting a few nights ago. He didn't believe in Jesus and got volatile before he left. We feared he might do something like this, but it is okay. We all knew where we were going if he did."

Beth held the woman's hand in hers as tears filled her eyes. They were tears of heartbreak for this awful thing that had happened to these five followers of Jesus. They were also tears of joy knowing they had put their faith in Jesus, and because they did, they would go to be with him. As the tears rolled from her eyes and down her cheeks, the woman continued.

"Beth, Jesus told me I would see you, and I was to give you a message. We have been studying the Bible day and night. Things will get much worse. Crises will come one after the other." She smiled before she said, "But I won't have to see them. I will be with Jesus."

Beth smiled back and nodded, tears now streaming from her eyes.

"Jesus said I was to tell you to get ready for what is coming. Store up food, water and supplies. Be prepared. The darkest days the world has ever seen are coming soon. Seven years..." As her voice trailed off, she left this world and went to be with Jesus.

Miriam lay the woman's head down gently on the seat of the car. The three of them rose to leave. The ambulance came flying in beside them. They walked away, motioning to the policeman that there were now no survivors, and continued toward their car. As they passed the two patrolmen on the way back, one said, "Told you it was an ugly scene. You wouldn't listen to us. I am guessing there are no survivors now."

"You are right," said Beth. "Thanks for letting us try."

As they got into their car, she told Miriam and Mila, "Our day is over. Let's get back to the shelter."

As soon as they arrived and walked inside, Blake said, "Well, you three are back early." Then seeing their faces, he said, "But I can tell there is a reason for that."

They shared the story of the woman. The room was quiet as they all allowed it to sink in for a few moments. Beth broke the silence.

"Blake, she recognized me."

"She recognized you? How? I mean, no one else has even come close to knowing who you are."

Kathie chimed in. "I thought Ally and I did an outstanding job on you. You don't look like Beth Jennings Thompson to me!"

"Well, she recognized me. But there may have been a reason for that. Jesus told her she would see me and was to give me a message."

"What message?" asked Anders.

"If all of you will sit down, and I will tell you."

Ally and the others who had gone through the interview process were expecting answers without delay. Aissa Messai was a decisive man. He was not likely to dwell long before deciding who would be his new personal assistant and what others would fill the remaining positions. The role of personal assistant was the most sought after, but there were no bad jobs in this organization. And Messai left no doubt that he would not tolerate jealousy and petty rivalries. Each of them must be grateful to have employment with him. He would not tolerate disloyalty either.

That part made Ally quiver. But she would be loyal at all costs... to *Jesus*. She checked her personal email again. She had a separate secure account that Evan set up for her. She would use it only for communicating with the Smyrnians. She could neither send nor receive emails to or from anyone other than them on the secure account.

Evan had warned her not to confuse the two accounts. She had now learned that all employees of Aissa Messai also shared a secure email account that was only available for use internally within the organization. Three accounts would be difficult to juggle. She would have to be as cautious as possible every single day not to send a message intended for the team to Messai.

There it was. A new message from the office of Aissa Messai. Her fingers trembled as she prepared to open it. This one email would determine the course of her life for the next six and a half years, or less. She hesitated briefly, then summoning the courage, she opened it.

"Dear Miss Fromm. It is our pleasure to inform you Mr. Messai has chosen you to serve in the all-important position of his Personal Assistant. Congratulations! Attached in multiple files you will find clear descriptions of every aspect of your job, and personal requirements, including the strict dress code, and others. Mr. Messai would like you in his office first thing tomorrow morning at 8:00. Do not be late. He is very excited about working with you."

She sat and stared at her computer screen in disbelief. She had asked Jesus to give her this position, but getting it was almost beyond belief. She needed to get started reading all the attachments. But first, she needed to call the team, including her parents, and let them know.

Beth stood before the group in the shelter. They fixed their eyes on her as she spoke.

"Things will get worse soon. Crises will come promptly. Each will follow on the heels of the preceding one. These will be the worst days the world has ever seen."

"No offense Beth, but we have already talked about that. We know full well that things are about to get worse," said Ben.

"But she said something else. We need to get ready. We must store up food, water and supplies. So my guess is, they will be in very short supply.

And it makes sense because we have had no rain for so long, the earth is parched. If the Spring rains do not come soon, it will get bad."

"Okay," said Evan. "We are long overdue a planning session, anyway. Let me get the whiteboard and let's list ways we will do those things. If Jesus sent us this message through a woman right before she died, we had better pay attention and get to work immediately. My guess would once again be that we do not have any time to waste. John, you are our resident survival expert. What are some things you have studied in the past?"

"Well, none of them are earth shattering. They are things we already know. The message is obviously a warning about an upcoming famine. There are two things about famines: One, lots of people die. And two, they are typically not brief. In the Bible, God warned Joseph that a famine was coming in the country of Egypt and would last seven years. There would be seven years of plenty during which Joseph was told to store up food to provide for the entire country during the seven years of famine. So, I am guessing we are being told this famine will last seven years. Sound familiar?"

"Very familiar," said Blake. "But we are already past our seven years of plenty. And we have to get ready!"

"That is correct, Blake. Instead of seven years to prepare, I am guessing we may have seven *weeks*, and possibly even seven *days*. So, we had better start now! The bigger thing is to plan exactly how we collect what we need. Let's start with water, since it is our greatest necessity."

Evan wrote *Water* on the board. "Obviously, we're supposed to know that there will be a shortage of water. What do we have that we can use to store water?"

"We need two types of water: drinking water and water for other essentials, such as bathing and washing clothes. Drinking water must be potable. That means as we store it, we must have a way to purify it. But it will need constant attention because it can still get contaminated and become unsafe for drinking. Has anyone seen anything we can use?"

"There is an old water tank in the barn," said Trey. "It is perfect for bath water and things like that."

Evan had listed the two types of water needed under the word Water. Underneath *Other Essentials* he wrote *Tank in the barn*. "That is a beginning," he said. "What else do we have?"

"I think we need to buy a large amount of the big water bottles businesses use for drinking water," said Ben. "We need suitable containers to hold it."

"Who will purchase those?" asked Evan.

Trey spoke up. "Rickie and I can fly out of state and buy as many as we can find. Then no one will be suspicious. If we bought them around here, everybody would wonder what we are up to."

"I agree," said Ben. "And we are forgetting one simple thing. We need to buy all the bottled water we can find. Trey and Rickie can bring a bunch back, and we can get more around here."

"We need to get on that tomorrow." John knew the urgency of these things.

"Okay. We will go tomorrow!" Rickie seemed proud to be a part of this survival effort.

"How about barrels?" asked Bruno. "We used to catch rainwater in barrels when I was growing up in Germany."

"There are three or four barrels in the barn loft," Beth offered. "If we can clean them up, they will be good for that."

"Yes, let's get those down and clean them up. We can use them to store water, but I doubt we will catch any rainwater. I think the woman told us it will not rain."

"You're right, John," said Evan. "So scrap the rainwater idea. But we still need to fill those barrels with water from the spring for other things."

They were all good with that part of the plan. Water supply settled, they talked about food.

"Two things," suggested John. "We need to purchase freezers and stock them with meat and other frozen foods. And we will need to grow indoor gardens. There is an art to that, but we can do it. We will have to ensure that temperatures stay around 70 degrees in that area and use fluorescent lighting. Then proper soil and compost are important. But if we get it right, we can grow a fine garden down here. I say we section off a specific spot for our garden in one bunker."

"You are right on the money," said Rickie, with his background in lawn and garden care. "We can grow great vegetables in a bunker, if we do it right."

"If I may," Mary interrupted, "we also need to buy up as many canned goods as we can. We have plenty of storage space. I have a bunch of canned goods at our house too, if we can get them. I raise a big garden and can lots of vegetables and juices every year. I also have jars and jars of jellies and jams. We need to bring all of them. They will keep in the right location down here. We can eat well on them for a year or two."

"Don't let her fool you," said John. "She has enough canned food to last us the entire seven years! The woman is a canning machine. I help her every year, so I can tell you all about that."

"We are on a roll here." Amelia was just getting into the mix. "I am a city girl, so I know nothing about raising a garden or canning. But I can shop with the best of them. Ladies, some of us need to go grocery shopping. We will stock this place with the essentials! We need a big vehicle to get it all back here. But no one should see us hauling all of that food."

"That's easy," said Trey. "My truck is big and has a bed cover. You can put a lot of food in it."

"I think we have enough," Evan beamed. "Everyone talk about who is doing what and let's get a 7-year survival plan in place."

Just as he finished, his phone chirped. Facetime call.

"It is Ally!" He almost yelled in his excitement. "Ally, we have been waiting to hear from you, especially your family. Talk to us! You look good all the way from Belgium."

"You are silly, Evan. You will never guess what happened. I got the Personal Assistant job!"

"No!" Mila uttered under her breath. But everyone heard her, including Ally.

"It is why I came here, Mommy. In fact, I believe I was born for this! This will allow me to be all the way on the inside and know every move Messai is planning to make. It will help all of you to be aware of his next moves before they happen. And you can stay safe."

"Little girl," said Bruno, "I am proud of you and scared for you at the same time. Will you promise me you will be careful?"

"I will be as careful as I can, daddy. This is a dangerous job, but I assure you I am more than ready for it. And I will keep you guys posted every single day."

John jumped in to inform his former student about the coming famine and need to prepare for it.

"I don't think we will have to worry about that here," she said. "Messai has everything he needs for years to come. I just wish I had a way to get some of it to you. But I can't. So, please store up as much as you can. We need all of you to stay alive and healthy!"

"We'll do that," John stated. "We have a secret weapon!" He pulled Mary into view of the computer. She smiled and waved at Ally.

"And your makeover partner will be hard at work too," said Kathie, also waving. "Some of these people need it." She laughed, and so did Ally.

"When do you start?" asked Evan.

"I have to be in his office at 8:00 in the morning."

The conversation continued until they ended it by praying for Ally.

Promptly at 8:00 a.m. the next morning, Ally walked into Aissa Messai's office dressed according to code. She wore a knee-length navy dress with heels and her hair and makeup perfectly done. It even stunned her when she saw herself in the full-length mirror earlier. She had never been one to dress up. *Tomboy* is how she would have described herself. Now she stared at a different version of herself, hidden inside her entire life. Messai had seen it in her the previous day when she sat in his office. She was now the businesswoman, not just beautiful, but gorgeous, even stunning.

Before she sat down, the look on his face revealed that he was happy with what he saw. His eyes looked her up and down as she stood before him, with a look that made her feel very uncomfortable and somewhat fearful of the most powerful man in the world. But she refused to let him see that. The look on *her* face was one of confidence and of a woman who was fully secure in who she was and in her ability to serve in this important role for the Secretary-General of the United Nations.

"You look amazing, my dear," he smiled. "Perfect for my personal assistant. I could not be more pleased. Now, are we ready to get started with our work? We have many important things on our agenda. I assume you read all the information I gave you."

"Yes sir, I did. And thank you for the complement. I want to look my best. I understand that my appearance and actions reflect on you and even impact the pursuit of your goals. Know that I will be exactly who I need to be every single day."

"Be sure to live by those statements, Ally, and we will get along just fine. We will accomplish the goal we both share, peace and prosperity in our world." She smiled in agreement. Her goal for those things were far different from his, and hers would come to pass. "Did you receive a copy of my calendar, and do you now have those things on your calendar, as well?"

"Yes sir. I have written all of them on a desk calendar and recorded them on my computer, tablet and phone with reminders set to ensure that we will miss none of them."

"Well done, Ally! I want to cover possibly the most important item before we go farther. You will often be a part of highly confidential meetings, situations and events. Did you sign the confidentiality agreement, and if so, do you understand what you signed and why it is so vital?"

"Absolutely, sir. Confidentiality is very important to me. I will keep those things strictly between us and any others who may need to be aware of them."

She was choosing her words carefully. For her, *us* and *others* included the Smyrnians. She would share any information that would be vital to the cause with them moments after she received it. Yes, she was good at this spy stuff. She always had been, and she would be now when it mattered most. She was confident in her abilities.

"Thank you. Now, first things first. I have scheduled a news conference at the top of the hour to introduce you to the world. They need to see my assistant for themselves. I know they will also be captivated by your beauty and thrilled with your intelligence. I am proud of you Ally and excited to have you on board and show you off to the world today. I hope we will have many years together."

"Six and a half years at most," she thought to herself. Then she realized that she needed to let the team back in the states know about the news conference so they could watch! There would be no break before it began, so she would have to find a few free minutes to send a quick text. She had to admit, Messai was charming. It was easy to see how people fell under his spell. She felt it pulling at her mind. She silently prayed for protection.

"A penny for your thoughts."

"Excuse me, sir?"

"A penny for your thoughts. You seemed lost in thought for a moment. You are not experiencing some anxiety because of the news conference, are you?"

"Oh, no, sir. Not at all. I was just thinking how fortunate I am to be in this position. I look forward to being introduced to the world as your new assistant!"

She said that with excitement in her voice and could tell it pleased him and put him at ease.

"Very well." Then almost as if reading her mind, he asked, "Do you need a few moments to freshen up before the camera crew and reporter come in?"

"If you do not mind, sir, that would be great. I want to look my best. I will not take long."

"Ally," he said with a smile, "there is no need for concern about how you look. You look stunning, my dear. You will be the envy of the world after today."

"Thank you again, sir. You know how to flatter a girl." She smiled shyly.

It was important to win his trust and make him believe that her commitment to him was genuine. She played the part well. Spies can do that.

"I will return in ten minutes, at most."

She left the room and hurried to the bathroom. Entering a stall, she pulled her secure Smyrnian phone from her purse and sent a quick text.

News conference. 9am. 3am ur time. Introducing me. Thought u may want to watch. Have to go. TTYL.

•　　•　　•　　•　　•

It was 2:35 a.m. in Missouri. Evan was sound asleep when his phone dinged with a text. Ally! What was wrong? He fumbled in the dark to grab it, knocked it to the floor, then picked it up. He read the text, still trying to get himself awake. He groggily thought about replying before he saw her final words. She did not have time to text more. He looked at his phone for the time. 2:40. The conference was in 20 minutes!

He jumped from his bed and sent a group text summoning everyone to the living room area of bunker one and informing them about Ally's text. Then he ran to each room in the bunker, yelling as he ran for all of them to look at his text. He sprinted out and did the same in bunkers two and three.

When he made it back to the living room, all of them were running in, out of breath as they did. Blake already had the news pulled up on the computer and connected wirelessly to a large screen TV. Evan did a head count and found everyone present. It was 2:55.

"Let's say a quick prayer for her," Mila breathed.

"Let me pray for my little girl," said Bruno.

They bowed their heads, and he said a one minute prayer. "Jesus, help my little girl right now. She is in the enemy's presence. Give her peace and the words to say, if he asks her to speak. Protect and guide her, Jesus. We ask this in your name. Amen." His tears were genuine as he spoke.

The Belgian reporter appeared on the screen and spoke in broken, but very good English.

"Good morning, Ladies and Gentlemen of the world. We are coming to you live from the office of UN Secretary-General Aissa Messai. He has called a special news conference to introduce us to his new Personal Assistant. I have not met her yet, so I will meet her along with all of you. The Secretary-General has a busy schedule, so without further ado, let us begin. I will hand things over to Mr. Messai to make this important announcement and introduction."

Sitting behind his impressive desk, Aissa Messai exuded prominence as he spoke.

"Thank you, Mr. Laurent, and good morning to all of you who are watching around the world. It is my pleasure this morning to introduce you to the young lady I chose as my Personal Assistant. She will be in charge of all matters related to my daily schedule and personal duties. And she will be by my side at all of my public appearances, so get used to seeing a lot of her. She is an impressive young woman, intelligent and strong. I am very excited about working with her daily. It is my distinct pleasure to introduce you to Miss Ally Fromm."

Ally walked over to join him as he arose from his chair and came around to greet her. The entire group of Smyrnians in the shelter stared in disbelief.

"That is Ally?" Evan asked.

"I can't believe that is my little girl," said Bruno.

The entire group sat in shock at the person they were seeing on the screen. As the camera panned in close enough to see her face more, it was definitely her, but she was not the Ally they knew. Gone was the tomboy, with her blue jeans and sneakers. The woman on the screen was stunningly beautiful and immaculately dressed. Evan said it for all of them. "Wow..."

Messai gave her the opportunity to speak. "Ally, can you briefly tell us why you applied for this position and why you wanted to serve as my Personal Assistant?"

"Yes, Mr. Messai. It would be an honor to do that. Good morning, ladies and gentlemen. It is my pleasure to speak with you this morning and give you a glimpse into who I am and how I will serve you by serving the Secretary-General. Mr. Messai and I share the same goal, namely the peace and prosperity of the world. We both desire to do everything we can to bring those two things to every nation and person, and we will endeavor to make that dream a reality. It is coming, so I ask you to join us in these efforts. We may see difficult times as we pursue our goals, but be patient and hold on, watch and wait, because I know without a doubt we will see it happen in a few short years, if not sooner. I look forward to meeting some of you as we travel around the world. I say to all of you, keep the faith, keep believing and seek truth. If times get difficult, do not focus on what is. Instead, look forward to what will be. When that comes, all of us who have overcome will celebrate together. Now, I will turn things back over to Mr. Messai."

"Thank you, Miss Fromm. Ladies and Gentlemen, I believe you can see why I chose this young woman for this important role. I am sure you saw the same things in her I saw. I will keep her close by my side and together we will make a difference in our world. Thank you for watching."

That was it. Succinct, but special. The reporter closed things out, and the conference was over.

"I can't believe what I just saw and heard," exclaimed Bruno. "That was my little girl. She was so beautiful and brilliant. But I fear the real reason Messai wants her. We must all pray that she is very careful. What is it that Jesus called it? Wise as a serpent and harmless as a dove? That is what my little girl needs to be. I only hope she can be."

"God has prepared her for this moment, Bruno. He will take care of her. She affirmed to Evan and me her calling and commitment to being a Smyrnian spy on our drive from Chicago to New York six months ago, not long after all of us had believed in Jesus. From what I heard, she is ready." John had seen what was in Ally and knew it was more than even she realized. But his confident words to her father betrayed the fear he felt inside. She would serve well, but the one she would serve was not Secretary-General Aissa Messai, but King Jesus.

There was no use going back to bed, so the group got an early start on their work preparing for the lean times that were coming. Mary and Kathie whipped up an amazing breakfast. They ate and were ready to go by daylight. They divided into teams, then each got to work on their assignments. The younger group was carrying water from the spring and filling the tank. That seemed like an eternal task, but the workers were many. The seven Abramson kids, two Fromm boys and Evan equaled ten. They found enough buckets for all of them to carry at the same time. They worked hard, and it was not long before water was rising in the tank.

Trey and Rickie flew out of state in search of large quantities of bottled water and five gallon water bottles. They would fill those from the Spring and carry them to the bunker that had a room reserved for drinking water, food and gardens. Bruno, Blake, John and Ollie were getting the barrels down from the barn loft and cleaning them up to get them ready for water too. They were all hopeful the spring would continue to flow, even during the severe drought. But it was already gradually slowing, so that did not seem likely. It made their water collection process even more urgent.

Beth, Amelia and Kathie drove Trey's truck to Sam's Club in Springfield to fill every inch with non-perishable food items purchased in bulk. Miriam and Mila rode with John and Mary to their house to bring the assortment of canned goods to the shelter. They looked so amazing they wanted to dig in to them right then! The teamwork was incredible. Everyone pitched in and filled their role. The work was being done. That would bode well for the future.

Evan wished to himself that Ally was here to be a part of it. He had seen something in her as she appeared on TV he had not seen before. How had he missed her beauty? She was his best friend, but at that moment, he wondered if she might have been more. He chastised himself for having the thought. He had such fear that Messai may want her for more than her intelligence. He saw the way he looked at her, even on the screen. Evan cared deeply for Ally. He wished he was there to protect her. He would miss her more than any of them could understand. And he feared for her more than he would show. How would she survive as a spy living and working under

Messai's nose? How would any of them survive? It was almost a guarantee, he thought, all of them would not. He hoped he was wrong.

They continued until they prepared as best they could. Food and water storage and gardening consumed half of one bunker, and that required creative use of space to fit it all in. For now, they would need to focus on the more important matters of spreading the word and going to war with the enemy. His name was Aissa Messai, and his power came from Satan. He outmatched them in their own strength. But there was one on their side who was greater. And the Bible promised they would be more than conquerors through him. They had to believe that.

Ally was proud of herself, and Messai was happy with her performance during the news conference. He had made that clear. He would take her out for a nice dinner at the most expensive restaurant he could find. There would also be a nice bonus in her first paycheck. She was already making more money than she ever dreamed possible. She would have to be careful that those things did not distract her from the real cause. She remained uncomfortable with the way Messai looked at her. She must keep her distance, even as she stayed by his side. What she said during the conference was true. Things would get difficult, but for those who believe in Jesus, tragedy would end in triumph. She longed to survive and see his triumphant return. She wanted that for all the Smyrnians. But it seemed less likely now than it ever had.

CHAPTER 16

While the survival preparation was going on, Ben was under orders to stay in his studio and get everything ready to reach out to the Jews of the world. By the time they finished, so had he. Everything was professionally installed and ready to test. He created his own network, which anything Messai might try could not hack or stop. He geared it specifically toward his own people. He would teach them that Jesus was the true Messiah, and many of them would believe in him. He subtitled the pastor's video in Hebrew so they would understand.

But the biggest key was sharing his own story of life as a strict Jew who saw the truth and turned to faith in Jesus. He would recite the prayers and read the Old Testament prophecies from the Hebrew translation so they would understand the depth of his Jewish background. His goal was to raise up an army of Jewish believers in Jesus. There was no better man for the job than him.

He would begin tomorrow promoting a new network only for Jews. The live broadcasts would take place every day at 7:00 a.m. Central Time. That would be 3:00 p.m. in Israel, but they would be ready to watch, or could replay it later. He chose that time because Jesus died on the cross at 3:00 p.m. and rose from the grave on the third day. The number three also held great significance in the Old Testament scriptures for the Jews. Noah had three sons. Three visitors appeared to Abraham to announce that Sarah would give birth to Isaac, the promised heir through whom their inheritance came. The Prophet Jonah was in the great fish's belly three days and nights. He now knew that the number three included the three persons of the Trinity: Father, Son and Holy Spirit. And he understood the importance that number carried with it into the New Testament narrative. Yes, 3:00 p.m. Israeli time was the right time to broadcast.

The next item on Blake's agenda was getting his source to the shelter. They needed him. Ally needed him. If anyone could get the inside scoop on activity within Messai's organization, it was him. Trey was ready to get in the air again, bound for New York to get the man. Blake was on the phone with the source before daylight, planning for that to happen.

"I know it has been a few days, but so much has happened that we are just now able to get Trey up there to pick you up. The good news is, you missed out on a lot of hard work."

"I am not afraid of hard work, but I am better at doing what I do well, getting the inside scoop on important stuff from people who do not want me to have it. You know I can stay under the radar, so I should be able to get right on that and stay on top of it. One important note: you said your pilot would get *up* here to pick me up. Be careful, Blake. That tells me you are *down* south somewhere. People like me pick up on little things like that. It gives us details we can put together and track you down. Those are the kinds of things I listen for as I gather information."

"Man, I have to be more careful, don't I? Honestly, I wouldn't have even thought about something like that. But I admit, I enjoy getting inside your head and learning a bit about how you operate. We need that. I will fill you in on a lot of things when you get here."

"I am ready to get started. Once you fill me in, I need to get out there and do my thing. I wish I could come today. I have everything packed, and I am more than ready."

Blake glanced at Trey, who was hearing the conversation. He mouthed, "I am ready to go!"

"Trey can leave for the airport now, if you want him to."

He turned and asked Trey, "What time can you be in New York? And what airport?"

"By the time I can get to the airport, have the plane ready and get clearance, counting three hours flight time, it will be probably be 12:00-1:00 when I get there. If he can be there, I can fly into Teterboro like I did before and do a quick fuel and go. That will save time. I think we can be back in Springfield by 5:00-6:00."

"I heard that. I will be there and waiting!"

"I will grab some donuts and a mug of coffee and get on the road."

"All right!" Blake said to his source. "It looks like I will see you this evening!"

Trey already had donuts and coffee in hand, had grabbed a jacket and was walking toward the door by the time Blake ended the call. He had to get the source to Missouri. He would be a huge addition to the team.

The shelter was ready to go, stocked for the lean times that were coming. Jesus had warned them through a woman who was dying as the result of a brutal shotgun attack on her and four other followers of Jesus as they were driving down the road. Their supplies should easily last for the entire seven years. They could stay in the shelter, be safe and have everything they needed. But they would not do that. As dangerous as it was, they had to be out in the world helping people and fighting an unbeatable foe. It was time to go to war, time to leave their safe place and walk into danger beyond their wildest expectations. Each of them who needed a change in the way they look had gotten one. They were all gathered, with Ben being the judge of whether their makeovers would keep them anonymous. Beth began by poking fun at Blake.

"Blake, are you in there?" she asked, pulling his long hair around his fully bearded face.

"I'm in here. I'm not sure I like it, but it appears I have to live with it for six and a half years."

"Let me get a look at everyone," said Ben. "I want to make sure your new looks can keep your identity secret. Blake, surely no one will recognize you as Blake Thompson under all that hair and your face covered by that scraggly beard. If I hadn't watched them grow like that, I wouldn't believe it either. It seems strange for the guy who always had to have his hair perfect."

"Thanks, Ben. I will take that as a complement, I think."

"And John, you are impressive with your gray hair and nicely trimmed beard. I know you can pass for anyone other than Professor John Baldwin."

"Why, thank you, sir. My name is Alistair Murphy. I am an attorney from Texas. Pleased to make your acquaintance."

"Ollie, old friend, you look for all the world like Sherlock Holmes in your raincoat and deerstalker hat. The mustache, beard and long sideburns are a nice touch too. And the glasses may be the key."

"Thank you, Bloke. Only I don't know this Ollie chap you mentioned. I am Hugh Walker, a detective from Great Britain. I can't hide the accent, but at least I have changed the look."

"I think it will work. Amelia, you are a member of Parliament? I would never guess that!"

"No sir, I am not. I am Charlotte Helmsley, Hugh's sidekick." She winked at Ollie. "He likes my curly bright red hair, don't you honey?"

"Yes, I do. I have always wanted a fiery redhead!"

"Ollie and I will work together most of the time. Just the way we like it!"

"Okay, you two are worse than Blake and Beth were when they got together. Give us a break." Anders rolled his eyes and shook his head before breaking out into a big grin. "No, it is nice to have a little twitterpation going on again."

"Anders, you have a bit of a makeover too. Nobody knows who you are, but then we can't have you recognized as Blake's cameraman, either. So we have given you a new name and accent."

"Yes sir. Since my parents were Dutch immigrants to the United States, I am going back to my heritage. I can speak Dutch with the best of them. And my name is Steffen Janssen." His Dutch was as good as if he had lived in the Netherlands or Northern Belgium his entire life. That would serve him well when he got to be there.

"So, Kathie, we get to you. Messai and his AMPP men believe you are dead. They think you died in that truck crash with John. Both of you must remain incognito. I hope Beth is not envious of your long blonde hair, especially after you cut all of hers off." Ben glanced at Beth with a concerned look. She just shrugged her shoulders and frowned.

"No sir, she is the one who suggested I go blonde and let it grow long." Now Beth smiled at Ben.

"I'm glad to hear that!" he said. "You look the part in your business suit with your satchel."

"Only my name is not Kathie. I am Susan Murphy, a financier. I am also from Texas, like my husband." She smiled at John. "I think I can get on the inside with a man so into money, like Aissa Messai, don't you? John is along to take care of me as he promised Doc he would."

"Yes, I do. Yours will be a dangerous job, if you try to do that. Okay, everyone, I think we are ready to go. I will continue growing my facial hair and curling my sideburns to look the part of a Jewish rabbi. You can't stop me from visiting Jerusalem from time to time. I hope Miriam and I can meet with some new Messianic Jews there when we go. I must be the leader of my people around the world, but especially there. She is Abigail Isaacs, and I am Rabbi Avraham Isaacs. I can't wait to get to Jerusalem. But my hair, beard and sideburns will need to grow a little more before I go. However, I will start broadcasting to my people right away. I think we are ready!"

Trey was in flight to New York. It was a beautiful sunny day with no rain or wind in the forecast, a perfect day for flying. As he flew, he reflected on how much his life had changed in the last few months. It had been easy for him to put his faith in Jesus. To begin with, he trusted Beth Jennings. He had been friends with her, and her family, for years. But he had also sensed there was something not right about Messai from the first time he saw the man on TV. He felt something he did not like when he spoke, something bad, evil.

The disappearances had bothered him, too. He could not make himself buy into the theory of an alien invasion, although he tried. Like Beth in her parents' house, he had felt good for the people taken, as strange as that was. Something about them made him feel warm inside. He often wished he had gone with them. That would have been foolishness in the thinking of everyone else in the world, but not to him.

When he flew Blake, Beth and Anders from Missouri to New York, they did not know he paid attention to the calming of the storm. But he did. It was like nothing he had ever experienced in his days of flying. To go from the roughest storm he had ever flown in and ready to make a crash landing to instantly being in calm air with a smooth flight? That did not happen without a cause. And the cause could not have been any natural occurrence. "It had to be *supernatural*," he had thought to himself. He had never been a believer in Jesus or church guy, but he had not ruled out the possibility of a God either.

The moment Beth explained it all to him and talked about Jesus, he got it. So he prayed to Jesus and asked him to be his Savior. He had experienced nothing like that. Jesus changed his life and gave him a purpose. He had flown combat missions in the military; now he was getting to do that for the Smyrnians. Every time he got in the air, he was excited. But the missions were about to get dangerous, possibly more dangerous than any he had flown in combat. He saw New York in the distance and knew Teterboro was not far. The source would be there to meet him. If all Blake had said about him was true, this was a guy Trey wanted to get to know! He started his descent into Teterboro.

Aissa Messai had called a special meeting of the United Nations Security Council in Geneva, Switzerland. Ally sent a memo to the members of the Council stating the reason for the meeting.

"The Charter of the UN empowers the Secretary-General to 'bring to the attention of the Security Council any matter which in his opinion may threaten the maintenance of international peace and security.' Mr. Messai has discovered a highly dangerous threat which we must deal with immediately. Your attendance at this urgent meeting is mandatory."

Beyond that memo, Messai had not made Ally aware of the reason for this meeting. It was unusual for her not to have specific details before every meeting of which Messai was a part. But this time, he had withheld that information. He had not offered it, and she had not asked for it. But she would be in the room with him and the council members, so she would know before this day was over. The meeting began with the chairman of the council calling it to order and saying a few words before turning things over to Messai.

When her boss spoke, Ally thought his voice sounded different from other times since she had worked with him. It was not the pleasant and charming voice to which she and the world were accustomed. If she had been listening outside the door, she would not have recognized who was speaking. The best description she could come up with was a low growl, almost evil. That should not surprise her, but it did. She wanted to get up and run, but she fought the urge. She had to stay in the room and not give him any indication that she was anything more than a loyal assistant who had his and the world's best interest at heart.

"Members of the council," he said in a low, gravelly tone, "according to our charter, it is my responsibility to bring to your attention any matter which threatens the maintenance of international peace and security. I have uncovered such a matter. We must deal with it immediately, and *harshly*, if we need to do so."

Ally felt her skin crawl, somehow knowing of what was coming next.

"There is a group of people who call themselves the *Smyrnians*."

She felt as if she may throw up. But she had to sit still and show no reaction.

"These people have been working against all of us and are attempting to turn the people of the world against the very things we are trying to accomplish. We have sought to stop them from these actions, but they continue poisoning the minds of gullible people and leading them into their web of divisiveness."

"I have already instructed the men from AMPP to find and arrest them. You will immediately recognize the names of their leaders: Blake Thompson and Beth Jennings, TV reporters from New York City. Their special programs which aired on February 2 created worldwide havoc and brought millions to their cause. Since that day, their numbers have multiplied exponentially."

"If we do not deal with them, they will continue to multiply until it becomes almost impossible to stop them. Fortunately, they have not gained a foothold in our shining example of what can be if we work together: the Middle East. I am asking for your approval to begin immediately taking any measures necessary to stop this threat."

"We have seen some perish already. John Baldwin, a professor from Chicago, and two others who had just joined them died in a fiery crash while fleeing from AMPP. Their intent was only to bring them into custody. Their choosing to flee proves they stand opposed to our goal of peace and prosperity in the world."

"We suspect some others and will seek anyone we believe to be one of them. We will search out their groups that meet around the world and stop them from spreading any further. That is the sole purpose of our time together today. I ask that you vote to grant me your approval."

Ally sat in silence, numbed by what she had just heard. She knew what was coming next. Messai was too powerful and persuasive to turn down. He held power over these pawns who were only there to do his every bidding.

The chairman spoke. "The Secretary-General is right. If he has found this group to be divisive and dangerous and a threat to international security, and if they spread that rapidly, we must deal with them immediately. Is there a motion that we grant him this authority?"

One made the motion, and another seconded. Discussion centered on ways they should carry out the order. When the meeting ended, they had given Messai full power to make those decisions and use AMPP to execute them by any means necessary to stamp out the group and put an end to the threat. Messai did not stick around after the meeting. He hurried to the limo that would take Ally and him to the airport. As they talked, his voice returned to normal and his demeanor to his usual charming self. Ally was getting a closeup look into the mind of a monster.

Trey left the plane for refueling and walked into the small airport to meet his guest. Instead, a group of men dressed in black suits greeted him.

"Trey Butler?"

"Yes, that is me. Is something wrong?"

"Come with us, please."

He knew who the men were. Aissa Messai's Peace Patrol. And he was well aware that their intentions had nothing to do with peace. But he had no choice except to go with them. As they walked, he looked around, wondering if any of the faces he was seeing may be the source. The men led him into a small room and asked him to take a seat. The military had prepared him for times of interrogation, so he was calm as they began.

As he walked outside the airport, the source hurriedly dialed Blake's number.

"Hey buddy. Did Trey make it on time? I can't wait to see you!"

"Yes, Blake, he made it right on the time he said he would. But things are not well. Four AMPP men met him as soon as he walked in and led him away. I couldn't hear what they were saying, but it didn't look good. We need to do something fast. Do you have any suggestions?"

"Let me think. Do you have a relationship with any powerful people in New York?"

"Yes! I am good friends with Senator Rosenberg. He will do just about anything I ask him to do. I don't know why I hadn't thought of that. I have to get off here and call him."

He hung up, leaving Blake feeling useless from 1,200 miles away. He did the only thing he knew to do: call the whole group together for prayer. They needed all of them praying together.

As they began, Evan's phone rang with Ally's ringtone. He said, "It's Ally. I have to get this."

"Put it on speaker," said Ben. "This is likely something we all need to hear."

He did, and Ally spoke softly, so softly they had to gather closely around Evan to hear.

"I have to talk fast. I was just in a special called meeting of the UN Security Council. They granted Messai permission to hunt you guys, and anyone else suspected of being a Smyrnian down, and bring you to justice using whatever means he deems necessary. You know what that means. You must be careful! Here he comes. I have to go." The call ended.

"That is why they have Trey!" said Beth in a frightened tone.

"We have to pray for the source to get in touch with the senator, and for him to help."

They started praying passionately, asking Jesus to intervene in Trey's situation at Teterboro.

The source's call went unanswered. He called again, then again. On the fourth call, the senator answered. "This must be important for you to call four times."

"It is, sir. I need your help now, right now. I am at Teterboro getting ready to board a charter flight and AMPP has just detained the pilot. I am telling you, this guy is 100% on the up and up. Can you please come or call and stop them? They must have him confused with someone else. Please sir, I need this flight to leave on time. And we are already late."

As they talked, Trey was being grilled by the men from AMPP.

"Sir, we have been watching your flight activity and found it to be unusual. We are investigating a group who pose a dire threat to peace and security. The UN Security Council gave the Secretary-General permission to put an end to their threat. You would not be a part of this group, would you? Let's just say your activity is *suspicious*."

"I assume you are referring to the Smyrnians. I have heard of them. I think everyone has. I have just been very busy, especially since the ban on flights ended. I can tell you I am glad to have the business. The ban put a hurt on me financially, if you know what I mean."

"Well Mr. Butler, we need you to come to the city with us. There is more we need to discuss."

Loud rapping on the door interrupted them. Someone was knocking impatiently. One of the AMPP guys asked, "Who is it? We are on official business with AMPP. Leave now. You are interfering with our ability to carry out our assigned task."

"This is Senator Rosenberg. I command you to open this door now!"

The man looked at the others. "Maybe we had better do what he says. The senator is a powerful man."

"He is not more powerful than Messai," said another. "I don't want to answer to him if we fail."

"Open this door now, or I will ask the officers with me to break it down."

The door opened. "I know this man," said the senator. "He is no threat to anyone's security. Release him now!"

"But sir," said one man. "We have our orders."

"Yes, you do. *I* am ordering you to let him go. He has a job to do, and you are holding him up."

Acting like little puppies with their tails tucked between their legs, they reluctantly complied.

"Now, leave this airport and do not interfere with this man's duty anymore." They hesitated. "I said leave, now!"

Once again they obeyed. When they left, Trey extended his hand to the senator and said, "I appreciate your help, sir. I don't know what they were thinking."

"Look son, I don't know you, but I know him." He pointed at the source. "And if he says you are okay, I will take his word for that. Now the best thing you can do is get on your plane and get out of here. Those guys do not mess around. They may come back with reinforcements."

Trey and his passenger sprinted for the plane and were in the air within minutes. As soon as they leveled out, he called Blake.

"They know who I am, so that means they know where I live and what airport I use. There is no way we can land there tonight. In fact, we probably shouldn't do that in the foreseeable future. Here is what I need you to do. I will fly into a small airport in Tulsa. We will spend the night. Send someone to pick us up at 8:00 a.m. I will leave the plane in a hangar there. I have done that before, so it will not be a big deal. They can't know we landed anywhere close to the shelter."

"I will come," said Blake. "I need to test this new look, anyway."

"That is fine. Just be careful and inconspicuous. I will let you know where we are."

Blake told the others what was going on, and Beth agreed to go with him. Both of their looks needed testing. If they did this without being recognized, they would be ready to go into battle. This may be just what they needed.

"Come, Ally. We must be going. Our pilot is waiting for us. Just one thing. Do I need to reiterate your commitment to confidentiality after our little meeting today?"

"Absolutely not, sir. I understand that fully. What happened in Geneva stays in Geneva."

He smiled at her attempt at humor. "Yes, it does, Miss Fromm. Yes, it does. You are the jewel in my crown. I am fortunate to have you. We must spend more personal time together after we return home." He smiled and took her hand as they walked to the plane. She had no choice but to walk with him hand-in-hand. She feared what may happen when they got back to Belgium.

Blake addressed the group at the shelter. "Look, we all knew this was coming. As we have said before, it is what we signed up for. I hope we will not forget who is in charge of these seven years. It is not Messai; it is Jesus. He started it when he took his people home. We were all left behind because we had not believed in him or given ourselves to him. He will finish it when he comes again to defeat Messai at the end of these seven years."

"In the meantime, we have to trust him and fight the enemy with everything we have in us. Beth and I will get Trey and the source tomorrow morning. Hopefully, that will go smoothly. In case it does not, I urge you to fight on and fight well. I trust that we will be back here, along with our teammates. All of you will be here praying for us. I know we can count on you for that."

"Blake, let me say this," said Beth. "We know everything, and I mean everything, is about to break. All the things the woman said will come true. I can sense that, and I am certain all of you can too." They all nodded in agreement. "It will affect the whole earth."

"The earth will be *shaken*." John interrupted her.

"You are right, John. It will be shaken in more ways than one, and we are ready. But we need to remember to pray for Ally, too. She is living with the enemy. And the enemy is evil."

"Have you noticed how much the violence has slowed?" asked John. "After only a few days they are saying the earth has returned to peace. I believe it is the calm before the storm. And the storm will be vicious. We may be the only ones who know it is coming. We need to let all the believers know. Evan, get it on the website in large font. It is coming, and it is very close."

Ally's plane ride back with Messai was uncomfortable. He had hardly taken his eyes off her. She feigned being sleepy, but opened her eyes occasionally to see him staring at her with a smile. She closed her eyes and pretended to be asleep for the rest of the flight.

The next morning Blake and Beth were up bright and early and off to Tulsa to get Trey and the source. It was a three-hour drive and possibly longer because they would drive the speed limit or slightly below. They held hands between them as he drove. She whispered, "I love you, Mr. Thompson. No matter what happens, remember that I love you with my whole being."

"I love you more than life itself, Beth. Wherever you are and whatever you are going through, let my love get you through it."

"I will," she said softly. On they rode until they reached an area near the hotel where the two men had stayed. They had held each other's hands the entire drive. Both knew they would never let go. They saw the men standing on the sidewalk a few blocks from the hotel. They pulled over and Trey and the source quickly got into the car. They looked carefully to make sure no one was following them as they drove up. Trey assured them they had taken every precaution to see that that no one had followed them either.

They made it back to the shelter safely, although somewhat shaken by what had happened. As they sat and talked that night, they spoke about what was coming. They were not sure what it would look like. But they were certain it was getting close.

Messai walked to the back of the plane with his phone, but Ally could hear him speaking. "How could you let them get away? Do you know where they went? Well, find out! I do not care if he was a senator. I am the leader of the world! Now find them, whatever it takes," he yelled. Not knowing which of them it had been, Ally silently thanked Jesus for protecting the Smyrnians.

CHAPTER 17

The world's economy had been strong following Aissa Messai's election as the Secretary-General of the United Nations. It was, in fact, a time of unprecedented prosperity, just what he had promised he would bring. For a few months, life was good. It was so good that people would not have believed it, if they had not been living it. Unemployment was almost a thing of the past for those who wanted to work and could work. Poverty level income jumped to middle class wages overnight. The middle class had more money than they ever had. More money was being spent than ever before, and businesses were flourishing. The housing and automobile markets were booming. The lending market was strong, with the number of people borrowing money at an all-time high. Optimism was soaring.

But that seemed to change overnight. The violence, brutality, rioting, looting and the deaths of millions of people, many of them followers of Jesus, had taken its toll. Businesses were closing. Prices fell sharply as deflation forced companies into bankruptcy. Investors panicked and a sell-off left the stock market in free fall. Thousands of individuals lost everything. The economic disaster led to plummeting incomes. Unemployment quadrupled. Housing prices declined drastically, and new homeowners found their home's value at half the amount they had financed. They could neither sell, nor make their payments, thus driving many into foreclosure. Families who had lived in nice houses were suddenly homeless.

Because of the collapse of the housing market and failing businesses, the banking system also collapsed. With no homes or money, people had nowhere to go. That led to alleyways flooded with people living in cardboard boxes. Others made their homes under bridges. Tent communities sprang up outside larger cities. Hunger and starvation became rampant. People rummaged through dumpsters and garbage cans in search of even the tiniest morsel, with no concern for sanity and disease. Fathers desperate to feed their children took food however they could get it, even if that meant stealing or killing. Extreme human suffering replaced abundance and success. Good times turned into hard times. Things had fallen apart as rapidly as they had come together. The woman's warning was coming true. And it was happening worldwide.

For Beth, Miriam and Mila, their tasks had gotten tougher when they traveled to help people. Most were in dire need. Beth longed to bring families who were broke and homeless to the shelter, but she could not take the chance of compromising their safe place. Seeing children living in such deplorable conditions broke her heart. And that was in smaller towns. It was far worse in the cities. Food prices soared. Only those who were wealthy could afford to buy food. Others went hungry. That was about to get worse.

Ally saw it too as she traveled with Messai. He would often make a point of visiting the tent cities or walking the streets, speaking to those lying beside them, dirty and hungry. It seemed they hung onto every word he spoke as he promised this was temporary and would end in prosperous times. She saw the hope in their eyes as they listened. She knew prosperous times *would* come with the return of Jesus. And those good times would last. For his followers, they would last forever. He often asked her, "Ally, do you believe prosperous times will come again?" Her answer was always a resounding "yes!"

Still, it was hard not to believe the things he said. The man was so charismatic, charming and believable when he spoke. She had to fight to avoid falling into his trap and surrendering to his will. The pull was so strong it was difficult to resist. Others easily fell under his spell; she must not. She leaned on things Jesus said, which the group had learned early in their Christian walk. Those verses referred to these seven years in which they were now living, following the Rapture of Jesus' church. She read them every night to keep her from succumbing and falling for him as so many others had done.

For then there will be great distress, unequaled from the beginning of the world until now—and never to be equaled again.

If those days had not been cut short, no one would survive, but for the sake of the elect those days will be shortened. At that time if anyone says to you, 'Look, here is the Messiah!' or, 'There he is!' do not believe it. For false messiahs and false prophets will appear and perform great signs and wonders to deceive, if possible, even the elect. See, I have told you ahead of time. Matthew 24:21-25 NIV

They were living in the time of great distress. It must be the greatest distress the world had ever seen. She was thankful Jesus would shorten it to seven years. If he did not, at the rate people were dying, she was certain it would wipe out the entire population of the earth. That time frame was the length of the Tribulation, chosen for the sake of her and every other follower of Jesus in the world.

The next verses were the ones that helped her keep her head on straight, as she liked to say. Someone *was* saying, "Look, here is the Messiah!" That someone was Messai himself! He was claiming to be the Messiah, but people did not realize that. And many had been shouting, "There he is!" They called him a savior, miracle-worker and God, but she and the Smyrnians knew none of those were true. He had performed great signs and wonders, including the economic boom after his election, and peace in the Middle East. And she was certain more would come.

Jesus had warned if it were possible, Messai would deceive even those who followed him. Ally was thankful it was *not* possible. They would never fall for his lies and deceit. She had witnessed how easy it was for people to believe in him. It might be easy for her too, if Jesus had not told them ahead of time how to recognize him, and given them the strength they needed to resist him.

The group in the shelter was ready to get out and into the fray. If Messai had his AMPP men chasing down the followers of Jesus, they needed to be out protecting them and fighting Messai's goons. Yes, that is what they were, goons, henchmen, cold-blooded killers. Going on the offensive meant going much farther than the local communities. It meant traveling to places in the United States, and around the world, wherever people needed them. They were getting messages from believers in Jesus everywhere who were attempting to hide out, but who also knew they could not hide forever.

The Peace Patrol was now being supported by security forces who had no regard for human life or anyone they deemed to be a threat to international peace and security. They were ruthless in their approach and had no mercy for those people. They seemed to enjoy their jobs a little too much. Besides, Messai had promised a reward for every person captured, so they were capturing them in droves. All the while, he convinced the world the Smyrnians were the enemy, and removing them was necessary for the world to become peaceful and prosperous again. But even he could not understand why the attacks did not stop them. They continued multiplying.

After finally convincing the others, Ollie and Amelia were heading to Israel, with hopes of also visiting other parts of the Middle East. He argued that he knew the place like the back of his hand and his way around like he did in his hometown of London. They were not nearly as sure of his disguise as he was, but they agreed it *was* good. Since Trey could not retrieve his plane and was a wanted man, they would have to fly from Springfield-Branson to Atlanta, and from there to Tel Aviv. They would stay in close contact with their secure phones. Messai had announced another trip to Jerusalem in the coming week, and they wanted to be there to see him. They would also get to see Ally! They wondered if she would recognize them.

But before they left, there was one item of business they had to take care of. They were ready to be husband and wife. It would be the second wedding performed by the Smyrnians. Ollie and Amelia's ceremony would happen in the afternoon and they would fly to Israel the next morning. Not everyone gets to spend their honeymoon in the Holy Land, reasoned Ollie. And it *would* be a honeymoon, albeit a working one.

Ben badly wanted to go with them, but his appearance needed to change more before he showed up there. Besides, he needed to build up a Jewish community of faith in Jesus before he went. Then he would go, meet with them and help them expand the movement nationwide. The thought of that caused him to tingle with excitement. That was why Jesus had brought him to faith as the first Jew to accept him during the Tribulation. And it was what he had called him to do when he met him in his house that miraculous night. He had the words *go and tell my people* embedded in his brain. He would never forget them and would never stop doing what Jesus had told him to do. He would get to Israel and lead the movement soon enough.

The Fromms were preparing to go back home to Germany. There was much to do, and Hans and Heidi needed them. A few house churches had started, but their country was still mostly untouched. The boys wanted to get the youth movement going. They could do it. They surprised Bruno and Mila with how they had matured since all of this first started, not just physically and emotionally, but also spiritually. They had a hunger to see their friends become followers of Jesus. So did the adults.

They all had a lot to do when they returned. They needed a safe place as soon as possible. They had not yet found a suitable location for a bunker, nor were they sure now that a bunker was the best thing for them. They would make that decision when they got home. AMPP still did not have a large presence there because there were limited signs of Smyrnian activity in Germany. That was true for much of Europe. The continent needed Jesus.

Blake and Beth were taking off for another part of the Middle East, namely Iran. Following the peace agreement, Jews were no longer considered infidels, and there were no other prevailing religions in the country, other than the predominant Islam. A few people had gone to the website and listed as having put their faith in Jesus after their special broadcasts. They would do their best to locate them and assist them however they could. They would have to be very careful, but they felt good about the difference in how they looked. They assumed they could fit in well.

Much to Blake's dismay, Beth would have to bring out the scarf. Her head would need covering to avoid any undue conflict which may lead to them being found out. She had studied the customs, along with the written and unwritten laws. She would also need to wear loose fitting clothing to conceal her figure, another must in the country. She had purchased a long black dress to wear for any small towns, but was taking more westernized clothing for the large cities. That would work well since their first destination was Tehran, where a group of believers met.

They would have to be together at all times, never out of each other's sight. Despite the dangers involved, they were excited about connecting with new followers of Jesus. Those people needed them and their help. Peace in the Middle East did not include followers of Jesus. It was only for Muslims and Jews. They still considered those who claimed Christ to be infidels and threats to worldwide peace and security, thanks to Messai. Yet they were ready for the journey.

Evan could not stay in the shelter any longer at this point. If the others were going, he was going. He was leaving Ben and Miriam in charge of handling communication with and between members of the team. He had one person on his mind: Ally. She was in Belgium, so he was going there. Anders was going with him. Evan wanted to be near her and see that she was okay. He would speak with her, if he could find a way. But even trying that would be very dangerous.

Anders' Dutch heritage would work well in Belgium, a country with a significant Dutch population. He would fit in well with locals and would help Evan fit in by being with him. Both of them were unknown to Messai or anyone else. So, they would have more free rein to get into places the others could not.

As with Ally, they would be right under Messai's nose, and he would not even be aware of it. They were eager to arrive in Brussels. The number of believers there was miniscule, but if they connected with those few, they may be of great help to each other. And they would check on Ally if they could get to her. Evan's greatest concern was to make sure she was safe. He did not trust Messai in the least.

In a last minute decision, they opted to take one more with them: the source. "No name," he had said. "Just call me Source." The man had been incognito for years, always able to get the inside scoop when no one else could, and having only one to whom he revealed it: Blake Thompson. Now, he was spying for the Smyrnians. He got on the inside in just about any situation. And he wanted to do that in Messai's domain. Blake had told him he would be a part of Ally's team. He was part of this team and gladly so, but he worked best alone. He was more effective that way. He would get on the inside, and Evan and Anders would help.

Trey's brush with AMPP made his going anywhere perilous. But if the others were going, they could not leave him at the shelter. That's just the way it was. Since he could not fly missions for now, he believed it was his purpose to go. He, John and Kathie would form an unlikely trio, but in actuality, they were not that unusual at all. Doc had asked John to take care of her, and the two of them had become fond of each other. They had no plans to marry; nothing like that. They just enjoyed each other's company and had fun together. John had decided she did not need him to take care of her. She was perfectly capable of taking care of herself. In fact, he may be the one who needed her to take care of him. They would still act the part of husband and wife, and Trey would be their driver. If flying was not an option, he would drive. He was an expert at both.

Rickie was getting Trey's plane and bringing it back to Springfield-Branson. As far as anyone except the team knew, he had purchased it from Trey and taken over his charter business. Trey had disappeared, fallen off the face of the earth. Rickie would now be the team pilot, which frustrated Trey. But he also wanted to be on the ground and in the thick of the action.

He, John and Kathie would make this first excursion to Atlanta, taking Ollie and Amelia to the airport for their flight to Israel, and saving them the flight from Springfield. After trying to find some believers in Atlanta, they would work their way back to Ozark, trying to connect with others in towns along the way.

Atlanta was a shell of its former self. The economic collapse had devastated it. Banks had closed their doors, businesses had gone bankrupt, and downtown looked like a ghost town compared to what it had been before. Atlanta had once been a bastion of Christianity, but losing so many people on September 11, 2029 crippled it and robbed it of much of its population.

Those who remained felt utter hopelessness. It was a fertile place to tell people about the one who could give them hope. It would also be a test of how they now looked. If they went unrecognized there, it was a good sign for their trips to other places, and eventually to other parts of the world. They would soon find out. Nervous? A bit, yes. But ready? Without a doubt.

Before any departures, the entire group gathered in one bunker for a wedding. This one would not be an elaborate affair, just a few friends gathered to celebrate the union of Oliver Barton and Amelia Clarke. And they guaranteed this one to be fun. Ollie was in full on Sherlock Holmes mode, raincoat, deerstalker hat and all. Amelia was rocking the Kitty Riley look from *The Reichenbach Fall*. They had both been huge fans of the old BBC Sherlock series back in the day. So their new identities were perfect, chosen for a reason.

The vows they had written to one another made the others howl with laughter. It was the most hilarious and unusual wedding any of them had ever attended. They had asked Trey to do the honor of pronouncing them husband and wife. When he announced, "Sherlock, you may kiss your bride," Ollie proclaimed, "Elementary, my dear Watson!" Amelia ran as he chased her around the bunker. After a brief sprint, she turned around and grabbed him with open arms and was the one doing the kissing. Ollie beamed. "I like this girl!" They finished with a celebration, realizing it was the last time they would all be together for some time, if ever. They all crashed for the night, sending Ollie and Amelia to the third bunker. Their real honeymoon would happen in Israel. The team packed and were ready to go their separate ways the next day.

That evening, Messai called Ally into his office. No one else was in and his door was open.

"Come in and have a seat Ally." He motioned to the sofa where he was sitting. "This is informal, so we will be comfortable. There is no need for you to sit in those uncomfortable chairs across from my desk. I have tried them and discovered how irritating they can be. I want you to know how much I appreciate you coming in late at my request. I will reward you for your time."

"I always try to be at your beck and call, sir," she said, feeling very uncomfortable sitting on the sofa next to him. This did not feel right at all. She considered excusing herself and leaving, feigning sickness, or finding another reason. But she needed to keep this job. If she was to be the spy on the inside, she must remain his assistant. He continued speaking.

"I am glad to hear that. It is exactly why I called you in tonight. You have become very special to me. I admire you for your efforts and willingness to do whatever I ask. You have made my life much easier. But I also admire you for your beauty. I can honestly say you are one of the most beautiful women I have ever known. And trust me, I have known some beautiful women."

"I have been thinking about our trips and some expenses we can eliminate. Because of the dire financial condition of the world we must not appear to be wasteful, as so many are hurting. For starters, we will fly commercial for a while instead of taking the private jet. That will set a good example. It is also foolish for us to stay in separate rooms. So, from this point on, we will stay in the same room. It is the prudent thing to do. We can better prepare for the following day. Good preparation is of the essence, don't you agree?"

Without giving her a chance to respond, he continued. "We will stay in the most expensive one-room suites available, with jacuzzi, minibar, all the amenities. Nothing but the best for you, Ally. I also detest queen beds, so I will book rooms with one king bed. Sleeping in the same bed will provide companionship for both of us on our many trips. So, I have made those arrangements for our upcoming trip to Israel."

"We will stay at the King David Hotel in the Presidential Suite. It has magnificent views of the Old City and includes a large jacuzzi and walk-in private Swedish sauna. I wanted to bring you in and inform you of those things before we depart, so it will not surprise you. I have always tried to be up front with you, and this is no exception. You understand, don't you, Ally?" He reached over and placed his hand on hers.

She fought the urge to pull her hand away from his, but did not. It was warm on top of hers and made her feel special. It mesmerized her. She had the sensation of being drawn to him. The chill filled the room. She had not felt it in months. Now here it was again. But this time a warmth that seemed to offset the chill accompanied it. It was as though she was having an out-of-body experience and was hovering above the sofa watching herself moving closer and closer to his side. She prayed silently:

"Dear Jesus, give me strength. I know the truth about this man. I need your power right now to give me a clear mind and form a barrier between him and me. Give me the words to answer him. Jesus, protect me please."

Evan did not want to interrupt the wedding. Everyone was having such fun, and it was Ollie and Amelia's big day. But a compulsion to pray for Ally overwhelmed him. It was as if she was calling out to him for help. He knew she was in trouble. So, he prayed... and prayed. He heard nothing they said during the wedding, oblivious to the others laughing and having fun. He was silently calling out Ally's name and asking Jesus to intervene in whatever situation she was facing. In his mind, he was screaming her name, even though no words were coming from his mouth. They came from his heart. He longed to be there for her and knew he would be soon. But for now, he needed to be there for her from 4,500 miles away. And he was.

The fog in Ally's mind suddenly cleared. The chill subsided. The warmth overcame it.

"Sir, that is not wise." She still did not remove her hand. "We cannot hide the things we do from the world. Maintaining your good reputation is essential. I believe it is important that we continue staying in separate rooms, as we have since I started working for you. You are right that a suite is unnecessary. A simple room with any size bed is fine with me. If it is a question of financial responsibility, I will be happy to pay for my room. You pay me well enough that I can afford to do that. I hope *you* understand what *I* am saying."

"Thank you for your honesty, Ally. It is one of the things I admire about you. But I have made my decision. We will be in Jerusalem for three days and two nights and will spend both nights in the Presidential Suite at the King David Hotel. Be prepared to work late while we are there, but also for some relaxation and good times. We work hard. A little play makes work easier." His smile was alluring, and his intentions clear.

"Sir, I will do as you say. But my role is to serve you by working as your assistant, fulfilling the job description you gave me when I applied for this position. That is what I will do, and I will do it to the very best of my ability. I love my job and would not trade places with anyone in the world. I only ask that you allow me to do what you hired me to do. I promise you I will do it well, as I always have. Thank you for your confidence in me. Now I had better go. Both of us need to rest before we leave on this trip. It is important that we be ready."

He gently removed his hand from hers. "You may go, Ally. I know you love your job. You do it well. Just remember, it is your role to serve me and attend to my needs. I want you to keep your job. There are plenty of others who would love to have it. And I am sure they would do anything I need them to do. But I want you. Keep that in mind. Good night, Ally. I look forward to our trip."

She left shaken and searching for answers. They would leave for Israel in less than 36 hours. She must have answers before then. She sensed someone praying for her. She knew it was Evan.

As the team prepared to leave the next morning, they said their goodbyes and renewed their commitment to stay in close contact with Ben and Miriam at home base. They must know each other's location and situation at all times, in case there was trouble. They would each receive an update at the end of every day. This was what they had been waiting for. They were mindful again of the fact that this could be the last time they would all be together. But they were invading the darkness that had invaded the earth. And one way or the other, they would win.

The next day they all boarded their flights and took off for their destinations. The Fromms were on their way back to Germany to join the Meiers in the work there. Ollie and Amelia were on their way to Israel to see

Messai in action and check on the status of peace in the Middle East. Blake and Beth were en route to Iran. They would also get a closeup look at how peace was going in that place which had long had a hatred for Israel and the Jewish people. But they also hoped to find a few believers there and encourage and help them in any way they could. Their mission had danger written all over it.

Evan, Anders and Source were excited about getting to Belgium, and to Ally. She and Messai would be on their way to Israel by the time they arrived. Ollie and Amelia would see her before they did, but they would be ready when she returned and would find some way to let her know they were there. She could relay firsthand information to them, which they would share with Ben and Miriam, who would pass it on to the rest of the team.

They hoped to protect Ally from the monster for whom she worked and was with every day. Trey, John and Kathie were ready to test their new looks in Atlanta and search for some believers. They hoped no one would recognize them, but knew if they did, it may be too late for them. They were still up to the challenge and excited about it.

Ben and Miriam fought the desire to be out like everyone else, but the time was not yet right for them. Thus, they were content to fill their roles at the shelter. Miriam would handle most of the communication with the team while he would communicate with the Jews about the truths of Jesus. Theirs was a vital role which all the others were depending on as they were out on the front lines of battle.

When Ally got back to her room, she sent a message to Miriam, who passed it on to the others. "Messai says we will no longer have separate rooms on our trips, beginning with this one. We will stay in the same room with only a king bed. Every room will have a jacuzzi. He left no doubt about his intentions. Apart from a miracle, I will be at his mercy. Please pray!"

Each of them received the word and were all visibly shaken. There was nothing they could do. They could not protect her without being there. But even if they were there, they would be powerless against Messai and AMPP. It was a job for Jesus and Jesus alone. They did all they could do. They prayed and tried to will themselves to trust him.

It enraged Evan when he got the message. He wanted to take Messai out. One bullet to the head ought to do it. He thought about the possibility and how he would do it. It would surely cost him his life, but it would save Ally's. Anders and Source saw his anger and tried to keep it from consuming him, but it was to no avail. They would have to pray for him as much as Ally.

When he slept on the plane, he dreamed of Ally. He dreamed that Messai had violated her in their hotel room. He awoke with a start, only to dream again. This time he was in a building across the street when Messai and Ally returned. As they stepped from the limo, he took aim and fired. Messai fell to the ground. He awoke again. The dreams continued throughout the flight. They were always the same. Ally hurting, sobbing. Awake... Dreaming... Messai dead on the ground, a gunshot wound to his head... Awake. He could not wait to get to Belgium.

Ally's sleep was restless too. She dreamed of Messai coming at her and of her fighting back. She awoke. The dream recurred several times. Then it changed. She dreamed of Evan. He was there for her! She could not see what was happening. It was again as though she was looking on from the outside as the two men fought. But this time it was happening in a dark hotel room. She heard punches landing and loud groans. She strained to see, but could not. A loud pop. A gunshot! Messai had killed him! "No," she screamed, trying to run. A hand grabbed her by the arm. She jerked to pull away. A voice. "Ally, I have got you. Messai is dead. Let's go!" Evan! He was the one who shot Messai. The monster was dead. She was free! The world was free.

They ran out the door and down the hallway. Steps behind them. Messai! She turned to look. There was a gaping hole in his head, but he was chasing them. He caught them just before they reached the elevator. The gun! He had the gun. Evan left it behind in his haste to escape. "Ally, you are mine," Messai growled. "Say goodbye to your boyfriend." He aimed the gun at Evan and pulled the trigger. A loud bang. She awoke in a cold sweat, as she had on a night several months ago. That time she was the one dying at the hands of Messai. All she could think about was being in Israel with a monster. "Jesus, help me," she prayed. She had nowhere else to turn.

The financial crisis was bad. But it was only the beginning of what the world would experience. Something else had contributed to it. It would bring devastation like the world had never seen. Many more would die. Even the Smyrnians would struggle to survive. It was coming fast.

CHAPTER 18

Spring had now come and gone, and another part of the woman's warning was coming true. The winter rains had not fallen. Neither had the snow. The earth was dry. People counted on the Spring rains, but they had not come either. Summer had been sweltering. Not that there was less rain than normal; there was *no* rain. Every day all over the globe, the weather forecast was the same: boiling hot and dry. How had it been so hot in Spring? No one knew. How did the heat extend to every place on the planet? There were no answers. How could the entire world have experienced total darkness, as in a complete absence of any light for 26 minutes and 51 seconds, during the lunar eclipse of December 20? Astronomers were clueless.

But it had all happened, just as the drought was occurring now. The earth was becoming a giant dust bowl. Dust storms were regular and so severe they caused hazardous driving conditions and the closure of airports, creating havoc for both ground and air traffic. Downed power lines and power failures interrupted lives and businesses. Dust found its way into buildings and automobiles, resulting in respiratory problems, especially for the most vulnerable. It also affected computers and other electronic equipment. In many places, it brought society to a grinding halt.

Then there was the food situation. The land was arid, brown and barren. Planting crops was useless. They would not grow. The grains, fruits and vegetables human beings counted on for their daily sustenance became nonexistent. It forced farmers off the farm to find work, but there was none due to the financial crisis facing the world. Livestock were dying at an alarming rate. Dairy products and meat had almost completely disappeared. Wildlife was also perishing, creating a crisis for those who depended on hunting for their meat. People who entered the woods typically found carcasses of dead animals far more than they found live animals. The only ones that seemed to eat well were the vultures. The hunger crisis that began during the financial collapse was at a point of critical mass. Grocery shelves were bare. Malnutrition was widespread across the earth. Children and adults were dying daily from starvation.

But even if people could find food, who could afford it? A simple bag of flour often cost a full day's pay. One trip to the grocery may cost a family their entire year's wages. With few jobs and low pay, buying any groceries available was out of the question for most families. Only the wealthy could afford to eat. Starving people resorted to inconceivable measures to survive. They ate family pets, and some took things a step further, practicing cannibalism. The crisis was worsening by the day.

The drought reached epidemic proportions, decimating the supply of water. Rivers and lakes dried up, as no rain had fallen for months. Dead fish lined dry riverbeds, and once flowing streams no longer ran. Coastal wetlands critical to the early development of many species dried up. Fresh water was all but inaccessible. Shelves were void of bottled water as springs that supplied it had stopped flowing. Wells had gone dry. People around the world were desperately searching for water. They had exhausted all reserves. Water rationing happened in every nation. Most households only had access to water one hour a day, and that was decreasing. The time was fast approaching when taps would no longer yield water. Chronic thirst became a major cause of death, as the world's population continued to decline. Dying of thirst is a terrible way to go.

Besides the food and water shortage, the arid conditions also brought raging wildfires that were inextinguishable. Billions of acres burned. Dry grass and trees were tinder for the fires as they swept through them and continued to rage, gaining strength as they spread. Much of the wildlife that had not died from lack of food or water perished in the flames. The blazes consumed many homes and businesses, as people who had lived through hunger and thirst died in the raging infernos. They reduced entire towns to heaps of ash. The earth looked like a disaster zone on every continent. It was like something out of a horror movie, only this was no movie. It was real.

Then the unexpected happened. Wild beasts that survived, driven by hunger and forced out by the fires, came into populated areas with a vengeance. No one who ventured outdoors was safe. Ravenous carnivores pounced on whatever they could find: humans, domestic animals, anything edible. Many who wandered outside in search of food or water, or to go to their jobs, if they were fortunate enough to have them, paid with their lives. People trapped in their homes shot and killed so many animals it littered lawns with the carcasses. But the more they killed, the more came. Ammunition was eventually exhausted as stock ran out. The beasts of the earth had turned on humanity and were on the verge of taking control. The hunter had become the hunted.

The earth was reeling. What more could happen? On September 11, 2029 over a billion people had gone missing, abducted by aliens based on the explanation of world leaders and experts in space exploration. They were wrong, but many still held to that belief. Then came the darkness, and with it something evil and sinister. The evil was now spreading and claiming as many victims as those taken in the Rapture on September 11.

The new year had begun well, but that had changed in an instant. Killing and a total disregard for human life became the norm. As that was happening, the drought was covering the earth and destroying not just the lives of people and animals, but the earth's ecosystem. The world was a dark and foreboding place. How could anyone survive? The Smyrnians would try to stay alive until Jesus returned, but the chances of that happening were growing slimmer by the day.

Evan, Anders and Source landed in Belgium in the early morning. The airport was eerily quiet. Few people could fly these days. The earth's crises had taken their toll on them. And it had almost crippled the airlines. Grounded planes and half-filled flights became the norm. Airlines had cut back on the number of flights and employees. So, on this morning they had no trouble seeing everyone who was walking through or sprinting toward their gate.

As the three of them walked from their gate and entered the terminal, Evan suddenly froze in his tracks. Anders and Source continued walking, but after a few steps, Anders saw it too. Source stopped, then turned and walked into a shop, pretending to look at magazines. He was smart enough to know something was wrong, and he did not want to give his partners away. He was a pro at things like this.

Both Evan and Anders stood momentarily staring at the couple coming directly toward them. Messai walked confidently, with Ally by his side. She looked stunning in her blue business suit, while his expensive suit spoke volumes about his position and power. Evan fought the urge to charge the man and take him to the ground. He understood that he could not do that, but his mind cried out to do it despite the consequences. He wanted to scream her name and run to her defense. Anders knew his partner was in trouble. He had to keep him from giving them away. He walked back to him and began speaking in a voice only slightly louder than a whisper.

"Evan, I know you are angry and hurting, but you can't give us away. Not now. We have work to do until they return. Try to get control of yourself."

His rage subsiding, Evan's eyes welled up with tears. Then she saw him. She stumbled against Messai, almost falling. He caught her and stood, holding her in his arms. Evan saw the man and heard his voice in person for the first time.

"Ally, my dear. Are you okay?"

It was not the evil voice he had expected. He almost sounded gentle and caring. It was no wonder she struggled to keep from giving in to him, and others so easily followed him.

"I am fine," she said. But he could tell Messai knew she was not.

"What is it? Can you get to our gate to sit down, or do you need to sit now for a while? We have plenty of time before our flight. We can get some food or something to drink. You may need to eat. I need you for this trip, so you must do whatever it takes to keep your strength up."

"I know why you need her," Evan whispered to himself. "She told us about your plans. If you touch her, I will take you out myself, no matter what happens to me because I did."

Messai led Ally into a little coffee shop that was open and still had a few items available. He sat her at a table. Leaving her there, he walked to the counter. Evan and Ally made eye contact. She mouthed, "Don't." He saw moisture in her eyes, too. Messai returned with sandwiches and coffee and sat, not across the table from her, but in the chair beside her. Evan motioned to Anders and the two of them walked into the shop and to the counter too. Hearing a voice behind them, they turned and saw Source standing there. He whispered, "I don't have a clue what is up. Can you let me in on it?"

Anders nodded toward the couple sitting at the table. Source whispered, "Messai!"

"And Ally," Anders whispered back.

Source stood stunned, then took Evan by the arm and said, "Let's go."

"No," said Evan. "I won't leave until they're gone."

The other two men saw there was no use trying to persuade him to leave. They got their order and sat at a table not far behind the pair. They heard the conversation.

"Eat your sandwich, Ally. You need your strength."

"Thank you, sir, but I am not hungry. I promise I am okay."

He unwrapped the sandwich and said with a much firmer voice, "Eat." She did, taking small bites, trying to force the food into her stomach.

"That is better. We have a busy schedule in Israel. But I have also put in some time for pleasure. Tomorrow we will be at the Temple and in meetings for the rest of the day. But this afternoon and evening will be for us. After we check in to the hotel and freshen up a bit, we will go out and enjoy ourselves. People there hold me in the highest regard, so there is no reason to fear."

"We will tour the Old City, then move to the new. I have made a reservation at a great restaurant. We will have a nice meal, then return to our hotel by 9:00 p.m. I planned to surprise you with that, but it is a good time to tell you. You are special to me, Ally, and I want to show you a good time. You deserve it. Then, as promised, we will share a room together. It is their best suite with a large jacuzzi and a minibar filled with the finest wine. Nothing but the best for you, my dear."

Source and Anders sat on each side of Evan, preventing him from getting up. His body was trembling with anger. He wanted to rush to her rescue, her knight in shining armor slaying the evil dragon. They must, they *would* stop him from doing that.

"I appreciate that, sir, but I am not sure I will be up to it. I may be coming down with something. For your benefit, I should get a separate room. You cannot get sick. Your presence is a must at every event you have to attend."

"*We* must attend, Ally. You will be fine, and we *will* go out and enjoy ourselves this evening. And we will return to the room together." His voice had become firm.

"Now, finish your sandwich and coffee, and let's get to our gate."

Then speaking softly again he said, "You are special to me, and I know this job is important to you. Have I not given you everything you desire since you took this position?"

"You have, sir, and more. But..."

He interrupted. "There are no buts, Ally. Now, come and let's be going. We have a plane to catch, and a wonderful evening ahead of us. You are not nervous about that, are you?"

"To tell the truth, sir, I am. I always want to do my job to the best of my ability and perform in such a way that allows the public to believe in the cause."

"Yes, my dear. You have performed well. And you will *perform well* on this trip too."

She said nothing more, amazing Evan with her composure under such dire circumstances. He hoped she would have the same composure, along with a steely resolve tonight. Messai helped her up, and they were on their way. The three men sat and watched as they disappeared from their sight. Before they did, Ally turned for one last glimpse at them. Her eyes revealed a longing to run to them. But her will to be a spy took over, and she walked with purpose through the terminal. She was ready. But was she ready for what she would face tonight?

Blake and Beth deplaned in Iran. They walked toward baggage claim, he with his more than shoulder length hair and thick beard and she with her short, dark hair and sunglasses. They appeared to be two American tourists who were carefree and excited about their time in the country. After claiming their bags, they walked to the car rental, getting a small and unassuming car. They drove straight to the hotel and walked inside, trying to not call attention to themselves. A few men sitting to their right stared at them as they passed by, then returned to their own conversation. After checking in, they hurried to their room, shut the door and set all the locks.

"Shew, we made it this far," she said, collapsing onto the bed.

"Do you feel as conspicuous as I do?" he asked.

"Totally. It feels like every eye is on us. It is not just what I fear they may want to do to us. I can't help but wonder if they *recognize* us. We need to stay focused on why we came here; to find that group of believers and see if we can help them, or at least encourage them. It is obvious times here are as dire as they are in the states. I have a feeling they need us more than we know."

"I am sure you are right. We may also need *them* more than *we* know. Let's get some rest, then we will try to figure out if we can find the house. Their report said they meet today."

After a brief nap, they freshened up and pulled up directions to the house. They had purposely chosen a hotel in the section of Tehran where the group met. That was it. In the entire city of the capital of Iran, there was one small group of people who had put their faith in Jesus. And today, they would meet Blake and Beth Thompson, alias Ryan and Kelly Davis. Was it a risky move to go to their home? Sure. Was it worth the risk? There was no doubt.

They walked out of the hotel and got into the car to make the less than two-mile drive. It would have been an easy walk, and both would have preferred it, but no one in their position and their right minds would do that. They located the house, parked on the main street and walked a short distance to a side street with no outlet and only a few dwellings on one side. The last one was the place they were looking for. Blake tapped on the door. They waited, hearing some rustling about going on inside. A voice spoke first in Farsi. They did not answer. Then it came in English.

"Who is it?"

"Ryan and Kelly Davis from America."

No answer from inside, nor did the door open. They knew they were waiting for the password.

"*Yeshua.*"

The door opened. Inside sat a group of about 20 people with open Bibles. When they saw Blake and Beth, their faces revealed their shock.

"It is us, Blake and Beth Jennings Thompson. We changed the way we look so people will not recognize us. If you look closely, you can see that it is us." The group seemed satisfied.

"We bring you greetings from the Smyrnians in the United States. We have prayed for you. I want to say thank you for keeping the faith in difficult times and a dangerous situation. You are an inspiration to us. We may be on Messai's top ten most wanted list in the world, but you are on his list just as much as we are. Now, tell us, what are you reading?"

"It is interesting you say that. We are reading in the second chapter of Revelation. It has interested us because that is where our name, Smyrnians, came from; the church at Smyrna. Thank you for choosing that name. It has shown us what our lives will be like. And they already have been. But then we moved to the next part, the letter to the church in Pergamum. We decided we would be like the people in that church. It says they did not renounce their faith in Jesus, even when a faithful follower of Jesus named Antipas was put to death for his faith. We will not renounce our faith, whatever happens. And the verse says that happened in their city, where Satan dwells. We too live where Satan dwells. There is little doubt they will catch us soon. We cannot hide forever. But they cannot kill us. Jesus said we should not be afraid of them because they can kill our bodies, but not our souls. We will serve him to the end, then go to be with him. That is far more exciting than living here in this place with the evil in the world."

"We feel the same way. But we will fight Aissa Messai for the entire seven years, if we can stay alive. However, like you, if we cannot, we know where we are going. Now do you mind if we sit and study the Bible and pray with you? Then we would like to know what you need from us."

They read and studied and prayed for over two hours. Afterwards, they brought out some meager food to eat. Neither Blake nor Beth had any idea what they were eating, but they ate it gladly with these followers of Jesus. The leader said, "I am sorry this is all we have. Food is scarce. We cannot afford to buy it. We are eating things we have saved up. And I apologize for having no drinks. Our water supply has run out. We are trying to find water anywhere we can."

"I guess that answers the question of what you need, doesn't it?" asked Beth. "It is the same in America and all over the world. We have no food or water to give you. But we can give you hope and let you know you are not alone in your struggle. We are with you through prayer. We want to encourage you to keep the faith. And continue telling people who Jesus is. Great will be your reward in heaven. We would like to pray for you before we leave. We will be in Iran for two days. Are there any other groups we can meet with?"

"There are none. We are still the only ones. But we continue to try. There is peace between the Muslims and Jews. That still seems strange. But there is no peace for us, only peace in our hearts because Jesus lives there. Please pray with us before you go. Will you get to come again?"

"We will come again tomorrow, if you are meeting. There is nothing better than being with other people who love Jesus wherever they may be."

"We will be meeting. This is a special time for us. We are meeting every day this week."

They prayed and prayed for the group, then left and cautiously walked to their car. They drove back to the hotel; themselves encouraged by these people who were completely sold out to Jesus.

Evan, Anders and Source made it to their hotel and got settled in. The other two tried as hard as they could to console Evan and calm him down. He was still seething at the thought of what may go down with Ally and Messai that evening and night. Although he had faith in his friend, he also knew she was in a vulnerable position, alone with the most evil man in the world and no one to protect her. He chose the only option he had. He prayed for her. It was the only thing that could calm him down. Anders and Source prayed with him.

He wanted to believe she would be okay, but he also understood that all of them were aware they may not live to the end of the seven years. He fought back tears, thinking this could be the end for Ally, before the first of those years had ended. He remembered her dream of being in the guillotine; the blade being released and her waking up just before it hit her neck. Could this be it? The time she had dreamed about? His eyes gave way to tears as that thought flooded his mind. His friends came and sat beside him, but they let him weep. Then something hit Anders, and he jumped up.

"Ollie and Amelia!"

"What about Ollie and Amelia?" asked Source.

"They are in Jerusalem!" He practically shouted. "We need to get word to them right now so they can be as close as they can get to where Messai and Ally are staying, possibly inside the hotel in case she needs them. Did Ally tell Miriam which hotel they will stay in?"

"No! We don't know where they are staying!" Evan snapped at Anders. "If she knew, why didn't she tell us?!" The tears had stopped, and the anger returned.

"I can find out," Source said in a soft voice meant to calm the conversation. "How do you think Blake Thompson always had a leg up on all other reporters in every big story? Me. I am not bragging; it's just the truth. I know how to get information. It is what I do. I will go right now and find out where they are staying."

"Just how are you going to do that?" Evan was struggling to control his emotions.

"Let him do his job, Evan," said Anders. "This is his role on the team, remember?"

"I suppose. I am sorry, Source. Go on right now and do that, if you can. We have to get word to Ollie and Amelia while they still have time to get where they need to be, come up with a plan and be ready if Ally needs them. And I know she will need them!"

"You don't know that," answered Anders.

"Well, they need to be ready!" Anders and Source agreed.

"Before I go, I need to tell you guys something," said Source. "I need to give you my name. If we are to be on the same team for up to seven years, you need to know. My name is Malachi. My parents chose it because they liked it. I had a friend who went to church. He told me it means 'Messenger of God,' and he believed that someday I would be God's messenger for a very important reason. I believe he thought I would be a preacher. I laughed at him and told him he was a fool for believing there is a God. He told me the Bible says the fool is actually the person who does *not* believe in God. I told him to call me a fool then because I would never believe in some *man upstairs* who 'created the universe.'"

"That ended our friendship, not for him, but for me. I wanted nothing to do with anyone who called me a fool for not believing in someone who does not exist. He was the first person I thought of when I saw Blake's special report that night. He is with Jesus now, but I wish I could tell him he is the reason I put my faith in Jesus. As a spy, secret agent, source, whatever you want to call me, I *am* God's messenger who can get information and bring it back to you guys. I *can* do that, trust me. I have never failed to get the scoop. I know how to do that. So, I am getting out of here so I can get it done now for the most important reason ever!"

"Thank you, Malachi. I have faith in you. I know Jesus brought you to himself for that reason and for days like this. We will pray for you to get the info. Call Miriam as soon as you get it. Then come back and tell us." The tone of Evan's voice changed. He now had a tiny ray of hope.

Malachi left in a hurry. No one knew who he was, so no disguise was necessary. He would, however, need a new passport and identification as soon as they got back to the shelter. That would be on top of Evan's priority list, if he could make it until then without someone finding out he was a member of the Smyrnians. If they captured him, he would never divulge that.

Ally and Messai arrived at the King David Hotel in Jerusalem, near the Old City. They would take an hour to freshen up and be ready for the afternoon of touring before taking a limo into the modern city for their night on the town. When that ended, they would return to the King David where Messai unquestionably had plans for her, plans in which she was unwilling to take part. She had racked her brain for answers or a plan of action, but had none. The pressure was on. She had eight or nine hours before he would satisfy his lust with her as the victim. They would be in the room together with the door locked, so she would be helpless at that point.

She hoped and prayed, but the pressure to find an answer kept her from coming up with one. The hour passed quickly, and they left the room for their tour. He insisted she wear something more revealing, nothing over the top, but more so than she was comfortable wearing. He wanted to show her off, parade her before the watching eyes of the world. Reporters followed them every step of the way, with cameramen often zooming in on her. They wanted the world to see the always sharply dressed businesswoman showing off another side of herself the world had not seen. It was apparent that something more was going on between the two. He could not keep his eyes off her and did not care who noticed.

Reporters were offering their thoughts on what would happen between the world leader and his *assistant* during this stay. Some were saying, "She *is* his assistant," then asking, "but assisting him with what?" Ally hoped her embarrassment was not showing. Who enjoys being paraded around town as a sex symbol in front of the millions of people who were watching these broadcasts? One of those was Evan Ryles in Belgium. His anger had returned with a vengeance, as had his fantasizing about killing Messai the moment he returned to the country.

Malachi entered the impressive skyscraper that housed Aissa Messai's office. Messai owned the entire structure and needed it for his full empire. He got on the elevator and pushed the button to take him to the penthouse. Reaching the floor and opening the door, he looked at the expansive area before him. There were no other offices on this floor. It was all the office suite of Aissa Messai. "Wow!" he thought. "This is impressive!" He crossed the large room, furnished with the most expensive decor, and arrived at an impressive mahogany desk that would not normally belong to a secretary. But with Messai, everything was always the best money could buy.

"May I help you, sir?" asked the secretary.

This is one thing that made him such a superb source. He spoke several languages fluently. One of those was Dutch, the primary language in the northern part of the country. And he looked the part almost as much as Anders. He would definitely pass for a local technician.

"Yes ma'am, you may. Let me see, how do I put this? I am here to check on something that is a surprise for Mr. Messai from his assistant, Miss Fromm. She wanted me to look into the possibility of installing a certain digital device into his desk that he will enjoy very much, and which will make his life a lot easier."

"Sir, I cannot allow anyone into Mr. Messai's office without authorization from either him or Miss Fromm. You will need to come back another day."

"Why do you think I am here today? Miss Fromm said she and Mr. Messai will be out of the country for two days, and she wanted to be sure I look into this today, and if possible, have it installed tomorrow before he returns. Can you call her and verify that?"

"I cannot interrupt her today. Mr. Messai had some special surprises planned for Miss Fromm to show his appreciation for all she does for him. He specifically instructed me not to disturb them."

"Miss Fromm told me the same thing. She wants to surprise Mr. Messai with something he will love. I thought she intended to leave word with you, with instructions to let me into his office. It is very much unlike her to forget something this important. If you can call her, please do. If anything is worth interfering with their day for just one minute, this is it. You don't want her disappointed, do you?"

"No sir, but the boss, excuse me, Mr. Messai, gave me specific instructions. I cannot..."

"Okay ma'am, if you insist, I will leave without following Miss Fromm's specific instructions for me. Whether you were, or were not told about this, matters not to me. But I assure you there will be repercussions for not allowing it to happen. I will express your refusal to her. Good day, ma'am. I have other important matters to attend to today for people who will allow me to do the things they have asked me to do. Not to mention that you are costing me a good payday." He turned to walk across the room as if leaving hurriedly and being frustrated and upset.

He was halfway across the room when she spoke. "Sir, if you promise to take only fifteen minutes at most, I will let you in. But you must be quick."

"Believe me ma'am, you will not regret that decision. I will recommend that Miss Fromm reward you for your faithfulness to her. I am sure you know she is a generous person."

The woman got up, and with concern on her face, opened the door.

"Now, if you don't mind, I must close the door in case someone comes in. Miss Fromm strictly forbade me to allow anyone to see me and what I am doing, including you. I am sorry about that, but I am following her instructions."

"Okay, but remember, only fifteen minutes."

He was in and behind Messai's desk in a flash and pulling up his computer. Password? What would Messai use for his password? He tried a few. *September112029*. Not it. *December202029*. That didn't work either. *Secretary-General1*. Nope. He remembered what the Smyrnians had told him about who Messai is. He tried again. *JesusChrist2029*. No good. Then something moved his fingers over the keyboard. Without even realizing what he was doing, he typed *IamMessiah666*. The computer came to life and opened!

Malachi knew what had just happened was not him. It was Jesus! It was the first time he had experienced anything like this. He had heard the others talk about it happening to them, but now he had witnessed it for himself.

Jesus was with him and had just performed a miracle for him, as he had done for people in the Bible. He sat in stunned amazement. Then he saw the time. Five minutes! That was all he had to find the hotel information and get out of Messai's office. "Jesus, guide me again," he whispered.

A desktop folder stood out to him as if it was the only one. It read *Travel.* He would not have chosen that one himself, but he knew now it was where he needed to look. He opened it and found more folders inside. One label read, *Jerusalem.* He opened it. More folders. One said *Hotels.* Bam! He clicked on it as he simultaneously glanced at his watch. Two minutes. Hurry, Malachi! As it opened, he saw the dates of this trip with several bits of information. One minute. No time to waste! There it was. *King David Hotel. Presidential Suite. Request: Complete Privacy. Guard posted at all times. Do not disturb for any reason.* He took a picture with his phone, then closed the file in a flash and shut the computer down. A knock on the door.

"Your time is up. You must come out now."

He was already walking toward the door. He opened it as the secretary stood with her hand still in the knocking position. It happened so fast it startled her.

"Yes, ma'am. I was watching the time closely. I told you I would finish in fifteen minutes, and that is exactly what I did. And you will be glad to know I saw everything I needed to see. I cannot do what Miss Fromm wanted at this point. The necessary changes will take longer than two days. I will make Miss Fromm aware of that. Hopefully, we can work it out when they are away on their next trip. He travels a lot, so I assume we will not have to wait long. He grinned at her. Now, I have to be going. Thank you, Elise. Again, I will make sure Miss Fromm is aware of your willingness to help her do something nice for your boss. I am certain she will show her generosity because you did."

"Thank you, Mr... I do not believe I caught your name."

But he was already going out the door and toward the elevator. It came much slower than he wanted. When it finally arrived, and the door opened, he entered and pushed the lobby button. As the doors were closing, he saw the secretary walking out of the office door as if to summon him. But it was too late. The doors shut, and he was on his way down. When he got off the elevator, he exited the building in a flash. As he passed the welcome desk near the door, the receptionist was speaking to someone on the phone.

"Here he comes now, Elise. Hold on, and I will try to get his name. Sir? Sir, I need to talk to you for just a moment. Mr. Messai's secretary, Elise, needs your name. Sir?"

Acting as if he did not hear, he exited the building and crossed the street. If he appeared to be a man in a hurry, he was. In his mind and his phone, he was transporting urgent information. By now Messai and Ally were finishing up their tour and preparing to begin their *special evening.* There was no time to spare. Her well-being, and possibly her life, hung in the balance. This is what he signed up for. The adrenaline rush he felt was amazing! He was in his element. He was *the source*, and from now on, he would be the source for the Smyrnians. He was making up for a lot of lost time. He ran all the way back to the hotel as fast as he could. He had the data they needed. They knew into whose hands it needed to go. Time was of the essence. He only hoped they would not be too late.

CHAPTER 19

As the Smyrnians battled on the front lines and the world reeled from all the devastation it had endured, something far worse than anything that had happened had begun in China with the entire world in its sights. It began with one man becoming violently ill and dying after a few days. Within weeks, it wiped out his entire family. Then it started spreading to people in their community and region, with cases now being reported throughout the nation. Medical science was powerless to discover a cause or deliver a cure. People were dying at an alarming rate.

Although the disease did its lethal work in a short amount of time, their deaths were excruciating. It bore a close similarity to the Black Death of the Middle Ages, which lasted just over three years during the 14th Century, but during that time, it killed over one-third of the people in Europe. Up to 800 people a day died in some places. In isolated cases, it completely annihilated small towns or villages. Estimates placed the number of deaths at up to 200 million before they could stop the plague. Black Death, now identified as the bubonic plague, was a thing of the past.

This was different, never seen. It had made its way out of China, with sporadic cases already showing up in other countries. It was reaching epidemic proportions and seemed destined to affect every place on the planet. If medical science did not come up with an answer, over 200 million people would die.

The Smyrnians were not unaware of its presence, nor were they surprised by it. But they focused on more pressing issues, which were affecting them personally. They hoped they would never have to deal with the plague, but that was likely inevitable. Its scope remained to be seen. The important thing was telling the people of the world about Jesus before it, or something, or someone else claimed their lives. But on this evening, they specifically focused on their teammate and trying to save her from Messai's vile plans.

Ally and Messai left the Old City and headed for their evening of pleasure in downtown Jerusalem. Dinner and a movie, with a flair only Aissa Messai could give it. As they got into the limo, he asked the driver to give them complete privacy as he slipped him a $100 bill. The driver assured him that would be the case. During the 45-minute ride, he sat close to Ally, far too close for comfort. At one point he reached over and put his hand on her leg. She gently pushed it aside, making him unhappy.

"Sir, you have such an important day tomorrow. Should we not be discussing your itinerary and how you will handle things?"

"Ally, my dear, can you not let business go for one evening? I appreciate your work ethic, but tonight is all about you and me. I want to show you a good time in appreciation for all you do for me." Then, smiling, he spoke silently to himself. "Ally, sweetheart, the only thing I am interested in handling tonight is you." She saw his smile, and though he spoke no words, she knew his thoughts. They were on her, and they had nothing to do with work.

Malachi entered the lobby of the hotel and slowed his pace to a casual walk. Nodding and smiling at people as he passed by, he made his way to the elevator and headed up to the third floor. He walked down the hallway calmly so as not to draw attention to himself, unlocked the door and entered the room. Once inside, he waved his phone at Evan and Anders and said with a big smile, "Got it!"

"No way!" said Anders. "How in the world did you..."

"The how is not as important as the where. And the where is the King David Hotel in Jerusalem, Presidential Suite. But the what is just as important." He showed them the picture he had taken.

Request: Complete Privacy. Guard posted at all times. Do not disturb for any reason.

"We have to call Miriam right now!" Evan bolted off the bed. "We have already told her we would call the minute you got back here." He was placing the call as he spoke.

"Evan?" Miriam answered. "What did you find out?"

"We have the information! Malachi, uh, Source, got it all somehow. You must get it to Ollie and Amelia right now!"

"Evan, I know this is Command Central, but you created these secure lines of communication, didn't you? I understand how we set this up, but would it not be better for you to call Ollie yourself? Your call to him will be just as secure, won't it? Time is of the essence here. No use wasting time by using me to relay the message."

"You're right, Miriam. I don't know what I was thinking. This is too urgent to waste time playing phone merry-go-round. Sorry to cut you off, but I have to call Ollie!"

"Wait, Evan. Tell me what is going on with Ally and Messai. Which hotel are they staying in?"

But he had already disconnected the call and was making another call.

Ollie and Amelia had arrived in Jerusalem a few hours earlier, tired from the long flight, but making plans to begin a few days of Holy Land honeymoon. They also needed to monitor Messai's activity and try to make some kind of contact with Ally. Their plan was to do that, then get back to the honeymoon. It is funny how plans can change unexpectedly. Ollie's phone rang, and he said, "It is Evan. I have to get it."

"Yes, you do. He would not be calling if it was not important."

"Evan! What's up, young chap? Are you trying to interrupt my honeymoon already?"

"Listen, Ollie. This is an emergency!"

"Is it now, or are you just trying to pull your old pal's leg?"

"No, I'm not. This is urgent. Please put Amelia on too and listen. We have to act fast."

"Amelia can hear us now too. Go ahead. What is the emergency?"

"Please, Messai has plans for Ally tonight that are not good. We saw them in the airport when we landed here. We sat close to them and overheard everything he said to her. He is taking her out on the town. They are probably getting started right now. After dinner and a movie, he is taking her back to the hotel, and his intentions are evil. Basically, if she does not do what he says, he will rape her, Ollie. If somebody does not step in and stop him, that will happen!"

"She has no plans to comply. You two are her only hope. I don't know how you can do it, but you have to find a way. They are staying at the King

David Hotel in the Presidential Suite. Malachi, or Source, I will explain that later, got the information. These are Messai's requests for the room: complete privacy with a guard posted at all times. And he asked that no one disturb them for any reason. You have got to get there, Ollie. Please…" His voice quivered as that last word trailed off.

"You can count on us, lad. I'm not sure what we will do, but we will do something. I'm sure it will be the AMPP guys providing the security. We have already given them the slip once and had fun doing it. I feel certain we can do it again. Do you not agree, luv?"

"Absolutely. Evan, sweetheart, don't worry. We will try our best. Honestly, I don't know how we can get past AMPP or get to her through a locked door. But Sherlock Holmes over here is good at this stuff. He will come up with some kind of plan. We just have to hope it will work."

"Please, you guys. Please be there for Ally. I am certain she will not let him touch her. And I fear what he may do when she does not. I am afraid he may even kill her in that room tonight."

"We will do whatever we can, Evan. But I can't make any promises. I know I don't have to remind you of this, but we are not fighting a normal enemy. We are fighting Satan incarnate."

"Please, just try. That is all I can ask. Try, for Ally's sake."

"You can count on that. I promise you we will try."

Ally sat across the table from Messai, still uncomfortable because of her attire, which was too revealing for her, and because of the way he kept looking at her. She was eating her food, knowing she must, but her thoughts were running wild as she did. Jesus had called her to be a spy for the Smyrnians and put her in the prestigious position she held as Messai's assistant. She had expected to keep this position for the entire final seven years of Planet Earth. She would do just about anything to keep it. But this was a line she could not and would not cross. However, she was certain in a few hours Messai would not just *ask* her to cross it, but *require* her to cross it. And she feared if she refused, he would *force* her to cross it.

His gaze had intensified throughout the day and had gone from infatuation to all-out lust. Her mind raced with potential escape plans. She had already tried, "I may be coming down with something and do not want you to catch it" and "We need to focus on work." He had pushed both aside as if they had merely been said in jest. It seemed he enjoyed her attempts to escape his intentions. He had now become like a lion waiting to pounce on his prey. Ally did not enjoy being the prey.

She considered crying out for help while sitting here in the restaurant, or excusing herself for a moment, then asking someone to take her somewhere safe. But Messai would never let her out of his sight, not tonight. Her only other option was to run and try to get away. But the AMPP guys would grab her in no time. So she sat and ate, feeling like an animal trapped in a cage with no way out.

"Ally dear, you seem so distant," Messai said charmingly. "Cheer up. This is your evening."

She tried to smile and act as if she was enjoying the food and their time together.

"There, that is better. Eat up. The fun has just begun!"

Evan was pacing the floor as Anders and Malachi tried to calm him down.

"Evan, there is nothing we can do from here but pray," Anders told him.

"What do you think I am doing while I am walking around this room? I *am* praying! I'm sorry, guys. I don't mean to yell at you. I'm just so worried about Ally and what may happen to her tonight. She is my best friend. How am I supposed to get her off my mind?"

"I understand that, Evan," said Malachi. "I wish we were there. But I am believing Jesus will somehow return Ally to us safe and sound. Look at all the things he has done for us already." He had told them how Jesus guided him to the right password and the right folders on Messai's computer.

"I know that. I am trying to trust him. It is hard when I'm here and powerless to do anything."

"Let's all keep praying. We can't be there, but Jesus is there, and we are asking him for a miracle." Anders' faith was still strong. But whatever words came out of their mouths, they all knew the first Smyrnian casualty of these seven years was possible before the night ended. Evan sat down and wept. The possibility of losing his best friend was breaking his heart.

Ollie and Amelia were on their way to the King David. They did not know what they would do. They had no plan of action. Ollie was very familiar with the hotel. He had stayed there many times. Had they known this was where Messai and Ally would stay, they would have booked a room there too. No, that was not a good idea. Even if they could get Ally into their room, they would be in the same building as Messai and his enforcers.

Their time to act was minimal. They got close and parked on a mostly deserted street five blocks away. 30 minutes. If their guess on timing was right, Ally and the predator should be there in 30 minutes. They sprinted to the hotel and entered through a side door that would allow them to bypass the front desk, Ollie in his raincoat and deerstalker hat and Amelia rocking her bright red hair in pigtails. They may have looked strange, but at least they were not distinguishable as Oliver Barton and Amelia Clarke. And if anyone asked, their names were Hugh Walker and Charlotte Helmsley.

She saw elevators on the left and started toward them. He grabbed her hand and pointed around the corner to a door leading to the stairs. She followed as they moved hastily, but stealthily. Once in the stairwell, he whispered to her, "The Presidential Suite is on the fifth floor. When we get there, we will try to get a look at the outside of the room and see if anyone is there." She nodded. This was uncharted territory for her, but after their daring escape in London, it filled her with excitement as her heart rate increased and her body shook. She did not know what may happen, but she was ready.

Opening the door, they stepped into the hallway and looked at an empty corridor. "This way," he whispered, motioning with his hand. They located the suite in a short nook to the left of the hallway. Getting closer, they could hear voices. An AMPP security patrol. They stood against the wall and listened.

"The boss has big plans for his sweet little assistant tonight."

"Yeah, she is in for a real treat." They laughed.

"This should be an easy gig. There is no way she is getting out of this room. And if she does, she is definitely not getting past us. Remember what he said. If she tries to run, we grab her and take her right back in. I kind of hope she does. That might be fun."

Ollie pulled Amelia toward the stairway again, and they hurried back through the door. There was an ironing station there, typical of those found in Jerusalem hotels. "In here," he whispered. Once inside, they talked softly so no one would hear, even though it seemed no one was around.

"We have to stop this, Ollie!" she exclaimed in a hushed tone.

"I know, luv. But how? There are two of them, fully armed. How are we supposed to take them out, get into a locked room, stop Messai and rescue Ally?"

She dropped her head. "I don't know. We just found each other, fell in love and got married. But we could die right here in this hotel tonight if we try something foolish."

"We have to stay in the stairway and listen for them to come in. Maybe we can use this so we can see." He picked up a small piece of hard plastic off the floor. "We can prop the door slightly open with it, but not enough so anyone will notice it isn't shut." They eased back to the door, and he inserted the piece of plastic, leaving a narrow slit through which they could barely see. "They should be here anytime," he said.

In Tehran, Blake and Beth were making plans to visit the group again the next day. As they did, they were praying for Ally, and for Ollie and Amelia. Plan and pray. Pray and plan. Ally was on their minds, as were the Iranian believers who were keeping the faith in a hostile environment, their lives on the line every day. They could neither feed them nor take them water, but they would try to encourage them and be with them one last time before leaving the country.

"We can both tell them our stories of how we came to faith in Jesus. They heard some of that when they watched our specials and have seen it on the website, but we can fill in the details for them. We need to tell them about Evan, and you have to share your story, beginning with your mom and dad. Then we need to hear their stories too. Actually, we can encourage each other."

"I think that is perfect, Blake. We need to get some sleep tonight, but there is no way we can sleep until we get word about Ally. I wish we were in Jerusalem to help Ollie and Amelia. And I wish I could see a way for them to save Ally from Messai, but no matter how hard I try, I can't."

"Neither can I. I can't bear the thought of that monster having his way with her in a hotel room. It makes me sick to my stomach to think of it."

They prayed, heartbroken for their young colleague and what she may have to endure before the night was over. Spying was what she wanted to do. Getting on the inside to get information for the team was her desire. She knew the danger she would be in. The time for her to pay the price may have come far too soon. They both hoped she would somehow find the strength to endure it.

The elevator dinged, and the door opened. Messai and Ally stepped out. He was holding her arm as they walked toward the room, as if to make sure she did not escape. They saw her face briefly. It revealed fear, yet courage. What would she do? Would she give herself to him to keep her position and continue spying for the Smyrnians? Surely not. But then, she would put the needs of the team, and the people of the world, above her own. They stood in silence, wishing there was something they could do. The pair disappeared from their sight and turned into the nook leading to the entrance of the suite. They heard him speaking to the two AMPP guys as he and Ally prepared to enter the room.

"Thank you for being here tonight, men. Be diligent and do what I have asked you to do, if I should need you."

"Yes sir, Mr. Messai. You can count on us. You just enjoy yourself and do not worry about anything. We have everything under control out here." He winked and smiled at Ally.

Once inside the room, he did not waste any time. Taking both of her hands in his, he said, "Ally, Ally, dear sweet Ally. I have been waiting weeks for tonight. I have told you how beautiful you are to me. Hopefully, this will be the start of something very good on all of our trips. I want you to be more than just my assistant. I need you to be my lover and perhaps someday, my wife."

"Sir, I have told you I cannot do that. I have been your loyal assistant and will continue to be that. I will work harder than I ever have. But please do not ask me to do this."

"Oh Ally, I am not asking you to do something you do not want to do."

"Thank you for that, sir. You will not regret it. I will continue..." He interrupted her.

"Ally, you do not understand. I am not asking you to do something you do not want to do. I am *ordering* you to do it. You have no choice, my dear. The guard posted outside the door is not there to protect us. They are there to make sure you do not leave this room. Now, I don't want to wait any longer. I will run the water in the jacuzzi. Water is short in the hotel, but they assured me there would be enough for us." He turned on the faucets, taking care to get the water to the perfect temperature. "Now, come Ally.

We need to get started so we will have time to get sufficient sleep and rest up for tomorrow."

"Sir, I told you..."

"Ally, *I* told *you*. Would you feel better if the lights were off? Here, I will turn them off."

The only light in the room came from the bedside lamp. He reached over and flipped the switch, then grabbed her, pulling her close. Before she could stop herself, she began swinging at him in the dark. She felt her fists making contact. He had not expected that. She felt him trying to grab her and hold her arms. She jerked free and swung wildly. She contacted his face. He stumbled and fell backwards onto the bed.

She ran for the door, and unable to see, ran into it, catching herself with her hands. Undoing the locks, she threw it open, catching the AMPP men by surprise. Knocking one of them to the floor, she started running toward the elevator. The other tripped over the fallen one as he started after her. As she ran, she heard Messai as he came out the door. "Get her and bring her to me!"

She reached the elevator and pushed the button, begging it to open. Someone grabbed her from behind and dragged her across the hall. She tried to free herself, but could not. Whoever grabbed her pulled her through a door. The elevator door had opened. The 2-man security detail saw it just as the door closed and they heard it move downward. They pushed the button for the other elevator and saw it was coming down.

One yelled, "Let's take the stairs. We can beat her to the first floor."

"No," shouted the other. "This elevator is here." The bell dinged, and the door opened. They jumped in and startled the three people inside. Seeing their uniforms, they cowered back into one corner.

"AMPP!" one man shouted. "Get out! We are in pursuit of an intruder."

The three exited pronto, as the door closed and the elevator started down.

Ally turned and saw the face of her attacker. "Ollie?" She wept uncontrollably. "And Amelia. But how...?"

"Don't worry about that dear," said Amelia. "Just do what Ollie tells you."

"Quick, down these steps. He talked as they ran. Once we exit the stairwell, turn left and go around the corner. There is a door that opens onto a side street. We will turn right on the street. Then there is an alley just up and on the left. It will take us to another street we can take and get back to the car from the opposite side of where Amelia and I came in."

"Forget the directions," Ally said, her sobbing slowing and her resolve returning. "Just lead and we will follow!"

"When we exit, hold the door and let it close quietly. Then we will walk calmly to the door so we do not draw attention to ourselves."

They reached the first floor, pulled the door open and entered the hallway. Amelia started walking, following Ollie, and forgot to keep her hand on the door. It shut with a bang. The AMPP men had just exited the elevator. Hearing the door slam, one of them yelled.

"The door to the stairway! It is her. Get her!"

"I told you we should take the stairs!"

"Shut up and run. We can't let her get away. The boss will kill us if we do."

"Run!" Ollie shouted.

"She is not alone! Someone is helping her escape. We can take him out and get the girl."

Ollie threw the door open, and he, Ally and Amelia sprinted into the street. As he ran, they heard the men burst through the door. They were following them, and it was clear they meant business.

"We are with AMPP. Stop now or die!"

Ollie led the two women as they turned into the alley, then exited out the other side into the street. He turned left, and they followed. Ally kicked off the heels Messai had made her wear and started running barefoot. The side street was dark, not having streetlights. The AMPP men were in hot pursuit. Unable to see them, they began shooting. Bullets pinged off the walls of buildings and the pavement below their feet.

"Left!" screamed Ollie, no longer caring that the men heard what he was saying. As they reached the adjacent street, the car sat waiting for them. "Get in!" he screamed as he pushed the key fob, unlocking the doors. Amelia leapt into the front seat and Ally dove into the back as Ollie started the car and sped onto the street while she was still trying to close the door. A bullet slammed into the passenger side mirror, smashing it and leaving it dangling on the side of the car. Ollie kept the accelerator pressed to the floor, leaving the AAMP men standing in the middle of the street.

"We lost them!" said Amelia. "Great job, Ollie! Ally, are you okay?"

"I am okay," she said, her voice trembling and trying to get her breath after the chase. "Thank you guys so much. I know I have blown my job as a spy, but I could not let him do that to me."

"I am glad you had the courage to fight back and get away from him," said Amelia. "I am so proud of you right now! Ollie, get us out of here and back to our hotel."

"Blimey!" shouted Ollie. "They called backup. They are coming up behind us fast."

"Not just behind us!" screamed Amelia. "Look up ahead!"

Coming toward them was another car with lights flashing. Just before they got to them, Ollie jerked the wheel to the right, throwing both Amelia and Ally against their doors.

"Here we go again," said Amelia. "We have done this before. Can we do it one more time?"

"We will sure try," exclaimed Ollie. Ally was hanging on tight in the back seat.

It was as if this was Ollie's hometown. He had told them he knew Jerusalem like he knew London. He was telling the truth. Taking side streets, onto a main road and back onto side streets, he drove like a madman. But he could not shake the AMPP vehicles. Now there were more. They stayed in hot pursuit, with additional ones who were joining the chase seeking to block them and bring them to a halt.

"Hold on!" he yelled. They did. With the pursuers out of sight momentarily, he peeled into a parking garage and sped toward the back wall, whipping to the right and into a parking space, cutting the lights as he did. They watched as two AMPP vehicles sped by on the street.

"Come with me," he said. "We are about a mile from our hotel. We can walk from here, but we will have to take back streets again. Here Ally, you will need this." He handed her his hat. "Put this on and pull your hair up under it. And wear this." He pulled off his raincoat and handed it to her. "Maybe they won't recognize us. They are looking for you. We need to get our things and leave the hotel. I have a dear friend who will help us. We have to get to him tonight. The problem is, it is about five miles to his house. He lives in Ein Karem. It is a tough hike. It will be better if I don't call him. We just need to show up. Can you two handle that?"

"What choice do we have?" asked Amelia. "Ally?"

"Whatever we have to do to keep from getting caught. Let's go."

They made it to the hotel and Amelia went inside to get their things. She was probably the least recognizable. She donned the raincoat and deerstalker hat, letting her bright red pigtails hang out from underneath it. She checked out, telling the desk clerk an emergency had come up, and they had to leave. As they waited, Ollie suddenly realized something.

"Ally, I have to call Miriam and tell her you escaped from Messai! She can let the others know."

He made the call, also telling her they were not nearly out of danger yet and hoped to get out of the country somehow. So, they all needed to pray hard for them. Miriam began calling the others, beginning with Bruno and Mila. Evan was next.

Back outside, Amelia met Ollie and Ally hiding in an alley around the corner.

"Let's walk," she said with a hint of sarcasm. "Maybe we can get there before daylight."

"I have a better idea," said Ollie, pointing to a running cab whose driver had abandoned the car to walk inside.

"Ollie, you are not thinking about stealing that cab, are you?" Amelia looked stunned.

"It has my vote," said Ally. "It is better than walking, and we don't have time to wait. Let's go!"

She took off running toward the cab without waiting for the others. Amelia was hesitant, but when she saw she had no choice but to go or get left behind, she reluctantly followed. They got in and Ollie sped away. The cabbie had not even come out of the hotel yet. He would discover soon enough that his cab was missing.

Speeding through the streets of Jerusalem, Ollie made his way out of the city and to the village of Ein Karem, arriving at his friend's place. Parking behind the house, he said, "Follow me, but stay out of sight until I motion for you. I want to feel him out first." They obliged. He knocked on the door. He left off the raincoat and hat so the man would recognize him. The door opened, and his friend appeared. He looked, trying to figure out who was standing on his porch.

"Oliver? Oliver Barton, is that you? You look different and frazzled too. What are you doing, and why are you showing up at my house at this hour of the night? What are you doing in Israel and even showing your face in public? It seems I recall you getting into some serious trouble."

"Alexander, I am sorry for such an intrusion, but I need your help."

"What can I do for you, my friend? You are always welcome in my home, you know that. But I would like for you to tell me what is going on."

"I need you to drive my wife and me, and a friend to the airport in Tel Aviv. We need to catch a flight out of the country ASAP. We can tell you the story on the way. I ask you to trust me."

"I trust you, Oliver. I will help you. Our friendship means much to me. You said wife. You finally got married? I am delighted for you."

"Yes, I did, Alexander, and I am thrilled. But we have gotten into a bit of a spot and need to leave the country at once. We have no time to wait."

"I will gladly drive you to the airport. Friends help each other. After what happened in London, I assume your life may even be in danger. I will not ask about that and about you becoming a member of the Smyrnians. I do not trust Messai. That is one thing about which I am sure. And I have always trusted you. That has not changed. Now, when can I meet your wife and friend?"

Ollie motioned, and Amelia and Ally stepped out. Amelia stood beside Ollie and took his hand in hers. Ally stood by her side.

Alexander smiled at Amelia and said, "You did well, Oliver." Then he saw Ally, and a stunned look appeared on his face. "You are Ally Fromm, Aissa Messai's assistant!" he exclaimed. "Oliver, what is going on here?"

"I will let Ally tell you."

She briefly shared the story of Messai's intentions, his attack on her at the King David and of their daring escape and arrival at his house.

"I saw the news. I could tell how uncomfortable you were in these clothes he made you wear. I have never liked him. Before we do anything, Elizabeth will get you into some different clothes, if that is okay." She nodded and followed him inside. The change of clothes made her feel better.

"I don't want to rush you, Alexander, but we really need to go. I hope I can book a flight as we drive. That should not be a problem with so few people flying these days. Our flight over was not even half full. Oh, and I need to ditch a car somewhere along the way. I can't leave it close to your house. I don't want to get you into any trouble with Messai and AMPP."

Ollie, Amelia and Ally walked to the back as Alexander quickly told his wife more about their plight and grabbed his car keys to leave for the airport. He exited the back door and saw the cab. Ollie shrugged.

"You stole a cab, didn't you, Oliver? That is okay. God will forgive you under the circumstances."

"Alexander, I must talk to you about something as we go. And if anyone asks who I am, my name is Hugh Walker. Now, any suggestion where I can leave the cab?"

"I know just the place. Get in, ladies. Oliver, or Hugh," he smiled at Ollie, "follow me."

Ollie followed impatiently. Alexander was one to obey the Law of Moses, and the law of the land. He drove the speed limit to the obscure location where he pulled over and allowed Ollie to leave the car in an abandoned lot. It was out of sight and never used. He got in to ride with Alexander, wishing he could drive himself. As they rode, he made a reservation online under the name Hugh Walker. A flight to the U.S. was leaving in two hours. They would be on it. But during the 40-minute drive, he had to mention the website to his friend and tell him to watch Benjamin Abramson's broadcast the next day. He smiled and said, "I will watch it for you, my friend." He told him to visit *smyrnians.com* first and watch a video they had posted which would tell him everything he needed to know. There was not enough time to explain in forty minutes. On they rode with Alexander methodically making his way toward Ben Gurion Airport.

CHAPTER 20

In Germany, Mila was weeping, but her tears came from joy, not sorrow. In Belgium, Evan was rejoicing as he ran around the room. In Iran, Blake and Beth were praising God for his protection and deliverance. The same was happening in Atlanta and at the shelter. But they all knew the ordeal was far from over because AMPP could still capture, or even kill, their three comrades before the night ended. So, even as they celebrated, they prayed.

"I want to go to Belgium and take Messai out myself," shouted Bruno.

"Now dear, you must not think like that. If I am correct, you can't kill Messai. He will be around for the entire seven years until Jesus Himself defeats him once and for all."

"You are right, Mila. But it doesn't stop me from wanting to do it."

•   •   •   •   •

In Belgium, Evan's feelings were the same as Bruno's. He wanted Messai dead and longed to be the one who would kill him. Anders and Malachi tried to calm him down, reminding him Ally was away from Messai now. Back at the shelter, Ben and Miriam sent an appeal for everyone to return. It would cut their missions short, but much had changed in a few days. They needed to be specific in their next moves.

Trey, John and Kathie would leave when they got their things together. Their time in Atlanta was unfruitful, anyway. Evan, Anders and Malachi would book a flight ASAP. Bruno and Mila were coming. They could not wait to see Ally! The Meiers would stay in Germany again. Blake and Beth would wait and fulfill their promise to be with the group in Tehran one more time.

Close to Ben Gurion Airport, Alexander stopped at a large market. Amelia bought a pair of scissors, black shoe polish and plastic gloves. Time was short, and it was her only option. It may not be the best one, but Ally's look had to change now before they attempted to make it through customs and security.

Fortunately, Evan had created an identity for her despite her objections. She had argued that she did not need it because she would work for Messai as herself, Ally Fromm. He had asserted you never know what may happen, thus you must prepare for every scenario. Now, she was thankful he had insisted. Her name was Sofia Weber. The photo was one of Beth after her change of hair color with Ally's face photoshopped in.

Now it was her turn for a makeover, which she dreaded but had accepted it must happen if they were to make it out of Israel. She sat quietly as Amelia cut off her beautiful, long blonde hair and left her with a rough cut that featured the short, mussy look. She objected slightly when Amelia put on the plastic gloves and began working the shoe polish into her hair, being careful not to get any on her face and as little as possible on her scalp. This had to look as natural as possible.

She finished as Ally sat in the front seat with the heat on and the fan at full speed. Her hair soon dried with only a blonde streak showing here and there. Still wearing the gloves, Amelia could at least give it a bit of styling. It would have to do. New passport in hand, she joined them and headed inside. The test would begin with passport control. They checked in and headed that way.

Messai was in a rage again as he spoke with the two AMPP men on the phone. "Imbeciles! Find them! Do not let them escape! You located the car in the parking garage. They cannot have gone far. They are on foot. Search every inch of the area. I have called in every AMPP agent and all security forces in Jerusalem. When you find them, bring her to me. I want to finish what I started. I will have no use for her after that, unless she submits and becomes my slave. If she refuses, I will dispose of her personally. Anyone who makes a fool of me as she did must either submit or pay with their life. If you do not find her, I will have you executed for your incompetence."

"Sir, she caught us by surprise. We never thought she would get away from you, so..."

"So, now you blame this on me? I gave you a simple assignment, and you failed. You have one opportunity to make up for it. If you do not, you will die in her place! I do not want to hear another word from you! Do your jobs and I may let you live."

Not being part of a group, Ollie, Amelia and Ally avoided being pulled to the side and questioned. They arrived at passport control. All three had fake passports, created by Evan, with their current photos. He backdated each of them eight months, exceeding the required six months. The station worker allowed all of them to come to the window at the same time.

She questioned each of them about the purpose of their visit, their time in the country, where they had gone and what they had done. The questions were easy for Ollie and Amelia, who were friends vacationing in Israel and had enjoyed all the country offered. Ally's time was not so easy.

Ollie stood nearby urging promptness as they would miss their flight if she did not hurry. Showing the woman their boarding passes, he pointed out that their flight left in 30 minutes. The woman looked closely at Ally's passport, holding it up longer than normal as if to make sure it was her.

"Can you tell me your name?"

"Stupid question," Ally thought to herself. But when she answered, the name Ally almost came from her lips. She caught herself and said, "Sofia Weber."

"Have you changed your appearance lately Sofia?" She sounded suspicious.

"No ma'am. I am having a bad hair day. And I have been sick the past two days." She tried to change her voice so the woman would not recognize her as Ally Fromm. Everyone could identify her voice. Her time in America had helped her speak with more of an American accent when she needed to. "Ma'am we are in a hurry. Please, we can't afford to miss our flight."

Ollie continued pleading for Ally to come on. The woman finally gave in and allowed her to go.

"I should send you in for questioning. Something doesn't feel right about you. But I know that would cause you to miss your flight. So I will let you go. This must be your lucky day."

Ally knew how blessed she was to get through so easily. She pulled out her Electronic Gate Pass and followed Ollie and Amelia as they placed theirs in the machine and moved on without hesitating. Ally's pass had her real name. That is the one thing Evan could not create, nor had he considered it. Ollie told her to say she had lost it and beg for leniency, if she needed to, but that did not become necessary. They just wanted to get on the plane and in the air, bound for the states, before AMPP or a security force discovered them.

After going through all the security steps, they arrived at their gate just in time for the last call. They hurried across the boarding bridge and found their seats, the last three to board. The plane was less than half full, so Ollie had chosen their seats several rows apart from each other so no one would see them together. If Messai's forces figured out they had left the country, they would search for a man with two women. So, instead, they would fly as one man and two individual women, all flying separately.

They would keep an eye out for each other and never get out of each other's sight. Unfortunately, he could not book a direct flight. They had a stopover in Paris that should be brief, barring any trouble. Once the plane was in the air, they were more comfortable. But they would not feel safe until they were in the shelter outside Ozark, Missouri with the others.

The searches of AMPP and the security forces had yielded no results until one of the two from the King David got wind of a stolen cab. They brought in the others and began an all-out search for the driver. They called cab companies until they located the one that had a cab stolen and discovered the location from which they had taken it.

Going to the hotel and questioning the front desk attendant, they discovered a Hugh Walker and Charlotte Helmsley had checked out hurriedly that evening. The two men reported that a man and woman assisted Ally in her escape. It was easy to put two and two together and figure out those two were Hugh Walker and Charlotte Helmsley. And the three of them must have taken the cab.

They put an APB out on the trio and the search was on again, this time with names. Messai himself went on the air with a special plea to the Israeli public, complete with a hefty reward for information leading to their discovery and arrest. Calls came in from all over, but none of them gave forth credible information as to their whereabouts, until a caller reported seeing a cab driving through a neighborhood of Ein Karem. He told of watching it pull into the drive and behind the house of one Alexander Ben-Ezra.

Alexander arrived back at home close to four hours after their flight departed. He had stayed and watched the plane take off so he would be sure they were safely on their way. Never one to get in a hurry, it had taken him over an hour just to leave the airport. He talked to a few people along the way and stopped to help an elderly couple get their luggage inside. Then he had stopped to get gas and pick up a few items.

Before leaving the market, he had called his wife to tell her he would be home soon. Her voice quivered as she spoke, but there was nothing unusual about the things she said. She only told him he needed to be getting home because it was late. As he drove, he wondered what Oliver had wanted to tell him. He would have to check out the website tomorrow and watch the broadcast he had mentioned. Oliver was very excited about it and eager for him to see it.

He entered his house and saw his wife sitting in the living room with a look of fear on her face.

"What is it, Elizabeth?" he asked.

A group of men from Aissa Messai's Peace Patrol stepped into the room. One said, "Alexander, we need to talk."

His surprise was obvious, but he tried his best to remain calm. "You have no right to be in my house. You have frightened my wife. She has done nothing wrong, and neither have I."

"Alexander, tell us about the man and two women who came here tonight driving a stolen cab."

"I am not sure I understand what you are talking about."

"Don't lie to us!" the leader of the group yelled. "We know they came here, and you drove them somewhere. You have been away for several hours. Where did you take them?"

He was thinking as fast as his mind would work. "He told me they needed to go to Netanya and spend the night there. My guess is, they are planning to fly out tomorrow. He said they could not get a flight tonight. I dropped them off in town. I am not sure where they went from there."

"You are lying. Aissa Messai is about peace, but these people have become threats to the peace he seeks to maintain. We always seek to avoid violence at all costs, but you leave us no choice."

He motioned to one man, and he walked behind Alexander's wife and put his gun to her head.

"Now, Alexander, either tell us the truth or he blows her brains out. You have ten seconds." He began counting down from ten to one.

Alexander saw the fear in his wife's eyes. He could not allow them to kill her. He valued his friendship with Oliver, but these men left him no choice. "I took them to the airport. They had a flight leaving tonight."

"Now, that is better," the man said and motioned for the other to lower his gun and back away. He was on the phone immediately. "They went to Ben Gurion. I want all available personnel there immediately. Search the airport. If they have already flown, get the flight number and destination. I can't imagine them getting a direct flight at the last minute. Find out where they're headed and dispatch AMPP and security people there to intercept them. If they have a stopover, get our people there. If that doesn't work, make sure there is a greeting party waiting for them in the U.S. Alexander, I appreciate your help. Should we find that you have been untruthful with us again, we will return. You shall not get off so lucky next time."

They were out the door before Alexander or his wife could say another word. He went to her and held her close as she sobbed. "They know their names," she said. "They got them from the hotel." There was nothing he could do. He had no phone numbers and no one to contact. There was only one thing he had to do, and he needed to do it right at this moment.

"Elizabeth, we have to watch something. Oliver wanted to tell me about it, but he said there was not enough time before we arrived at the airport. However, he gave me a website which has a video we must watch. Then we need to see a broadcast by a Jewish rabbi. I have no clue what he was talking about, but I know in my heart we need to see it now. It cannot wait until morning."

He pulled up smyrnians.com. He had seen on the news that Oliver Barton and Amelia Clarke had become a part of that group. He had often thought about it since, knowing his own distrust for Aissa Messai. But he trusted Oliver Barton. He had never lied to him or let him down, not even once. He owed it to him to watch this video and listen to Ben Abramson. His name sounded like he must be a good Jewish man. Elizabeth sat beside him as they watched the pastor's video, with Hebrew subtitles supplied by Ben, allowing them to understand what was being said. They sat quietly, neither of them saying a word until it had ended. She spoke first.

"Alexander, how can we believe in Jesus? It goes against everything we have held as true all of our lives. But what he said makes complete sense. It is hard to deny."

"Oliver told me to watch a broadcast by a Jewish man named Benjamin Abramson, too. But it is not on until tomorrow. We cannot wait."

Looking at the pages on the website, he found one that said, Archives. Clicking on it, he found multiple videos by Benjamin Abramson. The first in the list was My Journey to the Truth.

"We must watch this, Elizabeth." When Ben appeared on the screen, there was something about him that drew them to listen to his words. As he shared about his life, his commitment to the Mosaic Law and rejection of all other religions, they listened intently. Here was a man who had been as they were his entire life. Raised as an Orthodox Jew from birth and following those teachings into adulthood, he had also taught them to his family.

When he shared his story of turning to faith in Jesus that unforgettable night in his den and how Jesus had commissioned him to tell his people, it pricked their hearts. When he read the passage from Josephus' Antiquities, they understood who Jesus was and that he came to earth and died on the cross for their sins, then rose from the grave three days later. They now knew without a doubt what the pastor said was true. Benjamin Abramson had experienced it himself and became the first Jew of the Tribulation to believe in Jesus.

They returned to the final part of the pastor's message and did what he instructed them to do. Though Ben had been sharing his message for several days, this husband and wife became the first Jews in Israel to put their faith in Jesus. The moment was as glorious as Ben's had been. The house flooded with brilliant light. Jesus himself appeared before them and asked, "Who has believed our message and to whom has the arm of the Lord been revealed?" (Isaiah 53:1 NIV)

Together they said boldly, "You revealed your arm to us, Lord, and we believe!"

Jesus spoke again, "You know what you must do. You alone can give the word that may save my servants tonight."

"What is it, Lord? What must we do? I do not understand," uttered Alexander.

Elizabeth grabbed him by the arm and pointed at the screen. The words filled the entire screen, shining forth in glorious light: benjaminabramson@smyrnians.com. But they had returned to the pastor's video. How did it go back to the ending of Ben's message? There was only one answer, and they both knew it. And they knew what they had to do. Alexander clicked on the email address and hurriedly typed a message to Ben Abramson. In the subject line, he wrote URGENT.

"Mr. Abramson, my wife and I just watched your story and the pastor's video and put our faith in Jesus tonight. I cannot tell you how grateful we are to you for showing us the truth. But that is not the purpose of this email. Jesus told me to tell you this. I can explain later how I know it, but for now it is urgent that you see this and take action. Oliver Barton is a dear friend of mine. He often comes to see me when he is in Israel. Tonight he, his wife and Ally Fromm came to my door. Trusting Oliver as I do, I honored his request and drove them to the airport."

"When I returned home, AMPP agents were in my house awaiting my arrival. They threatened to kill my wife if I did not tell them the truth. I attempted to avoid it, but they eventually forced me to say where I took them. They made calls while standing in our living room. They ordered AMPP agents to intercept them either in another country, if they do not have a direct flight, or in the United States. The three of them are flying into a death trap and are not aware of it."

"Oliver gave me their flight plans before they left my car and entered the airport. They will stop in Paris, then fly to Atlanta, Georgia. AMPP has without a doubt discovered their schedule, as they know their aliases. I only hope they have not already captured them in Paris. If they avoid interception there, a large group will await them when they arrive in Atlanta. I hope you receive this email in time to take action. Please email me back and let me know you received it and inform me of any way we can help. Sincerely Yours, Alexander Ben-Ezra."

The plane landed in Paris, and Ollie, Amelia and Ally exited and hurried through security and on to their gate. Security personnel once again allowed them to pass through without pause because of the need to catch their international flight. However, they soon saw a delay listed for their flight. They sat nervously waiting for the call to board. The delay dragged on and on. There was nothing to do but wait. The plane was sitting outside, so there seemed to be no reason for such a delay. They desperately wanted to get in the air headed for the USA.

After what seemed like forever, the call came to board. The three of them walked on hurriedly, while trying to not draw attention to themselves. Soon the plane was in the air, bound for Atlanta. Ollie had been fortunate to get a flight there instead of New York. From Atlanta, they would be on their way to Springfield, then to Ozark and the safety of the shelter. What they did not know was, an AMPP patrol had just missed them in Paris but had allowed them to continue their flight. They would have a group there to greet them the moment they stepped into the terminal in Atlanta.

Ben was wrapping up things in his studio and preparing to get some sleep, if he could. That would be difficult for any of them because their minds were on Ollie, Amelia and Ally. As he prepared to close his computer, he saw an email come in. The title read: URGENT. He opened it and saw it was from an Alexander Ben-Ezra. A smile came to his face as he read the first part and saw that Alexander and his wife had just put their faith in Jesus. He quietly thanked God. Then it hit him. To the best of his knowledge, they were the first Jews in Israel to do that. His excitement nearly got the best of him as he prepared to run to tell Miriam and the others. Before he did, he noticed the next line:

"But that is not the purpose of this email." Looking further down, the names Oliver Barton and Ally Fromm jumped out at him. His heart rate quickened. After finishing, he left the room, calling for the others to join him. They did so immediately, knowing something was wrong. Aware of the situation three of their colleagues faced, they stayed on edge, fearing the worst, but hoping for the best.

"What is it, Ben," asked Miriam. "Did you receive some news about them?"

He told them about the email and filled them in. "They got a flight out of Israel, stopping in Paris, then on to Atlanta. But AMPP is onto them and has ordered a squadron to intercept them when they get off the plane. They may have already gotten them in Paris."

"Turn on the news," said Miriam. "I guarantee you Messai will want the public informed and on the lookout for them."

He turned on the TV. The first thing they saw was a live report from Charles de Gaulle Airport in Paris.

"I have with me Sergeant Jean Dubois of Aissa Messai's Peace Patrol. Sergeant, I understand your group was here to take into custody three escapees from Israel. But it appears you may have arrived too late after their flight had left. Can you give us any further information about that?"

"I cannot give any details about this situation. I can only say what most people already know. We are on a worldwide manhunt for three individuals. And we will stop at nothing to find them and bring them to justice. Allow me to put it this way: we know they are on a plane and where that plane is going. When it lands, AMPP personnel will be there waiting for them."

He refused further questions, and it appeared the reporter had no additional information about their flight. But Ben knew. They had to do something. But what? How could they possibly stop a squadron of AMPP forces and free their comrades?

His phone rang. It was Evan.

"Ben, we just saw the news! They are onto Ollie, Amelia and Ally! Do we have any idea where they are going?"

"We have all of that information, Evan, thanks to a new believer in Israel who sent me an urgent email a little while ago. From the news it seems AMPP missed them in Paris and will be ready for them when they land in Atlanta. And you can bet they will be out in force."

"Ben, do something! I wish we were there, but we're not. Please Ben, save them!"

"We just got this news too, Evan. Trust me, we will try our best to come up with a plan. But who are we to go against AMPP?"

"We will think and pray from here, and get a flight home as soon as we can, but something has to happen. If they get them, they are all dead! We can't let that happen! Are Trey, John and Kathie still in Atlanta?"

"They are on their way back here."

"Tell them to turn around and get back there as fast as they can. Can Rickie fly you, Miriam, and John and Mary to Atlanta? If they just flew out, they have around nine hours till they land. Come up with a plan to stop AMPP from capturing them! Please, Ben..." His voice broke.

"Let me get off the phone and call John right now. I will see if I can get them back to Atlanta. We will come up with something, Evan. I have no clue what it will be, but we will do our best. If they get us all, so be it. We can't let AMPP capture them without at least putting up a fight."

"I don't want them to get all of you. Just please do whatever you can. Please, Ben. I can't bear the thought of them falling into Messai's hands. He will make an example of them to the world."

"Just pray for us, Evan. And let me get off here so we can get moving."

Ben called John first. The three of them were two hours into the trip, but would turn around immediately and head back to Atlanta. They would think hard and stay in touch. They were itching for some action themselves.

Next he sat down with Miriam and the kids, joined by John, Mary and Rickie.

"Rickie, how fast can you get all twelve of us to Atlanta?"

"We can fly tonight, if everybody is ready. We have a big group. It will be no problem to get us all on board now, but what will we do with three more passengers on the way back?"

"We'll figure it out," said Ben. "I guess we have to take Trey's truck again." He rolled his eyes.

Blake and Beth were up and anxiously awaiting the time to get back to the Iranian group. He got a call from Evan. He did not even have time to speak before Evan started talking.

"Blake! Ollie, Amelia and Ally got out of Israel and are on a flight to Atlanta."

"That is great! I am so happy. I wish we could be at the shelter when they get there!"

"Blake, listen to me!"

He had never been so direct with him before. Blake was silent and listened.

"Messai has their flight number and destination. A group of his men will be there to take them into custody the minute they get off the plane. The entire team needs to be there with a plan to do something, if they can. John, Kathie and Trey were heading to the shelter, but they have turned around and are going back to Atlanta. Rickie is flying everybody else there right now. They will all be there, but what can they do against an AMPP patrol? Every one of them will be in extreme danger. They could wipe out half of the Smyrnians tonight. We have to pray."

"I can't believe we're not there to help them! I feel so helpless being this far away and not being able to do anything. We will pray, but I want to do more. I want to be there and fight for them!"

"Well, you're not, and neither are we. But we still have to stay in touch, all of us, the entire team. We all have to think and try to come up with some kind of plan. Wait. John is calling me. I have to go." Just like that, he was off the phone.

"Blake," Beth pleaded, "we have to think of something. We can't allow this to happen. The Tribulation is not even a year old yet. We all knew what we were getting into. And we seriously doubt that all of us will survive the entire seven years. But not now. Not this soon."

"I'm thinking, but my mind is blank. Let's brainstorm and see if we can come up with something."

They began talking. The others were doing the same. It was Miriam who had an idea just before they left the shelter for the airport. "The kids!"

"What are you talking about?" asked her husband.

"The kids. I will explain as we go. We must all put on our orthodox clothing so we will appear to be fully Jewish. Nobody knows who we are. We need to look like a normal Jewish family traveling somewhere. And Rickie, John and Mary, all three of you are under the radar. You will be a big part of this too."

Ally got up from her seat and walked to the bathroom in the back of the plane. She was only sitting a few rows from it. Looking into the mirror, she did not recognize the person looking back at her. How had things changed so fast? For weeks she had been the assistant to the Secretary-General of the United Nations, the de facto leader of the world. She had felt special dressed in her sharp business attire. Even though Messai's glances made her uncomfortable, they were also flattering. In a mere day, she had gone from prestige and power to the pitiful person she saw in the mirror. Had she failed? Jesus had called her to the position and allowed her to get chosen. It was her purpose during the Tribulation, to be a spy for the Smyrnians, on the inside of Messai's empire. She had gotten to do it for such a brief time and been able to relay so little information back to the team. But she could not succumb to the monster's lustful desires. For that, she had to take a stand. When he attempted to force himself on her, she had to fight back.

She straightened up and smiled at herself, looking into the mirror. This was her fight. Messai was her enemy, and she would fight him to the very end of these seven years, if she survived that long. And if she did not survive, she would still be the winner. "So, pick yourself up, Ally," she said aloud to herself. "The fight has just begun. The enemy is on the prowl and hunting for you right now. You *must* win this battle. You *will* win this battle!" She may not look like Ally Fromm, but the fighting spirit that made her who she was, returned. It showed on the face that looked back at her in the mirror. "Lord," she prayed, "please let those who are with us be more than those who are with him. The battle is not ours; it is yours. I trust in you. Give us a glorious victory this night through our Lord and Savior Jesus Christ, the *real* Messiah. We have staked our lives and future on him. Amen."

CHAPTER 21

Two hours before Ollie, Amelia and Ally's flight arrived, fifteen Smyrnians gathered at Hartsfield Airport in Atlanta. Miriam brought them together and shared her plan. Seven Jewish kids would cause bedlam just before the three left the boarding bridge and entered the terminal. Ben and Miriam would be in the middle of it, trying to corral them. Sweet, older John and Mary would try to help. When the AMPP guys tried to intervene, Mary would attack them with her purse, swinging it at them like an angry grandmother protecting her grandchildren. With the patrol distracted, Trey, John and Kathie would surround Ollie, Amelia and Ally obscuring them from view and whisk them out of the terminal to their waiting car. They would then drive some 75 miles to Ben Epps Airport in Athens. Rickie would make a quick up and down to pick them up and fly all of them back to Springfield.

When the plane arrived, everyone was in place. A text from Ollie signaled they were ready to exit the bridge. John stood ready to text him when the Peace Patrol became sufficiently preoccupied. The moment of truth came. The four youngest Abramson kids began running around the terminal wildly with their three older siblings chasing and trying to catch them.

Enter Ben and Miriam, who were in orthodox Jewish attire, as were the kids. Miriam was yelling at the top of her lungs. The kids ran around the AMPP patrol, in and out, using them as shields to keep from being caught. Ben was trying to bring calm to the craziness. One of them grabbed an AMPP man's gun, acting like a policeman chasing bad guys. The man ran after him, but could not catch him. The others came to his rescue. One grabbed the boy and held him.

Enter, Mary. She began flailing at the man with her purse, yelling at him to let the boy go. One of his buddies attempted to grab her.

Enter, John. "Let go of my wife!" he yelled. The entire terminal turned into a madhouse with people running all over the place trying to help break up the madness. Some found it humorous, while others were taking pictures.

Enter John, Kathie and Trey. Exit Ollie, Amelia and Ally. No one, including the guys from AMPP, noticed them slipping along the outer wall and hurrying down the corridor. They only had carry-on luggage, so there was no need for baggage claim. If they had it, they would have left it, anyway. They ran out the doors and leapt into the waiting car. Trey drove away, being careful to obey the speed limit within the boundaries of the airport.

Inside, the uproar continued. They would keep it going as long as they could get by with it to allow the others to get as far away as they could before the patrol discovered they were missing. After putting up with this far too long, an AMPP man pulled his gun and fired it into an empty seat in the waiting area. Everything came to a halt. People were screaming and running now, creating even more bedlam.

The patrol came back together and formed a line at the exit of the bridge. It took a moment for them to realize the passengers had already deplaned and left. One yelled for two of them to go on board the plane and search for the three escapees, thinking they must have seen them and returned to the plane. A thorough search and conversation with the crew revealed that no passengers remained on the aircraft. The two men came running back with the news. The terminal was empty. Gone were the Jewish family and others who had come to their rescue. Most people had fled out of fear after the gunshot.

"Search everywhere!" yelled an AMPP man. "Bathrooms, restaurants, baggage claim!" He made a call and ordered a lockdown of the entire airport. "No one is to leave or enter until we have located the rebels!" As they searched, Trey, John and Kathie got farther and farther away from Hartsfield and closer and closer to Ben Epps. Rickie and the others were in the air before anyone had a clue they were part of a plot to allow Ally, Ollie and Amelia to escape. The exchange happened smoothly in Athens and Rickie climbed into the air with 12 passengers, bound for Springfield-Branson Airport. John and Mary joined Trey, John and Kathie for a long ride back.

From Belgium and Germany to Iran, the other Smyrnians were celebrating what had just happened. Ben called each as they prepared for takeoff. Miriam was a hero. Her plan had worked to perfection. Soon they would all be together in the shelter, all but Blake and Beth. They had unfinished business in Tehran. Some believers in Jesus were expecting their visit this day.

Evan, Anders and Malachi, alias Source, had booked a direct flight which would leave Belgium in a few hours and take them to Newark, New Jersey. From there, they would fly to Springfield-Branson and be with the others by nightfall in Missouri. Being incognito as they were, they expected no problems. Bruno and Mila's flight would leave that night. Blake and Beth hoped to join them all at the shelter within two days. They would take some time to celebrate after their arrival, then make plans to get back into the thick of the action.

$$\bullet \quad \bullet \quad \bullet \quad \bullet \quad \bullet$$

Aissa Messai was possibly more angry than he had ever been. Something had to change with his Peace Patrol. Their ineptness at doing their job was unacceptable. They were often more like a comedy show than a control force for his agenda. He needed new recruits and would begin the search for them immediately. He could not afford to wait. Leadership would have to change. Additional training was necessary. He would dispose of some current members, including the men who had allowed Ally and her two co-conspirators to escape from Jerusalem, and those who let them get away in Atlanta. That would serve as a lesson to others who joined his forces of the importance of their roles in maintaining peace, enforcing his will and expanding his reign around the world. They must obey his every command and show no mercy to those who opposed him. He would miss Ally, but then she had not been his first choice. He was Aissa Messai, and he would have what he wanted. This time he would not settle for second best.

The World Health Organization had just declared the plague which had begun in China a full-blown pandemic. It had jumped continents as people traveled the world. Medical Science was trying unsuccessfully to find a cure.

No current medication fazed it. People were now dying at an alarming rate. They quarantined those who became infected, but it was too late. They had already passed it on to people who were spreading it to others. National governments desperately tried to slow it down or keep it from affecting their countries. Some of those efforts were working, keeping it isolated to certain areas. Airlines required health screenings before allowing passengers to purchase a ticket. That had slowed travel worldwide. Yet, there was little doubt in anyone's mind that the disease would eventually touch every nation on earth.

• • • • •

It was time for Blake and Beth to meet with the Iranian group again. They were excited about sharing their stories with them and hearing their stories. To be on the safe side, she donned the long, black dress and scarf, and he wore black pants and a dark shirt. Even though they were in Iran's largest city, they thought it better to fit in than look like westerners. They also put all of their things in the car, not wanting to leave them in the hotel. Blake drove carefully and parked in the same place as last night to be inconspicuous. They walked to the small street and down to the house. He knocked as he had before. No answer. He knocked again. Still no answer.

He spoke softly, "It is Ryan and Kelly Davis." There was still no sound from the inside, only an eerie silence. No shuffling of feet or movement of any kind. No voices. Maybe they had changed locations or decided not to meet today. Perhaps they were waiting for the password. "Yeshua," Beth said, being sure to keep her voice down. Still, nothing. She and Blake looked at each other.

"We need to leave," she said, her intuition kicking in. "We can come back later,"

"I don't understand," whispered Blake. "They said they were meeting every day this week. And they knew we were coming today. Something must have come up."

"Blake, let's get out of here. We can send them an email. We have that address too, remember?"

"I suppose you are right. But I just don't get it. They were expecting us. Something has to be wrong." He reached out and touched the handle. It was unlocked. "I am going in."

"No! Don't do that. We can't just walk into someone's home."

He pushed the door open. It was dark inside with no lights on. Being at the end of what amounted to an alley surrounded by buildings was not conducive to good lighting. Not wanting to give any cause for alarm, he did not use any light from his phone as he walked inside. His eyes would adjust to the low light soon enough. Once inside the room, he whispered, "Is anyone here?" Again, there was no answer. Beth had stepped inside too and stayed close behind him.

"Blake, we should leave. We shouldn't be here with no one home. It is trespassing."

He took another step and stumbled over something, almost falling. As she stepped out to catch him, she slipped on something wet and barely kept herself from going down. Their eyes were adjusting now so they could see the room. At first, it appeared to be bags or possibly rolled up blankets lying all over the floor. That would not be unusual for Iranian culture. But as their vision became clear, they witnessed the scene. Bodies, everywhere.

Blake clicked the light on his phone. The sight before their eyes broke their hearts. Every member of the group they had met, studied, prayed and eaten with yesterday lay slaughtered on the floor. Someone had slit their throats, practically decapitating some. They lay in a circle in pools of their own blood. The slaughter happened as they studied the scripture.

Open Bibles lay beside them, with notebooks containing their thoughts on what they had been reading. They had also written the names of people they were praying for. *The Smyrnians* was at the top of each list. These people had been praying for them! One woman, apparently the last to die, had written, "Forgive them Jesus, for they do not know what they are doing."

Gone... Murdered for their faith in Jesus. They knew it was coming. They told them yesterday. They just did not know it would come so soon. But it came, just as it would come to many more believers in Jesus throughout these seven years.

"Blake, we have to go!" uttered Beth. "We can't do anything for them. They have already left us. My heart aches for them. But I just want out of here."

He grabbed her and held her close. "Beth, I love you. I will always be here for you. Let's get in the car and head straight to the airport. Maybe we can get a flight today. We need to get back to the team at the shelter. I will call them as we drive and tell them we are coming home."

The door burst open, catching them by surprise. The members of an AMPP patrol charged inside with their weapons drawn and surrounded them.

"Do not move. Hands on top of your heads."

They complied. From behind, two of the men grabbed their hands, pulled them down roughly and cuffed them behind their backs.

"You are a little late to help them," one man said, pointing to the bodies on the floor. "But you must also belong to them because we have orders to take you into custody. Be thankful you didn't end up like them."

Blake tried talking to the men to diffuse the situation. "I'm not sure why you were told to arrest us. We are Americans, Ryan and Kelly Davis. We're traveling the world and wanted to see Iran. We only planned to be here for a few days. If you will let me explain..."

"Shut up!" the man yelled. "Our orders came from the top. We just carry them out. You are coming with us. Boys, take their phones and prepare them for transport."

Two of the men searched them until they found the phones. "You won't be needing these," he said as he tossed them to the man who seemed in charge. The two who had handcuffed them pulled blindfolds over their eyes and tied them tightly around their heads.

"Now, let's go. We don't have time to stand around here and talk. Start walking."

Blake was afraid, not so much for himself, but for his wife. What kind of husband was he? He could not even protect her when she needed him. What was he going to do now? His mind ran amok with questions, for which there were no answers. There was no way to get word to the team at the shelter. They would wonder if something had gone wrong when they did not call. But they would not know where they were or what had happened to them.

He and Beth had looked forward to seven years of marriage. They were so happy. Would it end in less than one year? Tears rolled from his eyes, soaking his blindfold. He listened for Beth and heard her quietly sobbing too. The men dragged them blindly outside and into a van parked in the alley. It threw them from side-to-side as it sped away.

Rickie landed in Springfield and unloaded his passengers. Trey had left his truck parked in the hangar, as promised. "Here we go, the back of Trey's truck again," said Ben. "I have had enough of that to last a lifetime. And this time there are three more of us."

"True, but after the ruckus you guys caused in Atlanta, your faces are everywhere if they have footage from security cameras. You need to stay hidden. Otherwise, I would let you ride up front with me. But in case we get pulled over, it is safer for you to ride back here with the lid closed."

Ben grimaced as he crawled into the back of the truck once again, but Ollie, Amelia and Ally were more than happy to climb in. They went first and slid all the way to the front.

"If we get stopped, I want to make sure no one sees me," said Ally.

The trip was smooth for a change, and they were soon pulling into the clearing and parking by the cabin. When they got out, Ollie got down on his hands and knees and kissed the ground.

"I can't believe we are here," he said. "I didn't think we had a chance this time."

"Ah luv, I never doubted you for a minute. You have a knack for escaping," Amelia said.

"I think we had better be thanking Jesus," said Ben. "Without him, you wouldn't be here."

None of them had any doubt about that. Once inside, they waited for Trey, John, Kathie and John and Mary to arrive. None of them would be content until all of them had returned safe and sound.

"We should call Blake and Beth, and Evan, Anders and Source," said Miriam.

"Evan called him Malachi the last time we talked," said Ben. "I guess the source has a name."

When they called Evan to tell them, they sat awaiting their flight. They were coming home!

Next, Ben called Blake. His phone went unanswered, then to voicemail. He tried again. Same thing. He called Beth's phone. No answer, followed by voicemail.

"Something isn't right," he said. "We have all committed to answering our phones when one of us calls. Neither of them would intentionally let our calls go unanswered. And I know both of them wouldn't do that. One of them would answer."

He called Evan back. When he answered, Ben said, "Would you guys try to call Blake and Beth? They aren't answering our calls."

After trying, Evan called back. "Same thing for us. What do we do? We have to find out if they are in some kind of trouble."

"There is nothing we can do right now. They planned to meet with the group again today. Maybe they are not taking calls while they are with them. If so, they will call us back when they finish."

"You're probably right, Ben," said Ally. "That time with the group is very important to them. I'm sure they will call us soon."

"I still don't like it," Ben said. "Iran is a dangerous place for people who are followers of Jesus. As much as I hate it, we have no choice but to wait."

John called shortly after that. Their trip was going well. There had been no problems, and they should make it to the shelter in a few hours. Now their concern was Blake and Beth.

The van came to a stop. Blake and Beth could hear the men getting out and the doors shutting. Then the back doors opened, and they felt themselves being pulled out. The men led them into a building, still blindfolded. A door opened, but they did not take Blake in. One man jerked his blindfold down. He blinked, trying to adjust his eyes to the light. It appeared they were in a warehouse of some sort. As his vision became clear, he saw that he was standing outside a room with a man on each side of him holding his arms. His hands remained cuffed behind him. Inside the room, he saw Beth. She sat on a stool, her hands also still cuffed. When they pulled her blindfold down and his eyes met hers, he could see the fear on her face. She was crying out for him on the inside, but he was powerless to do anything about it.

"Take him to the other room," one man commanded.

"No!" he yelled. "I am not leaving her!"

"Don't worry," the man said. "We will take good care of her."

He walked over and laughed in Blake's face. He struggled as they dragged him away. They took him down another long hallway to a room far away from Beth. With the handcuffs still on, they shoved him in and slammed the door. He turned and tried pulling on the locked door from behind, but it was useless. Beth needed him, but there was no way to get to her. He had promised to never leave her side. Now she was alone with them. Sitting in a corner of the room, he dropped his chin to his chest and wept.

Beth sat on the stool, trying not to look at her captors. The one in charge said, "Okay, boys, let's get her out of here. The boss wants her. And we all know the boss doesn't like to wait."

From behind, a man slipped a rubber mask over her mouth and nose and secured it with a strap around her head. She struggled to pull away, but it was too late. That was the last thing she remembered. The men lifted her up, carried her to the van and placed her inside.

Blake heard the door open, and four of the men walked inside. He fought against them as they turned him around and threw him against the wall. Something slammed against his head, and he sank to the floor. The men walked out as he lay unconscious with blood oozing from his head.

The van wove through the back streets of Tehran until it left the city and drove through open country, arriving at an abandoned airstrip. A private jet sat with the engines running. On the side it bore two letters, which left no doubt to whom it belonged: *AM*. It was *his* private jet.

The men carried Beth's limp body into the waiting jet and lay her on a bed in the back. A man removed the mask, inserted an IV into her arm and attached it to a bag of anesthetic liquid, which would guarantee her sleep for the next six hours as they flew. He inserted another needle into a vein in her other arm and drew two vials of blood, which he handed to the driver of the van.

"You know what to do," he instructed. "Get it done and make sure the boss has a copy of the report before we arrive in Belgium."

The man gave a thumbs up and hurried away on his mission. The jet started rolling and gaining speed, racing down the runway and lifting into the air with Beth Jennings Thompson inside.

Blake opened his eyes and saw concrete. He was lying on the floor with blood around him. His only recollection was of the men coming in and throwing him against the wall, then feeling like his head had exploded. Still woozy, he sat up and steadied himself. He discovered they had removed the handcuffs. The door was open. Why would the door be open? As he stood, his hand came down on something on the floor beside him. His phone! Why would they give him his phone? None of this was making sense to him. The place seemed quiet.

Beth! Weak, dizzy and somewhat confused, he struggled to his feet. Holding onto the wall, he walked through the open door, trying to remember which way they had brought him. A significant loss of blood likely contributed to his weakness and confusion. Crawling would be better. Easing down to his hands and knees, he dragged himself down one hallway. Nothing looked familiar. This was not the right one.

Going back, he saw where the men had brought him. Dust covered the floor and showed clear signs of struggle and footprints. He followed the footprints. They led him to the room where Beth had been. It was empty. She was gone, and so were the men. Something lay on the floor beside the chair where she had been sitting. He crawled over to look. Her phone. Someone had smashed it, destroying it. That left no possibility of tracing her. He became desperate. The building was hauntingly quiet.

Emboldened by a surge of energy and fueled by a spirit of desperation, he got to his feet. He searched everywhere but found nothing or no one. "Beth!" he yelled, his voice reverberating through the hallways. "Beth!" Only silence. He stumbled outside. There were no vehicles, and nothing but other unoccupied buildings. He had to find Beth. Where had they taken her? There was no way to know. Choking up with emotion, he did the only thing left to do. He pulled up his phone and called Ben, who answered on the first ring.

"Blake! Where are you? What's going on? We've been trying to call you. Are you okay?" There was no answer, only sobbing, on the other end. "Blake, talk to me! What is wrong?"

"They took Beth, Ben. They took her, and I don't know where she is." More sobbing.

"What do you mean, they took her? Who took her? What happened?"

Gaining some composure, he told the story. Finding the group slaughtered. Beth and him taken by the men from AMPP. Being knocked out. Waking in a puddle of blood. Searching everywhere for Beth. Finding only an empty building. He wept again.

"Blake, did you hear anything they said that would give you a clue where they may take her?"

"Nothing. I heard nothing."

"Can you get a flight back here? We will all go and search for her until we find her."

"I am not leaving without Beth."

The big jet circled the airport and landed in Belgium. It taxied to a private hangar where a limo waited. The men removed the IV from Beth's arm, having ensured she had enough anesthesia in her system to keep her asleep for at least another hour. Then they carried her to the big car and gently placed her in the back, sitting on each side of her as she slept. The driver pulled away headed for their destination.

Beth's lifeless body sat in a chair in the spacious living area of the spectacular mansion.

"You did well."

"Thank you, sir. I always try to ensure that we carry out our jobs precisely as you request. We take our roles as your special forces seriously."

"That is exactly why I chose you to be the commander of this unit. You have never failed me, not once, unlike some buffoons who have served in AMPP. How did the mission go?"

"It went according to the plan, sir. They returned to the home, just as you said they would."

"You disposed of the entire group, right?"

"Yes, sir."

"Good. That means there are no groups remaining in Iran. We will gradually rid the entire world of them. How about him? Does he have any idea?"

"None, sir. We left him there with his phone and an open door. A little bump on the head kept him unaware of the events going on around him until we were long gone, if you get my drift."

"I do," the man chuckled.

"Did you get the test results?"

"I did. The email came shortly before you arrived, and they printed it for me. The results left no doubt who she is. When she objects, I will gladly show her the proof."

"Are you ready for us to wake her? We can do that whenever you want."

"Give me another minute to look at her. She is beautiful, isn't she?"

"Yes she is, sir. Stunningly so."

"And now she is mine, all mine. I have wanted her since the day I laid eyes on her at the United Nations meeting. As I caught her gaze when I walked past her to the podium, I knew she was the one. Frankly, he did not deserve her. I do. Okay, you may awaken her now. I am ready."

"My men will stand guard, sir, should she try to escape."

"Thank you. I assume there will be no need for that, but it never hurts to be sure."

The man walked behind the chair, reached around Beth and held a small packet of ammonia inhalant under her nose. She roused, turning her head, trying to avoid the pungent odor. Her eyes opened, and she sat up, trying to determine where she was.

CONCLUSION

"Beth Jennings. I have eagerly awaited your arrival. Welcome to your new home."

She heard the voice, then saw the face. Messai! She glanced around. This must be his mansion. She remembered her new identity.

"You have the wrong person. My name is Kelly Davis."

"Now Beth, you cannot lie to me. I know who you are. I have wanted you for a long time. Ally Fromm was nice, but she was only a substitute for *you*. She was my assistant. But you will be mine, all mine. You are the one I have desired, the one I longed for."

"I told you my name is not Beth. I am Kelly Davis, a Humanitarian Aid Worker with People of Peace. We share the same goal as you."

He held up a piece of paper and smiled. "I knew who you were, but to prove it, I took some of your blood, extracted the DNA and did an identity test. How many guesses do you need as to the results?"

His smile was evil, yet alluring. He saw the stunned look on her face as he brought the paper and held it in front of her.

"See for yourself, Beth. The results are unmistakable."

She looked at the paper. He was right.

"I also have this picture of you. You did well concealing your identity, but when I held this picture to your face, it was a perfect match. You cannot mask your beauty with a change of hair color and style. I will let your hair return to its natural blonde and grow long again. That is the Beth Jennings I fell in love with."

"Get used to your new home, Beth. You are here to stay. No one knows where you are, and there is no escape. I promise I will take excellent care of you and give you everything you could ever desire. I can allow no one to see you in public because someone may recognize you. But you will be here waiting for me every time I return home. Yes, welcome home, Beth. You are mine, all mine, forever."

A tear rolled from her eye. He gently wiped it away, knelt down and embraced her. She felt the warmth of his embrace as her mind struggled to come to grips with this new reality. The shelter in Missouri became a fleeting memory. *Home.* This was home now. The tears flowed freely.

COMING NEXT
EPISODE THREE:

INFERNAL CHAOS

As the Tribulation enters its second year, the lethal epidemic extends its reach and claims massive numbers of victims. Then, as if the earth has not reached the limit of what it can endure, another catastrophic natural disaster strikes, killing millions more around the globe. All the while, Aissa Messai unwaveringly proclaims his message of peace and prosperity, even in the face of worldwide pandemonium. His power continues to increase as he solidifies his grip on the world. Having just captured his most sought-after prize, he feels unstoppable. The Smyrnians continue to fight, seeking to help people see the truth. They battle Messai and his murderous "peace patrol," while desperately trying to survive six more years. Amid it all, another long-feared global crisis looms on the horizon. It will be worse than any of the others. When it comes, the question is not who will survive, but can *anyone* survive?

OTHER BOOKS
BY DAVID O. BULLOCK

When a supposed alien invasion suddenly takes billions of people from the earth, a band of warriors arise to battle an insurmountable foe in Episode One of this thrilling series. Join them as they face the fight of their lives that will become a fight for their lives. When you enter the struggle with them, you will find your own life being challenged and changed as you read.

When things look hopeless, there is always hope on the horizon. Discover the connection and watch as your despair and discouragement give way to hope and excitement for your future!

Don't live the chicken pen existence, picking corn off the ground with all the other chickens. Rise up and soar like an eagle! In this motivational novel, you will find inspiration to get from where life has taken you to where you want to be.

ABOUT THE AUTHOR

David O. Bullock was raised on a farm in rural Kentucky. He left the farm to become a pastor at age 20. He holds Bachelor of Ministry and Master of Divinity degrees. David is married to his high school sweetheart, Glenda. They are still madly in love, have two daughters and six grandchildren and live in their hometown: Somerset, Kentucky. He's crazy about the Kentucky Wildcats, Cincinnati Reds, Cincinnati Bengals, Diet Rite and coffee.

davidobullockwriting@gmail.com
facebook.com/david.bullock.376
Twitter: @BullockWriting
linkedin.com/in/david-o-bullock

NOTE FROM THE AUTHOR

Word-of-mouth is crucial for any author to succeed. If you enjoyed *Invasion of Darkness*, please leave a review online—anywhere you are able. Even if it's just a sentence or two. It would make all the difference and would be very much appreciated.

Thanks!
David

Thank you so much for reading one of David O. Bullock's novels.
If you enjoyed the experience, please check out the beginning of the
series!

Rise of the Smyrnians by David O. Bullock

Blake Thompson is the top reporter for a major television network. When up
to one-fourth of the world's population suddenly disappears, it appears an
alien invasion has finally taken place. As the world deals with the devastating
loss, Blake sets out to discover and report the truth and also help prepare
humanity for possible future attacks.

As facts unfold, an unlikely band of warriors known as the Smyrnians arises.
These include Blake's cameraman, Anders Norstrom, his rival in the news game,
Beth Jennings, college students Evan Ryles and Ally Fromm, professor John
Baldwin and others. Together they will battle what appears to be an
insurmountable foe. They will face not only the fight of their lives but a fight
for their lives.